HALLOWED CIRCLE

LINDA ROBERTSON

Pocket Books

New York   London   Toronto   Sydney

Pocket Books
A Division of Simon & Schuster, Inc.
1230 Avenue of the Americas
New York, NY 10020

This book is a work of fiction. Names, characters, places, and incidents either are products of the author's imagination or are used fictitiously. Any resemblance to actual events or locales or persons, living or dead, is entirely coincidental.

Copyright © 2010 by Linda Robertson

All rights reserved, including the right to reproduce this book or portions thereof in any form whatsoever. For information address Pocket Books Subsidiary Rights Department, 1230 Avenue of the Americas, New York, NY 10020.

First Juno Books/Pocket Books paperback edition January 2010

JUNO BOOKS and colophon are trademarks of Wildside Press LLC used under license by Simon & Schuster, Inc., the publisher of this work.

POCKET and colophon are registered trademarks of Simon & Schuster, Inc.

For information about special discounts for bulk purchases, please contact Simon & Schuster Special Sales at 1-866-506-1949 or business@simonandschuster.com.

The Simon & Schuster Speakers Bureau can bring authors to your live event. For more information or to book an event contact the Simon & Schuster Speakers Bureau at 1-866-248-3049 or visit our website at www.simonspeakers.com.

Cover design by John Vairo Jr.

Manufactured in the United States of America

10 9 8 7 6 5 4 3 2 1

ISBN 978-1-4391-5678-0
ISBN 978-1-4391-6657-4 (ebook)

This one is for Logan.
Because you do so much.

Acknowledgments

Java-n-Chocolate Thanks
as always to my writing group OWN: Ohio Writers
Network. Michelle, Laura, Melissa, Rachel, Emily, Faith,
Lisa, Tracy—for reading, honesty, and hanging out.

Margarita Thanks
to Paula Guran, my editor. Because she's absolutely the
best and editors work too hard not to be thanked profusely.

Tour du Jour Thanks
to Scollard, for being a knowledgeable research consultant
past, present, future.

High Frequency Thanks
to my friends Ed (at NRRRadio) and Colleen for all the
shout-outs.

Shreddin' 7-string Guitar Thanks
to Jim Lewis, for being there *every* day. No matter what.
You made that guitar on the cover! Ain't that the coolest???

Reverent Gratitude
for the Many-named Muse. You *rock*.

It's your decisions about what to focus on,
what things mean to you, and
what you're going to do about them
that will determine your ultimate destiny.

—Anthony Robbins

CHAPTER ONE

"**W**hat do you mean, you nominated me?" I held my breath.

"Oh, dear. Shouldn't I have?"

Lydia Whitmore, a dear old witch who lived about ten minutes from me, was on the other end of the phone line. I could imagine her startled expression. With her kindly smile and snowy hair, always secure in a precise bun, her looks epitomized those of the cookie-baking granny. She also cornered the local market on being the goody-goody, saccharine-sweet variety of witch—what society's more mundane humans wanted all us witches to be.

She had called to inform me that the Witch Elders Council had announced their plans to find a replacement for Vivian Diamond, the Cleveland Coven's high priestess who had mysteriously gone missing.

Not that it was a mystery to *me*: I'd handed Vivian over to the vampire she'd betrayed. Chances were she'd be missing a very long time.

To determine the new high priestess the Council was, according to Lydia, planning a formal competition called the Eximium. Lydia had, incredibly, nominated me as a competitor.

"Lydia, I don't want to be the high priestess."

"Pshaw and gobbledygook!" Lydia said. "You're perfect for it, Persephone! Knowledgeable, experienced, personable. And such a charming smile, dear. You'd make a fantastic high priestess."

"I'm flattered," I said, rubbing my brow, "but I can't do it. I wouldn't have time right now."

"Oh, that's right! You have the child, don't you?"

"Yes," I said. My new role as foster mother wasn't the only reason I had no intention of getting involved with the Council, but maybe it would be enough of an excuse to dissuade Lydia.

It had only been three weeks since Lorrie Kordell, a wærewolf who used to kennel in my basement during full moons, was murdered. Her daughter, Beverley, ended up with me. We'd had the funeral a week and a half ago, and Beverley started school that following Monday. The legal gears and wheels to officially establish me as Beverley's guardian had been set in motion and we were just starting to get a sense of what "normal" was going to be for us. Beverley needed stability and the security of a routine to ground her despite all that was new in her life. "I don't want to start anything that will take more of my time from Beverley right now."

"How's she doing, poor thing?"

"She's still grieving, and she will for a while, but she's tough stuff. We'll make it." I truly cared for Beverley. When her mom got a job in the city and quit kenneling here, I'd missed more than just the popcorn and Disney nights I'd shared with the kid. "So, Lydia," I asked, intentionally changing the subject, "how'd you end up nominating entrants for this . . . *eggzemmyoom* thing anyway?"

"Because I'm the oldest!" Lydia laughed. "WEC wants savvy, smart, and pretty *young* women as covenheads nowadays, what with the internet and media always poking around the high-profile urban covens." She pronounced the acronym for the Witch Elders Council as *weck,* like a kid who can't make *R* sounds saying *wreck.* "They know I deserve the authority, but can't keep up with the social scene. This is their way of coddling me for what I can't do."

Over the last few years I had become friends with Lydia, who happened to be the previous owner of my old saltbox-style farmhouse. She'd sold off pieces of her land and bought a double-wide, then stuck the FOR SALE BY OWNER sign in the front yard. We met shortly after I called the number written on the sign. One-level living suited her knees better, she'd said. The only downside, according to her, was "trading the charm and earthy smell of a root cellar for a sterile, wire-shelved pantry." A kitchen witch, she canned the vegetables she grew in her garden and made the best black raspberry jelly I'd ever tasted, period. When she shared her scrumptious goodies, they always came with a little checkerboard gingham ribbon tied around the neck of the Mason jar. I was certain that fabric came from her worn-out dresses. She could've walked onto the set of *Little House on the Prairie* and assumed a place as an extra without being questioned. All she lacked was a sunbonnet.

"I tried to tell them from the start that Vivian was a no-good hustler," she continued. "I tried to stop her from being in Cleveland's last Eximium, but my objections went unheard. After she reconfigured the membership into nothing more than a who's-who list of wealthy local socialites, though, they understood."

"I know," I said. Lydia didn't know the half of it. Vivian had done wrong by the coven, but that was only a minor part of her no-goodness. Vivian not only set me up and used me in attempt to gain an Elders Council seat, but she had murdered Lorrie and been responsible for the near-death of Theo, another friend of mine. That's why I'd turned her over to the vampire.

Truthfully, it wasn't like I could have kept him from taking her, so "I turned her over to the vampire" may be overstating my role in the situation.

My part of it aside, the vampire had taken her and she hadn't been seen since. Now, Hallowe'en was coming and there was no high priestess to conduct the all-important annual Witches Ball. It was the single biggest fund-raiser of the year for the coven and its largest publicity opportunity. Having a stand-in or temporary priestess just wouldn't suffice—or so Lydia claimed the Elders had said.

"I wonder what happened to her," Lydia mused.

"I think she disappeared after she dropped Beverley here. Maybe the role of godparent was too much for her." That was the angle the media had taken. Any story that left me out of the loop was a good one and I was sticking to it.

"Will you adopt her, Persephone?"

"Sure, if she wants, but I think we'll just keep me as the legal guardian. She needs to settle in and just be a kid."

"See, dear, you're such a responsible soul! *You* should

be the one to lead the coven, not a stranger to the area. You know Clevelanders are slow to warm up to outsiders, and I don't want another fast-talking swindler misusing the privilege."

Vivian had carried a vampire's mark—I call it a "stain"—and that should have prevented her from attaining any authority in the first place. Under the influence of a vampire *and* in authority over witches? *Totally* bad idea. Vivian had pulled it off only because of a magical stake she created to keep her vampire master at bay. Now, due to her involving unsuspecting but responsible little ol' me in her plot, the stake was destroyed, she was with the vampire, and I, too, carried a nefarious stain.

Ethically, I didn't deserve being high priestess any more than Vivian had, but that wasn't something I wanted to advertise. "Lydia, honestly, I don't want the authority." Not the whole truth, but not a lie either.

"That's exactly why your name's in. They asked me to nominate someone local from the coven to take over and I gave them your name—"

"But I'm a solitary! I may be local, but I'm not really part of the coven! I never even attended the esbats, let alone the sabbats or—"

"You're still the best person for the job, Persephone Alcmedi, and if you want out, you'll have to come to the Covenstead and formally decline it. Good day."

The phone went dead in my hand.

So . . . if she didn't get her way, dear old granny-witch was going to be difficult.

It's always the sweet ones you have to watch out for.

CHAPTER TWO

I'd been to the Covenstead only once, almost a decade ago when I officially signed the adult roster and designated myself as a solitary—a witch who practices solo with no coven affiliation, but who still can vote on matters affecting the witch community. Back then, the building, situated on four semirural suburban acres, was little more than a concrete-block cube with garage doors on four sides that could be opened to let nature in while keeping the rain out. Now, a surprisingly attractive circular building topped with a geodesic dome was centered on the manicured lot. Stone walls rose from subtle "natural" landscaping that surrounded the dome; a wide paved parking area ringed the grounds. The rest of the terrain was as meticulously perfect as a golf course with large elder, ash, oak, and thorn trees in each corner. The acreage could easily accommodate outdoor rituals and the indoor facility offered the coven comfortable shelter during cold northeast Ohio winters. All in all, it seemed the perfect blending of witchcraft symbolism—nature, the circle, the triangle—enhanced for the comfort of those who could afford it.

Vivian had left her legacy by exploiting the deep pockets of her preferred flock. They bankrolled the bulldozer-demise of the old structure and funded the construction of the modern gymnasium-sized facility to replace it.

As I drove around it, the repeating triangle shapes of the dome reminded me of the Earth's global geodesic lines, the ley lines. One ran across the back of my rural twenty acres and its energy fueled my house wards as needed.

I parked my Toyota Avalon—I loved all things Arthurian and chose the model for its evocative name, not its style or gas mileage. Cool early evening air swirled around me as I opened the door and got out. Rain was expected later tonight. It was my plan to get home and cut some corn stalks for decorations before it started falling.

The Covenstead had four pairs of oversize wooden doors—each placed to coincide with a compass point. The giant E carved into the middle of the pair of doors in front of me confirmed I was approaching the eastern entrance, as if the darkening evening sky behind me wasn't clue enough. Over the entry was a wooden plaque elaborately carved with a leafy "Green Man" face and the inscription: "Merry Meet and Merry Part."

Despite its weight, the door opened inward easily with a push.

Inside, it was nearly pitch black. Overhead, dim pinpoint lights twinkled like stars in the heavens and illuminated the points of a pentacle inlaid in the floor. Made with the deep, reddish tones of cherrywood, the symbol was centered on an otherwise pale pine floor. The flooring where I stood just inside the door and that of the area surrounding the wooden circle was of a durable exposed aggregate, a pebbly mix of earthy shades. The room seemed so vast it felt like an empty sports arena, thrumming with potent silence.

Hello? The ley line whispered timidly to my senses, as if it were hiding far away.

The ley line on my property had spoken to me once, the first time I walked in the rows of corn behind my home. Since then, it always sent a barely noticeable pulse in greeting when I ventured into the cornfield, like a neighbor waving from across the street. Those who weren't sensitive to magical energy simply didn't feel it. They wouldn't hear it calling either. Those who were sensitive to it usually felt it as an indication of something bad, the sort of feeling most folks described as "this place gives me the creeps."

"Hello," I whispered back.

The smell of ylang-ylang filled my nostrils and I could sense remnants of energy. As I stepped farther in, eyes adjusting to the dimness, my every footstep seemed amplified.

I became aware of sound to my left.

Several stairways led up to a railed catwalk encircling the structure about ten feet above the floor level. How convenient: a well-placed media area where cameras could get a good view of rituals below. My, my, Vivian and her crowd had thought of everything, hadn't they?

But the sound I heard came from below. Wide descending stairs between the eastern door I'd entered and the southern door to my left leaked light and what was now discernable as chattering people and a ringing phone. I started down.

"Venefica Covenstead." Pause. "Yes, we received your fax."

At the bottom of the stairs were arrows, universal rest-room signs, and the glass wall of an office area, its door propped open. Inside, a bleached blonde sitting at a desk rolled her thick-lined eyes as she held her pen poised above a pad of paper. She seemed familiar, but I couldn't place her. Another woman stood leaning on an elbow-high counter and a pair of women sat on cushioned seats along the wall flipping through *New Witch* and *Green Egg* magazines.

"Okay," the receptionist said. "I'll make a note of that in your file, Ms. Taylor. . . . you're staying at the Motel 6 near the airport. Sure, we'll contact you there."

The woman waiting at the counter sniggered at the words "Motel 6" and turned to me. She looked me up and down, taking in my hiking boots, jeans, black tee, and dark flannel shirt in a quick assessment. "Getting the grounds ready for the winter?"

"The grounds?"

She flapped a hand in the air. "Here. The Covenstead grounds." She sounded annoyed with me, as if I weren't keeping up.

She thought I was the groundskeeper? I said, flatly, "No."

"Don't tell me you're here to sign in for the Eximium?" She crossed her arms, made a second up and down evaluation of me, and laughed.

Okay, so I had been outside preparing to cut fodder

shocks when roughhousing with Beverley and Ares, our black Great Dane, took precedence. Then Nana had yelled there was a call for me. After taking Lydia's call I came straight here. I wasn't expecting a dress code. "And if I am?"

"Are you?" she asked curtly.

She was tan, tall, and rail thin. Her glossy blue-black hair was straight and down to her elbows. Her expertly applied makeup was done in natural colors, except for fire-engine-red lipstick. The expensive white blouse was crisp; the flipped-up cuffs gave it a nonchalant flair. Her dark designer jeans were tight and pressed so they had a razor-sharp line down the front; the bottoms were folded up in wide cuffs to show thin ankles—a dainty gold chain around one—and pumps that matched her lipstick.

Lydia's earlier comment came back to me, the one about WEC wanting "savvy, smart, and pretty young women" as covenheads for good media exposure. But only someone wearing her ultra-stylishness as a mask would bother to iron jeans like that.

I stuck with my short answers. "Yes."

"And are you staying at the Motel 6 too?" she asked with an utterly insincere smile.

"No."

"Good. I hope you procured more prestigious accommodations. A high priestess does have to have some pride, you know. I'm at the Renaissance downtown. You?"

She was really bugging me. "At my home, actually."

"Oh." She drew out the word and her blue eyes narrowed. "You're the local nominee. How nice." She put out her right hand. "I'm Hunter. Hunter Hopewell."

Everyone in the room looked up when Hunter put her hand out to me. I knew something was about to happen.

Witches, especially pushy aggressive witches, do this . . . thing. It's similar to the guy-code, machismo, pissing-contest-in-a-handshake, where the strength of the grip proves who's the manlier. In the witch version, since the right hand is projective, she was going to zap me with her aural energy to see if my own was weaker or stronger. Though I know about this, I don't have cause or desire to practice it, so I hesitated, considering.

I thought of a conductivity demonstration back in high school. The whole class linked hands and on one end, someone touched the experiment's low-voltage electricity source. On the other end, someone touched the metal chalk tray. Everyone got shocked. In my class, I was the one to touch the metal. Knowing what was about to happen made that assignment fun at the time. Like most teens, I had enough of a juvenile sadistic streak to enjoy seeing certain classmates get a low dose of electricity.

Calling up that sadistic inner teenager, I threw a jolt of my own into my palm, reached out, and grabbed Hunter's hand with that same amount of high school glee.

Nothing happened.

She squinted again. The corner of my mouth crooked up. The nothing that happened meant we were even. Or, at least, that my new stain nullified her jolt.

The phone buzzed and the receptionist answered with, "Yes?"

"I didn't catch your name," Hunter Hopewell said, releasing my hand.

"I didn't drop it."

The receptionist placed the receiver in its cradle and turned her seat toward us. "Lydia will see you now."

Hunter moved to go around the desk.

"Oh, not you, Ms. Hopewell. I meant Ms. Alcmedi."

That the girl knew my name and pronounced it correctly surprised me. I thanked her and then it hit me where I knew her from. "Mandy, right? From Vivian's coffee shop in Cleveland?"

A sheepish smile flashed across her round face and disappeared.

"You changed your hair." It had been an indistinct pale brown.

She petted the unhealthy length of platinum blond hair stretching over her shoulder. "Yeah. Vivian's idea."

I wondered if Vivian helped her make any other bad choices. Poor girl. A compliment should've sprung to mind, but it just didn't. The overprocessed frizz she was stuck with couldn't flatter anyone and I couldn't just *lie*.

She appeared as if she might cry. "Are you okay?" I asked.

"I just miss her so much."

"Oh." What was I supposed to say? If I tried to console Mandy after I'd helped the vampire get Vivian, the words would taste ashy.

"I've been Vivian's intern-slash-protégé for almost two years. You'd think that, of all people, she'd give me a hint before she split." She rolled her eyes again even as she wiped at the corners. *At least someone had thought well of Vivian.* "I didn't think you'd remember me," she said.

I did. The coffee she'd made me had been terrible. Of course that had been the day I found out about Lorrie's murder, so maybe it was my mood souring my palate more than the beverage. Shrugging, I said, "I didn't at first. The new color threw me. I'm surprised you knew me."

"Vivian didn't often talk to people in her office at the shop. . . ." Mandy paused. "How's the kid?"

"Adjusting well," I said and started around the desk. "Thanks for asking."

"I was here first," Hunter protested.

"Yeah, I know," Mandy said through gritting teeth. "You've been here exactly thirty-three minutes and"—she glanced at the wall clock—"fourteen seconds."

"So the local contender is getting preferential treatment already," Hunter declared. "Why do you people bother having an Eximium if you're just going to hand it to your local contestant?"

From the office doorway, I looked over my shoulder at her quizzically.

She said, "I was here first and I should be seen first."

"Wah. Get over it," Mandy said.

Hunter made a derisive sound and ratcheted her chin up.

"You know," I said to Hunter, "a high priestess ought to know the difference between pride and conceit." I shut Lydia's door.

Sitting meekly in an oversize chair behind a massive mahogany desk, Lydia gave the impression of frailty but I knew better. She stood to greet me. Her usual summertime gingham dress had been replaced with a white turtleneck under a wide-collared forest green sweater, paired with a long, tan corduroy skirt. It was obvious the changing season had left her cold.

After a quick hug, I sank into the seat across from her and asked, "Are they all like that?"

"No, thank the Goddess, but she is the worst."

"Good."

"No, Seph. Actually, that's bad."

"Why?"

"Because, dear, she'll take the Eximium and become high priestess . . . with you opting out of it and all."

A hard frown tightened my face. I suspected I was about to be inveigled. I'd have bet that she knew I'd protest the nomination. She likely waited to call me about it until Hunter walked in the door, knowing that I'd rush down to decline. Meanwhile, Lydia had made Hunter wait so she'd be irritated and our paths could cross on those exact terms because then I'd be more motivated to concede and be in the Eximium. Damned sneaky old witch.

"What?" she demanded, gauging my hard expression. "Don't tell me you didn't instantly size her up and peg her for what she is."

"Lydia."

"Jolted you, didn't she?"

"She tried."

"I knew it!" Lydia's expression brightened considerably and she smacked the desktop. "Got nowhere with you, did she?" She tapped gnarled fingers on the desk. "She's jolted everyone in this office, except poor little Mandy. Even reached across the desk trying to shake Mandy's hand, but Mandy ignored her. She just kept typing and said, 'If you want to impress me, stick both of your thumbs up your ass and walk on your elbows.'" Lydia chuckled. "She can be so bland, that girl, then she spouts something like that!"

When I stopped laughing, the moment sobered and I said, "Seemed like Mandy was going to cry there for a moment."

Lydia sighed. "She's lost without Vivian." Leaning closer, she put one arm up on the desk, cupped her mouth with a hand, and whispered, "She's moody too. Probably bleeding." Leaning back, she went on at normal volume, "Still, if Hunter couldn't jolt you, that just confirms to me that you need to be in this competition!"

I couldn't tell her the reason I nullified her jolt was more likely due to the vampire stain I now carried. "This is all very . . . I don't know. But—"

"I know, I know. You're here to opt out." She pulled open a drawer and began digging around. "Vivian was so organized and in a week I've managed to undo it all. Poor Mandy is so aggravated with me." Her delicate digging turned into rough rummaging. "Where is that form?"

"Form?"

Lydia nodded, still searching in the drawer.

"Why do I have to fill out a form? I didn't fill one out to be nominated."

"You don't fill it out. I do. The Elders require formal notification if they have to make the local choice themselves."

"I don't understand coven politics."

"Of course not; you're a solitary." She shut the drawer and opened another. "I had it a second ago. . . ."

"Why can't you just pick someone else?"

"Not allowed. If my choice refuses, then the Elders

come in a few days early to evaluate everyone from the coven and nominate one of them." She fixed me with an expression of annoyance. "A waste of time, to be sure." She resumed hunting through the newly opened drawer. "Vivian filled the coven with influential people who would run it like a country club, where exclusivity is more important than spirituality. The rest of us were pushed aside and belittled. Some moved away, some became solitary. Some have their own covens now, though not WEC endorsed."

"The Elders will surely include them in the evaluations. I mean, one of them will be more suitable, right?"

Lydia shut the drawer forcefully. "I know what I'm doing. And I know that with you out, Hunter will take the Eximium. She will be the high priestess. She strikes me as the type who will use the exposure to further inflate her ego."

"Lydia, I don't want the coven left to further internal disintegration. I can see this means a lot to you and I do want to help, but I have enough responsibilities. I've had a lot thrust upon me recently. Other than Beverley, I have to take care of my Nana now and—"

"Demeter?"

"Yes, she—" I started to go on but she cut me off again.

"I thought she was in a home?"

"They kicked her out. I'm sure her pushy attitude and nicotine cravings had *nothing* to do with it."

Lydia caught my sarcasm. "Oh, of *course* not."

"Wait—you know my Nana?"

"I used to. A long time ago, dear. A very long time

ago." She smiled fondly as if at a good memory. "Plucky as ever, is she?"

"Plucky? Um, more like mulish and obstinate. You should visit—"

"Oh, I don't think she'd appreciate that."

"Why not?"

"Well, we didn't part on the best of terms." She paused. "That was her on the phone, wasn't it?"

"Yeah."

"Didn't even occur to me at the time." Lydia relaxed into her chair, the warm-hearted smile on her face continuing as she waxed nostalgic.

"As I was saying," I forged ahead with my list of duties. "In addition to Nana, there's Beverley, the dog, the house and yard, and my newspaper column is now nationally syndicated." My column devoted to making readers aware of the plight of those maintaining their "normal" lives despite being wærewolves was finally paying off. The syndication was, unfortunately, thanks to the vampire who stained me, but still, my broker was going to be a happy boy. He might even learn to pronounce both my first and last names correctly. "So the pressure is high."

"That's the one under the pseudonym of Circe Muirwood, right?"

"Yeah." Lydia, who had sold the house herself and not used an agent, had asked me many questions before she agreed to sell me her farmhouse, citing it was her responsibility to make certain that such a decidedly witchy home not end up in the wrong hands—what with its nearby ley line and all. And in the interest of *keeping* it in the right hands, she'd been interested in how I'd pay the mortgage and whether my work was steady. I'd told her about the column.

"You're casting a rather positive light on wærewolves with that column, aren't you?"

"Yes. Many of my friends are wære." I was accustomed to people being negative about them for no good reason. "Does that bother you?" Maybe it would get me out of the competition.

"Not at all. I've been close to many wæres in my time, it's just that, well . . . Demeter isn't fond of them."

"Witches and wæres—" I began.

Lydia joined me in finishing, "—weren't meant to mingle."

I laughed.

Lydia did too, then we sobered. "Is that still her mantra?" she asked.

"It certainly was, but lately she has been warming up to one of my wære friends. Surprised the heck out of me."

"How does she feel about your column?"

"It's my main income and the means through which I'm supporting her, so she can't gripe. Of course, that won't stop her."

Lydia was silent, considering, but her disappointment was clear. "I see. You do have a lot of irons in the fire." She tapped her hand gently on the table. "I had hoped you would do this. I trust you because you haven't been subjected to all the politics or tainted by them."

"If things were different, Lydia, I *would* do this." What Lydia didn't realize was that I was tainted. Bearing the stain of the master vampire Menessos meant I couldn't do this. Shouldn't do this. It would be unethical. Plus, I was already afraid Menessos would find some reason to further insinuate himself into my life. Becoming a high priestess with political clout might be reason enough.

And there was more. According to Nana and Johnny—a wærewolf friend who was oddly knowledge-able about mystical things and yet another complica-tion in my life, albeit a pleasant one—I was the Lustrata. The walker between worlds. I was still learning what, exactly, that meant. Johnny had moved into the attic room, at first as a guard of sorts, but also to help guide me in this new role. Nana had been insisting that I pres-ent myself as the Lustrata to the Council. I wasn't about to do that until I knew what in Hades being Lustrata meant. Who knew how this Lustrata stuff would affect being a high priestess, politically, personally, spiritually, whatever.

I exhaled resignedly; I'd come out here to decline this and should—

Wait. This sly she-devil of a pagan was full of tricks, wasn't she? "Lydia, since *you* fill out the form, I came out here for what? To sign it?"

Her regret disappeared, replaced by peevishness. She crossed her arms and turned away, brow furrowing. "You didn't have to come out."

About to give her my I-don't-appreciate-being-made-to-jump-through-hoops speech, I stopped when, beyond the door, someone yelped loudly.

I started out of my seat to see what was going on.

"Sit down, Persephone," Lydia said gently.

"But—"

"Hunter just jolted someone else. Another contestant must have come in."

I eased back into my chair. "Can't you disqualify her or something?"

"This is the way high priestesses have come to be, dear. Best with their broomsticks. By wick and by wand. Oh, the tests have evolved with the times, but if she earns it, proves better than her peers, she leads. Even if she's too young. Even if she's a persnickety, silver-spoon-fed Midwestern girl who doesn't have a chance at understanding the nuances of this city and these people."

We sat in silence.

Beyond the door, Mandy shouted, "Ow!" Followed by, "You bitch!"

Lydia looked woefully at me.

"Fine," I said. "I'll do it."

CHAPTER THREE

Desiccated cornstalks shifted in the night breeze, the sound scraping my ears as I stood at the edge of the field behind my home. Hallowe'en was coming. One week. I stood on the cusp of seasons, feeling the world adjusting, preparing for hibernation and the barren cold.

The goddess Persephone, my namesake, descended into the underworld for six months of every year. Her mother, the goddess Demeter, caused the world to grow colder and dormant, creating winter, while she mourned her daughter's absence. Like my namesake, I'd departed from my "normal" world and entered another.

But I wouldn't be returning. At least, not as the same person I was before leaving.

My life had become the polar opposite of what it had been a month ago; a warped caricature of what I used to know. Everything was backward, as if I'd been hibernating all this time only to awaken just at the onset of the world's bitter, frozen season. The green world was dying, a contradiction to the forced growth in my life.

Nevertheless, Hallowe'en was my favorite holiday and I was going to make the best of it. That meant decorating for harvest with pumpkins and gourds. It meant making caramel apples. It meant that, despite the coming cold, I would create a warm home environment . . . for Beverley.

So, my feet were planted at the edge of the cornfield. The predicted rain hadn't yet come, but I could feel it in the air. The wooden handle of my sickle felt smooth in my sweaty hand. A pile of stalks lay nearby, neat and stark against the dark grass. Night had fully come. The moon was new early last week; now it was officially a first quarter moon, a sharp crescent glimmering between thick, gray clouds. I was gathering cornstalks to make fodder-shocks for my front porch. Collecting them under a darkened sky matched the season's tone.

Unlike the front-yard Chinkapin oaks that had already begun dropping their golden leaves, in the grove the white ash and white oak trees still held most of their purple, bronze, and red ornaments. Something about the ley line crossing the field there helped them hold on to their leaves a little longer.

Amid their roots lay the access point I used to power my home wards. Though it was not a nucleus—an intersection of lines—it was close to such a hub and the earth-energy flowed strong. I could tap it due to lifelong training, learning to feel and discern the different energies, to draw out the latent energy stored in gemstones and crystals and shape it to my will. My experience had grown to incorporate bigger sources, like the line. I hadn't had cause to use it for more than the wards except twice: once to save my friend Theo's life and once to re-establish my home's innate security against vampires.

As Nana was prone to say, *Once is a mistake, but twice is a habit.* I didn't want using the ley line to be habitual.

Thinking of habits, I allowed my gaze to drift toward the house. Beverley's light remained on. Nana was still reading to her. I'd barely spoken to Nana since returning from the Covenstead, but a long discussion was inevitable. I would have to tell her what had happened, but it could wait a bit longer. I didn't want to further interrupt our new evening customs.

Our evening regimen started with Beverley going upstairs to shower with Ares on her heels so he could lie on the bathroom floor, waiting. Nana followed her up and, when Beverley finished, Nana helped her comb and dry her glossy, dark hair. They always played a board game, then ended the day with Nana reading aloud while Beverley settled in. They both seemed to enjoy the routine; I'd watched them, undetected, from my darkened room. Beverley was getting a better version of my Nana than I had known growing up, like Demeter 2.0 or something.

I didn't want to mess it up, not even for one evening. Getting Nana's input about the Eximium was important to me but, at the same time, I didn't want to tell her about it at all. She'd surely find a reason to be against my decision.

The breeze increased, but didn't flutter the corn. Only the treetops danced.

Come.

The ley line spoke!

The grove's branches swayed, beckoning me. Then all at once the field was inviting me, stalks undulating, tassels nodding, pennant-like leaves waving me in, encouraging me to step into the row, into the arms of the stalks.

Intrigued, I laid down the sickle and succumbed to the summoning. Immediately the row stilled as the dried leaves reached high, making an aisle for me, opening as if this procession of one moving toward that seat of power in the grove was a most welcome guest.

My steps, punctuated by the crunching of dead weeds underfoot, released aromas that combined the smell of harvest: the scents of soil and a field of vegetation left to deteriorate and rot, withering in the wind of ever-cooler days. In the embrace of the stalks, my fingers trailed outward, feeling their dry husks, the texture of the season.

The ley line sent a pulse to acknowledge me. I expected a faint hiccup, like a little gust of wind, but this was much stronger, like the tremor of a small earthquake under my feet or the bass drum at a rock concert thudding out its rhythm against my chest.

Something was different. Why?

You are different.

I walked on. Great. The ley line knows I'm stained. Just what I wanted, to feel more like a freak.

As I reached the edge of the grove, rain began sprinkling down.

If it began to pour like the weatherman predicted, I'd be drenched before I made it back to the house. Eyes on the sky to gauge the clouds, my toes struck an exposed tree root. For all the pomp of my journey here, my arrival was doomed to gracelessness. In my attempt to catch myself, my palm grazed the ridged bark of the ambushing oak. I stumbled into the grove and went down on my knees.

In an instant, a blue-tinged field formed around the interior of the wood and the space surrounding me.

The smell of saltwater filled my nostrils and the cry of gulls and the crash of waves filled my ears. Raindrops beaded and rolled on the lightly glowing exterior surface. Its spherical shape made it seem as if I was inside a bubble. What the hell was going on? A blue mist rose from the ground not far in front of me. It swirled rapidly together, twisting and pushing like some creature inside a balloon, stretching and growing.

"I pray thee, forgive me this trespass."

The voice was female, soft and melodic. In a few seconds, a two-foot-long mermaid floated before me. Her lower half was layered in pearlescent blue scales. The skin of her upper half was a shade paler and gleamed like it was embedded with glitter. Her raven hair lifted as if she still floated in water. She wore only pearls, a dozen necklaces of various lengths, one strand rounding beneath each breast.

"I am Aquula."

"You're . . . you're a mermaid? In my cornfield?"

She giggled and it was the sound of pebbles clinking as the tide recedes. I glanced up; the rain was hitting heavier on the bubble.

"I am a fairy." Her childlike voice came in a whisper, as if sharing a secret. "A water fairy."

Historically, it was customary for witches to call upon the fey as quarter guards for their circles. In modern times, however, calling the fey could get a witch killed.

Allergic to asphalt and iron, the fey had wanted to return to their own realm completely. They no longer wished to be bound to witches who could jerk them without warning from that world—where time ran differently—for the purpose of protecting a circle. Long before the other-than-merely-humans had come out of hiding, back in 1971, the Concordat Munus affirmed that the fey had, for lack of a better term, unionized. They were not to be summoned by witches ever again, or the witches would suffer the consequences. Elementals had agreed to stand—in spirit form—as our protectors in place of the fairies.

While the fey remained free to visit our world, such sojourns were rare due to their allergies.

I'd seen fairies on TV, but never in person. I was drawn to study her otherworldly face, so delicate and innocent. But I knew the fables. The fey only *look* frail. That misconception of frangibility had led humans to lose their fear of something very dangerous. "Why are you here?"

"I am here because of Menessos." She followed his name with a tremulous "Ahh . . ." sounding like a lovestruck teen.

"Oh. Great." There was no enthusiasm in my tone.

"He is quite lovely, is he not?"

Okay, so he was the walking, talking body double for Arthur Pendragon, my myth-based fantasy man who had romanced me in my dreams for as long as I could remember. He might be hot, but he was still a *vampire*. My fingers tapped on my thighs. "I suppose."

"Suppose?" She flipped her tail and seemed to swoon, falling slowly to the side, her hair gliding fluidly up.

Outside the bubble, the rain fell harder still. "He is gorgeous to my eyes, but I forget myself." She floated upright again. "Thou art Persephone and thou hast tempted him back into the circle."

That was what Samson D. Kline had told me, shortly before Menessos beheaded him. Later, Menessos confirmed it. "I didn't know he'd been refraining at the time."

"Regardless, I thank thee."

"I'm glad you're happy about it." Maybe she would keep him busy and away from me.

"I am his southern quarter guardian, and now I know I shall see him again."

Did she not know of the Concordat?

"The guardians of the north, east, and south are fearful, now that he hath returned to the circle. But I yearn for his beckoning." She paused, expression dreamy.

I realized she and the other three "guardians" did indeed know of the agreement with the witches. I already knew Menessos was not just a vampire. He was a vampire-wizard, a sorcerer. I had no idea how or if the Concordat applied to him and it sounded as if the fairies were none too sure themselves.

Her expression turned serious and she eased forward to slip a cold hand to my wrist. Her dark eyes, eerie with much larger irises than a human's, searched my face. "Be warned, sweet Persephone: the others have taken to plotting. And while I would do naught that would earn my master's wrath, the others seek only to dispense with their binding by any means. Thou art precious to him, else he would not have entered thy circle. This hath not occurred to my counterparts, sweet Persephone, but it will," she said gravely. "I beseech thee to take precautions and protect thyself."

"I will now," I said.

"I cannot linger." Even as she said the words, the rain slacked off.

I wondered if my world was, to the fey, like my personal meditation world where a jackal named Amenemhab counseled me. "Go, Aquula. And thank you."

She faded back into a mist. With a low pop, the bubble burst. The smell and sound of the ocean faded. While the fleeting raindrops pressed the mist back into the earth, the branches overhead shielded me.

I sat in the grove thinking. Vivian's stake had been destroyed by my hand. Menessos owed me. Acceptable repayment, as far as I was concerned, would simply be him staying the hell away from me. But if his enemies were going to think of me as a tool to be used for retaliating against him, maybe I needed to call in the favor he owed me.

I started back into the rows of cornstalks to make my way back to the house; it was barely sprinkling now. A few steps in, I heard a twig snap elsewhere in the field.

I stopped.

Probably a deer . . . unless it was one of Menessos's loyal beholders. If he commanded, any of those vampire-wannabe-muscleboys would keep an eye on me for him.

This was *my* land, my twenty acres, damn it! I should feel safe taking a walk here, not paranoid.

Of course, if it were the fey already making their move . . .

Or . . . Menessos himself had told me of his enemies

searching for ways to manipulate him via the connections he made . . .

A breath caught in my throat.

As I started moving slowly through the field toward the house, distant steps mimicked the rhythm of my own, attempting to disguise their presence. My hearing was definitely improved by the damnable stain I'd received, but I was far from grateful for that or any other "enhancements" it granted.

I came to an abrupt stop to avoid walking face-first into the broad web of a corn spider, then heard a *snap* behind me. Silence.

Stay calm. Think.

Gauging the last sound, I guessed my pursuer was about fifty feet behind me.

Adrenaline flooding my system, my flight instinct screaming, I bolted under the web and forward, using the biochemical boost to run for my backyard as fast as I could, swatting stalks out of my path. Though running blindly, I knew my steps were swifter than ever before.

Another bonus from the stain.

Air flowed more easily and deeply into my lungs, oxygen and adrenaline passed quicker into my muscles. My body was functioning like a new and improved machine, every component of the whole working more efficiently and smoothly, as if some residue that had always impeded the higher level of operation had finally been cleaned away. Like a long overdue oil change.

Was that residue my humanity? My soul?

I stopped dead in my tracks.

Another huge corn spider, black and yellow, hovered

in the center of a dazzling web less than an inch from my nose.

Dropping to my knees, I fought to control and quiet my breathing and crawled underneath and beyond the web. I could hear steps approaching, following, but cautiously. Still, I'd be found. It was only a matter of time.

It was close. I *sensed* it.

I shot up and ran. Behind me I heard squealing, swearing, flailing. A big spider and its web across your face can elicit a startled reaction even from the toughest. But it wouldn't stop whoever it was for long.

I took off again, sprinting through the crackling stalks, feet sure under me even on the rain-slicked soil. I pushed for more speed, telling myself this was a race, not a chase. And I ran, ran for the clearing ahead, ran for home.

My mind flashed on a different cornfield in my memory, reminding me of how as a child I'd fled like this on an equally dark night. Then, I was running away from all the fear and uncertainty in my life. My mother had gone, left me with Nana. I felt so unloved and everything was terrible. Instead of walking to Nana's apartment after school, I left the little town behind, tromped through woods, crossed a wheat field, a dirt road, and pushed into a cornfield. I never considered going back. Not even when night set in. I grew cold and scared, but instead of stopping, I literally began to run.

I collapsed that night, exhausted and sobbing, between the rows. The Goddess came to me there. The memory reminded me of Her comfort. That was something to hold on to, something to be inspired by.

I'll make it. I will!

My pursuer was gaining ground behind me, panting breaths like a locomotive rhythm in my ears. I suddenly felt exposed, like playing "It" and I so hated that game. *It is just behind me . . . if it catches me, I'll be It!* I could no longer trick myself into thinking this was just a race. Fear kicked in and a different chemical flooded into my blood-stream and seemed to soak up my energy. My breaths didn't do enough. My legs felt like lead.

Call on the ley! But I couldn't think of a spell-rhyme.

CHAPTER FOUR

"Persephone!"

"Johnny!" Expending the oxygen to call out cost me. I could feel my pace slow.

My pursuer was right behind me. I felt fingers grasping at my back, reaching for my flannel shirt.

"Persephone!"

Johnny was closer now. Thank the Goddess!

I burst from the cornfield and slammed right into Johnny. I think he tried to hold on to me, but I fell. Breathing hard, all I could smell was the grass in my face. My heart thudded against my rib cage like a Bumble Ball.

"Someone's out there." I rolled onto my back.

"I know, I can smell 'em. Erik." He nodded at Erik— the drummer for Johnny's band Lycanthropia—whom I hadn't noticed until then. The stalks rustled as Erik stormed into the field.

"Are you all right?" Johnny crouched beside me.

"Yeah."

He grinned and said, "Yeah! The way you came across that field—holy shit! I didn't know you were a speed-demon. I bet you could outrun a wære. Does the U.S. Olympic Committee know about you?"

Fighting to catch my breath, I couldn't laugh at Johnny's wisecrack. Besides, all I could think was: the speed, the hearing, that extra sense—Goddess knew what else—were undeniably "gifts" of Menessos's stain.

"Hey, what's with the frown? You sure you're okay?"

"Yeah, fine. Just catching my breath."

"Frowns always happen for a reason," he said. Straightening up from his crouching position, he stared down at me and crossed his arms. "Fess up."

"Just winded and scared." I sat up, in the damp grass, still breathing hard. "It's nothing."

That wasn't true. There was plenty to frown about. Johnny didn't realize I still carried Menessos's stain. He thought the stain had been burned away by the pain and consequent empowerment the stake had brought me. Johnny was partially right: I *could* have been unstained, but the vampire's bonding had fused itself to pieces of me I didn't want to part with.

Johnny didn't know the stain was now integral to my being. I could not be free of it without losing too much of my self.

I hadn't told him because he was still licking his wounds over his fight with Menessos. While I knew Johnny genuinely cared for me, he wasn't fond of the flowers and art and not-so-small fortune's worth of other gifts that the master vampire sent me after I destroyed the stake rather than use it to end Menessos's existence.

How could I say to him, "By the way, Johnny, I can still feel Menessos in the marrow of my bones"?

Maybe if I understood more about this Lustrata thing . . . but all I had were questions and no answers. Nana said the Lustrata was supposed to have a stain in order to have a reason to be a part of the vampire's world. Maybe Johnny thought I'd just pick one up from a more agreeable vampire later.

"C'mon, tell me what's causing that furrow in your brow or I won't help you up." Johnny stood over me, somehow combining his teasing smile with stubborn concern as only he could. His eyes, tattooed with the markings of the ancient Egyptian god Horus— the Wedjat—twinkled in the light that came from the house. He wore tight black jeans and an unbuttoned black-on-black shirt, flat black with stripes that were just a bit shinier. Under it, a white tank clung to his lean body, revealing the curve of pectorals, the dip under the sternum, the wave of abs. In the near-dark, it was all just levels of shadow, but those contours made me yearn to touch him, to rip off the shirt and reveal the myriad tattoos underneath so I could trace them with my fingers, with my tongue. The tight jeans with their pocket accent chains and scarlet wolf's-head patches paired with the leather biker boots completed Johnny's bad-boy rocker style. Oh. Yeah.

"I can't tell you. If I do it'll just embarrass me and you'll rub it in."

"Oh, I've got something I want to rub in all right." His pose faded and he reached down to give me a hand up, but somewhere in the stalks Erik gave a loud yelp. Johnny twisted away, ready to charge to the rescue of his drummer.

"Fucking spider bit me!" Erik shouted from somewhere in the field.

Johnny turned back and offered me his hand up again. "Anyway, Red, that run was impressive." He had started calling me Red—as in Red Riding Hood—a few weeks ago, when Nana moved in. He joked that visiting me "at Grandma's house" made him feel like the big, bad wolf. Except it was *my* house and Nana hated to be called "Grandma."

I slipped my hand into his and he easily had me back up on my feet.

With a devious smile, Johnny said, "Oh, look! You're covered in grass." He began brushing the little green blades off the arms of my flannel shirt, then stepped behind me and fluffed my dark hair gently. It made a shiver flow through me. Wiping debris from the back of the shirt, his hands swept lightly all over me. "It doesn't want to get off," he said. I could practically feel him thinking, *But I do.* He returned to my front and crouched, one hand brushing down the outer leg of my jeans while the other rested—surely only for the sake of balance—high on my inner thigh.

As he worked, I watched his face, remembering how swollen his eye had gotten after the encounter with Menessos. He'd earned it, lying to me by omission. But I couldn't forget his earnestness, his sincerity. Johnny believed in me more than I believed in myself.

And he wanted me. For all these months, he'd kenneled alone. And according to Celia and Erik, he hadn't even responded to the advances of any females—and there were plenty who advanced—at the band's live gigs.

So.

It seemed he'd been waiting for me. Hopelessly heart-challenged, relationship-disabled me.

Me.

Now we'd lived under the same roof for two weeks and although he made his desires clear every chance he got, he'd never forced the issue, never been overbearing or less than a gentleman, albeit a seductive gentleman with an unending talent for innuendo-laden conversation.

For a wære, sexual abstinence was ridiculous. Their libidos were stuck on hyperdrive—and he'd been denying himself, mastering himself. Or taking a lot of cold showers waiting for me to wake up.

Well, I had fully roused, and so had my yearning for physical satisfaction. Long ago, while in emotional pain, I dealt with a broken heart by convincing myself that my libido had overdosed on sleeping pills and would never get me into such hurtful trouble again. But my desires had awakened from the long coma and now seemed intent on making up for lost time. Problem was . . . had Johnny awakened them or had my stain been the blaring alarm clock?

The rain-wet waves of his hair beckoned and my fingers strayed to those misplaced tendrils at his brow, caressing them away, lifting the cedar and sage scent of him to my nostrils. I wanted to touch so much more of him. Right now I yearned to—

No. He deserved my anger for the danger he'd put Nana and Beverley in!

I almost groaned aloud in frustration. For the last two

weeks, that had been the biggest battle in my personal mental war about Johnny.

No one was harmed, my conscience reminded me. That was true—Nana was indignant about the whole thing and Beverley had spent her "hostage" time playing video games so she seemed no worse for the incident—but that wasn't the point. They *could* have been harmed, even killed, due to Johnny's deceit.

And I was also still waiting for him to explain to me how he'd managed an at-will partial transformation. He'd turned his hands to claws during his brief confrontation with Menessos. A wære just shouldn't be able to do that.

Under any other circumstances, it meant a wære had gotten close to a witch's spell energies and stirred up an incomplete transformation. Incompletes invariably lost their minds and never got them back. They remained stuck in a state between human and animal, crazed and vicious. Because of this, police officers were expected to shoot them on sight.

In addition to that un-wære-like talent, Johnny always kept his human sensibilities while transformed. He was unique in many ways.

We'd been becoming more than "just friends" since saving the life of our friend Theodora, but when he pulled a fast switcheroo with the stake, I learned he was willful to the point of deceit if he thought it necessary. I couldn't fully trust him.

And furthermore, if he was deserving of trust and discovered I was still stained and would forever be controllable by Menessos, could he trust *me*?

The Wedjat tattoos sharpened as he squinted slightly,

his focus intensifying. Surely he detected my phero-
mones. Desire. Anger. A scent cocktail that a wære
would crave.

Our mutual sexual attraction was trying ardently to
overwhelm rational thought. I clung to my shield—made
of trust issues that *should* keep us divided and that fear in
me that was unsure which part of me spawned this deep
yearning—but my grip weakened more each day.

"Such a sad smile from my Lustrata," he whispered.
He stood, hands sliding up my legs, hips, then under
the flannel to rest at my waist. The aroma of cedar and
sage grew stronger, then as his hands came to my neck I
detected something else.

"I smell metal."

He smirked. "It's from the guitar strings."

"I never noticed it before."

The damn stain had amped my sense of smell too.

It was a vaguely familiar scent to me, now that he
named it. I'd tried to learn to play on an acoustic guitar
as a teen, and I'd picked up a dorm neighbor's electric one
occasionally when the weather kept us all inside. I knew
some chords; that was all.

Johnny leaned in, ready to kiss me.

Erik burst from the field at a run. When he saw us,
he stopped, realized what he was interrupting, and said a
quiet, "Oh. Uh. Sorry."

"Well?" Johnny looked at Erik.

"Whoever they were, they were fast. Practically flew
outta here."

Flew? My spine stiffened.

Johnny's hands squeezed me reassuringly. "The scent?"

"Nothing I could identify," Erik said. "You?"

Johnny shook his head. "No."

"I'm going to increase the perimeter of my wards," I said.

"Good idea," Johnny said to me, then to Erik, "You okay?"

I slipped away from them and started gathering my cut stalks.

"Just a spider bite," Erik answered.

"Aww," Johnny teased, "little vampire-bug sink fangs into you?"

"That spider," Erik retorted, "was fucking mega-ginormous."

"Mega-ginormous?" I asked.

"Beyond giant and enormous," Erik replied.

"He drums *and* makes up his own words," Johnny said proudly.

Erik snickered. "It *is* a word."

"Right," we both said in response.

Defending himself, Erik said, "It is! I saw it on the Web."

Poking fun at him, I said, "If that spider was named Charlotte and she was writing on her web, I hope you didn't squash her."

"On the *Internet,*" Erik clarified.

I turned to them with the stalks in one hand, the sickle in the other.

"Holy Hecate," Johnny said.

"Huh?" Erik asked.

"Look at her!" Johnny pointed.

I turned to look behind me.

"Not behind you—*you*," he said, laughing at me. "You look like Hecate with her sickle and stalks."

"Yeah, right, because Hecate is *always* depicted in plaid flannel." Switching subjects to one I knew they'd not ignore, I said, "You guys hungry?"

"Of course," Erik said, still rubbing at the spider bite. "What do you think we're doing here?"

"Yeah," Johnny said. "Demeter promised to monitor the beef roast I put in for dinner and save some for us to eat after practice." He grinned broadly as he joined me and picked up a few stalks from the ground that I'd missed.

Though I'm a happy vegetarian, I know wæres need red meat. "I knew something was up with all that meat."

"If you want to know about the meat that's up—" Johnny whispered.

"I don't need to hear about your kielbasa."

"Okay, so rather than an oral description, you'd prefer actual hands-on experience with my 'ball-sa.' I'm good with that."

Even after a few weeks of this kind of innuendo, I still marveled at how quickly he could invent it. No clever reply came to mind. I went for the mundane. "How was practice? Got 'Debauchery' worked out?"

"Yup. So much so, we headed out to an open jam night at Peabody's." Johnny slipped half the stalks from my grip. We started walking around to the front of the house.

"What did the crowd think?"

"Kicked ass!" Erik said.

Approaching the porch, I pulled the lengths of twine I'd pre-cut from my pocket. Johnny passed his portion of fodder-shocks off to Erik so he could assist in the tying. Of course he had to put his front to my back and reach around me to "properly" bind the stalks to the porch posts. His body and his hands were very warm against mine.

"I didn't know you were familiar with Hecate," I said.

"Any goddess with a fondness for big black dogs is one I like," he replied.

I directed his rearranging of the few pumpkins I had, making sure I got a good view of Johnny's backside as I did, then announced, "All right. We can head inside now."

"What if I want to put more than my head inside?" Johnny asked, his voice lowering.

"Will you two just get a room already?" Erik complained, pushing past us with a groan.

Johnny laughed at him; I blushed and started to follow but Johnny held me back.

"Erik, there's ointments in the upper cabinet of the bathroom," I called, indicating the half-bath under the stairs. "Something there will be good for spider bites."

While Erik went to review my supplies, Johnny leaned in, saying, "That's a good idea he has there, you know," and gave me a soft kiss.

"That's eighty-three to go," I said. I'd promised him a hundred kisses, so I was keeping count.

"I thought I had eighty-seven left?" He opened the door and we strolled toward the kitchen.

"Nope. Eighty-three."

Nana was still upstairs with Beverley. I dropped my flannel overshirt on the bench back and slid in at the dinette; I expected Johnny to go for the food. Instead, he slid in beside me, forcing me to scoot over to accommodate him.

"You're full of surprises," he said, wiggling his eyebrows and putting his arm on the back of the bench nonchalantly. He was so comfortable in his own skin. I envied that. He dipped his chin down and managed to make it seem as if he was looking up at me. It was very male, very sexual, and I knew another sexual allusion was coming. "Your running impressed me tonight, and I must confess," his voice dropped low again, "knowing you have such strong thighs and a penchant for moving fast makes me very excited."

It took an effort to keep from visually checking his groin to see just how excited.

He sat up straight. "But that"—he pointed at my face—"we have to work on."

"Huh?"

"Everything you think shows on your face. To be the Lustrata, you're going to have to hide those thoughts, disguise those doubts, and show no emotion."

My forehead bunched up.

"See? Again, you react to my words. It's not like I don't want you to react to my words, but if you're facing an enemy, they'll play you like a violin, just by seeing your expressions."

"Then I'll wear a mask. Like Zorro. My secret identity will be safe."

"I'm serious."

Okay, so this must be Lesson One in filling the Lustrata's shoes. "I understand, I just think hiding my emotions might become a habit that wouldn't be good."

"As time goes on, you'll probably end up with fewer wrinkles."

I hit him in the ribs.

He chuckled. "I'm kidding." He reached up and smoothed my hair. "Nothing, not even time, will mar your beauty in my eyes."

It was easy to shut down inside my own conflict. Giving in would complicate so many things. We had trust issues already. What about our separate expectations? I wasn't sure what mine were, let alone his. And there was Beverley to consider. I was a role model for her now. My life was challenging enough already; adding to those worries unnecessarily was selfish. I needed to take care of Beverley and Nana, to get things in order for them before I opened myself to something selfish.

"That's my girl," Johnny whispered. A wry twist took his lips and a wistful tilt of his head made him seem sad. "I knew your expression would go blank if I mentioned how your beauty affects me."

CHAPTER FIVE

H e was taking it all wrong! "Johnny . . ."

"What?" he asked. Practicing what he preached, he did not allow a single expectation to show in his expression. He was right. I did shut down if he complimented me.

"Beverley needs me to be receptive to her. She'll think I'm mad all the time if I show her nothing but blankness." That had been my experience with Nana anyway.

"First of all, Bev's not an enemy. With her, don't worry about it. And second, when she becomes a teenager, this ability will be your best ally. Trust me."

I shut my eyes when he said that word. "Trust." His fingertips, callused from years of playing the guitar, slid over my bare arm. I smelled metal again. Winter could sleep away months. Spring could sprout everything anew, but my stain would never diminish. Nothing would ever be the same. How could I tell him the truth without losing him?

My eyelids parted slightly and I nodded, watching his fingers work their way to my wrist.

"We need to start some fight training too."

My spine stiffened and I met his Wedjat gaze seriously. "I *can* fight."

The white-gold hoops caught the light as he arched his brow dubiously. One was still missing from where Menessos had torn it out.

"I've done my share of fighting," I assured him.

"Got a punching bag with my picture on it somewhere?"

"Not yet," I retorted. "In college."

"Oooo. Rough dates?"

This was bringing up some memories I wasn't particularly fond of, but he might as well know. "In college, I dated a man named Michael. His younger brother, Chris, was inadvertently turned wærewolf by a girlfriend he was trying to kennel. Chris was targeted by wære-haters and Michael resolved to do something about it. He enlisted my help. I used divination to evaluate risks and determine the best way to proceed, and I did the occasional spell to send negativity back to its human originator. Basically, we bullied the bullies back and they left Chris alone. It was all they would understand."

Johnny's head bobbed up and down. "That's been my experience with bullies."

"Word got around. Soon, we had all the campus wæres training together for self-defense—methods that took wære strength into consideration and made sure they wouldn't severely hurt mere humans."

"Yeah, wasn't that about the time that famous actor was outed as a wære when he defended himself a little too aggressively against the paparazzi?"

"Right. That actor ended up serving time for manslaughter. Anyway," I continued, "we even persuaded Ohio University to designate a dorm specifically for wære students and convinced those students that it was in their best interests to be together."

"But you aren't wære . . ."

"I took the self-defense classes along with them and I even acquired some conflict experience."

"Conflict experience?" He almost chuckled. "Sounds like a code phrase girls use for slumber parties or brownie points earned for returning home alive after shopping on Black Friday."

I poked him in the ribs again. "That's sexist."

"No, that's witty. Was this before Celia and Erik were turned?" Celia had been my roommate in college. Later, after they were married, Erik had started drumming for Johnny. That connection was how Johnny had originally started kenneling at my place.

"Yeah. Michael and I were supposed to join them on that trip, but we broke up."

Peering sidelong at me, he asked in a sly tone, "He broke up with you or you broke up with him?"

Giving my heart a quick re-examination in terms of that relationship, I decided it was all healed up. It didn't hurt to talk about it. "The former."

"Ouch. Let me guess—he was an ass."

I rolled my eyes. "Duh. Standard post-breakup verbiage."

"Anyone that would hurt you must be an ass."

He was playing with my hair again. My cheeks began to warm.

"Can I ask why you broke up?"

With a heavy sigh, I gave myself over to the idea of sharing *all* my history. "Michael opened a second center in downtown Athens, without a word to me about it. I told him it bothered me he would do that. I just wanted to be kept in the loop, but he took it as if I meant he needed to clear things with me. One thing led to another. Within a few weeks, we not only broke up, but he fired me. He wound up with the woman he hired to replace me."

Johnny didn't say anything, just gave my hand an affectionate squeeze.

"I've always thought that if he and I had gone camping with Celia and Erik, perhaps with our training we could have saved them from being turned."

"Or you might have become wære too."

That wasn't a thought I'd even entertain; I *could* have made a difference.

"If that were the case," he added, "you wouldn't have a kennel in your basement and we'd never have met."

I didn't say anything. It was true, but I couldn't be glad Celia had been turned wære so that, years later, my path and Johnny's could cross. Celia had wanted to be a mother so badly and being infected forced her to give up her dream of having children. I knew how devastating that was for her.

"So," he went on. "When were you gathering your 'conflict experience,' exactly?"

Ignoring the taunt, I replied, "About four years ago."

"Have you kept up with this training?"

"No, but 'out of practice' isn't the same as 'untrained.'"

Johnny leaned forward, face close to mine, eyes smoldering. "I say we should go upstairs. You can show me your moves and I'll evaluate your strengths and weaknesses."

My reply mocked innocence. "There's no room for sparring upstairs."

"Combat can happen anywhere," he whispered seductively, sliding his body closer to mine.

His wære libido howled to me, my stain, and any part of me that would listen. Heat flared all through me. My breathing sped up. I wanted him to kiss me, to take me upstairs.

Get a grip on your hormones, girl! I scolded myself, but it didn't work. *Better yet, get a grip on his—*

"Anywhere," he repeated. "On . . . hard . . . surfaces and soft ones. In wide open spaces, or . . . tight . . . places. You always need to be ready for an encounter." He made an "encounter" sound like a lifetime of bliss.

My resistance was kitten-weak. The only way to resolve it was to give in and see if it was me or the stain.

I could almost feel his lips on mine—

"Beverley is sleeping," Nana announced, shuffling in wearing the thick terry robe that matched her pink fuzzy slippers. Erik came in behind her.

Johnny rose quickly and in seconds, he and Erik began filling their plates.

Nana sat in the spot Johnny had vacated and rubbed at her knees. Going up and down the steps was not good for her. I needed to do something about that.

"Where did you rush off to today," she grumbled, "or are you still being all mum about it?"

"Oh, is something up?" Johnny inquired, emphasis on the word "up," as he slipped his plate into the microwave.

Nana did that on purpose—asking in front of Johnny, knowing the pressure of their combined curiosity would be impossible to stand against. Might as well tell them. "Today I was nominated to be in an Eximium for the title of Venefica Covenstead High Priestess."

"You've been what?" Nana asked, incredulous.

"You heard me," I said.

"Wait. You might get to replace Vivian? Poetic justice strikes again," Johnny quipped. "Hey." He pointed at me. "That can be your slogan. Like Batman and Robin are the Dynamic Duo, and Superman has the bullet-stopping, building-leaping intro, you can be the Lustrata, Administer of Poetic Justice."

I ignored Johnny. "The interim priestess nominated me." I didn't want to mention Lydia's name, until I knew the circumstances of Nana's estrangement from her.

"Why you? You're a solitary! Not to mention that sooner or later you're going to have to reveal yourself as the Lustrata to the council!"

She made it sound dirty. Of course her words caused Johnny to vigorously wiggle his eyebrows at me.

"Why doesn't this interim priestess just do it?" Nana demanded.

"She claims to be too old for it."

"More the reason she should lead," Nana harrumphed. "Age equals experience and nothing guides better than wise experience."

"Aside from her, the coven membership is mostly newbies and pretenders." I wasn't about to mention the current preference for youthful, telegenic coven leaders.

"Vivian's assistant—"

"Is barely twenty."

"Lord and Lady, was Vivian that ignorant?"

In response, I gave Nana a hard look. She knew the answer to that one.

She pulled her cigarette case from the deep pocket of her robe, took one out, and proceeded to light it. Her eyes searched nothing as she took a long draught and thought things through. Exhaling the smoke, she said firmly, "You can't be in this Eximium."

"Yeah, Red," Johnny added. "This may not be a good idea."

"I *want* to do this. I already agreed."

"Well, you will just have to get out of it," Nana said in the tone that meant her word would be the end of it.

I bristled inside but, taking Johnny's advice, I made my face blank. My brows didn't lower. My arms didn't cross over my chest. I calmly said, "I know what I'm doing."

Peeved, Nana feigned indifference. "You're the Lustrata," she muttered.

"It's under control."

Johnny frowned. With his Wedjat tattoos he looked as if he were plotting the most devious of deeds. I'd figured out, though, over the few weeks he'd been living with us, that this "evil" expression only meant his mind was racing. I was happy to see it. He was rethinking his position and giving some consideration to mine.

Then the microwave dinged and all else seemed forgotten as the wære zeroed in on his red meat. Admittedly, the roast smelled delicious. I almost wanted some.

Erik, successfully pretending that he wasn't listening,

slipped behind Johnny and put his plateful of food in the microwave to heat.

Nana didn't give up. "Your duties as Lustrata would certainly be impeded by such a demanding position."

Johnny's face brightened and I knew he was thinking of a dirty remark about a "demanding position." He didn't say it aloud in front of Nana. But, Goddess help me, I thought it myself anyway.

"So," Johnny carried his plate to the dinette and sat across from me. For an instant I felt cornered and wondered if they were going to gang up on me. "What do you know that we don't, Red?"

I was grateful he phrased it that way and hoped Nana took the hint. "I'm not trying to win. In fact, I know I won't. I'm just doing it to knock out another strong contender who has the wrong attitude for the job."

"What attitude?" she asked.

"A bullying one."

"So you're bullying back?" Nana snapped.

"I didn't say it was a great and principled response, but bullies don't respond to ethical behavior. Their actions are wrong and for the wrong reasons. They're like animals about it and all they will respect is strength."

"So you're bullying back and justifying it." Another snap.

"No. I'm just going to beat her so she doesn't advance to the next round, then I'll lose in that following round."

"And it's fine for *you* to judge her as fit or unfit?"

So much for Nana taking hints. "She displayed it to everyone."

"That wasn't my question, Persephone."

I didn't back down. "I know what's right and what's wrong, Nana. Proceeding in this competition is the right thing to do and I'm doing it for the right reason."

"And what reason is that?"

"That coven was manipulated by Vivian. It's time that a real leader takes the reins and guides a sincere group forward, instead of someone who's power hungry and looking only to build a résumé. The true practitioners will come back if a suitable leader, someone strong and smart and experienced, is in place."

"This woman you're bullying, is she not smart or experienced?"

I shrugged. "She probably is."

"Aren't bullies strong?"

"I see what you're saying, Nana, but a dictatorship isn't the way to go. Power like that corrupts. We don't need any more of that."

"So you're suggesting that to avoid forceful leadership you will subvert that leadership by force? Do you hear yourself? Leading by force works for the vampires. It works for the wæres. It worked for Vivian for a long time. Look at the Covenstead she built. Look how she used the local media to create positive hype. Look how—"

"Nana. Maybe you should compete instead of me."

She thumped her fist on the table. "I had a coven once. I'll never do that again."

Into the silence that followed I offered a humbled, "I didn't know that." Another tidbit to file away.

"If this woman wants the job and can win it, let her have it! The contest will prove whether she is worthy and will dismiss her if she isn't. Who are you to interfere, solitary?"

Around a mouthful of roast, Johnny said, "As Lustrata, she *is* supposed to make judgment calls."

Nana glared at him.

"Thank you," I said to him. It earned me a share in her glare.

"I'm proud of her, Demeter. Worst-case scenario," he said, "this bully beats her and becomes the high priestess anyway."

"Right. That's the worst-case scenario . . . a bad high priestess." Nana stood, lifted her arms, and turned her face heavenward. "Crone, open their eyes!" When her arms dramatically fell limp at her sides, she faced Johnny. "The Lustrata *cannot* be beaten in an Eximium! When she decides to finally share that she is the Lustrata with the Council, they'll scoff. And when she goes before the Elders as part of that competition—it's standard, they always do that—what if they realize she's marked?"

"Stained," I corrected.

"Goddess, why are you so pigheaded?" Nana almost snarled.

I was pretty sure I knew: if pigheadedness was an inherited trait then I'd inherited it from her, but pointing this out would only make this argument last longer and get us further off-subject. My mouth stayed shut.

"It's a mark, Persephone, a *mark*," Nana insisted. "You know as well as I do that it would compromise you. Having that authority will only entice the vampire back to your door."

I realized Johnny's spine had stiffened.

Oh, shit. I'd been outed.

CHAPTER SIX

"You'll be Bindspoken," Nana went on, "and they'll put your name under the Faded Shroud! That, of course, will be really good for you."

Nana using sarcasm was unsettling. Add in the fear that Johnny knew I was still stained . . . I was ready to vomit.

She shuffled toward the hall, then turned back to me. "You're going to need the Council on your side, Persephone. Setting yourself up to fail one of their major tests won't win their trust. And that's something you're going to need."

I sat there in the wæres' dumbfounded silence. They both quickly returned full attention to their food. Erik had wisely stayed away from the dinette, opting to hold his plate and eat leaning against the counter. This meant they were on either side of me and it seemed their forks scraped on the plates in stereo, loud in my ears. Was this the stain too? I could hardly bear it.

By then, Nana had made it to the stairway. Her groaning as she climbed the steps joined with the scraping forks. No wonder stained people are so idiosyncratic. All these amped senses were giving me OCD.

"What's Bindspoken?" Erik asked. "And that shroud thing?"

Glad for something else to concentrate on, I said, "If your name is put under the Faded Shroud, WEC will no longer recognize you as a witch. No membership, no benefits, no voting on witch issues, no attending rituals. You're not 'recognized' by them ever again, and you're denied the right to perform magic for others. Not even to read their cards. It forces you to be a solitary, but ignores you while you go on about your life. No big deal if you are already a solitary. 'Bindspoken,' however, is like imprisoning your witch abilities. They bind your power. Kind of like hardening and sealing the aura until it's a wall, so that you're effectively severed—magically speaking—from the universe."

Saying the words made me realize how devastating it would be. If I was Bindspoken and the ley line called to me, I wouldn't hear it. I wondered if it would sever a vampire's binding without making me give up the good parts of myself.

Without another word, I left the guys in the kitchen with their savory-smelling meat. My feet took a route through the other rooms, away from the stairs, so Nana didn't see me in the hallway and start in on me again. Not that she'd likely have had the breath to shout at me while on the stairs. I sank onto the corduroy-covered couch in the darkened living room.

My mind flitted about, searching for some other thing to think about.

This living room was my serene space, although I hadn't found much time for serenity in the past few weeks. I kept all my books on Arthur and Camelot here; the deep red walls were decked with framed posters of nineteenth-century portrayals of legendary characters. The furniture was a mix of antiques I'd found in yard sales and more modern comfort. The room reflected me more than any other in the house.

I thought about the attic room Johnny had moved into. He'd finished it out since moving in a couple of weeks ago. It had drywall and a subfloor to start, but now the walls were painted the color of powdered rosemary and mock-hickory Pergo had been installed as flooring. He kept it neat and made his bed—a twin mattress and springs on Hollywood rails without a headboard or footboard. It occurred to me that his feet must hang over the end, he's so tall. His seven-string guitar sat in a stand next to an amplifier in the corner. A folding octagonal poker table, various plastic bins, and shaggy beige area rugs completed it. There was nothing homey about the room, no photos, posters, or knickknacks, as if he were a throwback to the Spartans. Since he was here as my guard, at least in part, it fit.

Not that I'd been paying him intimate visits there. But I did drop off the occasional basket of laundry he'd left in the dryer.

Thinking about Johnny's bedroom was not bringing me the tranquility I sought.

I sat up and opened the drawer in a side table and found a lighter. After meandering around the room lighting three tangerine- and ginger-scented candles, I returned to the couch. In the flickering light of the candles, my thoughts came to rest on the painting over the mantel.

It was an original John William Waterhouse oil painting, *Ariadne*. It must have been worth a fortune; Menessos had sent me the painting after I chose not to stake him. Hanging it here above my hearth in my rural farmhouse was incredibly impractical, but I loved knowing it was here for me to study and daydream over. If I ever had time to sit and daydream, that is.

Documents concerning the insuring of the artwork, at Menessos's expense, had arrived by courier a day after I'd received the painting. With it was a notification that some bonded professional group would be installing security devices. A phone number and an email address that was supposed to be Menessos's private account had been included, in case I needed to discuss the matter. Though I suspected Menessos had something up his sleeve with all this, like maybe he was bugging the place to keep tabs on me, having the painting here meant so much to me it might be worth it. I'd finally let the security company schedule for next week.

In the painting, Ariadne reclined, sleeping, with jaguars at her feet, and in the distant harbor, a boat was sailing away. Though subdued by candlelight, I knew the red of her dress matched my room perfectly. The frame was almost decadent: thick ebony wood with gilded and elaborately carved corners. My poster frames had gold paint on the corners. Menessos's wealth assured the gold on this frame was 24-karat gold leaf.

I thought of the tale . . . how Ariadne's father, King Minos, demanded as tribute from the Athenian king, Aegeus, seven young men and seven maidens who would be devoured by the monstrous half-man, half-bull

Minotaur. Ariadne fell in love with Theseus, the son of Aegeus who had volunteered to be among the sacrificial youth in order to slay the monster. She gave Theseus a spool of thread to help him find his way out of the maze of the Labyrinth where the Minotaur lived. Theseus slew the Minotaur and escaped, taking Ariadne with him to the island of Naxos. There, the gods shrouded his mind and made him forget her. He left while she slept.

I suddenly remembered something: Nana had done a Tarot reading for Johnny and the crossing card, the "current problem," was the King of Wands. On Nana's deck the King of Wands was pictured as Theseus. In my interpretation Menessos was the King of Wands: Theseus.

For Johnny, Menessos was a major problem.

Realizing that Menessos had sent me a painting with a woman who loved Theseus on it, a woman who gave up everything to be with him only to be abandoned, made a chill crawl up my spine.

"Thanks for the ride, man," I heard Johnny say. He and Erik came down the hall.

"No problem."

They stopped at the front door. "Sure you won't stay for a beer?" Johnny whispered the last two words; Nana didn't like the idea of alcoholic beverages in the house, so we kept the beer in the old refrigerator in the garage.

Erik laughed. "Nah. Gotta get home while Celia's still awake or there'll be no sex." I smiled in spite of myself; I was glad my friend was loved.

"Ah," Johnny said appreciatively, peering into the living room at me. "Pleasure with a special someone. Can't say I remember what that's like." He made whining puppy sounds and gave me a sweet, adorable expression.

"Yeah," I said. "I hear it's just like self-pleasure only it's sweatier and it's supposed to take longer, but that's not always the case."

They both cracked up, but I hushed them with a reminder that Beverley and Nana were trying to sleep upstairs.

Erik said, "Good night. I'll see you at Feral's tomorrow for rehearsal." Phil "Feral" Jones was the bassist for Lycanthropia.

"Right. See ya tomorrow." Johnny shut and locked the door. Shortly, Erik's Infiniti started and the gravel in my drive crackled under the tires. With a low rev, he drove away. In the next instant I mentally checked my perimeter wards; all set. I'd increase the perimeter tomorrow.

Johnny stood in the doorway to the living room. The forty-watt hall light silhouetted him as he reached up to place his hands on the molding over the entryway. A physique-enhancing stretch, it made for a very nice silhouette. A handsome darkness, a living shadow, watching me like the savage predator he was deep down inside.

If only Nana hadn't outed me.

The stain I still carried—"a filthy vampire's mark" as Celia had once called it—made me feel repugnant in his sight. That's why I didn't want him to know. I'd wanted him to see *me,* not the stain.

When I first met Johnny, all I saw was his ominous tattoos, not *him.* I'd been shallow and unfair. Johnny wasn't either of those, but knowing that the connection between Menessos and me still existed might be more than he could handle.

"Red?"

"Yeah?"

"Demeter has a point."

I hadn't expected the Eximium to still be the subject at hand. "I know." I yawned, then stretched. "I just wish she didn't have to make her points the way she does."

He eased into the living room to share the darkened space with me, but my serene room suddenly felt like a jail cell. He might ease into it, but we were going to talk about *my stain*. It was unavoidable now.

His hands slipped into his pockets. "I want to start sparring with you."

"You fight a lot?" I asked. Bands, bars, beer, and wærewolves. It wouldn't take much to start an all-out brawl.

"With the exception of that vamp, not lately."

That vamp.

"That wasn't a good example," he said quietly. Johnny hadn't done so well in that fight, but he'd healed in three days. "He's not a normal enemy."

"Master vampire-wizard. No, not exactly an everyday sort of guy."

His shoulders slumped. Johnny seemed to take my words as if I were complimenting the manipulating bastard. Or maybe his ego still smarted remembering how badly he'd been beaten. "We need to make sure you're ready, as the Lustrata, for this contest."

Despite my longing for his touch and knowing how sparring would give us an excuse to be close, I had to admit, "I'm sure there's not going to be hand-to-hand combat in the competition for high priestess."

"I understand that, but the martial arts gives you a mental edge. That couldn't hurt."

"Well, yes, but—"

"When is your Eximium?"

"Starts at dawn this Saturday."

He calculated. "Three days isn't enough time," he whispered as he pulled his hands from his pockets.

"Why do I have to be ready 'as the Lustrata'?"

He came and sat next to me with safe inches between us, hands on his thighs, fingers galloping. "I thought if you knock this other woman out in the early running and then win, you could bow out at the end and announce that you are the Lustrata. Win-win."

My shoulders tensed even tighter. "No. I'm not going to announce anything. Just because I've come to believe it doesn't mean the Elders are just going to accept my word. Anyone could make that claim. Simply claiming to be something doesn't make it true—or you'd have been a mega–rock star a long time ago."

He acquiesced with a grin. "You mean I'm not?"

The glow from the candle warmed the colors of his face and gleamed on the curls of his dark hair. The Wedjat tattoos became less like art and more like shadow.

"You'll have to announce it sometime."

"Why? Why can't I just do this incognito? WEC will probably have some test for me to take as verification or to use as a means to denounce me. Or, worse, they'll examine me like a bug under a microscope. I don't want that, Johnny."

He considered it. "How about we plan to evaluate tomorrow morning, form a plan, and just hit it? With only a few days to consider your strengths and weaknesses, what to do about them, how to approach them, our options are minimal timewise."

I nodded in agreement. Trying to keep the subject off me, I asked, "How do you know so much?"

Johnny tapped his temple. "It's in here. Don't remember where it came from and I can't access my past, but the part that works is filled up with rock'n'roll and the Lustrata." He shook his head. "I've known every minute of every day since I woke in that park, with these tattoos, that I would find the Lustrata. That I would instruct and serve her. That I was . . . prepared . . . just for her." His rapacious, masculine expression stole my breath. "For you."

He saw *me,* and the glistening light of the Lustrata wasn't dimmed knowing I had a stain. Hoping my eyes shone with as much sincerity as his voice held, I said very seriously, "I hope I can appreciate that as much as you deserve."

A boyishly lopsided smile sprang to his face. "I know how you can start."

"Yeah?"

He reached to caress my cheek. "Yeah."

He guided me closer as if I were floating like Aquula—

I jerked away. "Shit!"

Exasperated, Johnny asked, "What now?"

"I forgot to tell you! In the grove, a water-fairy came to me. She warned me. Said three other fairies were plotting against Menessos and might strike at me to get at him. That's who might have been out there in the field tonight." I started to get up. "I'll need to ask Nana tomorrow if anything in the Codex could help and I have to warn Menessos."

Johnny caught my arm and kept me sitting. "Why do you need to warn the vamp?"

Staring pointedly at his hand on my arm, I let disapproval show in my expression.

He straightened and released me, his arm sliding across the back of the couch. Twisting into the corner, he pretended to be relaxed, but his pose was too rigid. "Let the three little fairies do their worst."

My head dipped forward. "They're more dangerous than you think!"

"Not to me."

"They might target *me,* or did you miss that part?"

"So we get you ready, I help protect you, and we ignore the threat to him."

"I have to tell him."

"Why?"

"Because it's the right thing to do."

In a flash, Johnny was off the couch, pacing before me. "I get the right-action-for-the-right-reason thing, Red. But this isn't either! This is nothing but showing obedience to him."

"It is not showing obedience, it's me being me! Doing the right thing. You thought the stain was gone. You don't trust me now because you know it's not."

"Of course I trust you. I don't trust him. You're marked, Red. *Still.* That's why you can run so fast." His arms went up as he figured it out, then his fingers ran over his hair. "Why you smelled the metal of my strings. He is here and he'll always be here. In you."

"Doing the right thing for the right reason is important to *me,* Johnny. It always has been, and that hasn't changed. If I don't act when I know I can make a difference, I fail. I fail at being a good person and fail at being the Lustrata."

"The *right* thing to do would be for you to acknowledge that you feel something for me that's remotely close to what I feel for you. I've asked for only a single grain of sand from you, Persephone, while I'm the whole fucking beach at your feet. You want to appreciate me but your thoughts are always turning to *him*!"

What could I say? I stood, walked to a table, and blew out one of the candles. The tang of smoke hit my nostrils sharply.

Behind me, Johnny continued in an angry whisper. "If you contact him, even to warn him, he'll find a way to reel you in a little more, manipulate you again. That's what fucking vamps do!"

Johnny came toward me, motion fluid and easy. "I saw you take the stake. I saw the pain transfer back to him. He could not dump it on you anymore. He would have if he could have. How can you still be marked?"

I didn't want to tell him I chose to keep the stain; he'd never understand how it was bound to the parts of me I knew I would lose if I were free of the stain. "I don't fully understand it myself, Johnny." That was true. "Maybe he pulled the pain back to himself to trick me into getting close enough to stake him, maybe he was hoping to thrust it back at me at the last second. . . ." I let it trail off.

He let out a long, slow breath. "Yeah. I can see that. But you destroyed it and he didn't have to follow through." He ran hands through his dark waves again as he turned and paced away. "Can't trust vamps. Ever!" he grumbled. His motion turned into another stretch, then his arms fell to his sides, limp. His shoulders were straight, and I admired the lines and curves of his masculine strength—even if it radiated anger at me.

Turning back to me, he asked, "Tell me the truth: do you have even a little bit of your own will to fight him?"

He wanted me to say yes, it was evident in his question. I wanted to say yes. But, Lord and Lady, I wouldn't lie. "I want to think so, Johnny, I hope so, but I don't know. If what happened when I held the stake that night didn't ruin the stain, maybe it weakened it, or changed it so I have more resistance. Maybe not. I won't know until I'm around him again, and I'm in no hurry to find out."

The dim illumination of the room added to his mysterious handsomeness, but didn't reveal anything of how he felt and neither did he. Johnny said nothing more, just turned and headed quietly up the stairs to the attic.

CHAPTER SEVEN

The following morning, Beverley sat at the dinette finishing her cereal. Her hair was in one dark pigtail high on the crown of her head. Nana, playing solitaire beside her, had tried to talk the girl into adding a ribbon and a bow, but Beverley refused. As she rose to bring the bowl to the sink, she asked, "Can we carve our pumpkins tonight?"

I flipped to the back of the check register I was balancing and looked at its small calendar. It was the twenty-fifth; would a cut pumpkin last a week? "It's a little early."

Beverley giggled. "Demeter said you'd say that."

Nana, who remained at the dinette, said, "And then what did I say?"

"To tell Seph that if the pumpkins start to wilt we can soak them in water."

I had forgotten that trick. "If you can correctly spell all of your vocabulary words after school, and recite your timestables, we'll carve pumpkins tonight."

Beverley did a victory dance and said, "Yes!"

"Go brush your teeth and get your book bag." Resuming the math chore, I was happy to see the checkbook a little fuller than usual for midmonth. That was one thing I had Vivian to thank for. She'd supposedly hired me to find and destroy Lorrie's killer and I'd done just that, although not in the way Vivian had expected: it was Vivian herself who had killed Beverley's mom. A big chunk of Vivian's half-payment of $100,000 had gone to settle Theodora's emergency room bill. I'd used some of the cash to buy new clothes and school stuff for Beverley, for Ares's puppy shots and accoutrements, for groceries and fuel. The rest remained in the duffel bag wedged under my bed. I hadn't decided what to do with it. It wasn't as if I were going to be getting a 1099-Misc to account for it as income. The thought of cutting into the side of my mattress and stuffing the bills in there had crossed my mind.

I put the checkbook back into my purse.

"She should take her coat," Nana said, shuffling the cards. "The mornings are getting chilly." Fixing me with her you're-about-to-be-lectured expression, she placed the cards aside. "And speaking of that, how long is that young man going to ride a motorcycle to work?"

Johnny gave lessons at a music store and also did sales, but that was part-time. His other job was for Strictly 7, a local seven-string-guitar maker. "I guess he used to walk. His apartment is close to the music store and it wasn't far the other way to the warehouse where he paints."

"Paints? He's an artist?"

"He paints guitar bodies, sands and buffs them, adds the electronic parts, and solders them."

"He's going to have to put that motorcycle away soon." Nana's surprise had faded into nonchalance a little too quickly. My suspicion piqued when she asked, "Does he have a car?"

"I don't think so."

"Guess he may have to move back to his apartment when the weather gets worse," she said.

My heart gave a little pang when she said that. I did my best to keep any reaction off my face. She was digging as carefully as a paleontologist, but she wasn't going to find a bone to pick this morning.

After dropping Beverley off at school, I drove to the local choose-your-own pumpkin patch and strolled about. Though I had a few already, none were big enough to carve. After finding three large carving pumpkins with good shape and color, I searched for some of different sizes. I liked the oddly formed ones; they had character. The bright morning sun made the orange globes look so pretty, I knew that against the green grass, flanked with the burnt yellow of dried fodder-shocks, it would be beautiful.

Stabbing and gutting pumpkins and gouging designs in their hulls promised to be a constructive way to expend some nervous energy. It would be both time consuming *and* a good way to avoid Nana. She clearly intended to ask me questions that made me uncomfortable and follow up by expressing all the reasons I should alter my plans.

I wondered how much the whole pumpkin patch would cost. But even with a truckload of them, I'd run out of pumpkins long before Nana gave up on her not-so-sneaky inquiries.

I settled for the three big pumpkins, five mediums, and a bevy of smaller ones. The Avalon's trunk was pretty full.

When I arrived home, the motorcycle was gone; I'd missed Johnny. I wondered if he might be avoiding me. Maybe he just had to get "supplies" for our evaluation.

I hauled the pumpkins to the garage and went in, having to push past Ares—ever an overly enthusiastic greeter and getting bigger by the day. In the kitchen, Nana sat at the table, wearing an oversized shirt of gaudy cabbage roses and brown pants with her pink slippers. It didn't surprise me to see the binder with the photocopied Trivium Codex open on the table before her. We'd used a spell from the Codex, an ancient book equivalent to the Holy Grail as far as witches were concerned, to heal Theo. Since Vivian had stolen it from Menessos, he took it back as soon as the ritual was completed, but not before clever Johnny had secretly photocopied it.

Nana had been translating the Codex from its archaic Latin into English, consulting with Dr. Geoffrey Lincoln, the vet who'd helped us take care of Theo and been involved in the ritual that saved her. The doc was more expert in Latin than Nana.

The coffee smelled fabulous and I realized my usual morning dose of caffeine was late. I pulled my favorite mug bearing Waterhouse's *Lady of Shalott* from the cabinet.

Nana said, "So, I was sitting here, and suddenly I hear 'Folsom Prison Blues'!" She chuckled. "It was Johnny's phone singing! Said it was his boss calling. Did you know those cell phones can have anything as a ring? What did he call it?" She tapped the pages before her. "Ringtone.

Yes, ringtone. Any ringtone from any song or sound ever. And different ones for different callers, so he knows exactly who's calling by what song plays."

I wondered if he had a special ringtone for my number. What song would he pick for me?

"Anyway, they got an order for a bunch of seven-string guitars for Germany. Ain't that rich? Global business, happening in your home in the middle of an Ohio corn-field with not a skyscraper in sight."

Nana wasn't grilling and badgering this morning? Maybe I'd been wrong about her. She wasn't pressing me about the Eximium. My shoulders eased, tension fading as I savored my coffee.

"Now tell me, Seph, how are you going to get out of this Eximium?"

I tried ignoring her, sorted through the grocery ads on the counter. "Asparagus is on sale. Two dollars a pound."

"We need to talk about this."

"Have you come across anything in the Codex about fairies?" I asked. Maybe inquiring about Aquula would distract her.

"No. Why?"

"Just wondering."

"Don't try to change the subject, Persephone. We were discussing you getting out of that competition."

"No we weren't. You were *telling* me to get out of it. And I'm not. It's the right thing for the right reason, and nothing you can say is going to change my mind."

I'd said it firmly enough that Nana closed the copy of the Codex with an angry flip of her hand and announced she was going upstairs to sew.

Damn it. She does her sneakiest thinking when she's quilting.

I went about my normal routine and parked myself in front of the computer. Email, the first order of business, turned up a message from WEC with *Eximium* as the subject:

> *Congratulations Persephone Alcmedi on your recent nomination to the Venefica Covenstead High Priestess Eximium.*
>
> *A nomination is a high honor and we expect your performance in this contest will prove your skill and potential. We always receive numerous inquiries as to the best way to prepare for an Eximium, but we can offer no advice except to be physically, mentally, and magically ready for any challenge.*
>
> *The Elders overseeing this Eximium look forward to meeting you.*
>
> *We expect you to arrive this Saturday at least one half-hour before the dawn.*
>
> *Blessed Be.*

While the physical training session I'd been looking forward to would keep my energy level up and work my concentration in ways that I hadn't in a while, I wondered what Hunter Hopewell would be doing to prepare. Surely nothing that promised to chip her nail polish.

That led my thoughts back to Nana calling me a bully.

Defiantly promising myself that I could beat Hunter Hopewell in nonphysical ways, I got out my Book of Shadows and studied gemstones and their correlations with herbs. I reviewed poppets, runes, and astrology. By then, my coffee was cold. I dumped it out and poured myself a fresh cup.

As I resumed my seat, the computer beeped. I had a new email. It was a revision request from Jimmy Martin, the editor for my "Wære Are You" column. Newspaper deadlines are forever tight, so I immediately tended to it, then did some preliminary Web research for the follow-up piece and left myself sticky notes.

Thinking about wæres, however, turned into thinking about Johnny and daydreaming about his hard, lean body and how sparring with him might lend me some insight into what other kinds of physical exertions with him might be like. And I was more disappointed than ever that he'd been called away to work.

Before I knew it, Nana was rambling in the refrigerator and making herself a scrambled egg sandwich as lunch. The day was getting away from me.

I went outside with my broom and reset my perimeter wards so they included the bulk of the yard as well as the house. That done, I put my broom away and carried my Book of Shadows upstairs. As I passed Nana's room, I noticed she was working with shiny green fabric. Not the type of material she normally uses on quilts.

Then I noticed a pattern package on the floor: Beverley's Hallowe'en costume. A mermaid.

Without stopping or commenting, I proceeded to my

room and put my Book of Shadows in its place, but my thoughts had returned to Aquula's warning. I still had to do more than protect myself. I had to warn Menessos. And I remembered the contact information included in the documents about the painting.

Aha! Though I wasn't about to call and leave a message, I could email him and not have to get anywhere near him.

I wrote and rewrote the email a half-dozen times to be sure it was as sterile and to the point as it could be. Cursor on the send button, finger poised to hit the mouse, I re-read it one last time:

> *A fairy of your acquaintance, Aquula, paid me a visit. She warned me that a certain three others of her kind are plotting against you. I thought you should know.*
>
> *Persephone*

I clicked the send button.

I had no idea how often he checked his email—and for some reason imagining Menessos logging in to check email seemed ridiculous to me. He couldn't possibly get it until nightfall, but that wasn't my problem. I'd warned him. Even if my conscience murmured that I was taking the easy-cheesy way out, I'd done *something*.

Beverley had accomplished her spelling and math goals so we set up the folding table in the garage, covered it in newspaper, and were just placing chairs around it when Johnny arrived. He slipped into the bathroom before I even saw him, and when he came out he was wearing a long-sleeved thermal tee, sweatpants, and sneakers. All of it was black, of course, even his socks, but seeing him in sweatpants made me think . . .

When we'd done the spell to heal Theo, I'd had to rummage through everyone's suitcases to find clothes to take down to the kennel in the cellar. The wæres had all taken wolf form and when morning came, they'd need human clothing. I remembered that there were no undies in Johnny's suitcase. Come to think, his laundry never included them either.

The sweatpants might be interesting. He had, of course, dressed in loose-fitting clothes in preparation for the evaluation.

I explained about the pumpkins. Johnny seemed happy enough to delay it and carve pumpkins first. He sat next to me. Beverley was across from us. I was elated by his nearness yet I felt shy.

"Yuck!" Beverley stuck her tongue out and made a face, but dug her hand into the pumpkin's webby innards and pulled up another handful of gelatinous goo and slick seeds. "It's so cold and slimy! I like it and hate it all at once!" She giggled.

I knew exactly how she felt.

"Ready to scoop it out?" I asked.

"Uh-huh."

I held the bucket while she had fun scraping out the sticky stuff. "We'll dump this in the cornfield for the deer when we're done." I let her play with the stuff in the bucket while I used a big spoon to smooth out the interior of her pumpkin, then mine. Beverley preferred to squeeze the goo through her fingers in the bucket.

Johnny spooned all the seeds loose inside his pumpkin's hull, then, upon approaching the bucket, announced he felt sick and acted like he was throwing up as he dumped the innards into the bucket and on her hands. Beverley thought it was hilarious.

Their faces were both lit with joy. It was a great moment, a memory to keep. After the first handfuls of pumpkin goo were flung at each other, though, I wondered why I hadn't seen it coming.

"Now, kiddies," I protested.

Johnny splattered goo across the front of my white V-neck shirt.

"Hey!" I said loudly, standing. I'd managed to keep my shirt and jeans clean until then.

They went stock still, busted little kids, the both of them. I stepped over and grabbed the bucket from him.

"If you're going to include me in your mess-making, I have to have some ammunition too!" I held the bucket with my knees and grabbed handfuls out to throw at them. Shrieking with laughter, Beverley grabbed the bucket back and a bucket-stealing goo-fight began in earnest.

Beverley threw a handful and it landed in my hair. I gave a squeal and turned away, right into Johnny's arms. In a perfect cartoon-hero voice, he said, "Don't worry, Princess, I'll protect you from the seed-spitting dragon!" In my ear he added, "But the one-eyed, seed-spitting monster you'll have to take care of yourself."

Orange goo splatted across Johnny's cheek.

"That's it!" he said, letting me go. Grinning, he chased her around the garage. Beverley screamed and laughed. When he caught her, he tickled her until he got the bucket away from her. He threw a handful at me. It splattered against my collarbone and slid down into my shirt, cold in my cleavage.

"No, no!" Beverley laughed. "The prince doesn't turn into the seed-goo-dragon! He just saved the princess from it. Now she has to kiss him as a reward!"

Johnny quickly turned and offered her a high-five. "That's a great idea," he said, setting the bucket down to come to me. "You heard her."

"Um . . . but—"

"Oh stop." Johnny leaned in and tapped his unsplattered cheek. "Plant it right there."

I made it a quick peck. "It still counts," I announced quietly, "as one of the hundred."

He winked. "Eighty-five to go."

"Eighty-one," I corrected.

He feigned confusion. "No, I'm sure I have eighty-five left."

"Are you trying to steal them or are they just not memorable anymore?"

"I cherish each one, which is why they're worth stealing." He moved in like he might steal another.

Then goo hit him in the chest. Beverley had reclaimed the bucket.

Minutes later, saddened by how quickly the innards of three big pumpkins could run out, we heard, "You three are a fright." Nana stood in the doorway, a spot of seeds centered on her cabbage-rose shirt and a deep scowl on her face.

"That's perfect because it'll be Hallowe'en soon," Beverley said, giggling.

"It's going to be dinner long before it's Hallowe'en," she retorted. "And all of you will have to get cleaned up first."

"Aw, but we haven't carved faces yet," Johnny said.

"Tomorrow," Nana said firmly. "Come on, Beverley."

"Okay." She trudged across the garage, but grinned at us from the doorway. "That was wicked awesome!" She darted inside. Nana shut the door.

CHAPTER EIGHT

Pumpkin seeds hung from my hair, spotted my jeans and shoes. Johnny was no better. "Kid's got a good arm, good aim," he said, picking seeds from his hair and trying unsuccessfully to flick them from his fingers into the bucket.

The goo in my cleavage was uncomfortable, so while he wasn't watching, I started digging it out in a very unladylike manner. "Seeing her laughing just feels so good." I thought of Lorrie; she would have approved of a pumpkin goo-fight. My eyes got a little moist, but I didn't have a clean hand to wipe them with.

"Yeah," he said, turning to me. Then, "What are you doing?"

"The goo got in my shirt. I'm just getting it out."

"Can I help?"

"You wish."

"Duh." He waited. "You're a mess."

"You should talk."

He brought the bucket over and started picking seeds out of my hair.

"Ow! You're pulling!"

"Sorry." He tried again. "It might just be easier if we took a shower and then cleaned up the drain."

We?

I stared hard at Johnny's chest and began picking seeds from his shirt and acted like I hadn't heard the statement.

"You're biting your lip," he said.

I was. I stopped. "If we get cleaned up there'll still be time to do a training evaluation, right?"

"Oh," he said in a high, condescending tone. "So you have to start clean if you're going to fight?"

"No."

He put up his arms, hands lightly fisted, and bent his knees into a ready stance. "C'mon, then."

I dropped my hands and shook my head as I said, "Johnny, I can't just—" I lashed out quickly, knowing he wouldn't expect it, and kicked him, following with a left-right-left that had him backpedaling across the garage. I dropped into a ready stance. "I protected new wæres from hostile wæreophobes."

He grinned. "Yeah. But how often did you fight wæres?" Johnny came at me.

I kicked, ducked, and stepped past him. He went the opposite direction, grabbed the water hose from its coil hanging on the wall, unreeling it from the bracket, and turned the handle to the faucet it was connected to.

"No," I said.

I heard the rush of water into the hose, but he hadn't turned the attached spray nozzle on.

"Oh yeah. I said you were a mess. I'm just helping," he said innocently.

"No," I said more firmly.

He lowered the nozzle, snorted, and raised it again. "You've got a white shirt on. That's almost a dare. I can't help myself." Water shot across the garage.

I lunged at him, squealing and laughing, hands out to block, and slipped past him to shut it off at the source. He blasted me from the back until the hose ran out of water. I unscrewed the hose from the spigot. Enough of that. It was cold.

"No fair," he whined and let the nozzle and hose sag in front of his crotch suggestively.

I turned and faced him. My wet white shirt clung translucently to every curve I had. His jaw dropped. I let his distraction work against him and sucker-punched his mouth, pulling it at the last moment so I didn't actually bloody his lip.

Though I'd slipped past his defenses, I wasn't getting back out of range. He grabbed my arm and twisted me into a restraining hold, pinning my arms behind my back.

"Never pull your punches with me! You can't hurt me," he said. "If you train holding back, you'll do the same in a real situation." He rubbed his body against mine. "I expect a full effort," he whispered. "Every time."

Taking his words to heart, I lifted my knees to my chest. He couldn't hold me curled up in the air indefinitely. However, this position strained my arms and abs, and I wouldn't be able to sustain it for long either. Johnny gave first, and bent forward. As he did, I pushed my legs down and threw my head back. My cranium caught him in his adorably cleft chin. I thought the blow would make him release me. Not so. He laughed and reminded me, "Wæres aren't as fragile as humans."

My mind raced, unsure what to do to get away. Different tactic. "When are you going to explain your partial transformation to me?"

His grip never loosened. "Maybe when you tell the Elders you're the Lustrata."

I wasn't going to tell them and he knew it; that meant he didn't intend to tell me. Angered, my struggling redoubled. It hadn't occurred to me that he might have taken the hit, even if I'd landed it harder, and used my closeness to restrain me. Impressing him had been my goal, but all I'd managed to do was make myself look weak. I couldn't break free. Still, I kept wrestling against his grip. I wasn't giving up.

My frustration multiplied and I ripped his long-sleeved thermal tee—accidentally—in the process.

"Breathe normally," he said.

"I am!" But I hadn't been. More like grunting, growling, and snorting.

He released me and stepped back to give me room. "No . . . you're panting."

I was so embarrassed and mad at myself. I'd insisted I could fight and now looked like a wet fool. My unfriendly expression—or the wet shirt—won me a leering smile even as I took the ready stance. But Johnny didn't.

He said, "Breathing is the way to control everything else."

I broke my stance. "What?"

"Clap your hands for me."

My hands went to my hips. "Do a dance and earn it first."

"I'm serious, just one clap."

I clapped.

"That was your somatic nervous system. The conscious part of your nervous system. Brain says, 'do this,' and the body does." He suddenly threw a fist at me, but pulled up far short. "Did you blink?"

"Of course."

"That was your autonomic nervous system. The automatic part. Now blink because you want to."

I blinked.

"Blinking and breathing are on both sides, autonomic and somatic. You blink naturally without thinking about it hundreds of times a day. But if your eye feels dry or itchy, you can consciously take over and blink away." He paced to my left, turned, and began crossing to the right.

"Now, your autonomic nervous system has two branches, sympathetic and parasympathetic. The sympathetic side is responsible for fear responses. Fight or flight. It gets your lungs more open, your heart pumping. But rest and repose is the parasympathetic system, and after a round of the sympathetic side dealing with a high intensity situation, the parasympathetic side can kick in with an aftereffect that makes you not only tired, but you may even get all distant and aloof."

"Okay, I had expected to be tired after all our exertions." I made it sound dirty.

"Right." He swallowed hard enough that I heard it. "But that's physically tired. This is another level. This is your nervous system, not just muscles, and you have the power to limit this reaction—to a point." He paused. "Breathing is something you have the ability to consciously control. And by doing what is called 'tactical breathing' you can exact some control over the nervous system's response. Three to five deep breaths—"

"I do that in my meditation. Cleansing breaths. Slowly in, deep." I filled my lungs, knowing that doing so would put even more impressive curves under my clinging wet shirt. "And then slowly out."

"You know, I think I'll watch you practice that deep breathing just a little more."

I said nothing, just breathed deep for him.

"Then you're already conditioned to do this, just apply them—I mean *it*—apply it in a new way. If your sympathetic system is making you scared or angry, those breaths will lower your heart rate. You will be calmer, and your ability to proceed with greater clarity will increase. Afterward the parasympathetic side effect will be lessened because you didn't lose control and let the sympathetic side completely take over."

I wondered if there was some correlation between the way a vampire's stain worked and the functioning of the nervous system.

Johnny checked the ripped shoulder of his shirt. I stole a glance at the front of his sweatpants. Either he must've been wearing tight undies or my wet shirt wasn't having an effect.

"In the field, the other night I freaked out and my legs got heavy. I couldn't run anymore. How am I supposed to keep that from happening when I have to breathe hard to run?"

"You crossed your personal line and couldn't stay in the zone." At my quizzical look, he explained, "Your heart rate went too high for your body to actively maintain that level. It's like your heart just isn't as effective and the oxygen isn't getting where it needs to go. This happens to everyone, though at differing points. Once you max that line, you're going to fall apart. With exposure to such situations in training—and this is what we are going to do—you can teach yourself to react better, to stay in the zone, and to maintain cognitive control." He removed the torn thermal tee and tossed it aside as he assumed a ready stance and motioned me onward. "Again."

We circled. My eyes went to the Celtic armband tattoos. Just above his navel, amid the dark hair, was a seven-pointed star, a fairy star. Above that, stretching across his pectorals, was a pair of wings sprouting from a circle on his sternum. In the circle was a five pointed star, a pentacle. Beneath the circle, tail feathers balanced the wing images. They were beautiful, but it was his naked chest, and not the tattoos, that awakened my desire.

Johnny leapt at me. I retreated, dodging blow after blow, finally ducking under one to go into a cartwheel across the garage. Taking up the rake leaning against the wall, I went at him with the handle horizontal like a staff. The rake end was aluminum, lightweight, but the fanlike shape created drag. I swatted with the handle end from the left, flipped it, and swatted with it from the right; faked a switch back to the left and cracked him in the shoulder with it.

"Ow!"

"Sorry," I said.

He turned and sprinted across the garage. I went after him, but he spun back with a shovel in his hands, blocking my strike with its thicker shaft. It was heavier than my rake, with metal on both ends, but being a wære he handled it with no problem and the more substantial shaft cracked my rake handle.

Johnny used this against me and backed me across the garage one step at a time, pushing the shovel's shank against my cracked rake handle. My rake was going to snap at any second. I kind of wanted it to, so we could be done with this, so I could put my hands on his body and—

Suddenly, the rake broke. The world slowed but my mind was still fast.

I pulled the two rake ends apart and struck at him, backing him up two paces before I sidestepped and shoved both the pieces into the D-shaped handle of the shovel. Using the broken rake pieces like handlebars, I swung myself low and past him. My momentum and the sudden weight on the shovel made his grip weaken. As I stood I pulled my broken handles with me, forcing the shovel in his grip to twist, then all of it clanged to the floor.

Johnny turned to face me and time became normal again.

"Time slowed down," I said, hands making the time-out gesture.

"That's good, it's normal. Your brain goes into survival mode. It screens out anything not directly pertinent to surviving. Things slow down. Sometimes the sounds are so loud you can't function. And sometimes your hearing fades until you can't hear the sirens or the shots being fired all around you. Sometimes you're the one firing the shots. You can't hear them, you can't feel the recoil, but you can hear the jingling of the shell casings falling on the cement at your feet." He seemed far away. "And then your ears don't ring afterward and you wonder if it was real at all."

"Johnny?"

He blinked. "Yeah?"

"Is that a memory?"

"I don't know." His hands ran over his dark waves of hair and he turned away. He sounded angry as he whispered, "Why can't I remember?" Everything about him—his posture, his tone—was so male. His skin glistened with sweat and his muscles were hard and ripped.

I wanted him. I wanted to take him in my arms. I wanted to wrap myself around him. I stepped in front of him, put my hands around his face, and pulled him into my kiss. He yielded without delay.

"What the hell are you two—"

We spun to see Nana at the door to the house.

She took in our positions, his shirtlessness, my wet shirt, and the broken rake and shovel in the middle of the wet garage floor. "Oh," she said, the hint of a smile leaking onto her face. "I don't think I want to know." She shut the door.

Her amusement rained down on me like an instant cold shower. For me, the moment was gone. When I turned back to Johnny, however, he was peeking down the V-neck of my shirt. Though caught, he grinned broadly. "You missed some seeds."

"I know." I backed up and started digging out what was left of the pumpkin mess in my cleavage.

"I take it you dislike gooey stuff on your chest, huh?"

I choked out a laugh, doubting that even a muzzle

could keep this flirt-addict's dirty mind from being heard. "It was drying and getting all flakey and icky in there. But now that you've used the hose, it's more like snot." I pulled the last wad of it out.

"I will remove that particular fantasy from my list, then."

I threw the pumpkin goo at him.

CHAPTER NINE

I couldn't sleep.

After showering and dinner, my eyes didn't want to stay open and, though it was early, my bed was the right place to be. Then, with the clock glaring twelve-twelve, sleep deserted me. I woke with sore muscles. Getting comfortable wasn't likely.

Rising, I moved stiffly to the stairs and was halfway down before I realized the TV was on in the living room. Johnny was sitting on the couch in the jeans, tank, and denim shirt he'd changed into after his shower. In the glow from the screen, I could tell he was focused on me. I became aware all I was wearing was a creamy yellow babydoll sleep shirt and matching nightshorts.

"What are you doing up?" I asked.

"Watching Emeril Lagasse."

I glanced at the screen. "Cooking shows this late?"

"Couldn't sleep. Why are you up?"

"Sore. The ibuprofen is in the bathroom down here." I entered the little half-bath under the stairs. Taking two of the pain relievers with a handful of water from the faucet,

I returned to the doorway. "Good night," I said. "Hope you get some sleep."

"Red?"

"Yeah?"

"I'll give you a back rub, if that'll help. I mean, the way you were swinging that rake around and throwing punches, it has to be your shoulders that are sore, right?"

"Right." I knew what he hoped this would lead to. Did I want to be led?

"C'mon," he said nonchalantly. He patted the couch beside him.

I gathered my hair to one side and sat before him on the floor instead. I watched the chef present the feast of harvest-time foods while Johnny's warm hands began kneading my shoulders.

"Your skin is so soft . . . my hands are rough."

"I like it." My muscles were responding, relaxing quickly under his diligent and firm touch.

He worked up the back of my neck, then down to the muscles below my collarbone. He paused with his thumbs stroking little circles onto my skin while his fingers lay innocent and still just where my breasts began to round. As he worked his way across my shoulders, he pushed the spaghetti straps so they fell to the side.

"Some massage oil that warms with friction would make this even better," he whispered.

I could feel his breath on my skin. "Yeah. It probably would."

"I might have some in my room. Let's go up there."

I started laughing.

He stopped rubbing. "What?"

Over my shoulder I said, "You have to admit that wasn't exactly subtle or slick."

He crossed his arms in mock indignation. "That oil is *very* slick."

I laughed again.

The TV went dark and mute.

"Tell me, Red," Johnny slipped his warm hands onto my shoulders again. "How would you have me win you over?" He kissed my ear then whispered, "Would you have me continue the suggestive wordplay for an hour to win your mind?" He licked my earlobe. "Would you have me overpower you and take you?" His hands squeezed tighter on my shoulders, an indication of the strength he could use to do just that. But I didn't fear him; my muscles reacted by melting under the pressure. He nuzzled lower and put his lips to my neck while his hands slid lightly to my breasts. Sensations flowed over my skin, igniting every nerve. "Would you let *me* have control? Would you dare that?"

Sitting completely still, I was very aware of my heartbeat quickening.

"I want you, Red," he whispered. He scented me, knew I was responding. His touch grew lighter still, then his hands left my shoulders and he sat back, not touching me at all. I looked up at him over my shoulder and saw that his dark eyes brimmed with desire.

His hands rested on either side of him, palms up and open. "Would you prefer to be in control?" His voice was so soft, so soothing, yet it readily stoked the heat of my desire. "Would you take pleasure from me on your own terms?"

I wanted him every way and any way. Nana and

Beverley were sleeping. Ares was in Beverley's room. We had time. He wanted me. I wanted him. I wanted him *now*.

I stood before him. Slowly, I lifted my nightshirt. In the soft glow of the yardlight streaming in through the window, I watched his face as the rising fabric revealed the curve of my breasts. I lifted higher. He squirmed a little and rested his hands once again on the cushions to either side of him, palms down this time.

I dropped my shirt to the floor.

I turned away, let the shorts drop, and stepped out of them. I was wearing nothing now but white cotton bikini panties.

I bent to pick up the shorts, keeping my legs straight, grateful for being flexible. Johnny's throat rumbled approval. I didn't straighten up, but shifted to see the potently male expression on his face, mouth slightly open, nostrils flaring as he inhaled my scent again. His eyes took in every inch of me. His fingers dug into the corduroy cushions, fisting the fabric.

When I stood up and faced him, he jerked his denim shirt off and threw it to the floor, revealing the Celtic knot tattoos around his arms. The black bands had small images of wolves worked into the design. My eyes drank in the lean, muscular figure of this man, this man I was about to—

Sliding one knee onto the couch, I put my fingers to his brow, playing with his hair. My hand ran through those silky waves and came to rest on his shoulder. Leaning down, I watched him assess my breasts, the mixed wonder and lust on his face. I whispered, "Touch me, Johnny."

One hand rose to stroke the curving mound. My breath came faster. He filled both hands with the weight of my breasts, lifting them, stroking, the heat of his touch inflaming me more.

My hand slid to the bottom of his tank top. I yanked it up, pulling it off as he moved to allow me to take it. Sliding my other knee onto the couch, I straddled his hard, muscular thighs. His arms, still raised from the removal of his shirt, came down around me, hands caressing my hair as he pulled me into a kiss. It started gently, a soft brush of lips, but as his mouth opened to me and I tasted him, a deep hunger built upon immense desire. I sucked at his tongue and licked at his lips even as my fingers found the jeans zipper and released it.

I pulled from the kiss. "You do it."

Our eyes locked, my fingers ran though his hair as he worked his jeans down. When he settled back onto the cushion, I eased onto his thighs again. His hands went to my back, gliding to my hips. My fingers trailed down his abdomen to the hot, velvety smoothness of his cock, rigid and erect.

Johnny sucked a breath through his teeth as I caressed the length of him.

I took him into my hands and my own need redoubled. I was already so wet. I wanted to explore him, to map every contour of him, but I wanted him inside me more. It had been a long time since I felt the heat of a man inside me.

Gripping my breasts, he squeezed lightly, thumbs rubbing my nipples. He leaned forward, kissing each breast, alternately sucking and using his teeth to graze each tip.

I moaned.

Taking that as a sign, he ripped one side of my panties, then the other. The fabric dropped away. "Take me, Red." His fingers stroked between my legs, spreading my wetness. My thighs quivered at his touch. "Fuck me," he whispered. His head fell back against the couch and he groaned. "Please, fuck me. *Now*."

Easing down, I felt him slide into me, so hard. His hands held my ass, fingers spread, and I could feel wære strength and need trembling all through him. He could have pulled me onto him savagely, but he didn't. He just kept his hands on me, firmly.

"Don't want to hurt you," he whispered. "You do it. Take me. Ride me."

He feared his own wære strength.

My knees spread farther apart and slowly I slid completely onto Johnny's cock. I jerked my hips up, then thrust down.

"More," I said, breathless. Johnny rose to meet my thrust. "Yes."

Grinding hard against him, over and over, felt so good. I threw my head back, captivated by how complete each stroke felt, how if I rolled my pelvis a little right *then,* right *there,* that sweet heat flickered through me. The muscles of his thighs bunched then flexed with each thrust. His eagerness fed mine.

Wanting to gauge his reaction to this moment, I studied his face. Last night, the candlelight warmed the color of his skin, made his eyes like shadows. Now, with only stray light pressing at the windows, the dimness was cold, the darkness more complete. But it was perfect for him. Although he seemed to watch from the depths of a cave like a predator hiding, his beast was ready to roar in triumph.

His lips parted. "I know what you want," he said. Suddenly employing his wære strength, placing his arms around me, he leaned into me and I felt his thighs flex as he pushed up to stand on his feet. My arms encircled his shoulders, my legs wrapping around his waist. Hands cupping my ass, he lifted me on and off of him, slowly, so I was aware of every inch. It left me shaking with desperate need. My senses flooded with hyperawareness, as in a moment of danger when time slows. I heard each gasp of breath like a slow breeze. I felt each touch, each pulsing sensation, a hundred times over. My need rose up like a fierce creature of desire. I began working my body vigorously, swiveling my hips, feeling strong and impatient as I rode him until I couldn't breathe.

Clenching him with every muscle, I would have screamed if my lungs had air. My body throbbed, reverberating with pleasure so intense I went utterly still, while Johnny continued to pound into me.

My orgasm was so ruthlessly concentrated, each time he lifted me, it seemed another started, though the previous had not fully receded before the next began. I gasped quick, shallow breaths, only to moan them away.

Suddenly, Johnny thrust into me and held me, his face buried against my neck, teeth clamping onto me, pressing but not biting. A growl burst from his throat, a deep guttural, rumbling growl of release matching the new heat erupting inside of me.

He lifted me again, thrusting hard, once. Twice. My

orgasm started anew. My legs squeezed around him and I cried out. He panted into my neck and started again, pounding himself relentlessly into my deepest self.

Johnny sat on the couch again, but this time my legs around his waist kept him from sinking into the cushions. We caught our breaths, still embracing, still intimately entwined, enervated, and wrapped in afterglow that could have lit up the night.

Johnny rubbed my back, hands so warm. "Wow," he whispered.

I didn't move. I couldn't. It wasn't just the physical exertion, the sublime sex. It was fear.

I felt lost and scared and as if I were teetering on the edge of a razor. If I moved, the *next* moment would start . . . and I didn't know what kind of moment it was going to be.

Was the magnificent sex due to the stain? A vampire's stain never made anything better unless you paid dearly for it. Sex like this could be addictive. Was the stain sinking its barbs further into me, controlling, changing, devouring me?

Or was this real? Was the man holding me, cuddling me—shit! Cuddling me!—was he everything he seemed to be?

Either way, nothing in my life would ever be the same. I'd just gone and completely altered my world again in a whole new way.

Johnny started playing with my hair. He craned his neck, trying to see my face; I didn't want him to. I needed another moment to build my resolve to master myself and be ready for whatever came next.

Johnny's hands firmly maneuvered me until I was sitting up on his lap and his fingers strayed over my breasts again. He sighed with tired satisfaction. "So beautiful in the dark."

I smiled, ambiguously. A compliment.

Wearing a lopsided grin, he tucked a lock of my hair behind my ear. "I could hold you on this couch all night."

"But Nana and Beverley will be down early!"

His grin faded and his expression went blank. "You're right. Why don't you go on up to your room and sleep." He caressed my cheek. "I'll go to mine."

Separation. Breathing room. Good. Time to gather my thoughts. I hoped my mind blossomed with so many thoughts I could bouquet a varied selection of wildflower ideas. Right now, my mind felt like barren desert sands.

Grateful, and fearful, I made myself meet his eyes.

He caressed my cheek. "The beach is always there, Red. High tide. Low tide."

So we were both thinking about sand. Mine was arid and lifeless; his was the transition from one fertile world to another.

I didn't need Freud to point out what that revealed.

I leaned in to give him a quick kiss, but his hand slipped behind my neck and held me there for a long one. His lips were so soft, yet firm. Even his kisses were earnest. When it ended, I eased off him and gathered my clothes and torn undies. Legs shaking and unsteady, I fled, without so much as a good night to him.

CHAPTER TEN

Distracted by my vacillating mind, I forgot to set my clock to alarm. I overslept.

I rushed down the steps. My feet stopped short at the bottom. Johnny was cleaning something off on the couch. "Morning, Red. I spilled coffee"—he coughed—"on your couch here." He gave me a wink. "Sorry."

We'd spotted the couch. I hadn't even thought of that.

"If this laundry soap mix doesn't get it out, I'll try something else, okay?" He peeked into the kitchen, then came at me as if he would steal a hug or a kiss.

I backpedaled.

He stopped.

"That's okay," I stammered. "It's a slipcover anyway. It can be washed."

"You all right?" he whispered, obviously puzzled.

"I—I don't want Nana to know," I whispered back. "She'll be merciless in her teasing."

"Are you up now, Seph?" Nana's voice croaked from the kitchen.

"Yeah," I said.

Despite his clear disappointment, Johnny gave me a "go

on" nod. I hurried down the hall. Beverley was pushing her unicorn lunchbox into her bookbag. Remembering how she'd cradled that lunchbox in her arms when we got her things from the apartment, my heart went out to her. She'd told me that Lorrie always made her lunch, and always clipped a cartoon from the newspaper to put in with it. I wondered if her lunchbox seemed emptier without it.

"Sleepyhead," she said.

"Yeah. Sorry."

"I made her lunch." Nana's cigarette smoldered on the edge of a round ashtray on the far side of the counter. "Brush your teeth," she added to Beverley.

"Right." She bolted down the hall and up the stairs.

I resolved to get a kids' joke book, to copy out a joke each day to put in Beverley's lunchbox. Not her mom's thing, but something else, similar. I promised myself I'd get that book today. "Thanks, Nana. I forgot to set my alarm."

Johnny entered and tossed the rag into the laundry room.

"Are you going to live here all winter, Johnny?"

We both straightened at Nana's question.

"Truthfully, Demeter, I hadn't thought that far ahead." He approached her. "With the wards reinstated, though, I guess there's no worry of that vamp or his flunkie coming back."

"That vamp" again. And by "flunkie" he meant Goliath, Menessos's emissary.

"I suppose I could move back to my apartment." He shot a glance my way to see how I reacted to the idea.

How *did* I feel about it? Goddess help me, I felt

incapacitated by my indecision. I needed to talk to Amenemhab and sort my feelings out.

"Are you tired of my cooking already?" Johnny asked Nana.

"Oh, hell no! I just thought the broken wards were the only reason you were staying. They've been fixed for a week now, so it must be something else."

She *knew,* or she caught the glance, or something!

"Yeah," he said naturally. "You're right. I probably should get out of the way."

"You're not in the way. Not mine, anyway." Nana tapped her cigarette into the ashtray, then took another drag, watching me. "I was just wondering if your reason had changed."

The sound of Beverley's feet on the stairs came again, this time in conjunction with Ares's paws as they clamored down together, rumbling like a herd of elephants. It was, for once, a welcome noise. "Gotta get her to school," I said, grabbing my purse and keys as I hurried out.

I sat in my Avalon staring at the garage. The motorcycle was gone again.

Facing Nana alone, not knowing what she and Johnny might have discussed, made me uneasy. I fully expected her to start in on me again about the Eximium, the stain, the vampires, Johnny, and anything else she might have thought of. She'd probably bombard me with all of it in order to wear me down. Worst part was she could claim Johnny said this or that and I wouldn't know if he actually had or if she was playing me.

Stay blank. Unreadable. Don't be goaded.

I planned to busy myself getting a start on the next column and running errands today. Then I could get to meditation and discuss things with my totem animal and spirit guide, Amenemhab.

I got out of the car and slammed the door.

"I've decided something," Nana called as I came through the garage door into the kitchen.

"What's that?" Doubtless she had a great plan that I somehow figured into. I walked through the kitchen into the dining room.

There was a pause. I took off my coat, hung it on the back of my desk chair, and then I heard the sound of her slippers shuffling on the linoleum. "I'm going to call my auto insurance man," she appeared in the doorway, "and have him add Johnny to my policy."

I refrained from reacting visibly, sat down, and flipped my laptop open. "That's very sweet of you, Nana." I wondered how Johnny had reacted to the notion of driving Nana's old Buick Le Sabre with the AARP sticker in the back window.

"I told him that I thought having him around was nice and that he should stay."

Her sneaky thinking during sewing must have paid off in a devious and complex trap she was laying for us.

"I said he could take my car to work this winter. If I need to go somewhere, you can take me in your car."

Aha. That was how I figured into it. Probably safer for other drivers on the road if my hands were on the wheel anyway. "Okay. That's a great idea." I started to check my email.

The phone rang. Nana reached for it. "Hello? Oh hi."
Pause. "Yes." Long pause. "Okay. I'll tell her." Pause.
"Bye." She hung up and said, "That was Johnny. He said
he's going to stay at Erik and Celia's tonight."

"Oh," I said.

She headed back into the kitchen.

Shit. Was he mad? Or what?

"Did he say why?" I asked casually.

"No," she said.

I squinted at her back and wondered if that was the
whole truth. She had paused on the phone long enough to
get some details.

"Guess we're cooking for ourselves," she grumbled.

Nothing important in email. After sorting through
sticky-notes with ideas for my next column, I selected one
and stared at my little desk statue of Seshat, the Egyptian
scribe-goddess, while I mentally considered the points I
wanted to make in this week's column.

I made a good start—so good that the morning got
away from me. And, miraculously, Nana never inter-
rupted. No hounding. No browbeating. Nothing.

I got my grocery list, grabbed cash from the duffel
under my bed, put my coat on, and left. At the superstore,
I gathered my groceries and impulsively added a digital
camera to the list. I'd have to get photos of Beverley's
Hallowe'en costume and school events and such, right?

I managed a stop at the bookstore to pick up the
national papers so I could see my column in print, and to
buy that children's joke book, before it was time to pick
up Beverley at school.

I hid the joke book and put the groceries away while

Beverley did her homework. Then she and I made dinner with the radio on, dancing around the kitchen singing into wooden spoons. We snapped a few pictures of each other and laughed at ourselves. During dinner she told Nana and me about recess with her friend Lily and a science project involving weather.

After cleaning up the kitchen, we went out to finish up the pumpkins.

"Aren't we waiting for Johnny?" she asked.

"Something came up and he won't be here this evening. I'm sure he won't mind if we finish without him."

I probably would have given more thought to why he wasn't coming back tonight, but Beverley was eager to handle a knife. That kept me well grounded in the moment. Remembering my youth and my first experience handling an athame in ritual, we had a serious knife safety discussion, then started stabbing into the dotted-lines designs we'd poked into the orange hulls.

When we placed the finished pumpkins on the porch, with tea-lights glowing inside, we oohed and ahhed for a while, congratulating ourselves on the fantastic carving we'd done. When we went inside, Nana joined us for warm cider and cinnamon-pumpkin muffins I'd bought at the store.

"These taste wonderful," Nana said after a bite. "I bet Johnny could make muffins even better, though."

Was I being baited? I didn't know, so I simply replied, "I bet you're right."

Nana and Beverley soon headed upstairs to begin their routine. I had a pumpkin-carving table to clean, and a totem animal to consult.

• • •

I went out to the garage and cleaned up the pumpkin mess, folded up the table, and stored it. I pulled a clean rag rug from the storage shelves and laid it in the middle of the garage floor. Squirting water from a plastic bottle, I made a wet-line circle around me and sat down on the rug inside.

"Mother, seal my circle and give me a sacred space.
I need to think clearly to solve the troubles I face."

Meditation being second nature to me, I slipped into an alpha state almost as easily as I flipped a light switch. Visualizing the grove of old ash trees beside a swift flowing river, I imagined myself walking to it, taking my shoes off, and sticking my toes into the cool water. Cleansing my chakras, I thought about the last time I'd spoken with my totem animal, the jackal Amenemhab, here.

He'd told me I was a big part of the Goddess's plan. I hadn't known a Lustrata from an Electrolux at the time and since we were discussing my dilemma with Vivian, I thought he meant the Great Mother wanted me to be an assassin. He even had me wondering if perhaps my absentee father was a killer for hire.

In retrospect, however, it seemed the jackal must have been smoothing a path into the whole Lustrata thing. If I were willing to justify being an assassin in the name of justice, then I couldn't shy away from being the Lustrata, right?

"Hello, Persephone."

The gray and tan jackal sat on the rocks beside me.

"Amenemhab." I wanted to call him M&M or Ah-min, or something shorter and easier to say, but it irritated me when people read my name and called me Percy-phone, so I always made the effort.

He panted, then closed his mouth. One side twitched up in a dog smile. "Never a dull moment with you, is there?"

"Not anymore." Pulling my toes from the water, I allowed the warm sunshine to dry them.

"Tell me."

"Johnny and I . . . well. We . . ." It was difficult to even imagine myself saying it aloud. "We had sex," I blurted.

"Oh. And?"

That question could have meant any of a dozen things. Totem animals are wily, and Amenemhab was very effective at getting things out of me. If I hadn't been feeling so shy and embarrassed about the issue I might have just answered with the first thing that came to mind. As it was, I decided to ask a question in return. "And what?"

"Was it good, how do you feel about it, and is that genuinely why you are here?"

Of course he'd cut to the heart of the issue. Exasperated, I said, "Fabulous, don't know, and yes."

"All right then." He stood and leapt from the rocks to the softer grass. He rolled around as if scratching his back, then twisted onto his stomach and seemed completely comfortable. "Go ahead. I am ready."

"For what?"

"For either the long story you tell about how *fabulous* it was and why that makes it wrong or bad or difficult in some way, or the torturous version of the same story where I have to ask questions and drag the details out of you." He crossed his front paws and held his ears pricked curiously. "Go ahead."

I groaned. How to sterilize the tale and break it down into the most necessary pieces? "It was not like it ever was before."

"Oh, you are getting very good at this! How so?"

"Multiorgasmic good."

"Congratulations."

Being congratulated about a sexual accomplishment felt weird. "Thank you."

"And how exactly are you trying to analyze this into being a wrong, bad, or difficult thing for you?"

"It was that good because of the stain."

"Are you certain?"

"When I've had sex before, it wasn't *that* amazing and I wasn't stained then, so yes, I'm certain."

"Mmmm. A very effective position to take, if you insist on turning the good thing into a bad thing." He paused to consider it. "This could be the root of all your problems, you know."

"What could be the root of all my problems? 'Cause if there is one single thing at the root of all my problems, I'll get a shovel right now and dig until all the roots are exposed, then hose them down with weed killer."

Nonplussed, Amenemhab said, "You can see others in black and white, you know right from wrong. You're willing to make a judgment call and are capable of acting on it, but when your notice is not on others; when it is only yourself you must judge; when it is your life, your intimacy, and your comfort zone being scrutinized by those judgmental eyes of yours, the black and white smear until all becomes gray."

I considered that. He could be right. "Okay. So help me see things clearly."

"A binding like yours will amplify a libido, but that mark isn't the only new part of the experience. Your partner was new."

"You're right," I conceded.

"Isn't there another part of these sexual circumstances that was unique?"

"Huh?"

"Have you ever been with a wære before?"

"No."

"Have you ever had intercourse in the position the two of you chose?"

"Are you seriously asking me *that*?"

"If you are going to overanalyze something new, then you have to be open about all the aspects that were new. Was it a new position for you?"

"When we started, no, by the end, yes."

"Hmmm." Amenemhab cocked his head. "What if it is as you fear? If it is due to the mark? What if it is all of these things? What if it is simply the chemistry between the two of you?"

"If it is the stain, I can't do that again; if it's our chemistry, I can."

He shook his head as if disappointed. "How do you ascertain this?"

"If it's the stain then it's controlling me. I have to find a way to stifle it, period."

"But you enjoyed it!"

I spread my arms. "Enjoyed it so much I'm here."

"So you won't repeat something you already did once and enjoyed"—he scratched a paw down his brow and over his muzzle—"because you think the mark might be making it feel better?"

"Don't be condescending."

"I'm not."

"You are. You make it sound silly."

"It *is* silly."

I made a face at him.

"Of all the things that have happened to you and changed in the last month, very little of it has been under your control. One thing you can control is your relationship with Johnny. Perhaps you are conflicted simply to exert some control because you can?"

"You're a little furry to be going Freud on me."

He sat taller. "You enjoyed sex so much it disturbed you and you're here. I'm obligated to 'go Freud' on you."

"You make it seem like I'm just being a silly, prudish girl. I'm not. I've got feelings for him. I was attracted to him even before the stain. Now my feelings are growing, and growing fast. Scary fast. I know I'm freaking out a bit. I'm afraid it's the stain that's making me feel this way, not just . . . us."

Amenemhab stood with irritated suddenness. "Do you doubt that taking your grandmother in was the right thing to do?"

Unsure where he was going with this and disliking

his impatience, I answered guardedly. "I knew it would be aggravating and good at the same time. So no, I don't doubt it was the right thing to do."

"Was taking Beverley in the right choice?"

"Of course."

"Was saving those parts of you bound to Menessos the right thing to do?"

"Yes."

"You had a choice, you know. You *chose* to take the actions that would save your other self. Now that you are more fully aware of the consequences, are you more or less certain that was the right thing to do?"

I hesitated. Without those parts of my self bound up with the stain, I wouldn't have any sense of right and wrong. I wouldn't have feelings for other people. I couldn't imagine being the kind of person who had no values, who could not care for others.

"Was it the right thing to do?" he pressed.

Softly, I said, "Yes."

"Then find a way to live with the binding, Persephone, for *it is yours*. Forever. Unavoidably." He paused. "You can, of course, waffle over every decision and you can pick and choose your relationships, selecting only the ones that avoid intimacy." He paused. "Not what I would recommend, by the way."

My hard look didn't faze him.

"Persephone, the real question is: why would you deliberate so hard to find a justifiable reason to avoid fabulous intimacy?"

I opened my mouth to answer, then stopped. I couldn't say it.

"Let me guess, you think you do not deserve it?"

I stared at the ground.

He pressed, "Because you think the binding has tainted you?"

I didn't answer, which was, in itself, an answer.

"I adore and applaud your altruism, but, please, do not disregard what you have given up! Being selfless is heroic, but being selfless to the point of self-destruction is futile. It undermines the triumphs gained in the selfless moments."

That made sense.

"Your body has been graced with the touch of something immortal—"

"Something *dead*."

"Stop searching for reasons to abhor it, Persephone. It is part of you now, and self-loathing will only consume what little confidence you have." His voice was firm.

I didn't know what to say; he was right.

"Yes, you have been forcibly altered. Yes, Menessos is at the core of it. But do not forget the Goddess put Her mark upon you long before the vampire. She chose you for this fate. She handpicked you to bear this. She knew the twists and turns that would befall you. She found you strong enough and worthy in Her sight. Perhaps you should open your eyes and see that fabulous intimacy as compensation for the rough road you're meant to travel." Amenemhab left me with that and loped away.

Out of the meditation, I sat in the middle of my garage.

The right thing for the right reason.

Put your big-girl panties on and accept it. I could do

this. Johnny had been after me for months, so he must have growing feelings as well. Beverley had encouraged our kissing, and Nana seemed to know anyway, so truly, who was I trying to hide it from?

Myself.

I'd find a way to tell him why I was being ridiculous and how I planned to fix it. Tomorrow.

Surely tomorrow we'd also discuss my Eximium plans, since something kept him from it tonight.

CHAPTER ELEVEN

Friday, around noon, my phone rang. Before Nana could get up from the dinette, I answered. "Hello?"

"Red!"

I grinned. "Hi, Johnny. I—"

"I have the best news. This is so awesome. Yesterday, Feral got word that some suit had been asking about Lycanthropia at the music store. So we did some digging, found out from a friend at another Cleveland guitar store that someone'd been asking there as well. So, we knew something was up and pulled an extra rehearsal last night before going out to a jam night to play. The suit was there!" Johnny said.

"The suit?"

"A&R. A rep scouting for artists and repertoire."

Sounded like good news. "And?"

"He said the Rock and Roll Hall of Fame is hosting some big meeting of label execs and A&Rs. Started yesterday, with various discussions, panels, and all that kind of shit. Label showcases. Industry stuff. Said they'd invited various unsigned bands to play short sets."

I leaned against the wall, listening to him; he was like

a kid, he was so excited. At least his absence here last night wasn't because I'd not kissed him the morning after.

"Some band they had scheduled to play tonight had to cancel because their guitarist slipped in the shower doin' his girlfriend and broke his wrist. So the suit's in need of a replacement band! He gave us a business card, wrote a private cell phone number on the back. He wants Lycanthropia to play."

"That's awesome!" His band had been on the edge of getting noticed for longer than I'd known him. "How'd he know to ask at the music stores?"

"Said since the cancellation came in he'd been calling all over northern Ohio talking to bars and local venues getting numbers on attendance, quizzing local radio stations about who got requested, and music stores about who sells. After assimilating that data, he was keen on picking us, but went to the music stores to ask personally."

Realizing the synchronicity made my grin widen. "So you get to be a local 'nominee' too, just like me, huh?"

"Yup."

"When is the show for the big shots?"

"Tonight."

I'd have bet he was jumping around like a little kid. "Wow, that's fast."

"Yeah, I mean shit like this, they've had it planned for months, but with the last-minute cancellation and all, us being able to fill in unexpectedly gives us a boost."

Then it hit me: "So, I'm not going see you before the Eximium."

"Red, I'm sorry." All that little-boy excitement had drained from his voice. "We're at the studio right now, rough-mixing the tracks for a disc so we can pass some out to the execs in attendance. Please don't think I'm crapping out on you."

"I understand," I said firmly. "That's okay."

"Don't lie. I can hear you're disappointed and after we . . . you know . . . and all. I'm sorry, Red."

"Stop apologizing. This is your dream, Johnny. Get those tracks done."

"Red—"

"The beach is always there," I said, copying what he'd said to me. "High tide, low tide, and done-with-your-disc tide."

He laughed. "I'll make it up to you," he said. "I swear."

"I'll hold you to that. Break a leg tonight."

"Deal. Is there a witchy version of 'break a leg'?"

"As Above, So Below."

"Hmmm. I get it, it sounds sagely and all, but I'm gonna stick with: Kick ass tomorrow at your Eggsy-competition thing. What was it called again?"

"Thanks. And it's an Eximium."

"I know with that starting at dawn you're not likely to come and see us—we're not going on 'til midnight and that's way too late for you—but in case you wanted to come down and maybe wish me luck or something, I put your name on the comp list anyway."

"And because Erik was giving them Celia's name and Feral listed six girls' names?"

"Well, maybe . . ."

After sweet good-byes, I hung up the phone.

Maybe we'd be okay after all. He sounded good. I sounded good. I think.

Behind me, at the dinette, Nana cleared her throat.

It sounded like the mustering of grouchy thoughts in preparation of her last-ditch effort to talk me out of the Eximium. Worse, it was followed by the long inhalation that began long-winded lectures. Thinking to head that off as long as possible, I turned, saying, "Find anything in the Codex about fairies yet?" I moved into the kitchen and started making another half-pot of coffee.

She rasped that breath away. "No. Why do you keep asking about fairies?"

"A water fairy came to me in the grove the other night."

"A fairy?" Clearly surprised, she sat straighter and leaned forward.

I'd successfully headed off whatever tirade she'd been prepping.

"I haven't seen a fairy since the Concordat went into effect," she said. "The grove . . . must've been riding the ley. Was it male or female?"

"Female. Blue. Her eyes were too big." I pushed the button to start the brewing.

Nana gave a small laugh and resituated in her seat to face me better. "You'd never seen one, had you?"

"No."

"Big or small?"

I indicated with my hands. "Two feet, maybe."

"They can grow bigger at will, almost to full human size." She pulled out her cigarette case. "She must've spooked you since you keep asking if there's anything about them in the Codex." She put the filter of one between her lips and flicked her lighter.

"She had a warning for me."

The lighter's flame disappeared. She jerked the still unlit cigarette from her mouth and demanded, "A warning about what?"

I strode around the counter and sat across from her. "Apparently our vampire-wizard never rescinded his bonds after the Concordat."

"Did she threaten you, trying to get you to influence him to break it?"

"No, nothing like that. She seemed infatuated with him and even said she was eager to be called on. It's the other three. She said they were plotting against him and she knew that I must be special to him, since he entered my circle. She fears they will act against me to get to Menessos."

Nana remained silent, tapping the dinette top, thinking. "That means an earth fairy, a fire fairy, and an air fairy . . . north, east, and south. I will give this some thought."

"I increased the perimeter. Should I boost the wards to make them stronger?"

"Your vampire's blood oath should keep them out. If they incur his wrath he will be less inclined to break their bonds."

"He's not *my* vampire."

Nana harumpfed. "Fine. I'll put iron horseshoes over the doors. You do have a ladder?"

"You get the horseshoes, I'll do the climbing and nailing." After a moment, I asked, "What if they try to take me hostage, saying they'll free me if he severs their bonds?"

She made a face. "They wouldn't take you. You're not a virgin."

I sat straighter, ready to tout something back, except nothing appropriate occurred to me.

Then Nana's expression turned serious. "But Beverley is."

Beverley! "What can we do to protect her?" My brain went into overdrive. Cold iron, St. John's wort, and four-leaf clovers came to mind. "If I could get little iron pellets, like shavings of some kind, I could sprinkle them all over the yard perimeter. What are BBs made of? Would iron interfere with the other wards?"

She waved dismissively. "I've got a flint arrowhead and a silver chain."

Flint with silver was an old Irish ward against fairies.

"I'll put the arrowhead on the chain and make Beverley a necklace. I'll have it empowered by the time she gets home from school and give it to her tonight with the warning she's to never take it off." She appeared thoughtful, then added, "And I think I know just the story to tell her tonight to teach her what she'll need to know."

"Thanks, Nana."

"Of course. She's the closest thing to a great-grandchild I'm ever going to get, apparently."

All consideration for blank expressions disregarded, my eyes about bugged out of my head. Where had *that* come from?

She lifted her cigarette and lit it. "Now, Persephone, about this Eximium . . ."

Damn. She got me. Hooked me deep, and now she was going to reel me in.

"Tell me, honestly. Do you want to be the Lustrata?"

"Do I have a choice?"

"No."

"Then, yeah, I guess."

"You accept it, that easily?"

"Not that easily, no. But kicking and screaming won't change it, so . . ." I shrugged.

"Just swear to me that your motive for being in this Eximium is not to have the council see you as a failure in some wacko attempt to get out of being the Lustrata."

"I swear. I told you the reason already."

Evidently she accepted what I said as she rose from the bench and said she was going to find the arrowhead and chain. Her fuzzy slippers flopping, she left the kitchen.

I got up and poured fresh coffee in my Lady of Shalott mug. I'd teased Johnny about him not being allowed to drink out of this mug because it was my favorite. Returning to the dinette after squirting a sizeable dollop of chocolate syrup into the cup, I sat and stirred my coffee.

I remembered Tennyson's lines about the Lady of Shalott.

> *There she weaves by night and day*
> *A magic web with colours gay.*
> *She has heard a whisper say,*
> *A curse is on her if she stay*
> *To look down to Camelot.*
> *She knows not what the curse may be,*
> *And so she weaveth steadily,*
> *And little other care hath she,*
> *The Lady of Shalott . . .*

My fingers traced over the image of the boat on the cup.

Metaphorically, I was weaving night and day, trying to make the many threads of my life into a web of happiness. *A curse is on her if she stay to look down to Camelot.* "Stay" meaning "stop" and Camelot being a metaphor for grandeur, a place of rich culture, of enlightenment. It made me wonder. Happiness lost, in Camelot. In the classic stories, Guinevere tried to cling to honor, but could not fight her passion for Lancelot any more than he could fight his passion for her. And it had ruined a kingdom.

My passion had ruled me but I was no Guinevere. And no matter who Menessos resembled, I had no Arthur to answer to, no king's reputation to protect.

Only the role of Lustrata to fulfill.

Though I still wasn't clear on exactly what bringing balance and walking between worlds entailed, Johnny seemed to be preparing me for hostile days ahead. I hoped I could grow into the Lustrata's laudable shoes. And quickly.

After dinner, when Nana and Beverley went upstairs to begin their evening routine, I finished nailing up horseshoes at the front door and the door to the garage. I had another pair to put up over the garage door and the garage's "man" door, but decided to let them wait. I went to the landing and listened as Nana told her story.

"There once was a pair of pretty sisters," she said, "who heard the sweetest music as they strolled in a field collecting flowers. Following the sound, they discovered the music came from a fairy ring. This was not a ring for your finger, mind you, but a circle of toadstools where the grass inside the circle has been flattened by the feet of dancing fairies. To the sisters' delight, the fairies were still there! Caught in their revels, they asked the girls to dance with them. One of the girls refused, but the other agreed to dance. After she skipped around the ring with the fairies three times, she slipped into the fairy world through a doorway that suddenly appeared in the middle of the ring. It was as if the ground had swallowed her and the fairies. The remaining girl wept bitter tears for her sister, but she was never seen again."

I climbed the steps to stand in the doorway of Beverley's room.

"Many years later," Nana went on, "the sister who didn't dance had a daughter of her own. This girl was pretty like her mother and loved to collect flowers from the field. Her mother always warned her to beware the fairy rings and gave her one of these." Nana held up a silver necklace with a small flint arrowhead. A circle of iron shared the hole in the top of the flint through which the chain ran. Silver four-leaf clover charms dangled on either side of it.

"For me?" Beverley asked.

"Yes. Be sure to wear it at all times and avoid any fairy rings you might find."

"Wow. I love this, it's so cool!" Beverley slipped it over her head.

I went in to hug her good night. "You will wear it everywhere, right? Even to school every day?"

"Yes! Wait . . . is something bad going on?"

"Not if you wear the necklace."

Her fingers curled around the flint. "I'll wear it. I

promise. And good luck tomorrow," Beverley said. "I know you'll do great."

"Thanks, kiddo." She accepted my hug readily. Nana was mum.

"Oh, and Seph," Beverley called as she crawled into her bed.

"Yeah?"

"Thanks for the joke in my lunch. Everyone at my lunch table wondered why I was laughing so hard, so I read it to them. They cracked up."

"What joke?" Nana asked.

"What do you call a fairy that never takes a bath?" Beverley asked.

"I don't know," Nana answered.

"Stinkerbell!"

Nana chuckled.

I gave Beverley another hug and went back downstairs.

Taking the ladder to the garage, I nailed up the last horseshoes. After putting my ladder and hammer away, I went upstairs to my bedroom, undressed, and took a shower. Clean and comfy in a nightshirt silkscreened with a maiden and a unicorn, I prepared for bed, my head still spinning with fairies and vampires, the Eximium and Lustrata-ing, Johnny and, well, Johnny.

Because the contestants were expected to arrive and assemble before the opening ceremony at dawn, I set my alarm for six A.M. Thankfully, Daylight Saving Time wasn't until November, so the sunrise wouldn't happen until seven-fifty-two, according to my Witches Almanac.

Thinking a good book would relax and distract me, I snuggled into bed with a new novel that promised to be a page-turner. Few pages had been turned, though, before my mind drifted from the story.

I wished there was a study guide for witches' competitions: a list of spells to know, moves to make, strategies to consider. Something, anything to help me mentally prepare. It's not as if I wanted to win, but defeating the savvy and obnoxious Hunter Hopewell was, no doubt, not going to be easy.

As for mental and physical preparation, I'd been hoping for a final training session with Johnny.

Johnny.

Thinking about him warmed more than the cockles of my heart, whatever those were. But past the physical pleasure, my brain buzzed on a new wavelength regarding him.

I wanted to tell him I was sorry about being scared of so many things.

I considered Amenemhab's "permission" to not feel bad about feeling so good. He made it sound like I *deserved* fabulous intimacy. While I was wary of how that mindset could be a catch-all excuse to authorize all kinds of bad choices, my heart trimmed it down to simply: "It's okay to accept what good things come freely into your life."

Johnny had chosen to be part of my life, and if we shared something genuine and fabulous, I was a fool to oppose it. With that understanding came acceptance and recognition of how integral he'd become to my life. He wasn't just my "beach," he was becoming the firmament, the bedrock of my life. Our lives. Nana's and Beverley's too.

And here I was, missing what might be the biggest performance of his life.

It was obvious I wasn't going to get to sleep anytime

soon. Why not surprise him, catch the gig, and deliver a few kisses not subject to the countdown? There was time. Then I could get some decent sleep before the morning.

Out of bed and on my feet, I went to the mirror. This was not the face of a potential rock star's girlfriend, and my hair needed help too. Just clipping it back was too harsh, so I switched to an elegant twist with some tendrils pulled out that softened the angles of my cheekbones. A little color on my cheeks, around my eyes, on my lips. Better. But my hair was still too "up" for rock'n'roll. I pulled more tendrils free in the back. A lot more; my hair has Greek-heritage thickness.

After I chose a tight pair of black jeans, my eyes scrutinized the closet in search of a shirt. What shirt said, "Forgive me for being scared"? A black, low-cut, push-up bra under a black long-sleeved lace shirt was a good start. I added a suit jacket. *No, still shows more than I want to reveal.* My dressy velvet vest worked. A hint of bra showed where the vest's V dipped, and the lace shirt stretched just right to accentuate my breasts. The long black leather blazer worked well as an overcoat. I grabbed my low-heeled black boots.

Carrying them from my room, I expertly avoided the squeaky steps on my way down.

I'd left the car in the drive, so, after making it quietly to the front door, I put my boots on while standing on the porch. Inside, the sound of the heels might have woken Nana.

Movement and shuffling in the corn caught my attention as I walked to the car. I paused for a moment and peered toward the field. I didn't often get to glimpse the deer, and tonight was no different. They had fled back into the woods.

In the car, I cranked the heater and headed for I-71.

I'd been to the Rock Hall enough times that finding it was no problem. Since this was a private event, there was ample and easily accessible parking. Even from outside I could hear the buzz of a band playing. However, they stopped before I could make it inside.

While waiting at the coat check, I watched people and evaluated the scene. A cash bar was set up to my right, and people were approaching it from my left, so logic dictated that the bands must be playing somewhere to the left. After winding through the lobby and walking under four wild little cars suspended from the ceiling that U2 used in their Zootopia tour, I discovered a stage set in a kind of alcove, just to the left of a central escalator.

It seemed the space was a perfect stage; the shape of the area would amplify the music and push it toward the crowd, a mixture of aging hipsters and younger rockophiles dressed in everything from designer duds to vintage tees and, of course, plenty of denim and black.

I took the escalator up to get a view, and found that from the moving stairway I could see behind the stage. The members of the band that had just finished were loitering in front of a propped-open door marked GREEN ROOM. I wondered if Johnny, Erik, and Feral were all in there waiting, warming up.

Checking the other direction, I glimpsed executive types, all chic in their dress-down business clothes at a gathering of tables perched at the edge of the loftlike overhang of the second story. Unlike the rest of us, they had wait service for their drinks. Most of them were making calls or texting on phones and BlackBerries. A few even had netbooks or laptops. They were separated from the mingling viewers by tall, curtained partitioning. Then the escalator plopped me onto the overhang and the recording-industry pros went out of sight. Two bouncer types stood before the curtained doorway. A silver-edged stand held a sign that read SPECIAL GUESTS ONLY. There was room, however, for people to watch the show or pass by as they wandered toward exhibits.

Curious about the show and hoping to catch a peek at Johnny before he went onstage, I stood at the rail watching stagehands remove some pieces of equipment and bring other equipment on. They hooked up endless cables, switched out microphones, and started a sound check. Much more went into even a short showcase than I'd thought.

There wasn't much else to see, unless I wanted to start roaming the exhibits. I checked my watch. There was time. Aimlessly sauntering past a few of the glass cases, I took in the vintage guitars, old concert posters, tickets, authentic stage clothes of various artists, and other memorabilia.

With my enhanced sense of smell, I caught a whiff of a scent I'd not noticed before. A combined odor, something like—

"Rock'n'roll with a touch of elegance." The voice came from behind me.

I turned.

Goliath.

CHAPTER TWELVE

I should have recognized the voice. It was as unmistakable as his luminous skin and eyes the color of summer forget-me-nots. His hair, so pale it was nearly white, was fastened back in a ponytail, and his scarecrow-thin body was adorned with a black suit, black shirt, and a tie that matched his eyes.

The scent had nothing to do with the exhibits. It emanated from Goliath. Though mostly hidden under masculine cologne designed to mask the stink, my increased olfactory capacity amplified the mixed aromas. All vampires smelled like rotting leaves. Well, all but one. Goliath's master, Menessos, had no scent.

His eyes flicked up and down my body, lingering at the V of my vest where the edge of my bra showed through the lace. I refused to feel uncomfortable before his scrutiny, though; he'd seen me topless—not by my doing—during the ritual that saved Theo, so this was conservative in comparison.

"Rock'n'roll with a touch of elegance?"

"Your attire. The master would approve of this ensemble on you. Or off you." The vampire leered.

"I couldn't care less."

He eased closer. Goliath embodied intensity, a vibrant aura of energy and violence that shimmered all around him like a neon sign flashing DANGER: STAY BACK 100 FEET. "You should care," he said. "His approbation is quite valuable."

I stood my ground, despite his six-foot-four intimidation. "You would know."

"That I do." The right hand of his master, Goliath had been selected and stolen from his home as a child because he had extraordinarily high intelligence. Menessos had him trained as an assassin and Goliath had become a very effective tool in the vampire's arsenal.

"How is Beverley?" he asked. Despite his murderous servitude to his master, I'd also seen Goliath be very tender toward Beverley. Goliath had been dating Lorrie before she was murdered and seemed to be genuinely fond of her child.

"Good," I said. "She likes the new school. Nobody there seems to know about her mother, so she can just be a kid. She's made some friends, does her homework without much fuss, and I expect her grades will be very good. We made jack-o'-lanterns yesterday."

"Is she dealing with her grief or bandaging it?"

"A little of both, I think." That he bothered to ask any of this further confirmed his affection for Beverley. "Some days are better than others, but we work through it." I paused. "She does all the kid stuff she's supposed to do, then something will remind her of Lorrie and she cries. I let her and we talk."

Goliath appraised me for a long moment. I wondered if

meeting his gaze was still a bad thing. He'd mesmerized me once . . . but now I was considered property of his master. He put his hands behind his back and stepped past me to look at a poster mounted on the wall. I turned to watch him.

"Your home will be good for her, Persephone."

I was flattered he would think so.

"I tried to tell Lorrie that Vivian should not be named the child's guardian," he continued. "Vivian comprehensively deceived her." His jaw clenched so tight I heard molars grind. "She is suffering for her crime. And she will continue suffering for it."

His hands, I saw, were fisted tight.

Aware of my notice, he loosened his fingers and adjusted his tie even though it needed no adjustment. "I believe in retributivism," he said. "Strong and cruel retributivism."

"You mean vengeance."

"Vengeful justice," he said, "is the only amnesty those who have been wronged can receive. Nothing can undo Vivian's crime, bring Lorrie back, or remove the impact on the rest of us who will miss her. But when I hear Vivian screaming, my pain diminishes."

The calm visage and mellifluous voice should have been commenting on something poetic and beautiful, not insinuating terrible torture. Unnerved, I asked, "So, what brings you to the Rock Hall?"

"We have associates with a record label in California. I am their escort for the evening. And you?"

"I imagine you already know."

"I do, of course. I knew that wære band was appearing."

For a moment, my heart stuttered. I hoped it was not

their associate who was extending a web of power ties onto the band. Menessos had extended such ties to my little newspaper column. My circulation had been a good nine papers, then fell to six just before Lorrie died. After burning Vivian's stake and sparing the vampire, my column was suddenly picked up by every major newspaper in North America.

Newspapers. Record labels. Menessos's connections were vast and interwoven. I considered the Lady of Shalott again, weaving her web.

I thought it best to change the subject. "May I ask you something?"

With caustic grace, he said, "You just did."

Vampires were so damned condescending and irritating. "I mean something personal."

His eyes became slits. "You may ask."

"Did it bother you when your master killed your brother?"

Goliath did not react. Absolutely nothing changed about him. It was the kind of reaction Johnny wanted me to learn to fake. "Anyone foolish enough to dare an attempt at harming the master will only receive wrath and terrible death."

"But Samson tried to harm Menessos thinking he might avenge you and save you from your master."

His mouth formed a firm line. "And the guitarist whelp, down there." He gestured toward the area where the stage would be. "Does it bother you that he deceived you? That he betrayed your trust and endangered both your obstreperous grandmother and Beverley, trying to save you from my master?"

Touché. "Yes. It bothered me a lot."

"A lot," he repeated, mockingly. "Ironic that you choose such small and insignificant words to describe what was single-handedly the most damaging event to my master's rule in the last century. It deserves more than a simplistic, monosyllabic response."

He was doing it again. "Why are you being so super-cilious?" I could use big words too.

"Your conspicuous concupiscence for the jumentous wolf is distasteful."

My obvious desire for the animal-smelling wolf was distasteful? I wanted to say another pair of monosyllabic words: *Fuck you.* I opted for: "Your magniloquence is desipient." Of course, my pompous language was just as silly as his. But I knew it.

He sneered and moved closer to me. "We are inescap-ably bound to him, you and I." He lifted his hand to my hair, pulling gently on a loose tendril as a lover would. "Most people in your position wisely fall on their knees at his feet. The rest generally flee and try to hide, denying what has happened. But you . . . you are learning to play the game." His hand fell away. "I commend you. I am eagerly watching this unfold." He stepped away. "I regret I must leave your company, Ms. Alcmedi, but I hope you have the most gratifying of evenings."

"Goliath."

He paused.

"Did Menessos get my email message about the water fairy?"

One corner of Goliath's mouth turned up. "Yes. Business as usual, Ms. Alcmedi. For us." As he walked away he added, "You, however, have but a short time to prepare and become accustomed to it."

"And now," the announcer's voice rang through the Hall as I arrived back at the overhang, "a local band!" The crowd cheered; the volume took me aback. "Is this who you came to see?" he asked. They cheered louder.

The loft section, this side of the curtain anyway, was nearly empty, so I easily resumed my place at the rail. Below, the area in front of the stage was absolutely packed with far more people than I would have previously guessed were here. Where had they all come from?

"Who are they?" the announcer asked.

"Lycanthropia!" the crowd shouted, out of sync.

"Who?"

A chant started, and after a few syllables, everyone was together. "LY-CAN-THRO-PIA, LY-CAN-THRO-PIA!"

It was stunning. These people were wild for Johnny's band! They weren't just another band, they were big shots.

The chanting continued, even louder, as the announcer waved his arms to encourage the throng. I realized then the enthusiastic fans were predominantly female. I'd thought my jeans and lace top were sexy, but hell, some of them were wearing bikini tops paired with skirts no longer than some of Elvis's belts were wide.

Now I wondered about Goliath's comment on my outfit. Maybe he'd been snarky and I hadn't caught it. I studied the energized women below. If what they wore was normal rock show attire then, comparatively, my outfit was Amish hoedown.

The announcer shouted, "Lycanthropia!"

The lights went down and sporadic beams of white blasted up from the front edge of the stage. Every so often a brilliant red beam would flash.

Erik, shirtless, stormed the stage and dropped to his seat behind a massive set of drums. Instantly he was blasting out a beat with both feet on the pair of bass drums, and throwing in trills on the toms, crashes on the cymbals. It was primitive and hardcore. Arms raised, the crowd began jumping up and down, bouncing as a group in time with his rhythm.

Feral ran onto the stage and started up a keyboard, a series of notes running in ebbs and flows even after his hands left the keys. He strapped on a bass guitar and started thrumming a low-tone harmony that had me tapping my foot. The two of them carried on for several measures, and then Johnny crossed the stage with an all-male swagger. He wore black leather pants and from where I stood, the leather accentuated the perfect contour of his ass and accommodated his strong thighs. A sleeveless black T-shirt showed off his armband tattoos and lean biceps.

The crowd—the women—screamed for him. He hadn't even picked up his guitar, hadn't played a note or sung.

Wow.

Shadowed behind the lights edging the stage, Johnny slipped the guitar strap over his head, adjusted the axe-shaped instrument, and readied his hands . . . and a chord rang out. Another and another, into a rapid-fire run on a scale that had his fingers flying up and down the fretboard. The music the three of them created hooked me and I was swaying before he even neared the microphone.

When he sang, his voice wasn't just on-key, it was filled with passion, as if he felt every word in his soul. By the time they got to the chorus I knew this was "Debauchery." They had been working on the lyrics for this the night Vivian broke into my house.

The song ended with Johnny holding a note vocally. Erik and Feral let it ring through the hall for a few long beats, then went right into the next song and Johnny followed along. Except for transitions like that, they didn't stop playing for the entire twenty-minute set. Johnny's black curls were dripping with sweat by the time they finished. Erik and Feral were no different. They poured every ounce of energy they had into the show.

I couldn't see beyond the curtains to see how the industry execs reacted, but the crowd was riveted.

When their set was finished, Johnny said a quick "Thanks, and good night." I moved for the escalator, had to wait. During the set, people had filled up the space behind me; they must have been in the exhibits. The crowd below continued to scream; I heard women crying out his name, saw them reaching for him.

Johnny took off his guitar, threw some picks at the crowd, tossed out some T-shirts and CDs.

Stepping onto the overcrowded escalator, I wondered how I could get to the Green Room. A security team took up positions just off the stage. Climbing up and walking over clearly wasn't going to happen.

The escalator lurched an inch and stopped.

People around me groaned and started down the

now-still steps like a staircase. My awareness returned to Johnny at the edge of the stage. He reached down, grabbed the hands of blond twins in Goth cheerleader outfits, and pulled them up onstage.

I stopped midstep. People pushed past me.

The women fawned over Johnny, rubbing his chest. He was grinning; his mouth moved but I couldn't tell what he said. They laughed. He slipped an arm around each of their waists and led them off the stage. They walked toward the Green Room, where one twin opened the door while the other wrapped her arms around him and kissed him hungrily. Then they pulled him into the room.

The door closed.

CHAPTER THIRTEEN

I couldn't move.

The door opened again. Celia came stomping out. I whispered her name to myself and, as Fate would have it, she suddenly looked up and saw me. She stopped. Her mouth moved as she said my name.

That fight-or-flight instinct kicked in. What had Johnny told me? It was part of the sympathetic nervous system? Screw him. He was going to find out there was no longer any sympathetic part of any of my "systems" toward him. Now in flight mode, I could move again. My feet descended the escalator as quick as the people around me allowed, and I headed for the front door and my car. Keys in my pocket, I didn't even wait to retrieve my blazer from the coat check.

Mr. I-Am-Your-Beach evidently had plenty of sand to spread around. Those two girls looked more than happy to trade in their leather pom-poms for sand buckets. Shovel away, Johnny!

I found my Avalon, got in, and slammed the door shut. In minutes, the Rock Hall and Cleveland were in my rearview mirror.

Only then did my cheeks get wet.

• • •

That was the longest drive home. Ever.

Just as I pulled into the driveway, my headlights flashed on something skittering away across the edge of the yard. I wanted to think *deer* but something in my brain said *fairy*. Spooked, I pulled up as close as possible to the garage—I didn't dare open it, the sound would surely wake Nana—and put myself on the porch in a rush. Even as I put the key into the lock I checked the power on my perimeter wards; they were strong.

I glanced up to make sure the horseshoe was still hanging over it, then quietly opened the door. Just inside, I removed my boots. I could hear Ares growling low in his throat from Beverley's room, so I started whispering his name as I ascended the steps. I opened her door a crack and reached over to his cage. "Good boy," I whispered to him. "It's just me." His tail whipped against the bars as I patted him. "Shhh, don't wake your girl."

Shutting the door, I tiptoed to my room. After undressing, I crawled into bed.

I shouldn't have had sex with Johnny! I knew it.

This was so stupid.

I had to sleep, to get up in a couple hours and be ready for the Eximium. I'd be meeting Elders. I'd be competing. I needed to be at my peak, not rock bottom. The clock said one-forty-eight A.M.

Fluffing the covers, flipping my pillow to the cooler dry side, I rolled over irritably. Thoughts arced through my skull like a plasma-lightning orb, scorching hope and igniting heartache.

By three-thirty, my mind had revisited every high moment of sexual tension, every flirty remark, every shy touch, every kiss, and even the orgasms. I'd analyzed all the postsexual conduct.

Even with my fear factored in, there was no understanding his actions. No logic. I had to chalk it up to male chromosomes, male ego, and—since this seemed to be their big break—a decision to do his best to live up to the rock'n'roll stereotype.

Well, I'd made a decision as well.

I was done with Johnny.

At six A.M., the alarm blared me out of my slumber.

I showered and dressed, towel dried my hair, and sat cross-legged on the floor at the end of my bed. With a silver candle for endurance before me, I took a moment to ground and center. Squeezing a tiger's eye in my receptive left hand, I drew physical energy from the stone. I was going to need some help to get through this day without bottoming out from exhaustion. With tiger's eye and enough coffee, I'd be good.

At six-thirty, I tiptoed from my room. That is, until the light from the kitchen clued me in that being quiet was pointless. Did I go deal with Nana or run out the door and avoid her?

Then I smelled it: she'd made a pot of coffee. My head hung. I'd barely slept; I *had* to have some.

Slowly, I walked to the kitchen. She sat at the dinette

wearing her robe over a flannel gown. The Codex lay open before her. A trio of stubbed-out cigarettes lay in the ashtray like bent and broken little people.

"You're up early," I said.

"Couldn't sleep." Her interest remained on the page as she wrote a line of translation.

I poured a cup of coffee for myself. "Refill?"

"Please."

After filling hers and replacing the pot, I sat across from her with mine. Let her do her worst. I wasn't changing my mind and I had java to back me up if my fatigue made me weak.

"You must have come across something good in there," I said.

"No—well, yes, it's all good, and since I'm up I thought I'd get this wrapped up. The doctor's stopping by this afternoon to go over the translation. But, no," she added, "it wasn't something in here keeping me awake."

I waited.

She was probably going to make me very mad momentarily, then pass the blame onto me with a "you asked" reply, but I walked into her trap regardless. "What is keeping you up, then?"

"My knee."

I hadn't expected that. "You take something for it?"

She nodded almost imperceptibly, still intent on the page before her. "Done me no good."

She sounded frail. Was this a trick? Was she going to try to get me to ditch the Eximium to stay here and take care of her? I scrutinized her face.

Her jaw was set, her mouth a firm narrow line. It

wasn't unlike her defiant angry expression, but neither was it the same. Her wrinkles had a new depth. Her bed-messed beehive hair told me she was in enough pain to not care about her appearance. That, and the angle of her shoulders, told me this was real pain.

My Nana was hurting and mere ibuprofen didn't help.

She was old. Eighty-four.

I couldn't make her young again. There was, however, something I could do—with Vivian's money. "How about we remodel the dining room and make it your bedroom? We could put doors on it."

She considered it briefly. "No bath. I'd still have to travel the stairs to bathe."

"We'll add a bath."

She sat her pencil down. "Persephone—"

"It's the right thing to do, Nana. I'll take care of it." Or we'd move. Other than my not wanting to, the down-side of moving would include—in all likelihood—a higher mortgage and then dependence on the money Menessos arranged for me by getting my column nationally syndi-cated. If he decided to "un-arrange" it, we'd be hurting.

For the first time since I entered the kitchen, Nana truly focused on me. She inhaled deeply as she studied me, and when she exhaled, it seemed some of the weight of her pain went with it. "I know you will." She paused. "I've been hard on you. Too hard, maybe. And you always do make things right. You don't stop until they're as they should be." She pulled the cigarette case from her robe pocket. "I need to accept that. You're not your mother."

"What?" My resentment for my mother roused fast, deep and sharp.

"When a situation looks like it's too much to handle, you go meet it head-on. Baseball bat in hand. When things get hard, Persephone, you don't run away." She reached out and took my hand. "You could've slipped out the door without coming in here, knowing I've disagreed with you about this Eximium. Still, you came to face me."

She didn't know that I *had* run away. I'd fled from Johnny and the Rock Hall like a cat fleeing a junkyard dog.

She said, "You're going to do the right thing today. I know you are."

"Thanks."

"Watch the others, Persephone, the ones around you when you go to the Eximium—and not just the other competitors. Watch the Elders. You are the Lustrata and, like it or not, they will eventually look to you for your service. So watch them, and see who is worthy to have the Lustrata call upon them."

CHAPTER FOURTEEN

After I arrived at the Covenstead, Mandy directed me from the office to a back hall. I had the feeling I was going back in time.

The walls were stone, the floor slate, and every fifty feet we went down three steps. The hall was curved, so we were probably following the perimeter of the Covenstead. Every six feet, half of a giant amethyst geode was set into the stone wall. A candle burning in the cavity of each geode illuminated the lavender spikes and lit the way. We ended up in a sub-basement level where all the doors were oversized and made of oak, with iron workings reminiscent of a castle or old church.

"There *is* plumbing and electricity down here, right?"

Mandy flashed me a smile. "Yeah. It is deceiving, though. Vivian—" She stopped. Mastering herself, she went on, "She wanted it to feel ancient, like it had been here forever."

"It does."

A few steps later, she paused before a door similar to all the others. "Here's the holding room. The restroom is across the hall, there," she said and pointed behind her toward an alcove farther down the hall. "Modern flushes, running water, heated-air hand dryers, and everything."

"Thanks." Lifting the door's handle, I pushed hard and entered a space about the size of an average school's classroom. Other contestants were already waiting. Everyone looked at me, evaluating me as they surely did everyone who walked through the door. It made me uncomfortable. We weren't here as friends, we were here as competitors all vying for the same prize. Well, they were, anyway.

The room was also stone-walled, and—being twenty-plus feet underground—it was cool, like walking into a cave where the temperature was maintained naturally. The scene made me think of a candle party at Goth boot camp. Black military-style cots sat in rows to either side, with a wide central walkway in the middle. Each bore a folded black name placard with silver calligraphy, atop a small pillow resting on a folded gray blanket with black-tasseled corners. Candelabra provided enough light to be functional, but didn't do much to relieve the overall gloom of the place.

I found my name and sat on the cot. The women returned to whispered chatting, cross-armed pacing, or fidgeting. I counted cots. Twenty-one. More than I'd expected. About fifteen were here already; Hunter was not among them.

They were an eclectic group; all shapes, sizes, colors. They all seemed a little older than me, early thirties or forties. Three of the women I'd have guessed were in their fifties. The attire was mostly jeans and sneakers, though a few went for dressy office style with pantsuits and low heels and a few others wore jog suits. One of the fifty-ish women wore a loose broomstick skirt and long-sleeve tee. Her skin was tan and the rust-colored shirt suited her well. Her long hair, some brown but mostly gray, was braided. The name card at the foot of her cot read: MARIA MORRISON.

At least my jeans and sneakers weren't a faux pas. I'd considered wearing a flannel overshirt again just to rankle Hunter, but ended up in a plain black tank under a copper Henley, and a zippered, dark-green sweatshirt with a wide collar. Layers, practical.

The door opened and another woman came in. She immediately struck me as Welsh: thick, shoulder-length blond hair in a bob style; pale skin; and brown eyes. A little over five feet tall, she wore camel corduroy pants, a yellow V-neck tee, and a khaki-brown hoodie. She was all the colors of a wheat field.

Like me, she glanced around, realized there were names on the cards, and began searching for hers. It was beside mine. She whispered quietly, "Hi."

"Good morning," I answered. She was young; barely twenty. It surprised me that anyone so young would be ambitious enough to compete for high priestess.

She picked up the placard. "I'm Holly." She flapped the paper once, peered at mine. Her brows puckered and I knew she was stuck on the pronunciation.

"I'm Persephone," I said.

"Oh, right." She smiled. "Apt name for a high priestess."

I shrugged. "Guess so."

Holly sat. Her knees bounced. She repositioned her feet. Her hands ran over her hair.

I yawned.

Everyone else here was excited and nervous. They wanted to be here. They wanted the title and position and believed they had a good chance of winning it. My preference would have had me in bed sleeping. My mind was reeling and my eyes didn't want to stay open. If Hunter didn't show up, maybe I could just go home.

Of course, as soon as I thought of her, the door opened and speak-of-the-devil walked in. No, actually, she strutted in. Her hair was fluffed and bound up in a stylish way, and her expert makeup enhanced the striking beauty nature had blessed her with. It was impossible to ignore her and, even dressed conservatively in sky-blue yoga pants and spandex shirt under a matching jacket, her arrival held the spellbinding quality that a high priestess's entrance should never lack.

It took longer for the others to resume their chatter than it had after Holly and I had entered. Hunter had likely hand-jolted everyone here, or tried, so we all took a moment to think something begrudging toward her.

"She zap you too?" Holly whispered.

I shook my head. "She tried. Nothing happened."

Her brows shot up. "Really? Wow. You're probably the best bet to win against her, then."

"I wouldn't say that."

"Why not?"

"Because I'm sure this test isn't going to come down to the best hand jolt." I glanced around. "And so is everyone else, or they wouldn't have shown up." I examined Hunter for a moment. "If all is right and fair it won't come down to that."

Holly leaned closer. "I've heard the Elders at the

Mother Covenstead are fighting among themselves. WEC is supposedly in danger of falling apart and they are vying to create alliances with the Covensteads, hoping to create power bases for themselves. Someone who can tap into power like that could be helped into position and then, of course, their loyalty to the Elder who put them there would be expected."

I faced Holly again, my expression darkening in irritation. Political maneuvering pissed me off and witches should know better. Our history was laden with being on the tortured end of such idealized endeavors. "I have no interest in what the rumor mill says and it won't sway my opinions."

Holly gaped at me. Despite the warm light from the candles, her Welsh features turned icy. "That's noble of you, Persephone, but I hope you're not noble *and* blind. You do see how they hate us out there, don't you?"

I certainly did, but the meek, small woman transforming into a crouching tiger surprised me. I utilized my newfound blank expression. "Us?"

"Witches, wæres, vamps, the fey. All of us. After twenty years, the novelty of having real monsters among the populace is wearing thin."

That notion wasn't unfamiliar to me but, from her, it was unsettling. Unless she retained lucid memories of being an infant, this was how the world had been her whole life. It wasn't a novelty to her.

"The media's once-positive spin has become ambiguous. Intolerance is on the rise," she continued. "If we don't combat it now, if we don't choose strong leaders they can't criticize—leaders who can see what's coming and act to head it off, who are savvy enough to use the media, who can be positive role models and live up to the expectations of their positions—then this 'going public' nonsense will blow up in all of our faces."

Her vehemently whispered tirade had taken me aback, but I tried not to show it.

Holly abruptly got up and headed for the door, probably for the bathroom.

The entry door opened before she got to it, however, and she slipped around the group of women who strode in and searched for their places. They completed the ranks of contestants. This much interest in the position, with women willing to relocate to a new city, was encouraging. After they'd found their cots the whispering slowly resumed. I glanced over the group. They were a restless, nervous bunch. It seemed I was the only one unmoving; fatigue was creeping over me.

Hunter was motionless as well. She watched me steadily, seeming to take my calm for confidence. She gave me an up-nod, like men do to acknowledge each other without nodding their heads in what might be taken as a submissive gesture. I offered her one back.

When Holly returned, Hunter stood. "Ladies." With that one word, she charmed the group into silence. "There are twenty-one of us here to compete for one position. One." She strode to the end of her cot and made eye contact with each of us in turn. "We are sisters in a common goal and one among us will be victorious. I'm sure you all want it as badly as I do, that you've all tried to prepare as hard as I have. Maybe harder! May the Goddess be at our sides, may we all reach our highest potential as we compete and, when it is done, may we all be friends." She reached to her left, then her right, and took the hands of the women nearest her. "What say you?"

A circle formed then, as each turned to take the hands of those around them. I stood and moved forward to take my part in it.

Hunter faced me. "What say you?" she repeated.

I knew a challenge when I heard one, even disguised as a call for friendship. She was very good, very smooth. Probably thinking she had this wrapped up, she wanted to win over the toughest critics first—those she competed against. Acting like she was the leader already, she put those words to me as if acknowledging I was the direct competition. So was she offering me a chance to put my foot in my mouth? A chance to show I could outshine the pizzazz she'd already shown? I didn't want to do either. My efforts here were meant to bring about the best outcome for the coven. I wanted nothing more than to knock her from the running and go home and sleep.

"May we all be friends," I repeated her words.

"May the Goddess be pleased," Maria in the broomstick skirt said, "and this community best served by what transpires here."

Hunter smiled convincingly at her, seeing her for the first time, but clearly realizing that here was another competent woman. She'd found the strength in the room.

Hoping I'd fallen off her radar at that point to be replaced by Maria, I watched the two of them measure each other up behind the polite expressions they wore.

More than money was on the line here. More than prestige and a respected office. This should be about someone attaining the position in order to pass on knowledge and instill ethical standards in those coming up.

But it wasn't. As Holly had pointed out, even if I naively didn't want to think so, power was on the line.

The door opened again. Lydia stood in the opening; her usual bun-bound hair lay loose and flowing over her white robes. She said, "It is time."

The Covenstead's giant domed interior was dark, save for a line of eight wrought-iron candelabra, each holding a trio of slender but tall white pillar candles. The iron stands flanked a rectangular dais where five thrones sat, each with a rustic broom resting to its right.

That same candlelight backlit a dragon statue placed at the eastern end of the dais. Like an ominous and fierce relic from an ancient time, the dragon seemed like a roughly chiseled block of stone. Tarnished iron and copper bands accented the base of each of two ivory horns, lending a draconic majesty. Obsidian eyes and ivory fangs and claws gleamed, making it seem almost alive. A large cast iron cauldron sat before the beast.

Lydia guided us contestants to form a line, steadfast and serious, running east to west like the dais. Then she took a position for herself at the west end of the dais. My eyes scrutinized the details of the elaborately carved, dark wood thrones. Two had the triple-crescent Moon Goddess symbol engraved on them; two had pentacles. All were padded with black leather and round silver studs fastened the dark skins to the wood. The centermost seat had a wider back, was significantly taller, and the Goddess-symbol of the full moon with the waxing and waning crescents on either side crowned it. Studying the design, I realized that the triple moons were large pieces of moonstone, and the center full moon disc was engraved with a pentacle.

We waited silently in that regal ambience. I'm sure we were given this time to be in awe of the moment, to consider those seats and reflect on our purpose, our competition, and the weight of what we were about to engage in.

Lydia said, "Welcome witches, to the Venefica Covenstead Eximium." She spread her arms wide. "The women who will sit upon these thrones are your Elders. The one who will sit in the center will have the highest rank among them. She will demand the most respect as she carries the greatest power. While each Elder will be involved in selecting a test you will be given, the center-seated Elder, given the title Eldrenne, will choose the terms of the Eximium's final test."

She paused.

"Once the Elders enter the Covenstead, no contestant may leave until the Eximium is over. Neither may anyone enter, save for select guests who are arriving to aid or observe the tests." Fingers folding together in front of her, her saccharine-granny smile perfect, she continued, "I give you this one warning: these tests will reveal much, not only to the Elders, but to yourselves and to each other. If you are wary, if you doubt, speak now, for you will be bound and required to participate in every aspect of the tests, whatever they may be, until such time as you fail to advance to the next round. You *must* compete until you are bested; refusal to participate for any reason will bring severe consequences. You will be permanently disqualified from future Tournaments. You will be expelled from your current coven membership and henceforth denied membership in any formally recognized coven. Depending on the circumstances, you could be Bindspoken."

Lydia let that sink in. Nana's warning rushed back to me.

"Should you choose to compete and become disqualified or lose a round, you will remain in a separate area until the Eximium is completed." Again she paused, then made eye contact with each of us in turn. "Questions?"

No one moved or spoke.

"I will ask this only once, so if you harbor any sliver of doubt in your mind, if you fear you may not be willing to comply with these rules, then answer now. Is there any among you who wishes to withdraw from the test and leave these grounds?" She waited.

Silence.

"Very well." From within pockets in the folds of her gown, Lydia produced a small vial. "The details of how this Eximium functions and its tests are secret. No one may divulge these secrets after it is complete. You must each donate three drops of blood, to be added to the binding spell of silence." Assuming a position next to the dragon, Lydia nodded to the woman in the broomstick skirt. "Maria. Come forward."

She approached Lydia, who indicated the cauldron. Maria reached in and came up with a dagger. Lydia uncorked the vial. "If you please."

Maria unsheathed the blade and made a quick, shallow slice on her thumb. Holding it over the vial, she allowed three drops to fall in, then returned to her place in line, dagger still in hand.

"Next," Lydia said.

On my turn, I did as everyone else had. The cauldron held many daggers and I selected one—they were all identical. Releasing it from the tooled leather sheath, noting the similarly tooled design on the blade and the razor-sharp edges, I cut my thumb and added three drops to the vial.

When everyone had made their donation, Lydia put the stopper in the vial and returned it to her pocket. Then she strode to the western end of the dais and gestured to the east. "Let the Elders enter the Covenstead!"

The eastern doors creaked open. Glowing rays of dawn fingered through, bringing crisp autumn air and birdsong with them. One by one, with infinitesimal slowness, four old women filed in.

It was a kind of parade, a cavalcade of witches, a procession of disguised power. They were not a pretty sight. Eyes sunken, skin sallow and waxen, wrinkled and scowling, they shuffled along as Nana did, their gnarled hands gripping their ceremonial staves tightly, aiding their slow progress.

Each wore ceremonial robes, flowing layers of gray and maroon and black. The lapels and cuffs of the robes were hemmed in silver designs: crescent moons for the first two, ankhs for the third, and pentagrams for the fourth. These variations meant something, gave clues to their status, but the symbolism was lost on me. I wondered if Hunter understood it.

White hair, either thick and slightly frizzy or softly curling ringlets, cascaded over their shoulders from under the wide brims of crooked, pointed hats, each with a band and silver buckle. The bands for the first two were maroon, the third was gray, and the last was deep, deep purple. Upon the bands were tarnished charms—badges they had earned. Among the charms, I saw spiders, crow's feet, centipedes, snakes, fireflies, dragonflies—there were more I could not see.

The very air they stirred reached me and it carried a promise: here, was unequivocal power.

The Elders were not to be trifled with.

Why had I ever thought I could hide what I was from these women?

CHAPTER FIFTEEN

The Elders took their places upon the outermost thrones, leaving the center empty.

"Enter the Eldrenne!" Lydia cried.

The doors to the east had shut, but now they creaked open again and a mist flowed through, curling across the floor. I could smell anise and nutmeg.

Another woman stepped into the doorway, head down, and paused like a shadow against the swirling mist. A raven sat upon her hunched shoulder. The staff she held was topped with a small crystal ball held in place by a weaving of wood as if the staff had sprouted branches that twisted together to form a beautiful, loose net.

Edging the staff forward, she eased from the doorway and began crossing the distance toward the dais very, very slowly. The bird launched itself to the air with a cry that echoed throughout the dome. The Eldrenne seemed never to take a step but to flow like the mist at her feet. Her other hand was held slightly out, palm to the floor, fingers spread. She wore large rings with big stones set in tarnished metals. They seemed very fitting on her twisted fingers.

The robes of the Eldrenne were gauzy black-on-black

layers that fit her frail frame as if there were nothing but a ghost below her bony shoulders. The edges bore elaborate embroidery in metallic black thread. Her hat was a scrawnier style, the narrow brim rippled slightly. The cone bent behind her and slightly under. A copper pentacle charm dangled from the tip. The band around her hat was shiny black, the buckle copper. Charms were spaced along the band, as well as up the cone of the hat. Some even dangled from the brim edges.

Her hair was a white waterfall, sleek and fine, falling into the mist where the ends were hidden. She approached the dais steps, floating up them smoothly, as if hovering. When she arrived before the center throne, she turned to the assembled group and the mist retreated, flowing up and under her robes.

The brim of her hat finally levered up as she lifted her chin. A silver veil with a large black appliquéd spider hid her face.

Free hand rising in a smooth, slow gesture, she revealed her face. Her sunken cheeks were pink; stark against otherwise pallid skin. When she opened her eyes, I gasped; her eyes were covered by a fine, bluish film.

The Eldrenne was blind.

She sat on her throne, the Elders to either side deftly parting her long hair so she did not sit upon it. The raven landed upon the high back of her seat and settled its feathers.

"Welcome, dear Elders and Eldrenne, to Venefica Coven. Merry meet," Lydia said, arms raised high. Placing her hands on her heart, she bowed her head. "We are honored to have you here, presiding over our Eximium."

"We thank you," the Eldrenne said. Her voice was tremulous, thin and breathy. "Merry meet to you all." She gestured to her left. "Morgellen."

One of the Elders with the crescent moons on her lapels, Morgellen, spoke. "Twenty-one of you have asked to compete." Her voice was firm and her words came quick. She was probably the youngest of the Elders before us; she sat straighter and had moved slightly faster. "The first test is mine to designate. Over the next few hours, you will all take a lengthy written test. It will assess your knowledge of basic craft as well as the advanced specifics needed to serve as high priestess. We will choose ten and a single runner-up to proceed to the next round." She thumped her staff on the dais.

A written test. How modern and unmystical.

Lydia ushered us all below, then spoke to us in the hallway. "Here is the testing room." She gestured to an open doorway as we passed. "Breakfast will be served immediately, in the dining room, here." Again she gestured and, this time, stopped outside the door. "After eating, you may remain there or return to the holding room, which is down the hall. You will be summoned to the test room promptly, so don't dawdle."

After being in the darkened dome, the kitchen's fluorescent brightness hurt my eyes. The breakfast coffee wasn't made yet, so I took that task upon myself and promptly set about making some. While filling the pot and transferring the water, I considered my personal goal: beat Hunter early and get us both out of the running.

That was the only way to avoid contact with the

Elders. But it was highly unlikely that Hunter would be in the bottom-scoring half of any witchy written test.

Crap.

I made coffee strong enough to degrease an engine. I was going to need it.

Part one of the written test consisted of ritual format, sabbats, pantheons, and moon phases. Part two covered spirit guides, astrology, divination, herbs, and gemstones. Part three was spell-casting, charms, potions, talismans, and amulets. And the fourth was for Rites of Passage, the Fivefold Kiss, Handfasting, Crossing, ethics. Each section had a hundred questions. Mostly, it was multiple choice.

> The Moon is waxing full in Libra, and the planetary hour is in Mars. You are burning incense made of High John the Conqueror and basil, and you have a violet candle, a circle of turquoise stones, and a jade elephant on the altar beside your statue of the Goddess. What kind of spell are you casting? A spell to:

> A.) defeat enemies in battle
> B.) achieve fair, swift justice
> C.) banish an illness
> D.) communicate with the dead
> E.) find favor of the powerful

And so on.

I got through it because the inside of my skull buzzed with caffeine.

Most contestants took one test, had a fifteen-minute break, and then started the next test. My plan, however, had me skipping the breaks and going straight through. My answers would be my answers, period. Being the kind of person who'd rather ride a bike for an hour and get where I'm going than to ride it for three twenty-minute segments, I just wanted to be done.

The first to complete all the four parts, I was released to go to the holding room—with a much-needed toilet break on the way—to rest until lunch. After lying down and stretching tight muscles to coerce them into relaxing, I shut my eyes and slept. Until quiet crying awakened me, that is.

It was Holly crying. Considering her, wondering whether I should inquire or let her be, I decided ignoring her would be rude. I sat up. "Hey."

She wiped her face with her hand. "I'm sorry if I woke you."

"You okay?"

"Yeah."

It was a lame question answered with an obvious lie, but asking "What's wrong?" would have been prying. Truth be told, I didn't want to know what she was crying about. If she wanted me to know and I didn't ask, she'd tell me anyway. So. Talk about something else. "Where are you from, Holly?"

"Wisconsin," she said.

All I could think of was cheese. Trying to avoid making some dimwitted remark about dairy products, I said, "I didn't realize that Cleveland would be such a draw. It surprised me there are twenty-one entrants. And from all over."

"You're the local nominee. Probably stinks to think someone from somewhere else could come in and take it from you, huh?" She seemed apologetic.

"That doesn't bother me. I've been a solitary witch for so long . . ." I had to make her think the Eximium was important to me though. "It's hard to think of me not being solitary. It probably stinks to think someone who doesn't have a background with vast leadership experience might take it."

Clearly confused, she asked, "If you're solitary, how'd you get nominated?"

I rolled my eyes. "Long story."

"Being a high priestess is all I've ever wanted. Since I was a little girl. My mother was the HPS in Madison." HPS is the standard Wiccan acronym for High Priestess, while HP means High Priest.

Her drive and ambition became clearer to me.

She wiped her eyes again. "I know I'm not going to make the cut here. The entrants are all very impressive."

"Holly, don't even think that way." Goddess help me, I sucked at pep talks. If I was going to parent Beverley, I'd have to get better at this. "Don't count yourself out before it starts."

"I just don't want to go home, cut in the first round. I want my mother to be proud of me."

"Does she love you?"

"Of course."

"Then there's no way you can let her down." I tried to sound reassuring. "Let me share something with you, maybe it'll help: I don't compete with others. If you're watching others to see what to do, you'll always see someone doing something you think you can't top. But if you're looking inside, you'll find the will, the drive, to reach the goal the best way you can—regardless of others."

Applause from the doorway made us both jerk.

It was Hunter. "Beautiful. Oh, that was just beautiful, Persephone." Her blue eyes shifted to Holly. "Honey, this *is* a competition. So your best has to be better than the others. Period. It's not all happy-happy, so deal with it. If you want to know what to do to win, just watch me." She grinned broadly. "Oh, and lunch is being served now." She stalked from the doorway.

"It's noon already?" I grumbled. The nap had helped, though. I did feel refreshed. Holly, however, held her shoulders bunched up with tension. I put my hands on her shoulders, pressed a little until they eased down a bit. "That's an opinion I don't share. Don't let her get to you."

"Easier said than done," Holly said, sniffling but smiling.

"I know. But that's her tactic, to dull your confidence and sharpen her chances. If you do the best you can without letting her get to you, then no matter what happens, when you see your mother she'll be proud of you and you'll be proud of yourself."

Holly glowered. "I hope *she* didn't get to finish her test." She meant Hunter.

I snickered. "Right. She probably sat there and reread each question to check every answer. She strikes me as being very thorough that way."

"You mean anal-retentive?" Holly offered.

I wouldn't take the bait. "C'mon," I said. "I'm starved."

"I wonder what her motives are. She's so aggressive; zapping people, taunting people. I bet she's sponsored by one of the Elders. If she is, they'll gear the tests to her strengths and then—"

"Holly. She's getting to you." She may have an inner crouching tiger, but it was a paper tiger.

"Right."

Lunch consisted of small chef salads and turkey sandwiches. I opted for two salads and a bottled tea.

Hunter continued her twisted version of networking during the meal. In a group, she was bright, cheery, and encouraging. I sat far away, kept my head down and my mouth shut. Except for munching my salad, anyway.

After eating, three more portions of the test remained. Part five had write-in answers, concerning sigils, alphabets, and symbols. Part six dealt with binding, banishing, alchemy, and elements. The seventh and final portion was essay answers on a myriad of subjects.

We were not allowed to run through these portions back-to-back. We tested, waited for all to be done and tried not to fall asleep, took the next, and so on. When the last test was turned in, Lydia addressed the group. "You may go now to the holding area. There you will remain until you are called to the announcement of finalists. Dinner will be served afterward. I strongly suggest that you use this time to nap if you can, as the remaining tests will likely take you until the dawn."

It was almost four P.M. I wasn't sure how much good

a single hour of sleep would do me, but I'd take what I could get.

Assembling in the Great Hall at five o'clock, we lined up in front of the dais as before. Morgellen held a paper scroll out to Lydia. "Let the names be read," she said.

Lydia took the scroll, and said, "For those whose names are not called, you may retire to the holding room after dinner. You will gather your things and be moved to another holding room, where you may rest and not be disturbed by the comings and goings of the finalists. For those whose names are called, you will return here after dinner." She lifted the scroll, broke the seal, and unrolled it. "These are the names of the contestants who will progress to the next round, in alphabetical order. . . ."

My name was first. Persephone Alcmedi.

Hunter was in that list, as expected. Holly was announced as the runner-up. She'd made the first cut, and being the youngest of us, that was impressive. I gave her a thumbs-up.

After a quick, light dinner of soup and sandwiches (I had potato soup and passed on the ham sandwich) we finalists were taken to the Great Hall and again stood before the Elders. "The eleven of you will compete in the second test. Should any of you be disqualified, the runner-up will replace you," the Eldrenne said. She gestured to her far right and said, "Elspeth."

The other Elder with the crescent moons on her lapels leaned forward. Her permanently frowned face pinched up derisively. "Twenty-one there were, now ten plus one there are." Her words were elongated as if she formed each sound very carefully, but it lent her an air of scheming. "The second test is mine to designate. Now that we have established who among you has the most book knowledge of our ways, you will all submit to a formal interview."

Damn it! That was the last thing I wanted to do: stand before them, answering their questions, hoping they couldn't sense my stain.

"Before these good Elders and the Eldrenne, I will consider whether you are well spoken and judge how you conduct yourself under our ever-watchful eyes. To serve your community as high priestess is to be visible to all and you must exhibit confidence in your demeanor, as well as possess the persona and image that will uphold our standards. Further, you must display an accessibility the media cannot manipulate—and they will try." She appraised each of us in turn. "We will choose five and a single runner-up to proceed to the next round."

Elspeth gestured to the cauldron, then toward the end of the line on her right. "Choose lots. They are numbered one to fifty. You start."

Again, Maria approached the cauldron first. When she looked down, she gasped and stepped back.

"You *will* draw a lot," Elspeth commanded.

"But—"

"Draw," the Eldrenne said, "or suffer the consequences."

It took Maria a moment, but she gathered herself and stepped up to the cauldron. Sinking to her knees, she stared down into the deep cast-iron pot. She darted her hand inside, gave a squeal and withdrew.

What was in there?

"An empty hand will forfeit," the Eldrenne whispered.

The woman reached in again and as she retrieved her lot she swiftly stood. Held at arm's length, her lot squirmed in her grip. I stared; she held a scorpion by its tail.

"What is the number," Elspeth asked, "on its belly?"

"Six."

Elspeth turned to the next in line. "Now it is your turn."

Maria scanned about for a place to discard the wriggling creature and realized she would have to hold it until this was done. She seemed unsteady as she returned to her spot. The women around me fidgeted nervously.

Remembering Nana's advice, I watched the Elders as this process continued. They were forming opinions of us as we reacted to choosing a scorpion from the pot. I determined not to show any fear. When my turn came, however, staring down into that cauldron, seeing their dark insectlike bodies crawling about, I felt fear.

Still, I watched them, trying to determine movement, to anticipate it.

A childhood memory of catching crawdads in the stream when Nana took me to a nature preserve flashed through my mind. Like a light breeze through a tunnel, calmness billowed into me and blew away the dust clouding my judgment. I reached into the pot, selected a scorpion, and lifted it. "Thirteen," I announced.

After the lottery was reviewed and the critters returned to the cauldron, I found out I was to be interviewed third out of the eleven. Lydia ushered us to the kitchen. "The interviews will begin at seven o'clock. You have free time until then, that is, after you ladies have washed up the evening dishes."

"Dishes?" Hunter asked pointedly.

Lydia's eyes narrowed. "Are you unwilling to wet your hands for the coven you may lead?"

Hunter's jaw dropped, then firmly shut.

"I didn't think so." Lydia turned to leave. "Again, the time before and after your interview is also free time and I suggest you sleep if you can. Return to the holding area. I will come for you there when it is your turn to be interviewed." She left us.

An awkward moment of silence filled the kitchen. I started opening cupboards hunting for the dish soap, found it.

"Let me wash my hands first," Maria said. She scrubbed her hands mercilessly in the sink. "Goddess, I hope there are no more scorpions!" she said and shivered heartily.

She received a bevy of seconds to her thought. "It's not like we'll have to deal with those on a daily basis," added a woman named Suzanne who spoke with a slight Southern accent.

Hunter let her crossed arms fall loose. "No, as high priestess, you'll just have to establish our community platform, state our goals, and implement solid plans to reach them while creating lines not only for outreach but awareness."

"Sounds like you memorized a pamphlet," Maria remarked.

Hunter didn't miss a beat in replying, "Trying to institute and apply that level of strategy makes snatching a single scorpion from a pot seem easy."

Suzanne squared her shoulders. "That is kind of what I meant. We don't have to deal with the unsavory image of the mystic medicine woman of centuries past. That kind of thing made us easy targets for superstition and haunts us yet. A high priestess is clergy. Aside from all the public outlets you mentioned, we also have to be available for our coven members, to counsel and teach them, and often deal with the foolish who want power but are clueless about our laws and ignorant in general. We must be vigilant for our cause."

I noticed Holly's head snapped up at that last and she squinted hard at Suzanne, as if the woman had just spoken some secret spy code phrase. Holly's hands were fisted.

I cleared my throat and interjected, "Comparatively, doing dishes is worry-free."

"If you like menial work," Hunter answered.

"I'm not above doing it," I retorted.

"But a high priestess has far more important things to worry about, as I've just pointed out." She added, "That's not conceit or pride, it's a simple fact."

"Are you ready for all that?" Maria asked, rinsing her hands.

"Are you?" Hunter asked back.

Maria dried her hands on a towel. "Of course, or I wouldn't have asked. And I've noticed that women who think highly of themselves—as in being too good to do the dishes because it might damage their pretty, fake nails—are easily baited and generally turn the hook

around and send it back trying to avoid tough questions."
She tossed her brown and gray braid over her shoulder.
"Think you can answer now?"

Hunter squared her shoulders and took a pose of
authority. "Yes, I am ready to be a high priestess, ready
for the responsibility and the work of the position. And,
if you must know, I have an allergic reaction to most
dish, hand, and laundry soaps. I use specialized products at home and I doubt that what they have here is the
same."

Maria tossed the towel to her. "Then you dry."

She caught it and said, "I would be glad to." She didn't
look glad to.

Holly spoke up. "No one even mentioned dealing with
vampires, wæres, wanna-bes, frauds, and the fey."

"Exactly," Hunter said triumphantly. "It all makes
washing dishes seem"—she looked down at the drying rag
with distaste—"absurd."

"So you'd rather deal with a vampire than safely wash
dishes?" Maria pressed.

"Yes."

"Have you ever faced an angry vampire?" I asked.

She spun to me. "I assume you have?"

"I have," I agreed. "And you didn't answer."

She realized she was busted again, but didn't back
down. "All I can do is my best. That's all any of us can do.
And when this is over, we'll know who the best of us is."

She still hadn't answered the question, but had said
something that sounded good and leader-ish anyway.
Around us, the side-choosing began, some of it mental,
some of it outward as women moved to stand nearer Maria

and me, or nearer Hunter. Goddess, help me. I hated politics. I wanted no part of it.

So, I gathered the dishes and started the water, but warily watched the assessment. Maybe I was assessing as well, but I wasn't choosing teammates as if we were on a reality show. I was wondering who could handle the position. For whom was I planning to pave this road?

CHAPTER SIXTEEN

Lying on my cot, wrestling with the drowsiness that came after eating, I was racking my brain for a way to shield against the Elders that wouldn't rouse their suspicion. I had to make it through the round. If I had a later interview, I could sleep and perhaps, with a fresher mind, come up with a plan. But that hadn't been my multi-legged lot.

After the interview, I'd have about two hours to sleep. If I wasn't cut after this round, that, I thought optimistically, should get me through the night.

A scream resounded through the stone walls.

Instantly on my feet, I was the only one up and moving forward. Yanking open the door, my feet had me in the hall before I knew which direction to go. The sound of another door pulled me around to face the restroom end of the hall.

Mandy backed from the alcove, trembling. One hand covered her mouth, while the other was held before her like a loathsome thing. Footsteps resounded behind me; Lydia was hurrying toward us.

"Mandy." I eased toward her. "What's wrong?"

The holding room door shut behind me, then shoved open again.

"Mandy," I repeated.

Her frizzy blond head turned to me, her distress evident. She blinked. "Persephone," she whispered. She held that outstretched hand toward me. Blood was smeared on her fingertips. "She's dead—she's—she's dead."

Lydia stopped beside me; I felt the other finalists crowding behind us.

"Who's dead?" Lydia asked. "Where?"

Mandy shivered. "The . . . the one from Georgia. S-Suzanne." She began to sob and pointed to the shadowy alcove near the restroom. I could see nothing from where I stood.

I heard the regular tapping of staffs behind us and turned toward the sound; Morgellen and Elspeth were rounding the turn. "Finalists! Return to the holding room," Morgellen called. I did not obey quickly. Lydia went to them and they whispered together as they moved forward. "Lydia, take Mandy to the office where she can clean her hands. Call the police immediately. Elspeth and I will wait here to secure the area."

The next hour passed in what seemed like only moments.

The police arrived right away and quickly marked off the area with yellow plastic tape. We were all herded into the holding room while they "secured the scene." They photographed everything and dusted for fingerprints. From the doorway of the holding room, we watched the body bag roll by on a stretcher. We were all stunned, moved, and frightened. We barely spoke at all.

Until the police came in with fingerprint cards and ink, I don't think it occurred to any of us that we were suspects . . . or that a killer might be among us.

We were questioned individually in the kitchen by a short, balding male officer with glasses. His badge had the name Moore on it. During my turn, he wrote down my name and asked, "All right, miss, where were you when you heard Mandy scream?"

"On my cot trying to sleep."

He scribbled in his notes. "And for the half-hour preceding that?"

I explained about being in the kitchen, then returning to the holding room.

He scribbled more. "Did you go to the bathroom at any time?"

"No."

"You just laid on your cot and stayed there?"

"Yes."

"Did you see anyone else leave?"

"I was aware of the door opening and shutting a few times, of walking back and forth, but I didn't see who. My eyes were shut."

He let me go back to the holding room alone, after asking me to send in Holly. The doorless stretch of hallway must have been deemed safe enough for us to walk alone—and no one could escape from it. As I reached the last curve before the holding room door, I heard Morgellen arguing with another police officer. "We are conducting an Eximium! Every one of the contestants has been given a dagger. Every Elder has one as well, though I cannot be sure if any of us brought ours. I didn't bring mine."

"We will have to have everyone's dagger," the officer said. "For forensic testing." He radioed to another officer and requested thirty evidence bags be brought.

"You may take the daggers and proceed with your investigation, young man, but we must continue with our competition."

"That may not be possible—"

Despite the horror I felt that someone was dead, I was ready to cheer about getting out of the interview with the Elders. But Morgellen cut him off mid-sentence.

"I assure you it is," she insisted, her voice firm. "We will keep to the Great Hall. You may do your work here."

"In all likelihood, ma'am, one of them is guilty! I want them all confined to the holding room below ground for now."

"I don't doubt that, young man, but the rest of them are *not* killers and a high priestess will be chosen from among them. These women are foresworn to compete, and face dire consequences should they refuse to participate, let alone leave these grounds before the night is over. We Elders see no reason to halt the contest."

"Someone has taken a life, ma'am. Your consequences are clearly less of a deterrent to the killer than the threat of life imprisonment or capital punishment."

"Perhaps, Officer Detrick, but our prize is probably the motive for the murder. Our proceeding may help you find the murderer."

I stepped into view as if I hadn't been listening out of sight. Still, I felt the weight of Morgellen's gaze as I passed.

Rejoining the others, I said to Holly, "Officer Moore will see you next." She left as I sat on my cot.

Overhearing Elder Morgellen and Officer Detrick confirmed to me that Suzanne had been stabbed to death and one of the ceremonial daggers we'd each pulled from the cauldron was the most likely weapon.

Hot, I removed my sweatshirt, folded it, and laid it under my cot. I smoothed the copper Henley down.

Why would anyone kill her? As I understood it, none of us contestants knew each other, beyond what would be revealed in holding-room chatting. I thought about each person in the room, considering Morgellen's suggested motive. Who might have done it?

I noted Holly's empty cot; she was answering Officer Moore's questions right now.

As the runner-up, if one person was out of the running, she was in for the next round and therefore had a one in ten shot at advancing. If she remained the runner-up, she would compete, but it would not even be counted unless one of the other ten refused.

Or died.

I remembered how she had glared at Suzanne in the kitchen when Suzanne spoke of being "vigilant for our cause." Among us, Holly was the only one who seemed to have any benefit from Suzanne's death. Did the paper tiger have real claws?

● ● ●

Morgellen had convinced the police to let the Elders proceed with the Eximium. I had no idea how she managed
it but the fact that she was an Elder left me wondering if
she would use her power to compel him into giving his
permission. Unethical, but considering the situation, I
wouldn't rule it out. Even if she was sincere in her belief
that we would aid in the killer's capture if we continued,
allowing us to do so with a killer loose among us was
quite a risk to take.

Another officer came to the holding room and bagged
and tagged each of our daggers individually. A watchful
and silent female officer stayed in the room with us when
he left.

When I was called to my interview at ten after nine,
my feet felt heavy. Escorted upstairs by Lydia and the
dagger-bagging cop, I trudged along, my legs like iron
weights. How could I shield? How could I hide? At the
bottom of the steps to the Great Hall, I stopped. This was
my formal meeting with the Elders. Nana had warned me
about this.

Would they detect that I was the Lustrata? That I carried a stain? Would I, in the next few moments, be con-
demned to be Bindspoken? Maybe that wouldn't be so
bad. Maybe it would nullify the stain.

But I couldn't imagine not feeling the vibration in a
stone, or the elemental's spirits standing guard in a circle,
or not hearing the call of a ley line.

Determined to clear my mind and keep my secrets my
own, I started up the steps. The handrail was cold under
my sweaty palm as I ascended into the dark, and turned to
the dimly lit center of the vast floor.

"Come, child," said the Eldrenne.

I went.

The candlewicks had receded deep; the flames were no longer atop the pillars, but housed inside thin walls of wax, dimming the already low light until the Elders' faces were shadowed under the brims of their hats, wrinkles deep and forbidding as they appraised me.

"Merry Meet," I said, bowing in formal greeting, "Elders and Eldrenne. I am—"

"You are Persephone Alcmedi, of Eris Alcmedi, of Demeter Alcmedi, of Clio Alcmedi, of Thalia Alcmedi, of Elpis Alcmedi," Elspeth said.

"Yes," I answered. My Greek witch lineage went back centuries. I was grateful she didn't want to list it all.

"As the local nominee, we all anticipated you would breeze through the written portion of the test, as surely the acting priestess made a wise choice in you. We were not disappointed. We are assured by your very nomination that you not only know the Rede well, but strictly adhere to it."

Fighting against swallowing the lump forming in my throat as it would be a telltale sign, I worked at mastering the blankness within me and without and making the lump shrink so it wasn't choking me.

"Being high priestess is many things," Elspeth continued. "What concerns us here is how, in some ways, it is akin to being the owner of a business. There is a budget to consider—funds must come in, and they must flow out as well. What would you do to keep that flow of funds coming, and what would you do with it once you were in control of the Venefica Coven finances?"

Whoa. I didn't actually want this job. Suddenly, I was willing to bet Hunter had a business degree. Vivian had run a coffee shop, so she had a degree of sorts, or experience anyway. What experience did I have? "I honestly don't have experience with a business's finances but I am self-employed, so I understand money management and documentation. I maintain savings, handle investments with the help of a qualified professional, and live within my means. Do you have guidelines, training, or assistance in this area?"

Elspeth's mouth crooked wickedly on one side. It was not a smile; more like a cat's mouth twitching before it pounced. "You readily admit then, that you are not experienced enough to take this position and would need help."

"Yes, if it is available. If left to my own, though, I'd pull the books and study what was spent where and for what purpose in the past, and compare that to the budget at the time. I could create my own guidelines that way."

"What would you do to raise funds?"

"Find a successful coven and ask their priestess to share her techniques with me."

"Bah!" She thumped her staff on the dais and shook her head, irritated. "Do you know what the annual goals for this coven are? The long-term goals?"

"No."

"Are you aware of the policies and politics? The promises and commitments made to local government?"

"No."

"Have you read the Coven's business minutes? Have you even shown up to a sabbat?"

"No."

She screeched questions at me in a rapid-fire manner, but there she paused. "What makes you think," she taunted ruthlessly, "the members of this coven would accept you as their high priestess?"

My face turned to the floor. I felt so damn small in that giant room, like a mouse that had left its hole in the wall and scurried into the middle of the room only to have a big cat leap in front of me. "I don't." I felt cold, as if a draft blew over me; I should have left my sweatshirt on.

The Elders began whispering and murmuring to themselves as if they were a mental group in a nursing home. But there was a cadence to it, a rhythm, and I knew it was more than mad ravings.

"The local nominee," the Eldrenne whispered and her voice silenced the others, "is not indifferent to her coven. She is a solitary, who knows nothing of the coven model."

My head lifted. She had her palm out to me. No wonder I felt a draft; she was searching my aura. "That is true," I said. I hoped like hell she couldn't see things I didn't want her to see. I centered my thoughts on what experience I did have.

"The acting priestess has nominated a woman who cannot hope to run the coven!" Elspeth cried in outrage.

The Eldrenne's blind eyes seemed locked on me; her lids narrowed.

I went utterly still.

The Eldrenne gestured dismissively and the cool draft dissipated. "Lydia's a wise witch. She would never waste her nomination," the Eldrenne countered. "Tell us,

Persephone Alcmedi, what qualities does Lydia see in you that make you worthy for this honor, despite your weaknesses?"

"I have many strengths," I said with conviction. "I am well known in my community for my skills with divination and counseling, especially with Tarot. I write a syndicated newspaper column, so I am well aware of local and national views on not only witches, but wæres as well. And I am always learning more about vampires and fairies. I have become something of a champion for the other-than-ordinary community, though admittedly I think that public battle will continue for some time. My long lineage affords me access to several Books of Shadows. I can organize people, set goals, form and implement a plan. I am responsible, fair, and hard-working." As I spoke, I realized I was getting angry and defensive. I couldn't help adding, "And I'm wondering why you aren't asking me about my spirituality and moral compass, which pantheon I prefer, and what elemental quarter-calls I use."

The Eldrenne laughed; it was a *heh-heh-heh* chuckle. "I think we know what Lydia saw in you," she said. Her hand returned to her lap and her face dropped down again. It seemed a kind of signal.

Elspeth resumed her questioning. "What is it you hope to accomplish, should you become high priestess?"

I hadn't thought about answering questions like this. I should have. Now was not the time to be formulating such ideas.

"You are hesitant to share your hopes?"

"No. No. It isn't that. I just . . ." I paused again, knowing I was not getting off to a good start. "Vivian pandered to the kind of witches who are mostly show and talk. I didn't like that and it kept me rooted in being a solitary. It seemed she snubbed those who wanted to practice the witches' ways of magic and spirituality."

Elspeth gestured to indicate the geo-dome. "Her 'pandering' paid off well for Venefica Coven."

"Yes, this facility is an admirable Covenstead." My hands slipped meekly into my pockets.

"You would snub those curious souls who gave deeply from their personal finances?"

"No, never." I paused. "I don't have a grand speech to pitch myself to you. What I know is that most of those who paid for this wanted a place to brag about, a place to be toadied to as they are at their country clubs and spas. Their donations were generous, but they were also strategic tax deductions." I pulled my hands from my pockets. "Vivian was good at schmoozing the wealthy. But, for the rest . . . take Mandy, for instance. That girl is a seeker, and she's thirsty for knowledge. She idolized Vivian, and Vivian took advantage of her. What does Mandy have to show for her loyal service? I'm not sure Vivian taught her anything. Mandy, and those like her, are the future. They are you"—I gestured at the dais—"decades from now. What groundwork is being laid for them? What ethics and standards are they being taught? Any?"

"So ethics and standards are important to you?"

"Yes. Personal responsibility, accountability, and a true sense of kindness. What is a high priestess if not a teacher? What will anyone learn from someone who cares nothing for them?" I hushed myself there. This was not a soapbox. I wasn't here to preach at the Elders.

"What else is important to you?"

"Justice." I said it without thinking.

Elspeth raised a white brow at me.

Had I just opened a trap for myself? Given them a clue I didn't want them to have?

"Justice," Elspeth repeated slowly, her expression pensive.

"Curious," another Elder murmured.

The Eldrenne lifted her blind eyes again.

Suddenly I said, "Someone died here tonight. Aren't we all feeling the importance of justice?"

"Yes," the Eldrenne said. "Yes, we are." Something about the curve of her lips said she was on track with my thoughts. She wasn't going to be diverted from that course by any attempt of mine to link it to tonight's crime.

CHAPTER SEVENTEEN

When my interview concluded, I was escorted back to the holding room. Drained and eager for a measure of sleep, I dozed off quickly. My napping filled the better part of an hour. It was enough to find unconsciousness, but not enough to stockpile energy or feel rested. I awoke to Lydia's voice.

"Contestants!" Lydia called from the doorway. "Witches! Join me in the Great Hall."

Climbing out of the cot was difficult. It made me feel a little better to see that I was not the only sluggish one. The rest of the group were moving slowly as well.

Holly stood with Lydia. Her scorpion's number had been the highest drawn, so hers had been the final interview.

"You are drained from a day full of testing and weary with worry over the needless death among us, but rise as the witches you are! Rise with strength, knowing that for what comes next, you will need it."

Her words inspired us and made us wary. We took our places, forming a line like good kindergartners. And, in childish fashion, Hunter stepped in behind me and whispered, "How confident are you about your business plan, Persephone?"

She obviously felt she'd aced the interview test and successfully impressed the buckles off the Elders' hats. Good for her. But rubbing my nose in it: bad for her. I was tired enough to be easily incensed.

Facing her, I scanned her up and down and said, "Business degree, check. Silver spoon, check. Massive ego, check. All great qualities for a high priestess, don't you agree? I mean, if they want the trophy-wife version of a leader, you're in. If they want someone who will do exactly what they are told because of misplaced loyalty to a politically motivated Elder whose ass you must have kissed, you're in. But what if they want someone who can guide the spiritual and magical development of seekers? That *is* the primary function of a high priestess, unless I'm mistaken. If *that's* what they're looking for, then your GPA, your family connections, and your look-at-me-I'm-upper-class makeover are irrelevant. And your get-out-of-my-way-I'm-coming-through attitude? It becomes a hindrance."

I turned away, relieved to find the line had surged ahead. I got to stride forward with purpose to catch up. In the hallway, Moore and Detrick stopped and watched us as we passed. I heard Lydia call out a reminder that the officers were not permitted in the Great Hall as we conducted the ceremony and testing. I still suspected the police officers' willingness to let us proceed had more to do with spellcraft than typical procedures.

When we arrived at the stairway to the Great Hall, I realized that Hunter had fallen to the back of the line.

The Elders were already seated on their thrones as we

re-formed our east-west line before the dais. They must have ranked the interviews already. My stomach knotted hard enough to rival the heartache I had successfully been ignoring until that moment. Scolding myself harshly, I concentrated hard on what was about to happen. Best-case scenario: I had to prepare myself for being cut from this without having accomplished my goal of knocking Hunter from the running. Worst-case scenario: the Elders or Eldrenne read or detected my stain and my Lustrata-ness and meant for me to be Bindspoken.

The Eldrenne gestured to her left. "Desdemona."

The Elder with silver ankhs embroidered on her lapels and cuffs said, "We have chosen, indeed, those who will proceed." Her voice was shrill and a bit squeaky. She handed a scroll to Lydia, who broke the seal and turned to read.

"In alphabetical order, the five finalists are: Persephone Alcmedi . . ."

I blinked in surprise, but held on to the sigh that would release my tension. I didn't want Hunter to know I'd been worried.

Lydia went on. "Lehana Bosico. Hunter Hopewell. Amber Lantz. Maria Morrison. The runner-up is: Holly Price."

Beside me, a woman whose name was not called shut her eyes and sighed disappointedly. For the first time, I realized my participation was knocking out contestants who truly wanted the job. Someone removed from the running in this round might have dominated in the next one. Then again, if I had beat them out—how qualified were they to start with?

Lydia returned to the end of the dais.

"If your name was not called, please return now to the holding room. Mandy will take you to the secondary holding room where you can rest."

Five women stepped away from our line and retreated from the Great Hall. We who remained looked at each other and closed ranks a little. I smiled at Lehana, who stood to my left. She grinned back and grabbed my pale hand in her dark one, then reached to take Hunter's hand on her left. To my right was Maria with the broomstick skirt, and I slid my hand into hers and nodded. In turn, Maria took Amber's hand and she took Holly's.

I considered Holly; she'd made it through the second round. Surely her mother would be proud. Surely she was proud of herself. But as runner-up again . . .

The six of us faced the Elders and, I felt, tried to convey that we were ready for the next test.

Desdemona smiled broadly, showing she was missing her bicuspids. She scooted forward on her throne and her hands shook as she excitedly rubbed gnarled fingers together. She spoke in verse with her strange, high voice and sounded completely insane.

> *"We have seen you take a written test.*
> *You have plans for the coven, but what comes next*
> *Is my test and in it, we will discover*
> *If you can think on your feet . . . and if you can govern."*

She stopped there, cocked her head at us, and bit her lip. An odd mannerism. It made me wary.

Her arms shot out, extended to either side, palms

open. I felt the static chill of power being called before me, felt it dancing from the dais as she said,

> *"Although we be a mourning choir*
> *For the one who has expired*
> *Know that all of thee are liars*
> *But only one in guilt is mired.*
> *And thus the contest we so desire*
> *Shall continue as required*
> *And next my test will transpire*
> *I bid thee now enter, vampires!"*

Power spiraled across the Great Hall. As she fisted her hands and jerked them close to her chest, the eastern and western double doors burst open. In the dark of each open entry stood a figure.

From the smell of decay riding the wind that gusted into the hall, Desdemona hadn't been lying. Vampires.

The Covenstead was protected, like most buildings, with the metaphysical barrier that kept out those with the curse of undeath. The soulless undead couldn't pass through unless invited in.

Desdemona had made the invitation.

My attention bounced back and forth, completely intent on the as-yet-unrecognizable figures in the doorway. Although obscured, their stature and wide shoulders showed both to be male.

Please don't be Menessos and Goliath.

The figures stepped from the shadows to the dim interior . . . and I was relieved to see both were unfamiliar. Of course, this could be even worse: they might sense the stain upon me and not have any qualms about revealing such information to one and all.

The vampires strode toward the dais. They were handsome men wearing fashionable clothing that combined I'm-hot-and-I-know-it with I'm-going-clubbing-to-find-a-piece-of-ass-worthy-of-me. Not that design and style could say all that alone; it was inherent in the very fabric of their beings. From their squared shoulders to the self-assurance of their gait—everything about them radiated confidence.

They looked us over with what elsewhere would be taken as lascivious intent. One exuded conceit with the lift of his chin and the firm set of his unimpressed mouth. The other made me think of a delighted frat boy who'd just strolled unnoticed into the ladies' locker room.

Although no one else seemed to be bothered by it, the stench of rotting leaves made me gag. They could have at least tried to cover it with cologne.

"Eldrenne, Madam Elders," said the unimpressed one. His voice was deep. Tall and muscular, he had the disproportionate chiseled features of a comic book hero. Even his blond hair, trimmed business short on the sides, was styled so that three perfect tendrils of the longer top fell forward in a trademark rugged way. He did not bow his head, but rather turned it sideways a fraction while cocking his head. It might be construed as a slight bow, but vampires were not ones to show obeisance to any mortal. "I am Heldridge and am pleased to participate in your Eximium." He signaled the other vampire.

"I'm Sever." He flashed them each a flirty smile, but didn't bother to offer them any pretty words that probably weren't true. Sever had golden brown curls that hung past his shoulders.

"Welcome," Desdemona said to them. To us, she said, "The test will entail the—"

The other Elders all reacted to her sudden stop, sitting straighter as their notice drifted beyond our contestant line.

A trembling resonance began low on my spine then fluttered upward like fingernails scraping over each vertebra. The fine vibration slid around each rib only to rejoin in my sternum, where heat began to build between my breasts. My mind flashed on images of the darkened living room, of Johnny's face before me while our bodies were entwined. My nipples hardened.

I blinked hard, willing the images to stop, willing this reaction to stop, but the heat dropped down, gliding under my skin to my navel and lower, between my legs. A rush of desire swept through my body—

The southern doors burst open behind me. Without looking, I knew who was there.

"Ladies—and my fellow vampires—please permit me to interpose myself." As the contestants around me turned, I did, too, and saw Menessos come striding in, projecting his innate patrician polish. "My presence may not have been solicited, but I trust it is not unwelcome." His walnut-colored waves brushed his shoulders as he moved. The thin beard, trimmed to balance his square jaw, perfected his image as a manifestation of Arthur Pendragon, the warrior from centuries past and my dreams. However, the elegantly cut modern suit that draped from his strong, broad shoulders and the white shirt—sans tie and fashionably unbuttoned—branded him as a New Age warrior, the Lord Executive of the Boardroom. In my eyes, he was a time-transcending champion, cunning and adaptable, trained to win at any cost. A man to be wary of.

From the dais, I heard a sharp intake of breath and the Eldrenne whispered, "Menessos."

That made me turn back to the dais. The other Elders exchanged glances. The Eldrenne flicked her fingers and her staff shot into her grip. She stood. Behind her, on the throne's high back, the raven spread its wings and cawed.

The other Elders came to their feet as well, staves in hand, eyes bright, ready.

The Eldrenne's mouth curved deeply downward, as if she could embody scornful contempt. "You were not invited."

Menessos laughed quietly, but continued into the hall toward us. "I have said as much, dear Eldrenne. I assure you, austere Elders, I have come only to be a participant in the Eximium, as vampires often do for such events. Would you banish me from the proceedings?"

She hesitated. "Local vampires are customary."

He gestured at Sever and Heldridge. "This territory falls under my jurisdiction."

She stamped her staff on the dais floor; it cracked like thunder and the orb atop it began to glow with a white light. "Why have you come?"

"It is my right to attend." Menessos stopped perhaps ten feet from our contestant line. "Do you yet begrudge me the past, Eldrenne? Will your bitterness never cease?"

They had history between them. Curious.

"You give me no cause for anything but bitterness, Menessos." She spat his name.

"What benefit could I seek in aggravating the wounds of decades past, Eldrenne?"

"Your motives are ever your own. To guess at them is to relinquish myself to thoughts just as depraved and self-ish. I will not sully myself to venture there."

"Your words sting me, Xerxadrea."

The other Elders gasped in unison; he'd addressed her by name. WEC had only a handful of Eldrennes and once they became Eldrenne, *that* was their name in public.

"Good," she replied. "It may not be the stabbing vehement agony you deserve, but a sting implies pain and if I have hurt you even a little, then I will relish it."

Menessos took three steps forward, hand out, palms open in a show of nonaggression. "If my pain pleases you, Xerxadrea, if you delight in hearing of it, then come down from your dais, witch. Come down and make me bleed of your own hand, that you may be happy once more."

Before I could even turn back to her, the Eldrenne glided past me to accept his offer.

CHAPTER EIGHTEEN

"Blood Oath!" Desdemona whispered. The other Elders took up the words and repeated them until they had a soft chant, each hammering their staff when they said "oath."

Menessos lifted his arm and bared his wrist.

The Eldrenne took his hand in both of hers. With a cry of victory, she shoved it upward as her raven swooped in. The bird beat its wings and hovered in the air, talons raking his skin over and over.

"By my blood," he said, standing calmly while the bird tore his flesh open. "I am here to harm none. I am here to participate fairly in your Eximium. And I am here to give you this moment, Xerxadrea. Let your bitterness be gone."

When the bird flew away and returned to rest on the high back of her throne, the Eldrenne pulled a black handkerchief from the folds of her robes and covered his forearm with it. She whispered and chanted words I could not make out. When she was done, she said over her shoulder, "Contestants to the kitchen to wait. You will be called shortly for the next lottery."

I was so glad for the chance to remove myself from Menessos's presence I had to force myself to keep to a sedate pace and not to run to the stairs and out of the hall.

The six of us had to grope most of our way to the kitchen in the dark. The candles in the wall geodes had either burned out or were unlit. We had only the fluorescent glow from the open kitchen door to guide us. I wondered where the police—and the portable lights they'd brought in to illuminate the alcove—had gone.

Between the walk in the dark, the scene we'd just witnessed, and the insecurity aroused by the combination of death, drama, and vampire presence, the six of us seemed somewhat shell-shocked.

Holly was the first to speak. She opened the refrigerator and, seeing apples, asked if anyone else wanted one. No one took her up on it.

"Coffee?" I asked. That's what I wanted.

"Good idea," Maria said, and came to help me while the others took seats at one of the long tables.

"Damn, but that was intense," said Lehana, sinking onto a folding chair. She spoke with an accent more pronounced than Suzanne's.

"Is that Jamaican?" Holly asked. I turned, thinking she was inquiring about the coffee I was spooning into the filter, but saw she was intent on Lehana.

"No. Haitian."

Holly rummaged in the drawer for a knife and took it to the table where she began neatly slicing her apple.

Maybe she was too young to understand the glory of good coffee. Then I realized she had just armed herself with a sharp knife. Again.

"So what flavor is your witchcraft?" Hunter asked.

"Why do you ask?" Lehana asked back, her manner cool but her eyes darkly serious.

Maria and I exchanged wary glances.

Hunter shrugged. "Just curious."

Lehana stood and peered down at Hunter, who sat across from her. "You think I am a Vodoun, a priestess of Santería, and you have a problem with this?"

Amber, at the head of the table, wordlessly rose and went nonchalantly to the refrigerator. If I'd been sitting with them, I'd have retreated too.

"I didn't say that," Hunter replied. She crossed her legs and draped one arm across the back of the adjacent vacant seat, all with an unruffled, you-can't-make-me-uneasy expression.

I noted her sense of ease, her body language. It reinforced her just-curious response; any other pose might have disqualified her defense.

Lehana's eyes slitted. "You want to find out what flavor my magic is? Come with me somewhere private and I'll give you a taste."

"Can't just tell me here?" Hunter tsked. "Secrets, hmmm? Afraid to expose yourself? Worried someone might pick up on the power-stone you're faking your way through this with?" Hunter stood abruptly. "I notice a lot of things, Lehana. Like your hand going to your pocket often during the tests. I noticed you holding something in your hand when you chose your scorpion—even caught a quick glimpse of it. A *vinculum* isn't easy to come by. I have to wonder, which Elder gave it to you?"

The fluorescent lights overhead flashed and went out.

Plunged into darkness, the underground kitchen became a blackened cave. Someone squealed. Someone else swore in a mutter.

"Does this mean bad things have happened in the Great Hall?" Amber's voice came from my left.

"Maybe it's just the lower level circuit or just the kitchen," Maria offered from my right.

Hunter said, "I'll go find out."

Remembering the dark hallway, I said, "Shout for the police. They've got to be somewhere out there and they will have flashlights."

I heard Hunter groping along the wall. "Door should be here somewhere." *Crack!* "Ow!"

"You okay?"

"Yes," she hissed. "Door's open, I walked into it!" A second later she shouted into the hallway, "Hello?" Her voice echoed down the corridor.

"If bad things are happening in the Great Hall," Amber pressed, "is announcing our exact location a good idea?"

"If the vampires wanted to find us," I said, "they wouldn't have any trouble locating us in the dark even if we were silent."

"Thanks. I feel much better now," Maria added sarcastically.

"Don't worry," Hunter said from the doorway. "An Eximium massacre would ensure bad PR, and neither VEIN nor WEC would sabotage the other politically. They may have their rivalries, but they understand that if they give mundanes a reason to turn against one group, the others will shortly suffer the same fate." She didn't pause before her voice resounded down the corridor again, "Hello? Anyone there?"

"Vein?" Maria asked.

"The Vampire Executive International Network—VEIN," Hunter said.

"Of course. What else could it be?" I said, crossing my arms and leaning against the counter. The solidity of it was nice in the dark.

"I see a light," Hunter said.

"Hello? This is Officer Moore. Who's calling?"

"The contestants!" Hunter answered. "We're in the kitchen. What's going on?"

"Not sure. The electric's out all over the building." His voice was closer now. "Everyone okay?"

"Yeah."

I could see the faint blue glow of an outline on Hunter and knew the officer was getting close.

"I'm sure the emergency candles are here somewhere," Hunter said, "we just aren't familiar with where they'd be." She backed into the room as Officer Moore entered with a flashlight held over his head.

"Well, we'll find them," he said and moved toward the cabinets, flashing the light around to take in the room. "Oh my God!" He rushed to the tables. "No one move. Everyone stay right where you are!"

In the glow of his flashlight, I saw Lehana in a chair, eyes wide and vacant. A large dark stain covered her chest.

• • •

Lehana was dead.

Holly, and the knife she'd been cutting her apple with, were missing.

She had evidently killed twice. Giving her the presumption of innocence when she was missing just wasn't logical. But neither was killing to get ahead in a competition, then disappearing and not being able to compete anyway. It made no sense! Except, she had exhibited some signs of militant extremism. Maybe she wasn't here to win either, but to ensure the placement of a certain kind of priestess. We might actually be after the same thing—but with decidedly different ways of achieving our goals.

I paced, angry and hoping Morgellen would poke her head into the room for just a moment. She'd pressured the officer to let us continue, and she might have even used magic unethically to ensure his cooperation. And another life had been lost.

The lights had not come back on, but Lydia had appeared with Officer Detrick and a flashlight and located the candles. While Detrick briefly questioned us—I think he took my pacing for nervous energy—by candlelight in the kitchen, Lydia and Moore disappeared into the hall. I could hear Moore on the radio calling for backup. And I heard the beginning of the reply, "Negative."

When our statements had been taken, Moore called Detrick to the hall while Lydia joined us. "I've replaced and lit the candles in the hall's geodes," she said. "We're going to take you back to the holding room. It has only one entrance, so you'll be safe there. The officers are insisting we lock you in for your own safety. One of them will remain posted outside the door." Seeing I was about to protest, she added, "It will be brief, I promise."

The halls seemed colder as we returned to the holding room, and the shadows that had at first seemed like appropriate ambiance had become frightening areas demanding scrutiny.

When we arrived, Officer Detrick went in first and quickly searched the room. Declaring it secure, he gestured for us to enter. We wordlessly gathered inside the door and watched it swing shut, then heard the crisp metallic sound of the bolt sliding shut.

The sound had a finality to it. Something all prisoners must feel when they hear a lock engage.

While I was glad our safety was taking precedence, I'd already decided that if I had to, I would call on the ley line and force that door open. I silently started plotting a spell-rhyme.

Maria, Hunter, and Amber sat on adjoining cots, each holding a candle. Another flickered near the door. I sat on my cot with my own candle. In the wavering shadows, I could just make out the pillow on the head of Holly's empty cot next to mine.

Maria and Amber were murmuring to each other. Hunter stood and crossed the short distance to my cot and sat next to me.

"You okay?" Hunter asked.

I reached under my cot for my sweatshirt, intending to put it back on. "Yeah, you?"

"Yes."

It had been my hope to basically ignore her. Since I had told her off earlier, being buddies wasn't something I expected to happen. Now though, Hunter's voice seemed less authoritative. I studied her.

She wore a goose-egg bruise on her brow where she'd walked into the door, but her expression was calm and blank. Still, her hands were trembling as she smoothed over her hair.

"You sure?" I asked, letting her see in my face that I didn't believe her.

Her expression softened, almost as if it relieved her to know she didn't have to put up a front for me. She took a deep breath, let it go. "No," she whispered.

Amber, her head down and fingers raked deep into her hair, said, "I can't figure out why Holly would kill Lehana."

That was such a "duh" statement, surprise and confusion must've shown on my face.

Maria clarified, "As in why *her* and not one of you two." She pointed at Hunter and me.

"Me or Hunter?"

"We all know you're the top two contenders." Amber's voice was shaky. "It would make more sense to take out one or both of you than any of the rest of us." She put her head back down, resuming a pose of misery.

She had a point, even if it was oddly flattering and disconcerting at the same time.

I wondered if I should voice my thoughts about how Holly might be eliminating contenders for political reasons.

"The *vinculum* Lehana had would trump any contender's efforts," Hunter said.

"What is that?" Maria asked.

"It's a small object, like a stone or a ring, that's

bespelled to link to another person. They're highly dangerous to create but, if successful, anyone could use the item to see into the other's mind and gain answers. Handy in social settings and tests."

"How do you even know about a thing like that?" Amber asked.

"In my hometown, a local politician got busted with one a few years back."

Hunter stared off toward the door; Amber's line of reasoning regarding Holly's motive clearly bothered her. "Holly is probably hiding somewhere in the Covenstead," she whispered.

Though we were locked in with a guard outside the door, I wanted to search for her. And stop her.

"Could she have convinced herself she'd win and then realized she wouldn't and decided to retaliate by . . . doing this?" Maria stood, tossed her braid back over her shoulder, paced a bit before realizing that walking made her candle shine too unsteadily. She sat again. "She can't actually think she can win this way."

"They wouldn't give it to her now," Hunter said.

People willing to take a life usually aren't thinking clearly, but I couldn't judge too harshly. I'd been willing to take a life, albeit the life of a murderer. I considered myself a rational person, with the added perk of being willing to make tough decisions. I decided to tell them what I was thinking. I couldn't risk silence and let anyone else die. "I talked to Holly only a little, but it seemed very clear in that small amount of conversation that she was highly concerned about WEC politics. Remember, Suzanne said, 'We must be vigilant for our cause,' before she was killed?" That elicited nods. "And we've now learned that Lehana had a tool that insinuated she was planted by someone of power." I thought of Holly's suspicion of Hunter. "Can you fight? Can you protect yourself, Hunter?" I asked.

"From a knife in the dark? Hardly."

Why didn't I feel as threatened?

It hadn't occurred to me to feel that threatened. I knew I could fight. Even Johnny would admit—

No, couldn't think of him.

"Then we just stay together," I said. "Until this is over."

We heard the door bolt slide open. Lydia entered carrying a candle. She moved wearily, making her way over to join us and sit on an empty cot. "I must tell you the truth. Only two police officers now remain in the building. The rest have taken their equipment and left."

That seemed highly inappropriate for a place with a murderer on the loose.

"Two?" Amber asked. Her voice was thin as a thread.

Lydia nodded. "When Officer Moore called for backup he was told the electrical failure was due to a power station outage. The whole damn county seems to be out." She shook her head. "All other officers are needed to deal with the emergency. They will get back to the Covenstead eventually, but Officer Moore and Officer Detrick are on their own for the time being."

"Are the doors still secure?" I asked.

"Yes. If Holly had tried to flee up any of the staircases, the Elders and the vampires would have detected her. We believe Holly is still somewhere inside." She added ominously, "But she's not getting out."

"Good," I said.

"Good?" Amber nearly shrieked. "How is that *good*? We're in here!"

"It means she won't get away with what she's done. She can't hide forever. Why don't we search for her?" I pressed. "Use the vampires and their keen senses—"

"Bah!" Lydia smacked her hand on her thigh. "They would never deign to be our bloodhounds. They think this is all very funny, watching us scramble on account of one young woman. Nor do we want them feeling we owe them for anything. Besides, we need them for the next test, which will take time—*night* time—and that's something we're running out of fast." She hesitated, then continued. "Here is the plan. We will go upstairs to the Great Hall and continue the Eximium. The officers remaining are moving furniture to block access to the hallway on either side of the office area. On this level, we are to confine ourselves to that area and use only the stairway near it. The elevator has been shut down."

Considering the Elders intended to get through this no matter what, and if the vampires were running out of night, that was as reasonable a solution as we could get. We'd likely be safe anyway as Holly must still be hiding in the lower levels.

If any of us had questions, we didn't ask them. We simply filed out of the room, candles in hand, following Lydia.

The Elders sat on their thrones, and the three vampires stood to the left of the dais. I tried my best to ignore

Menessos, but his presence undeniably beckoned to my awareness and shaped my perception of the moment. Even without being visually focused on him, my body knew where he was, knew when he turned or shifted his weight. My aura prickled with every blink of his eyes, discerning even the finite movement of air his lashes created.

Nana had to find something in the Codex to minimize this. Or I had to develop a shield or something. I wasn't willing to believe that I had to deal with this super-charged awareness permanently. There had to be a way around it.

To the right of the dais sat several dozen bread box–sized chests. They were all different, from wood to metal to cardboard, some decorated or carved, some plain. I hoped there were no scorpions inside.

"Since Holly is missing and Lehana is dead, there are only four of you to compete," the Eldrenne said. "Despite this, in order that we may maintain the testing schedule, only one of you will be eliminated this round, and three will proceed to the next round." She gestured to her right. "Desdemona."

Pointing a gnarled finger down our short row, Desdemona spoke in that slow, squeaky voice that made me think of the Wicked Witch of the West. So long as she didn't call us "my pretties," I'd be okay.

"A room, a scene, a situation—
Further details closely rationed,
Motives mixed among the undead,
You'll be misguided and misled.

Do not falter, fail, or mis-think
Or, no doubt, your blood they'll drink.
You'll not see us, though we'll be there,
To judge persuasion, poise, conviction—and compare."

The last she said very slowly, straightening. "The lottery, embark . . ." She gestured to the cauldron. "You," she pointed at Maria, "with the eyes, dark."

Approaching the cauldron, Maria peered inside and gave a sigh of relief. Readily she reached in and came up with a skeleton key. Hunter, then Amber, then me. There were a handful of brassy slender keys left in the cauldron.

"Find the number upon the key.
Match to the chests, there will be three.
Of them, just one may you select,
As one, you open and collect."

The four of us inspected the keys; mine had a number one. I located three chests bearing the number one on them. First, a wooden chest: old and worn wood with many nicks and scrapes, leathery straps rounding it with buckles to reinforce the stability, tarnished hinges and lock. It had character, but it wasn't that big. Perhaps a foot long, eight inches high, eight wide. Round topped. Not heavy. Reminded me of a pirate chest. I could detect nothing moving inside, which was good. I didn't want to find a critter inside.

The second box with a number one was a steel box, gray, with a silvery flip-switch that held the top shut, and a lock beside it. It was very sleek and modern, but very plain. It was little more than a lidded cake pan with a hinged top and handle. Very practical.

The last box was white, with ornately carved designs and bejeweled corners. It was like a small house, the top peaked like a roof. The handles on either side were very feminine and curvy.

"Line up after making your selection," Desdemona called.

While I didn't expect we were going to keep these boxes, if that happened to be the case, I liked the little pirate chest the best. I picked it up and carried it to my place in line.

Amber and Maria had already selected their boxes; we waited only a moment more for Hunter. She'd chosen a very femininely decorated box. I wasn't surprised.

"Open them," Desdemona said, "and begin your inspection."

CHAPTER NINETEEN

Trying not to think about the story of Pandora, I sat my box on the floor and slid the key inside. The others were trying to open theirs while standing, but Maria saw me and mumbled, "Good idea," and knelt down to do as I was doing. To me, it was a precaution against anything jumping out at me. Hunter and Amber followed suit and placed their selections on the pine floor before turning their keys.

We glanced at each other to affirm we were ready to lift the lids "as one."

The candlelight would not illumine much, so I cautiously turned the box away, hinges toward me. With it backward, I slowly opened the lid to reveal—

"A scroll," Maria said.

"They're all scrolls," Hunter affirmed.

Desdemona cleared her throat daintily, then said:

> *"On the parchment, rolled and sealed*
> *Find a truth that cannot be revealed—*
> *Though the vampires will use wiles and wit*
> *In hopes you will give in and surrender it.*

Also there is sound advice
Adhere, and it may suffice
To help you obfuscate, twist, confound
And see you through this wicked round.

Test order is dictated by the brass token.
Bring your scrolls, with seals unbroken."

Lydia asked, "Numbers?"

"One," I said, holding up my key. Hunter would follow me, then Maria, then Amber.

Lydia handed each contestant a length of white yarn. "For your key," she said. "Vampires and Persephone, if you would follow me. The rest of you, I will return momentarily to lead you below."

Scroll tucked under my arm, I looped the string through the key and tied it around my neck as I walked behind Lydia. She took up a candelabrum with three tapers as she started down the stairs, and lit the way. We went into the conference room of the office. "Persephone, you remain in the hall a moment." She led the vampires into the conference room, lit enough candles around the room so that it was almost bright, then exited and shut the door behind her.

"Your scroll," she asked, hand out.

I gave it to her. She inspected the seal, though I hadn't had time to read it since opening the chest. I grinned at her.

"What?" she asked.

"That's an awfully by-the-book inspection for someone who suckered me into this whole thing."

"Gobbledygook." She handed the scroll back. "When I leave, break the seal, open it, and read." She spoke as she lit a pair of tea lights in decorative lanterns hanging in the hall. "You have a few minutes to gather your thoughts and form a plan, but get in there quick as you dare. Keep the scroll with you; don't let them see it. There's a hint written at the bottom. Unroll the scroll and hold your hand over the end of the page. Heat activates the ink." She patted my arm. "This night has been more dangerous and deadly than I ever imagined." There was an apology in her eyes, but it remained unspoken. "Blessed be," she said.

"Thank you, Lydia." I took her hand and squeezed.

Then she left.

Tapers illuminate much better than tea lights. The short hall dimmed into near darkness without Lydia's candelabrum. After a fleeting thought of whether Holly could possibly be lurking nearby—a thought I scolded myself for having—I cracked the seal and unrolled the scroll and held it near the lanterns.

It read:

Scene:

A coven member, high-ranking, has been hit with various misfortunes lately: her husband died, she lost her job, she has a disease that requires expensive drugs that she cannot pay for without a job and insurance. She contracted with vampires to make blood donations regularly in exchange for cash. Even then, she has been forced to skip doses

*of her medication to make it last longer. The vam-
pires have ceased accepting her blood. The medicine
is "tainting" it. As the vampires have advanced her
money, she now owes them and cannot pay. She has
a five-year-old daughter.*

Secret:
*The coven member has been told her disease is
worsening, and she will die in a few months.*

Unrolling it fully, I held it against the wall and
pressed my hand over the lower section. The words faded
into view.

Hint:
MAY
CATCH
OYSTER
ECLAT

What kind of cryptic, hellish hint was this?

I reheated and reread that last part three times. I read
it backward, I tried rearranging the letters of each word
to make other words. "May" could mean "possibilities" or
the month of May. "Catch" could imply its literal meaning, catching a ball or a cold, or it could mean mentally
understanding. "Oyster" made no sense to me, but "eclat"
meant reputation, acclaim, so maybe they went together,
insinuating the oyster's reputation for libido enhance-
ment. All in all, these clues made my head hurt.

Putting my game face on, I went into the conference room remembering how collected Hunter had been when confronting Lehana about her magic and the *vinculum,* and hoping I could convincingly exude that level of confidence.

I scanned the room. Sever seemed at ease in a chair with his feet propped on the table between candles. Heldridge paced, shrouded in shadows, at the far end of the table, while Menessos held a small candle close to a framed painting on the wall. He appeared to be studying it. Even without his awareness centered on me, his proximity created a reaction that warmed my body in a way that could have been comforting if not for my aversion to being manipulated.

"Gentlemen—"

I politely called them each by name, intentionally mispronouncing "Menessos." Didn't want these others, or the Elders watching, to think I knew him at all. "What can I do for you?" I asked, keeping my eyes on their chins.

Heldridge came from the shadows toward me. "One of your witches owes me."

The brighter light made the angles of his face harsher. "Who?"

He smirked. "We'll call her Ann."

"What is it that Ann owes you?"

"Blood, money, or some combination of the two."

He was going to play his role as "intimidating," so I sat opposite Sever and relaxed into the seat. My role was going to be "unaffected." Hard to do with Menessos in the room, but I was going to do my best and get through this without delay. "And you have discussed this with her?"

"Of course." Heldridge looked down his nose at me. "I wouldn't be here if I were satisfied."

Looking down at me did not reinforce his attempt to intimidate. As our roles went, this was the high priestess's territory, and therefore *my* place he was invading. I had to be comfortable. Cocky, even. And I could do cocky. "And you came to me for your satisfaction. I'm flattered."

"I want my money!"

Most people who expose their anger expect a similar emotional response. Instead, I smiled sweetly. "I'm not a banker. Did you misread the sign on the door?"

Heldridge growled and ran a hand over his head. It messed up the trio of tendrils on his brow.

"Miss," Sever put his feet down and leaned across the table. "My friend here has a contract with . . . Ann. She's not upholding her end of the deal." Sever seemed like a good ol' boy. Not pompous or elegant, but he didn't lack sophistication. "It's simple, really."

"If it were simple, Sever, you wouldn't be in my office. What is it you expect me to do about this illicit little arrangement between private citizens?"

The two of them exchanged glances; Menessos continued examining the art.

"Ahhh," I said. "There's a business involved."

Heldridge slid a hand into his pocket. "My club. The Blood Culture."

"Apt name."

"Of course. It's easily reached from both the Cleveland Clinic and University Hospitals."

I held up a hand. "Let me guess—a lot of nurses are donors?"

"On their way home. Very convenient."

I said, "You don't want police involved, but you want my help in getting you what you want." I paused. "Perhaps you should explain this more fully. What kind of arrangement did you contract with Ann?"

Heldridge barked, "Details aren't necessary." He turned away from me, back to the darkness.

"You are afraid to tell me the details? Why? Are you afraid I will tell the police?" I tapped my cheek. "Perhaps they'll shut your business down?"

"They wouldn't dare! If the blood-drinkers in this town don't drink with *me,* people *die.* The cops wouldn't risk what would occur if my doors didn't open!"

I was willing to bet that most of this, except the "Ann" part, was true. Heldridge probably did have a club and nurses probably did donate.

"You're missing the point," Menessos said quietly.

His voice stroked me physically, as if he'd breathed warmly into my ear. I ignored it as best I could. Time was a factor in this test. "Spit it out, Heldridge," I insisted as I stood and approached him. "What do you want from me?"

"I want you to take your witch, straighten her out, and sober her up so we can take her blood as contracted!"

That wasn't possible. But his demand showed they didn't know that the taint was disease and drugs, not booze. With affected cynicism, I said, "You want me to take her to rehab?"

"Or she gives me my money back!"

"So you prepaid for her blood?" Devil-deals like this didn't surprise me at all. I readily believed they did shit like this all the time.

"Quarter of a pint, every other Friday, for the next year."

Was that safe? Not that they would care. But fictitious Ann didn't have a year to live. They weren't getting paid, either way. "A quarter pint every other Friday isn't going to send a slew of vampires into the night searching for victims."

"No, but I can." Heldridge's threat was convincing.

Sever cut in, "Vampires party on the weekend like everyone else, doll. Our drinks don't come off the beer truck in boxes full of pretty-labeled bottles. We have to make arrangements. The demanding thirst never wanes. So if supply wanes, we act."

"It's business," Heldridge added, straightening his tie to match his ramrod posture. "Usually, the living get to live on unhindered."

If it were legitimate business, he could put a lien on her property if she had any, as if she were a contractor who didn't do the work she was paid to do. But it wasn't legitimate; though I'd bet if I researched it I could find this kind of situation covered in new legislation on the dockets. A degree in business would probably have provided me some ideas on this too.

"Perhaps," I suggested, "you should just write this off your taxes as a bad debt." I knew something about writing off losses.

"I told you," Heldridge sneered, "I seek satisfaction. An accountant's solution won't satisfy me."

"Sometimes, in business, you take a loss."

"*I don't lose!*" he seethed.

"Rehab is not the answer. First, it takes time. Second,

she may not dry out. And, if she does, she might fall off the wagon." I folded my fingers together. "I'm betting you already have a solution that will satisfy you in mind. But you don't want to say it, you want to steer me toward it so you can agree with me when it becomes my idea." I paused. "I don't have time for that. And I'm not easily led, Heldridge, so quit wasting everyone's night. Just spill it."

"Spill it?" He reached for my throat, stopped inches away when I neither flinched nor blinked. "Spilling your blood might satisfy me."

"But that wouldn't profit you."

He grabbed my throat and squeezed. "It isn't always about profit!"

Menessos was suddenly there, throwing Heldridge to the floor.

CHAPTER TWENTY

"I will rectify this," Menessos said, and winked at me. He grabbed Heldridge's arm and dragged him to the other end of the room. Sever, encouraged by the twitch of Menessos's finger, joined them. Once Heldridge stood and smoothed his ruffled suit, the whispers began.

Glad to breathe again, I touched my throat lightly and leaned against the table. I'd been warned they could blood me.

But Menessos wasn't supposed to come in here and solve this for me. He wasn't trying to help me, was he? Trying to maneuver me into position as the high priestess so he could benefit?

I wouldn't put it past him.

While they chatted, I repeated the words to myself: *May, Catch, Oyster, Eclat.*

Menessos turned and sauntered toward me. "We have reached an agreement," he smiled alluringly. I even saw a hint of fang.

As each step brought him closer, his growing nearness stoked the heat in my body, kindling the desire

that tightened places low and deep inside me. *Forget it!*
"Good." I said, crossing my arms. No matter what kind of
response I was having to him, this test was being watched
by the Elders. Giving them even a hint of my connection
to Menessos could ruin everything.

"We will accept the child as an offerling—"

"What?" I demanded, shoving my rising desire down
on its ass. I came to my feet again.

"She will be given to us—"

"A child?"

"Yes."

"No." I shook my head. "Absolutely not."

"You," Menessos said pleasantly, continuing as if I had
not protested at all, "will discreetly look the other way. My
people accept it, yours accept it, and we all move forward."

"A little girl's life?" I was stunned by what he was suggesting.

"A virgin child's blood will sell for ten times that of
her mother," he replied.

"That's abuse! Sticking her with needles to bleed her—"

"Your witch is a drunkard. That kind of life is argu-
ably more abusive."

"You have no right to—" I stammered, remembering
they did not realize the woman was as good as dead, and
altered my words.

Menessos took advantage of my hesitation and filled it
with his own thought. "What kind of life could the child
possibly have with her mother?"

"Your point is taken, but you've no right to judge the
situation of that home. An' it harm none!" I protested. "I
will not let you harm her!"

"Who said anything about harming her?" he asked, innocently charming.

That desire rose up, brushed itself off, and rushed at me again. I squinted suspiciously at him. His eyes sparkled and he seemed to be laughing at me.

"'An' it harm none, do what ye will,'" he quoted the Rede. "Do you subscribe to the belief that it implies 'harm least'?"

Some wiccans and pagans added the line, "An ye harm some, do as ye must," to the Rede, meaning if some action was deemed absolutely necessary, some minimal harm befalling others *might* be acceptable. Others felt that there was always some measure of harm involved in any spell-work and that the Rede merely implied a witch should endeavor to do as little harm as possible. I said, "No one should ever knowingly, willingly, purposefully seek to harm another."

"But it happens. People have tempers. Some are weak."

Where was he going with this? He was setting me up. And his soft voice sounded so reasonable, so warm, inviting me to agree with him.

"Some drink liquor and abuse their children. That is, without a doubt, harm, yes?"

"I am not aware of any abuse in their home."

"Abuse takes so many subtle forms, Persephone. Neglect can be as bad as physical harm." Menessos's voice was low and soothing. "Making a child watch daily, live daily in the environment of their parent's slow self-destruction, that is mental harm. Would you agree to that?"

"To the statement, yes, to it applying to their situation, no."

"People get hurt every day, Persephone, dear, idealistic Persephone."

Every time he said my name, it was as if his voice physically touched me. Gooseflesh rose along my arms.

"Perhaps you have heard the saying, 'An' ye harm some, do as ye must'?"

"I am aware of that additional line in some traditions." Had he been reading me?

"The harm has been done," he said benevolently. "We will take her, teach her, and raise her to be wise and strong and beautiful. She will have a fuller life than her mother could ever provide."

"No." My voice lacked the strength needed to give the word real weight.

"We will see to it that she is loved, attended, and nurtured in ways her mother is currently incapable of handling. We have many options." He gestured to the other vampires who indicated their agreement. "I know of couples who are childless, but do not wish it to be so."

I thought of Celia and Erik. Did he mean wæres? He was suggesting they would—in theory—foster this hypothetical child into a home of wæres! But in exchange for what? "You will deliver her to a life of servitude to the undead."

"You would have her stay in a life with no future. As good as dead!"

"You would make her a pawn—"

"No! Her mother made her a pawn," he snarled. Heat flared on my sternum. "I would make her wealthy and her every need would be met."

"Still a pawn," I countered coolly, "just a classier version of the game."

"This game will be played regardless, Persephone. What version would you choose to have this child play?"

My stomach churned. "Merciful vampires" administering a fate free from wont . . . this was brutal to my conscience. My only consolation was that this was a hypothetical situation. Not real. *Not real.*

Or was it?

Could this kind of deal-making have been behind Goliath's kidnapping? Had a family secret been covered up by the payment of a child?

"As above, so below, witch," Heldridge shot in. "Does your Goddess never cause harm?"

"She would choose to harm least," I whispered. By allowing unpleasantness to transpire in small doses, a tenuous balance would be maintained.

My secret hint was that her mother was dying anyway. There was no mention of extended family to adopt the girl. Could I make this decision? As high priestess, I would have authority and would be expected to use it, even when unpleasant for me. The job is what the job is. But if this kind of thing was under the jurisdiction of a high priestess, it was news to me.

Neither option was good. Still, I had to make a choice. . . .

Make a choice. *May . . . catch . . . oyster*—! *May-ca-choys-tereclat.* Make-a-choice-directly.

I knew what this was all about. I knew what to do.

"Fine. I will agree to look the other way while you take the girl on the following conditions: One, she is fostered with a wære family of good conscience and a history of secure kenneling—a family of whom I approve.

Two, you may take blood from her only in safe amounts and only without her knowledge. I'm sure you have ways of doing that. Three, on the full moon just prior to her eighteenth birthday, you return her to me, where she will remain for no less than two cycles of the moon. She will yet be mortal, human, and alive. I expect to find her healthy, both mentally and physically; to be well educated, socially adjusted, and happy. I will perform a rite of passage. If she chooses not to return to your fold, if she chooses to remain away from you and not become an offering, she will be rescinded. You will count your debt paid and allow it."

Heldridge's unyielding glare was icy. "You ask us to become foster parents so in the end you can convince her not to become an offering?"

"If you've sold her blood, taken in non–health-threatening amounts, the cost of her rearing should be less than your profit. In fact, that should be part of the deal. A complete annual accounting, verified by an outside source, of what you have earned from her blood and what you have spent on her upkeep."

The vampires exchanged glances.

Before anything could be said, however, the door to the room opened. Desdemona stood beyond it.

> "Well done, contestant. Your performance will
>> be evaluated,
> And you will proceed to the next round if you
>> are thusly fated."

The test was over. I'd shown that I could and would make a decision, even when all the options were flawed.

I moved immediately toward the door. I was *so* out of

there, so gone before something else happened with the stain.

Menessos caught my arm and held it, keeping me from leaving. I wanted to jerk away, to huff angrily, defiantly. But the instant his flesh touched mine, this first touch since I'd chosen to keep the stain, since I'd destroyed the stake, he sent a heated caress deep inside me, sinking through skin, through muscle, and deep into bone, warming me as if I'd swallowed the summer sun—

Menessos jerked his hand away.

Was that the vampire version of the jolt Hunter had given to everyone in the contest?

He stared down, studying me. His scrutiny was not unlike that he'd given earlier to the art in the room, but suspicion lurked under the surface of his cold-steel irises. Even as I stared boldly into his imprisoning eyes, I felt no draw from them, no threat, but saw they were paler, icier than I remembered. "That was brilliant," he said. "Manipulating us into attending properly to the needs of a child whose parent wronged us." He paused, a wicked twist claiming his lips. "This concept, I will have to consider all possible applications. I can utilize such arrangements immediately." The menace in his tone was unmistakable. "Can't you, Heldridge?"

I suddenly remembered the pain that Menessos felt when I'd tended the wound where Samson tried to stake him. Angered he would manipulate my ideas to his devious aims, and more so that children might be involved, I gave in to an impulse: I grabbed his raven-scratched arm and squeezed. But this time I anticipated the heat of our contact and threw my witch-jolt out to shield against it, effectively diminishing it. I felt his ridged and torn flesh squirm under the pressure of my grip.

In a blink, his eyes had gone nearly white. His fanged mouth opened in an indication of pain, but he made no sound.

The fingers of his uninjured arm suddenly snatched onto my shoulder and he jerked me close. Heat billowed around me, between us, without passing my shield. His wicked expression returned and his voice came low and threatening, "Whatever the outcome of this Eximium, I *will* see you again, witch."

As I brushed past Desdemona in the reception area, she put one of the tea light lamps into my hands. Outside in the hall, I paused for a deep breath to cleanse my aura of the fear and feel of Menessos. I wasn't sure if I was supposed to wait for the Elder or Lydia or a policeman to escort me, but I wasn't going to wait either. Forcing myself onward in the dark, I hoped the outage didn't reach all the way to my more rural home. Nana would wake up to a cold house. It wouldn't help her knee.

Going with that thought to keep the vampire from my mind, I promised myself I'd get right to work getting a contractor out to start work on renovating the dining room for her.

As I started down the hall, I heard a sound from the darkness ahead.

It was a sound like the susurrus of fabric as someone walks along.

I stopped. "Hello?" *Holly?*

Nothing.

I held the lamp behind me. The space darkened, but my eyes adjusted slowly. I saw nothing.

Without further incident, I made it to the door of the newly designated holding room. It was an office supply room. The three cots barely fit—each was pushed tight against the shelves and boxes of the three doorless walls. There was an iron stand with a platelike top just inside the door, the two pillar candles placed on it provided soft light. Maria was on the cot to my right, snoring. She was alone.

Hunter and Amber must have gone to the restroom or something. Hunter would have to come back here to retrieve her scroll before she went to Desdemona's test. Still, leaving Maria alone seemed rude. I sat down on the left-side cot, placing the lantern beside my feet and my scroll on my lap. The others' scrolls rested under their respective cots.

In the dark, as my ears grew accustomed to Maria's regular snores, I gave in to my fatigue and lay down, clutching the rolled paper scroll to me.

The sound of voices in the hall brought me sitting upright, just as Hunter and Amber stepped in. "You're back," Hunter said as they neared.

Something seemed different about her. I couldn't put my finger on it. "Yeah."

"Was it terrible?" Amber whispered, placing a third pillar candle on the plate.

I hesitated, yawned. "It wasn't easy."

"At this point, it can't be easy," Hunter whispered. "Any of it. Or there would be no point." She slipped the scroll from under my cot and headed back to the door.

As she placed her hand on the knob, there was a knock. Hunter quickly stepped back to allow space for the door to open. Lydia stood in the doorway.

"Are you ready, Hunter?"

"Yes."

"Good luck," I said. I handed her my tea light lantern.

"Sure. And thanks."

Again, she seemed quite happy. Odd.

"I'm going to see if I can copy her," I said to Amber as I pointed at Maria.

"Don't blame you." She sat on the vacant rear cot.

My eyes were shut before I'd fully stretched out on Hunter's cot.

Moments later, as I was again beginning to doze, I heard Amber sit up, stand. My head lifted and my eyes opened. "Where are you going?" I whispered.

"Restroom."

"I thought you just came back from there with Hunter?"

"She had to go then. Now I do."

"Let me go with you."

"No, rest. I'll be fine." She retrieved the pillar candle from the stand near the door.

"Alone?"

"I was just there." She rolled her eyes at me. "It's just the other side of the stairs. Besides, the policemen are still around. Don't worry." She left.

My toes twitched in my shoes; I felt torn. Let Amber go alone, or leave Maria alone. Again with the no clear choices. So I stood and went to the doorway, determined to stand there with the door open, listening, waiting.

The hall was so dark. My ears strained for a sound, any sound other than Maria's snoring.

A minute passed. And another. Too many.

I took another candle from the stand and left Maria, walking down the hall. Pillar candles are unhandy to carry and not very bright.

"Amber?" I called softly. The shadow of stairs lay ahead. She'd said the restroom wasn't far past this. "Amber?"

A shadowed alcove in the wall held the restroom door. Amber would be in there.

I heard movement inside.

My hand slid around the chilled metal handle, pulled.

Amber stood there, one hand on the counter not far from where her pillar candle sat. The other hand clutched at her chest. Her eyes were wide. She fell to her knees. Her hand dropped from her chest, red spreading down her shirt. Her mouth opened and moved, but no sound came out. She leaned, falling.

I shot through the door, rushing toward her, candle dropping from my grip as I reached to catch her. I managed just enough to keep her skull from bouncing on the floor. "Amber! Amber, no!"

My hand went to her chest. Blood welled over my hand. Amber clung to my wrist. Then her grip went slack. "No! No!"

"Yes."

I turned.

Holly, in the doorway of a stall, held a knife. In the light from Amber's candle on the counter, the blade's edge gleamed black with blood, dripping to the floor.

Her face was flecked with dark spots, as was her hair, her V-neck tee, and her hoodie. The essence of a life, taken, in drops.

My first instinct was to rage at her, to scream and demand answers. To beat the shit out of her. But my mouth opened and what came out was, "*This* is what would make your mother proud?"

Her mouth became a firm line. "Yes." Her eyes gleamed as she stared down at me.

"I don't understand."

"She was murdered by scheming witches like her. And like you." Instantly her knife hand shot up, dripping blade-point down, and she came forward.

CHAPTER TWENTY-ONE

In one swift motion, even as Holly's arm started stabbing down, I rose and used my momentum as I kicked out, knocking her knife hand up and away. She turned her face toward her arm, surprised, and I punched her hard in the jaw. She fell and the knife skittered away.

Holly was young, small, and clearly inexperienced as a fighter. She could have killed her victims only by surprising them. I felt bad for her as I pounced on her and took her by the hair. I whacked her head on the stone floor to daze her. Then, still sitting on her, I jerked one of her shoes off, ripped the shoestring out, and tied her hands behind her back, tight. I took her other shoe and unstrung it; then I bound her ankles, pulled them up, and knotted the ends of the strings together.

"Oh my god!" she groaned. "Oh my god! That wasn't supposed to happen."

"Yeah, I bet." I stepped toward the restroom door.

"Holy shit!"

It wasn't Holly's voice. Slowly, I turned.

Amber was sitting up, staring at Holly. Amber began to laugh.

"You're okay?" I stammered.

"Yeah." She ripped open her shirt and pulled an elaborate fake "chest" away from her own. As she turned it around, she revealed it was some bizarre device with plastic tubing all through the back.

Over her shoulder, she said, "I didn't invoke my stone!" as if talking to the toilet in the stall behind her. She giggled again, turning back to me. "And I'm so glad I didn't. I would've missed the show. Somebody finally kicked your ass, Holly! Goddess, you should see your face."

I stood there, dumbfounded, motionless. What the hell was going on?

The back of the restroom—both the floor and the wall itself—rolled open like a garage door and the fourth Elder stepped into view, eyeing me suspiciously.

"For twenty years, I've been re-creating this test in some fashion for every Eximium I've been a part of. Never have I seen the like."

"All right already," Holly exclaimed. "Untie me! I think she chipped a tooth!"

"What the hell is going on?" Realization began to seep into my brain, but I couldn't believe it.

"I love this part!" Amber said, getting up and stepping to the open doorway. She pulled out a half-full gallon jug of red fluid and began refilling the chest mechanism. "No one died here tonight. Not Suzanne, not Lehana. Not me." She grinned. "We are all part of the fourth test."

I blinked rapidly. "The paramedics, the police—"

"Part of our group."

"Then . . . Suzanne and Lehana . . . you and Holly . . . aren't real contestants?"

"Never were." She capped the mechanism's well, put the lid on the gallon jug. Removing her shirt, she replaced the chest mechanism, attaching it to her bra with Velcro. From a hanger, she took a shirt identical to the one she'd been wearing—except this one had no blood-stains—and put it on.

"Excuse me!" Holly protested.

"Oh!" I dropped beside her and worked at the knots, but they were too tight from her straining against them. I reached for the knife, hesitated.

"Here," Amber said, handing me a pocketknife. "That one's a fake."

I cut the strings and Holly immediately went to inspect herself at the mirror. "Sorry," I mumbled.

"Do not apologize, child." The Elder, leaning on her staff beside her, was grinning at me. It was unnerving. "I am Vilna-Daluca. Your solution to our play is one I will have to ponder before I can decide how to judge it."

"Damn," Holly said, fingers poking at a bruise swelling on her cheek. "You're going to have to start asking contestants if they know judo, Vil."

Vilna-Daluca laughed heartily. "I'll personally drive you to the dentist tomorrow if it is necessary."

The Elders drive? Why did *that* stick out to me as ludicrous in this moment?

Probably because everything else was tripping my weird-o-meter into the red zone, my thoughts centered on that trivial thought. What kind of car did Vilna-Daluca drive? Did she wear the robes—no, no, that was just silly. I'm sure even the Elders were like normal old women when they weren't doing witchy things.

Probably played bingo and dominoes and everything.

"Fear not, Holly, you will heal," Vilna-Daluca said, but her interest was centered on me.

Oh, shit. I showed them I could—and was willing to—fight. I went for a subject change. "What normally happens?" My voice conveyed meek innocence.

"You should have cowered, or screamed, or fled," Holly said. "Fighting back is unheard of. Detrick?" she called.

The police officer opened the door and poked his head in. "Yeah?"

"He would have been blocking the door," Holly pointed at him. "So you couldn't escape."

"It's over?" he asked.

"Duh," Holly said.

"How'd she do?" Detrick asked.

Holly pointed to her swelling cheek. I'd punched her *and* whacked her head on the floor. That was going to swell a lot.

"She decked you? All right!" He gently punched my arm. "Slugger! Were you filming, Vilna?"

My eyes went wide.

"Yes."

"I'll mop up the fake-blood mess in a minute; I wanna see." He shuffled past us to the area behind the wall.

"Yeah, I bet," Holly retorted.

"You're bleeding," Vilna-Daluca said to me. She indicated my hand.

I had a cut on my knuckle. It wasn't bad; I grabbed a paper towel to wipe it.

"Yeah, worry about *her*," Holly mumbled. To me,

she continued explaining, "After you'd tried to run and couldn't, I would have moved in. If you had broken down and cried, I would have scolded you for being weak and trying to lead a coven. If you tried to talk me down—which I thought you were starting to do—I would have reconsidered killing you, we would have talked a bit more and seen where you went with it."

"Oh-ho!" Detrick hooted from the back area. "That had to hurt!"

Holly went to join him. I dropped the paper towel into the trash and eased across the space to peer into the back. This was a classroom like the others, but the "restroom" façade had been constructed around the door to facilitate the setting. There was a whole production room set up back there! The paramedics, Lehana, and Suzanne lay sleeping on cots farther back in the room. "It's incredible," I whispered.

"C'mon," Amber said. "Time to go get Maria."

As we walked back to the holding room, Amber explained, "We each have a stone, we're supposed to invoke it when it's our time to 'play dead.' It gives that appearance to anyone who's checking us. Lehana is new to the troupe and played with hers; Hunter picked up on it. That surprised me. But she thought it was a *vinculum*. I guess that is the most obvious guess, what with Holly planting her seeds of mistrust with WEC and all."

"Completely had me." Now I understood what had been different about Hunter when they came back to the holding area—she'd had this part of the test while I was with the vampires. She was dealing with the vampire test now, while Maria slept. Amber and I stepped inside;

Maria continued snoring. "So you have to set up again for"—I whispered and pointed in the direction of the snoring—"now?"

"Yeah," she said. "But first," she pulled her purse from under her cot, "let me show you this." An atomizer was in her hand. She sprayed it. "Your turn to nap," she said.

I woke up sometime later on the cot.

Hunter was shaking my shoulder. "Wake up!"

I didn't want to. "Hmmm? I'm up." I sat up. "You just back from the vampire test?"

"Yeah. Lydia brought me back. Amber had already started the scenario with Maria." She very nearly giggled like a delighted little girl. Maybe Hunter got giddy when she was tired.

I stretched. I was so short on sleep I was beginning to go numb. "What time is it?"

"It's after four."

I sat up and glanced toward Maria's empty cot. "And you're not trying to sleep? Why?"

"Oh, I have to talk to someone about this! I mean, Goddess, that was outrageous! We were punked by the Elders!"

She'd woken me to share in her enthusiasm, but I couldn't. Being roused from a valerian-aided snooze left my eyelids as heavy as I ever remembered them being.

"Lydia told me that Amber would wake Maria and tell her it was almost time for her turn," Hunter went on. "Then Amber would start the scenario for Maria, and afterward they'd see her to the vampire test. She'll probably soon be transferring to the office for that test."

I felt downright groggy. "I need caffeine," I said, thinking but not adding, *if you insist on keeping me awake to talk.* "Suppose we can go to the kitchen and help ourselves?"

"Don't see why not, whether or not Maria has moved on to the vampire part, we won't cross her path between here and the kitchen. But there's still no electric."

"Damn." I paused. "Did you notice if it was a gas stove?"

"Think so, why?"

"I *need* coffee." Bad enough to make it the hard way.

We took our candles, pushed some boxes and furniture aside in the hall, and proceeded to the kitchen. When we arrived, however, I found the overhead lights did work. I headed for the coffeepot. "I bet the power outage was all a part of their show."

"You're probably right."

I got the coffee brewing and sat at the table to wait. Hunter said, "I should probably thank you for the reality check earlier."

I looked away, feeling embarrassed as I remembered what I'd said. Then I decided that I was being stupid. She *had* needed it and she wasn't angry now. I faced her and snorted a little laugh. "Promise you'd do the same for me?" The smell of the coffee was perking me up.

"Yeah." She laughed softly. "I do have a business degree and I did grow up with a silver spoon. My mother probably spoiled me a little because of my allergies;

maybe it helped create that ego." She paused. "You're very perceptive."

"Usually gets me in trouble, helps me make enemies." I tried to play it down.

Hunter remained serious. "I want to win, Persephone. As much as you do, I'm sure. I want this more than anything, and I swear, if I win, I *will* do this right. I'll be all that a high priestess is supposed to be—not a trophy-wife version of a leader."

I had, as Nana would've said, "knocked Hunter off her high horse" with my speech. The least I could do was give her a hand up so she could brush herself off. "I believe you," I said.

"So what's your story?"

The coffeepot dinged to signal it had completed brewing. I got up to pour a cup. "Journalism degree. Raised by my grandmother—no silver spoon." I indicated the pot. "You want a cup?"

"Please."

I returned to the table with two Styrofoam cups and a yawn. "Not a moment too soon," I mumbled and took a long sip of the dark liquid. "Mmmm."

"Oh my," she said. "That's strong."

"It'll put hair on your chest."

Hunter gave me an amused look over the edge of her cup.

"Pour some out and add water if you want, but I need it this strong to shake off that valerian spritz and get through the rest of this."

We were still sitting at the table with our Styrofoam cups when Lydia brought Maria in. "In fifteen minutes, the Elders will convene. The Eldrenne will reveal to you the final test." She let the door shut. Maria joined us and sank heavily into her chair. "You want some coffee?" I asked.

"Is it as strong as you made it this morning?"

"Stronger."

"Good."

I got up to get it for her; she called me a dear.

"So?" Hunter asked Maria, grinning.

"I can't believe I just went ignorantly into a fake murder scene and followed it by walking fully understanding into a fake round-table with real vampires." She fanned her face. "My heart can't take so much pressure all at once and my mind's still reeling."

I set a cup before her, and the creamer and sugar packs; she thanked me as she mixed up her brew. She stared into her cup as she stirred. "Lydia said these tests would reveal much to the Elders, ourselves, and each other. She was *sooo* right."

"What did you learn about yourself?" Hunter asked.

Maria made an unhappy face. "Faced with a real, violent threat to my life, I'm a chicken shit."

"What about you?" Hunter asked me.

Up to this point, I'd been enjoying the company. My high school friendships were nonexistent and, while my college friendship with Celia remained a meaningful one, I'd not had many opportunities to sit and talk with other witches, except Lydia. She was grandmotherly. This was different. Like co-workers chatting about the job. It felt very normal and good while it lasted. Now, I had the feeling that Hunter wanted to know how we did in both of these tests so she would have a better idea of where she stood. "I'd rather not say."

"You couldn't have done worse than me," Maria said. "I'm honestly surprised they are letting me go to the next round. I mean, technically, the three of us competed already. Amber wasn't an actual contestant."

That's right. One final round. What if I won this? *Goddess, don't let me win.*

"C'mon," Hunter goaded me.

Maria glanced over at me and said, "You've nothing to be ashamed of."

"I'm not ashamed." I sipped my coffee nonchalantly. "I just . . . I don't know."

"Well, I'll tell you what I think," Maria said. "I think that after seeing the cut on your knuckle, that swelling bruise on Holly's cheek makes more sense to me."

I put the cup down and hid my hand in my lap, not that it did me any good.

Hunter's brows shot up. "You fought?"

Trying to appear meek and mild to offset feeling like a brute, I asked, "What did you do?"

"I used psychology and talked her down." She relaxed against the backrest of her folding chair as if she'd just been told something serious. "Never occurred to me to take her on."

Maria cackled. "You didn't think of it? *You* jolted everyone who'd shake hands. And *she* was the one to think aggressively." She pointed at me without lowering her Styrofoam cup.

"As far as judging goes," I said to Hunter, "I'm sure your actions are perfectly aligned with what they're looking for in a high priestess." I hoped she'd forgive me for my earlier insults. I faced Maria. "And yours was probably more desirable a solution than mine. They're probably running a background check right now to see if I have a rap sheet."

"Do you?" Maria asked seriously.

"No!" I laughed, but the sound of it hung in the air maniacally and I wished I could take it back.

"How'd you decide to fight? 'Cause she's petite?"

"It just kind of happened." Great. We'd been having a nice moment, bonding. But even among my sister witches, I was a freak.

"What about the vampires?" Maria asked Hunter.

"They are all damn sexy. Especially Sever."

"What?" Maria exclaimed.

"Oh, not that I would ever do *that*—I'm not looking to be any fang-boy's sangria—but being alone in the room with the three of them was as wonderful as it was terrible." She lifted her cup. "Focus on the positive," she said, and giggled before sipping.

"I focused on their chests and not to gauge their pectorals," Maria said. "It was all business in there. I didn't dare let myself see their faces. Not even enough to see if they were handsome or not."

"Trust me, they are."

Silence. Even staring at the table, I felt them turn to me. Before either worked up the nerve to ask, I blurted, "No comment!"

They both cracked up.

Lydia pushed open the door. "Ladies."

The Covenstead Great Hall interior was now almost dark. It was nearly five in the morning and the tall pillar candles had burned down to glowing nubs on the high, flat candelabrum discs. The room felt quieter, and the regality of the dais had faded sleepily like a dream ending.

Lydia led us to the center of the room, gave us back our daggers, and took her position at the left of the dais. I glanced toward each of the other contestants. One of us would be the high priestess of Venefica Covenstead soon. One of us would have to start her time in that role by organizing a grand Witches Ball in a very short amount of time. I hoped it wasn't me.

The Elders sat like bowed and bent statues upon their thrones, tired old women who'd been up all night, their faces shielded from the meager light under wide brims.

The vampires now sat in stately chairs lined on an elegant area rug placed to the right of the dais. Sever perched on the end of his seat, elbows on knees and hands clasped. It seemed Freudian, as if he were indicating his eagerness to leave. Heldridge appeared uncomfortably rigid like an Egyptian hieroglyph, but seemed utterly bored. Between them, the epitome of relaxed patience, Menessos gazed at me the way full-bellied lions watch antelope: *When my appetite beckons, I will devour that.*

"There are three paths in Hecate's sight: past, present, and future," the Eldrenne said. Her raven cawed softly. "And now there are three of you."

She said no more, but tilted her head as if listening to something far away. She stamped her staff gently on the dais and the crystal orb began to glow. The light claimed her face slowly, glowing eerily on the blue film over her eyes. Her gnarled hand, shaking, lifted, aimed at us. It seemed the blind woman searched for a handhold to grasp . . . she was searching, yes, but not for steadiness to aid her as she left her seat. I felt the cold static of power reach through my clothes to my skin. I was aware of Maria giving in to an involuntary shiver next to me.

Light, if light can be thick and gray, began to form behind the Eldrenne, a mist swirling upward, each molecule glowing within. The light from her staff twinkled here and there on the mist, making it seem as if it were not mist at all, but deepest, blackest velvet rolling in the wind, with diamond dust glittering about the surface.

Suddenly, I could smell raisin and currant cakes.

Menessos sat straighter. His movement caught my attention and I glanced from him to the Eldrenne, then on to the magic behind her. It undulated once, like a dancer had taken position—a dancer hiding under a cloth kissed by ocean breezes.

A sound came to my ears, low and deep like the voice of Time.

The four Elders lowered their heads until all I could see was hat and brim.

The mist moved again, and it seemed a figure walking. Though it moved no closer, each step made the figure's details become more realized, and it grew in size until twenty feet tall, head topped with a conical hat, the tip of which neared the domed ceiling.

A beautiful, haggard face, kind but resolute, studied us.

"My call has been heard by many," a voice said. It

was the voice of every Elder, of the Eldrenne, the voice of Time Eternal, the voice of the Depths of Nothing and Everything. It licked my bones and tasted my soul, my essence, and my stain. It swallowed my fear and my hope and left me standing there naked and exposed in its sight, a vessel as open and empty as when I lay sobbing in the row of the cornfield as a child.

"Hecate," I whispered.

CHAPTER TWENTY-TWO

"The path I laid at your feet, you have traveled. And now you gather to Me." Hecate's voice reverberated within me.

The velvety mist-figure stretched her arms over our heads. Palms up, mist and power poured from Her hands like the tails of rocketing fireworks, but ever-burning. The sparks showered to the floor before us and rippled like water from an upended bucket. The sparkling lights reached our feet and floated up and over us. It touched my skin as if my clothes weren't there, sinking in like the faintest pinprick kisses. She restored all She had taken from me and gave me more, filling me up with Her understanding, Her courage, Her approval.

"My blessings on you, witches who hear Me. Witches who hasten to my bidding. Witches mine."

She flowed through the dais as if it were intangible. As she came toward us she shrank to human size, though one arm stretched to caress Menessos's cheek. "Be forgiven," came a whisper as soft as the wind.

Just as She neared, just as I hoped to see details in Her face, Her eyes—the velvet mist became just mist, and it dissipated as if it never were.

The Eldrenne sat straight; the Elders lifted their heads. "And now my test for you—" the Eldrenne said.

Both Hunter and Maria stood just as before. No one displayed—in word, gesture, or attitude—any reaction to Hecate's presence or disappearance. "Witches who hear me," She had said. Who had heard? Who had not?

"—my test is to create a protrepticus."

A pro-trep-what?

She gestured to the cauldron and thick black mist shot from her hand to cover the top. "Select an item. Maria has gone first many times. Let Hunter choose first."

Hunter went forward in an obedient, if cautious gait. She stared down into the cauldron.

"Fear not, child; nothing inside will sting or bite."

Hunter reached in and pulled out a round, palm-sized item of silver. With a confused expression, she opened the item. "It's a purse mirror."

"Maria."

Maria pulled a locket from the cauldron.

"Persephone."

The black mist swirled over the cauldron, effectively blocking the contents from sight. I reached in and came up with . . . a cell phone.

"The item in your hands will become your protrepticus."

Beside me Maria said, "Excuse me, Eldrenne. I'm not familiar with that term. Can you explain a pro— pro—?"

"Pro-TREP-ti-cus," the Eldrenne said slowly. "The protrepticus is a device that houses an aide of sorts. It will be very beneficial to the high priestess." With one gnarled finger, she gestured over her shoulder. "Behind the dais, three tables have been set." As she spoke candles on the darkened far side of the room flickered to life.

"Everything you need is waiting for you. You may begin now."

Again, Maria spoke up. "Are the spell instructions on the tables, Eldrenne?"

The Eldrenne laughed in a slow, mirthless way. We three caught on: this was the bad part.

"Like any witch worth her salt, I have no doubt that if you are standing before me now, you could pick up a spell you've never seen and be as successful as a master chef with a new recipe."

"Are we to construct our own spell, then?" Hunter asked.

"Again, any of you could achieve that, couldn't you?"

Uncomfortable, I waited. I wasn't going to ask anything. She'd tell us what she wanted us to know. Maybe the other two had figured that out as well. The Great Hall was silent for a long minute.

"This test is meant to separate the winner, to lift her up and mark her as the high priestess of a WEC-recognized coven. This test is more than witchcraft, more than social skill, more than shrewdness and resolve. This is a test of raw talent. The kind that reveals whether we are dealing with mere witches, or if a sorceress is among you."

"Sorcery?" Maria whispered.

"Yes," the Eldrenne whispered back. "This is the Venefica Coven; after all, 'Venefica,' translated, means 'sorceress,' so we expect the high priestess to be able to fulfill the role as intended. An *ordovia* awaits you, but it

will take more than your ability to read and follow direc-
tions to succeed. Begin now."

Ordovia was the old term for spell scroll. Most witches
used their Book of Shadows for spell-keeping. Perhaps
ordovia was more specific to sorcery.

Hunter went to the first table, the one on the left,
Maria to the middle one, and I approached the remaining
table to its right.

This was it. Last round. My entire goal here was to
knock Hunter out of the running and it hadn't happened.
Did I leave this round a loser and let whatever would
be, be? Maria was competent. She might make it. But I
didn't honestly believe that. She'd sounded too discon-
certed by this test. Hunter would win.

I glanced at her as I stepped up to my table. In the
course of these tests, she'd convinced me that she could
not only do the job, but *be* a high priestess also.

I'd been wrong about her. I wasn't too big for my
britches to admit it.

So why was I doing this?

To keep from being Bindspoken.

I had to proceed. Or at least act like it. *Just go through
the motions enough to convince the Elders.*

Before me the table, illuminated by a single taper candle at either end, was set with various unlit candles, bowls
of salt and water, incense sticks, and little sprigs of herbs.
A scroll, the *ordovia,* lay front and center.

Placing the cell phone on the table, I thumbed the
WEC-embossed seal. I remembered explaining sorcery to
Johnny before the spell for Theo. I'd compared it to sand
on a beach. "The sand touches the sea and the air," I'd

said, "and stretches along the coast and inland to the soil. Witchcraft is like that: it receives the waves of power—the gods and goddesses of the various pantheons—and touches the energy of nature, influences it, to shape witches' will through rituals and spells. But sorcery digs through witchcraft, burrowing deep into places you cannot see to find the treasure—the power—below the surface. It consumes that power, directly creating immediate change, not just influencing a future one."

"Witchcraft is sand," he'd replied. "Sorcery is buried treasure. Got it."

Sand on a beach . . . Johnny.

My chest felt tight at that memory, but I forcibly mastered myself again.

Sorcery, Nana had taught me, was to be used only as a last resort in moments when immediacy absolutely demanded it. The power was overly eager for release and wild when loosed. As if that weren't enough, its effects could be intoxicating. Many witches tasted it and became addicted, finding more and more excuses to use the immediate and instantly gratifying sorcery, working until it consumed them.

At home, the ley line in the grove powered my wards and I wasn't afraid of it—that was a simple redirection, a mere droplet of power. That droplet had the power to numb my whole arm for the moment it took to use. And I'd learned that while the initial touch of a ley line is prickly and sizzling, like putting your hand into boiling water, that sensation quickly turned into numbness. Extended exposure led to the next phase, where that heated "almost-pain" then dulled to an intoxicating warmth. You got a not-quite-inebriated feeling, a slightly euphoric buzz. I understood how that could take hold and create an addiction.

So, I was wary. Venefica Covenstead, like all coven-steads, was built on a ley line nucleus, an intersection of lines. It had far more power to offer than the single line I tapped.

Even as I thought about it, the energy acknowledged me with a tiny pulse. It whispered and I understood it was deep, a monster buried in the lowest subterranean depths to protect the world. It was caged, trapped power, slowly being poisoned by its captivity. It begged to be called on, to be touched and loosed, to flow free and roil with ecstasy. It would become contaminated, polluted, if it did not flow, if I did not hurry and release it.

The *ordovia*'s waxy seal snapped as my fingers applied pressure, and the scroll's thick paper unrolled in my hands.

I am your buried treasure, the whispering power said. *Like the chest you selected and opened with your key, you recognize the potential in what is not seen by others, you recognize what we could be together . . . and I recognize what others do not see in you, Lustrata! Call on me, raise me up! I will do your bidding and we will be infinitely potent.*

"Shut up," I whispered back. The grove's line was not a manipulating power. But then, it wasn't confined either. Nuclei, clearly, were far chattier than lines.

The paper was blank.

Remembering the heat of my hand had made the clues appear on the other scroll, I held this one nearer the candle flames. Sure enough, the letters sparkled and appeared.

PROTREPTICUS
Summon a Spirit.
Procure its permission.
Bind it to your bauble.
Seal it safely in.

It sounded so easy. Like a recipe: mix, pour, bake. But it left out the ingredients, the amounts, the bake temperature, and the time. This was not going to be a simple task.

The items on the table were pretty standard stuff for such an unstandard spell. My plan started forming. Stones, black thread, chalk . . . but nothing to write on.

The floor.

Summon a spirit.

With the chalk in hand, I sank to my knees and drew a rectangle on the wooden floor. Inside, I wrote the letters of the alphabet in two rows, numbers below those rows, punctuation marks below that. Drawing a large *deosil* circle, big enough to enclose me and the rectangle, I stepped outside it and drew another larger circle beyond it. Beyond it, I drew a third circle.

Studying the items on the table, I considered the herbs first. Honeysuckle and basil. Both had protective properties, but basil aided astral travel, which I wanted to avoid, and it was banishing, whereas I needed to bind. Honeysuckle aided psychic power, intuition, so I chose it and left the other behind. Transferring items from the table to the inner circle, I took the salt and water, the orange candles and the white candles. Lastly, I appraised the stones; all were beneficial, so all were moved to the inner circle.

I placed an onyx in the north, turquoise in the east, sunstone to the south, and jade in the west. Each got a white tea light candle, lit from the taper on the table, before I took up the bowl of salt. I spun, tossing salt wide across the floor.

> *"Triple rows and sealed up fast,*
> *my hallowed circle now is cast."*

After using the honeysuckle bundle as an asperging tool to flick water in each direction, I then held the orange candle up in salute to each compass point and said,

> *"Earth from the North, Eastern Winds, Southern Flames,*
> *   Water from the West . . .*
> *Elements—hear me!—keep my circle blessed.*
> *Safely shut me in, please,*
> *Shut all else out.*
> *Protect me now.*
> *Truly I speak, truly I see.*
> *So mote it be."*

With the protective niceties in place, I sat and put my hands to the chalk circle containing me.

Reaching out for the ley line, I called to it, humming.

It was there, far below. Hunkering, hiding in the dark, yet watching me like a starving animal watches someone enticing it with meat. It had been waiting, yearning for someone to call it and here I was, alive and strong, searching for it. But the other contestants, they were searching for it also. It was suspicious.

They locked me away, it whispered. *So far below.*

"Open for me," I whispered back.

Unlock me. Unleash me!

"I have no key."

No key! The despair in that whisper was pitiful.

What kind of lock would Vivian use? My mind ran through various magical seals, all of which I discarded for their ease or lack of effectiveness for something as big as a ley line nucleus. Vivian had access to the Codex. She could have altered many sorcery-laden locks beyond anything I knew. But that would be no good to any contestant.

Contestant. The line had said "they" locked it away, not "she."

I had an idea.

"I have a key," I pulled the skeleton key on the white string from under my shirt.

That's it! Touch me.

With the key in hand, I visualized reaching my left hand down, down through the Covenstead floor, through the basement levels, through the foundation, through layers of earth and rock and there . . . there were the ley lines, low and deep, tingling in the palm of my hands, scraping like a flint about to spark. I stopped and visualized a buffer around my hand, a static kind of glove for handling the cords of a nucleus. The visualized ley lines were white-hot cords and suddenly in my mind's eye I could see them all interconnecting, six lines joining and dropping into the earth, like strings of Yule lights knotted and impossible to unravel.

Ahhh, yessssss.

All these lines were energy, all had the ability to access the dead, some more than others. Among these cords was a highway to the Summerland, a threaded conduit for traveling—if you weren't bound to a physical body, that is. In astral travel, where the spirit leaves the body, a sorcerer could visit the dead, other entities, and perform all kinds of nonphysical tasks. Of course, there had to be protections in place so that nothing slipped into the sorcerer's body while the spirit was absent. This bit of chalk, salt, and water wasn't up to that level of protection. I had to call spirits to me.

Which cord was it? Which string to pluck?

Spirits have a certain feel. The nerve endings just below skin discern them the same way they gauge temperature. Though intangible, the information registers in the brain. Most people wouldn't recognize the texture of a spirit, as they discern more strongly on the reaction they have to it: the hair on the nape of their neck rises and, possibly, goose bumps rise. Anyone who's ever been in a truly haunted house knows that the malign variety of spirit also strokes their flight response.

With the static buffer covering my palm, I sorted through the cords; patiently searching for that texture, like steam and silk, the one that evoked the reaction in me. Finally, I found it. Visualizing the static glove holding tight to that cord, my hand slipped a measure away—no sense risking getting pulled in.

> *"Arise spirits, hear my call,*
> *Arise between the drawn walls.*

Listen now and hasten near!
I've an offer for you to hear."

Reaching for the little stones with my right hand, I came up with a rainbow moonstone in my palm. As an afterthought, I grabbed the carnelian and sat it before me, for courage. Using the moonstone like a mini-planchette on my makeshift witchboard, I began to spell the words.

Am making a protrepticus.

A spirit-house.

Who will live in it?

I watched the edge of my circle. The ring just outside this one shimmered as if there were dust in the air illuminated by flickering sunbeams. Spirits came and peeked in, little orbs flashing by, more than I could count.

Who is willing?

The parade of orbs continued; it was fascinating. In my heart, I began to hope that Lorrie would come by and be willing. It would be a way for Beverley and her to communicate and stay in touch. But that was an exponentially long, long shot.

What was I thinking? I was supposed to fail this round.

Go now.

Never mind.

I had participated. The Elders could not punish me if I lost my nerve, if I sabotaged myself, or if it appeared that no spirits would take me up on my offer.

Thank you.

A light glistened on my face.

An orb was hovering about three feet off the ground in

the outer circle. It remained steady. Others did not follow, did not pass through. This one waited.

Go on. Return.

From the little collection of stones, a pointy quartz crystal trembled and slid across the wood floor to the chalk letters before me. I lifted the moonstone out of the way. The crystal looped along in little circles, pausing briefly to spell out:

Too late for that.

Oh shit.

Proceed.

Concentrating on the orb, I whispered, "You give permission?"

You did not ask for it.

"I just did."

Verbally.

Great. A difficult spirit. "You want me to spell it?"

Offering.

My brows hunkered down. Right. To take something from the beyond, I have to balance it by giving something back to the beyond. This was where, in ancient cultures, the sacrifice came in. But I had no animal to trade, and wasn't sure I would have been able to if I did. I had stones, herbs, chalk, and candles; all tangible items.

"What offering is appropriate?"

Your soul for mine.

"No way. Absolutely not."

Ha ha.

What the hell? A difficult, jokester spirit? "No deal."

Promise me vengeance.

"Vengeance?"

Avenge my wrongful death.

"I don't know the details, or even the era of your death. I cannot promise vengeance, but I can promise to investigate to the extent of my abilities."

More than investigation. Action! Punishment!

My curiosity was piqued. As Lustrata, this would be acceptable. "What if you are lying?"

Was murdered!

"Yes. I will investigate and if you are wrongfully dead and if a course of action exists that I can take to avenge your death—without harming me and mine—I will."

The crystal spun in place three times.

Agreed.

"You will be housed in this." I held up the cell phone, hoping it would decline to live in the contraption.

Agreed.

Now all I had to do was bring the spirit into the middle circle, put it in the cell phone, bind it there, and seal it in. The "easy" part was done. The next part would bind me to this phone, and to this spirit who wanted vengeance.

I really didn't want to be the high priestess.

CHAPTER TWENTY-THREE

I drew a little square in the air just above the ground at the edge of my circle. "Open now the door." I pushed the cell phone through into the space. "Sealed again is the door." No sense taking the risk of a nasty spirit getting to me and having to fight unnecessarily.

I drew another door, higher up, and orb-sized, imagining it opening in the wall of the circle beyond.

"Spirit, there is the door.
Pass now, from outer circle into mid.
Spirit, enter now the door.
Come forth, as ye will and as I bid."

The orb floated forward, pushing through the space where I had indicated the door should be. It entered the middle circle.

"Sealed again is the door."

Now . . . how to fail?
"Spirit!" The Eldrenne's voice made me look up. She

stood three steps beyond my set of circles. I glanced at the other contestants. Hunter was working; Maria looked frustrated. As an afterthought, I shot a glance at the dais and wished I hadn't. The Eldrenne still sat on her throne.

And yet she was here as well.

Bi-location. Probably only I could see her here; she might have had mirror images with each of the other contestants as well.

"Do you understand the purpose of a protrepticus?" she asked the spirit.

The crystal slid around the floor and spelled:

Triple three fold.

The Eldrenne nodded sagely. She asked me, "Do you understand the ownership of a protrepticus?"

"No," I said honestly.

"You will keep it with you at all times"—she held up a hand—"you do not have to take it into the shower, but it must be within six yards of you. Water will not harm the spirit, but if the spirit's house rusts, you'll deal with rust in your pockets, so tending it properly is expected. The item will not require an actual electrical charge but it will feed off your energy; the more you use it, the more it will take. Until you get used to it, be careful."

"Will it take a significant amount of energy?"

"You're holding a spirit in this world and sustaining it, in an item."

"That's a yes?"

"Yes."

My intake of breath was telling.

"Are you unwilling?" she asked sweetly.

"Do I have a choice?"

The Eldrenne's mouth quirked up on one side. "Proceed or be Bindspoken."

"That's a no, then."

"What do you choose, Persephone Isis Alcmedi?"

"I choose to ask what 'triple three fold' means, specifically."

She laughed. "I like you, Persephone." She clasped both hands around her staff and said, "There are three souls involved here, yours, the spirit's, and mine. The protrepticus does three things to each of the three of us. It binds us, obligates us, and allows us. It binds spirit to object, witch to spirit, and Elder to witch. It obligates the spirit to work on your behalf, obligates you to tend the object and sustain the spirit, and obligates me to allow you admittance to any and every WEC meeting and grants you a voice and a vote. And, lastly, it allows the spirit to continue participating in 'existence,' allows you access to Council Elders, spells, and information as needed, and it allows the Council to communicate directly with and locate you if necessary."

Consensual SM aside, for most people bondage is a bad thing. Magical binding is no different. In fact, the binding of anyone to anyone else or any*thing* is, generally, frowned upon by witches. All bonds tamper in some way with freedom and that's always a negative. It was why the stain made me feel dirty and angered me so much. In order to avoid more of that, and to preserve the secrecy of the stain I already had, more questions needed to be asked.

"What exactly do you mean when you say it binds me to the spirit and you to me?"

"The spirit must be sustained by you, it must be nearby at all times."

"What if I forget it at home? What if it falls out of my pocket and is run over by a car? What if my dog eats it?"

The Eldrenne shook her head. "If the protrepticus passes beyond the realm of six yards from your aura, the spirit's connection will be severed and the spirit will return to the other side. If your dog eats it, you must remain within the distance until it is passed through the dog's system, and then you must collect all the pieces. I would suggest you then wash them thoroughly." Ick. "The same if it were run over by a car; gather and place the pieces into a leather pouch and keep it with you."

"That's it?"

"I will know, so no, that won't be 'it.' "

Aha. "Okay. And the 'binding of you to me' part?"

Despite blue film on her rheumy eyes, I'd have sworn she stared right at me. "It is equivalent to claiming you into my *lucusi,* my sacred grove . . . my own coven."

So. This was supposed to be an honor. I didn't know her policies, so I didn't know if I agreed with them, but I undeniably liked her. And if being bound to her didn't reveal the stain, then maybe she could help me not succumb to Menessos. They had a history. I was sure she knew things I'd want and need to know. Nana told me to watch the Elders and see who the Lustrata thought was worthy of being called on. Of the five Elders, I'd have to choose the Eldrenne.

"You hesitate, child?"

"How is the binding to be done?"

"I bind myself to you exactly when you bind yourself

to the spirit and object, and I do so in the same manner, so it is a binding of your choice. If you choose to proceed."

I wondered how many Bindspoken witches there were out there, who had opted out at this moment.

There was no such thing as a "loose" binding. Layers of it, but none were loose. The vampire mark was a binding; if he marked me again it would be like adding another layer of control and connectedness, until it had the capacity to be complete. It's an all-or-nothing kind of thing. But how to do it to keep her from seeing or feeling the vampire's binding? I wasn't sure that was possible. But if I stopped, I was surely Bindspoken. To be the Lustrata, I couldn't be Bindspoken. The only chance of avoiding that was to proceed and hope she *didn't* come to know of it.

"I will proceed."

Grasping the black thread from the items I'd moved to the smaller circle, and then taking up the crystal the spirit had used to spell with, I stood and closed my eyes. Boosting my personal shields, I said:

> *"My inner circle wall is dropped,*
> *But this spell is not stopped."*

Imagining the barrier between myself and the spirit and phone dissipating, my eyes opened. The spirit remained hovering where it was, glowing softly, and waiting. It made no move of aggression. Good. Good sign. I moved closer and went down into a crouch with one knee on the floor, the other up should I need to move fast.

Unwinding a length of black thread, I severed three

long pieces with candle fire and slipped them under the cell phone. Feeling a tug, I glanced over my shoulder. The image of the Eldrenne was holding three hairs she'd just pulled from my scalp, rolling them in her fingertips.

> *"Willingly you submit, willingly I grant.*
> *You into this device I now implant.*
> *I claim responsibility for your care.*
> *Sustaining you with energy I will share."*

I placed the crystal on the display centered in the gray cell phone. The spirit-orb lowered until it hovered just over the crystal. I circled the phone with a ring of salt, then lifted the strings up, saying,

> *"Three strings hold you."*

I began to tie them and said:

> *"Three knots bind you."*

Sparks scintillated in every direction as the strings went tight around the orb. I pulled it as tightly as I dared, amazed that the orb was tangible. One knot, two, and three.

The orb was throwing light like a sparkler on the Fourth of July. Quickly, I drew the dagger Lydia had returned to me and cut my index finger.

> *"Three drops seal you."*

Behind me, I heard the Eldrenne begin chanting. Salt crawled from the bowl like an army of tiny white ants and encircled me.

> *"Willingly you have competed.*
> *Willingly your measure I have meted.*
> *Into my* lucusi *you are now impressed*
> *For you have truly passed the test*
> *I claim responsibility for your care.*
> *Sustaining you with knowledge I will share."*

She opened her hand, and the rainbow moonstone I had been using rose from the floor and flew into her palm. She slid my hairs around it.

> *"Three hairs hold you."*

She began to tie them and said:

> *"Three knots bind you."*

My spine arched and I felt bright inside. Sparks scintillated before my eyes, sparks that weren't real, not outside of me, but existed only inside my head, inside my spine. Stretched tight, every firework trail burned under my skin. The first knot she tied felt as if it were around the vertebra between my shoulder blades. The second knot tightened around my chest at the sternum, expelling all the air from my lungs. The third knot coiled around my neck, then dropped to my sternum, tightening like a noose, choking me.

I couldn't breathe.

An eternity passed before she whispered, "And three drops seal you."

My need for air grew.

Blood dripped from her old finger onto the rainbow moonstone; I felt it. I felt each drop like a giant forge hammer crushing me, flattening me like molten steel, until the binding became fused to each and every cell in my body, an amalgamation that could never, ever be undone.

Wind suddenly spiraled up around me, a tornado inside the cylinder of my circle. The stones and salt blasted the edges around me. The brightness inside of me shone from my every pore, illumined my skin, and flashed from my eyes.

I couldn't move. All I could do was feel and think . . . and all I could think was, *Is this how the Eldrenne's eyes got filmy?*

When the light faded, I collapsed to the wooden floor. The little stones hailed down, pelting me. Chalk dust and salt floated down. I coughed. Exhaustion overwhelmed me and I gave in to it.

When I awoke, it seemed Maria and Hunter were doing exactly the same. "Awaken ye witches!" the Eldrenne called.

My circle was still up. I spoke the release of it, barely holding off a yawn and stretch until the task was done. Standing, brushing chalk dust and salt off my clothes and shaking it out of my hair, I faced the dais.

"Vampires," she said.

Menessos, Sever, and Heldridge rose from their seats and strode toward us. The two lesser vampires flanked Menessos; I enjoyed watching him walk toward me. He moved fluidly, so confidently.

I suddenly realized how his self-assurance impressed me. There were many people in my life with qualities I admired, qualities I knew the Lustrata needed to outwardly demonstrate. I promised myself that as the Lustrata I would study, train, and adapt. I wanted every possible advantage in my arsenal.

A few yards away, Menessos slowed, stopped. He gestured to Heldridge, who approached Hunter and shook her hand, spoke. When Heldridge moved to Maria, Menessos gestured Sever on.

"It was a pleasure to meet you, Persephone," Heldridge said to me. He wasn't convincing.

What was appropriate to say? "Likewise."

He bowed his head slightly and strode toward the seats. Sever stepped up to me next. "Best of luck to you, Miss Persephone." He flashed that little-boy grin.

"Thank you, Sever." He, too, stepped away.

I pulled up my witch hand-jolt shield and wrapped it around me as Menessos came to stand before me. Surely he was shielding as well, because my body detected only a mildly desirous reaction as he slipped his hand into mine, and lifted it to his lips. The chivalrous gesture made me think of Arthur, and how before I'd ever met this vampire, Menessos's visage was the same as Arthur's in my dreams. He whispered, "I shall be seeing you, Persephone Alcmedi. Soon." His breath on the back of my hand was like the desert wind on my aura. But that heat couldn't get through.

The Eldrenne stood, stamped her staff once on the dais floor. "Hasten into the night, drinkers of blood. Your honored participation is acknowledged with gratitude. May you drink and rest before the dawn."

The eastern doors opened.

"By your leave," Menessos said. He gestured and was preceded in exiting by the others. At the doorway, he glanced sweepingly over the contestants, and down the row of Elders. Then he was gone. The doors clanged shut.

"Lydia," the Eldrenne said. "Bring the others."

Lydia curtsied once and walked away toward the stairs.

"Finalists, come before the dais, please."

I bent to pick up the cell phone, glanced down the line. Hunter was picking up the compact. Maria didn't pick up anything. I looked askance at her; she shook her head "no" at me. She hadn't done it. My heart sank for her.

We three lined up before the dais and in moments Lydia returned to the top of the stairs, followed by Mandy and all of the other contestants. They formed a long line to the left of the dais.

"Three of you competed in the final test," the Eldrenne said. "One of you did not succeed." She paused. "Maria. Come forward."

Maria took three steps closer.

"You competed well."

"No spirits answered."

"That is their way, child. Sometimes their unwillingness to participate is to the competitors' benefit."

"Yes, Eldrenne."

"Stand to this side," she said, gesturing for Maria to stand on the right of the dais.

The Eldrenne released a slow breath, leaning heavily on her staff. The raven adjusted its position on her shoulder, fanning its wings once. "Long years has it been since a final round produced two successful witches. It goes to a vote." She turned. "What say you, Morgellen?"

Morgellen stamped her staff and said readily, "Hunter Hopewell. Her score was highest of them all."

"What say you, Elspeth?"

She stamped her staff. "Hunter Hopewell. Her education, qualifications, and experience are superior."

The Eldrenne turned to her other side. "What say you, Desdemona?"

Desdemona sat forward and stamped her staff. "Persephone Alcmedi. In the company of vampires she was unafraid, and her inspired solution was tailor-made."

"What say you, Vilna-Daluca?"

Vilna stamped her staff. "Persephone Alcmedi. True courage is rare. Combined with selflessness, rarer still."

"The tie is mine to break," the Eldrenne said. She thought for a moment, then eased down onto her throne again. The bird hopped up to the raised back and cawed. The Eldrenne rolled her staff in her gnarled fingers so that the orb-top spun round and round. She whispered, lips moving, no sound I could hear coming out. The other Elders did not copy her gesture. Who was she speaking to? Herself? For a long minute she conversed with no one, head tilting in thought, then whispering more.

The bird cawed again.

Her old face lifted, conical hat tilting back until her

face was turned up to the orb, mouth open, and blue-filmed eyes glistening. She cackled, long and loud and worthy of ancestors gathered 'round a cauldron under a darkened sky singing of toil and trouble.

She lifted the staff and stamped it hard. A clap of thunder resounded inside the Covenstead.

"The new high priestess of Venefica Covenstead will be . . . Hunter Hopewell."

When the applause from the other contestants died down, the congratulations I spoke to Hunter were true and heartfelt. She'd proven to me she was worthy and capable of the job. She'd acted and reacted like a leader from the start. She'd asked questions and sorted through the contestants to find her competition, to assess the threat. What bit of ego got in the way, Maria and I honed down with our comments. In the end, Hunter showed me that a strong woman is often seen as a bitch, even when she's succeeding and doing the very things expected of her.

I locked that realization in memory; the Lustrata wouldn't be immune to such reactions from others.

As the other contestants came forward to congratulate her, I stepped away, relieved by my loss. Maria hugged Hunter, glanced about, saw me, and approached.

"I was rooting for you," she whispered.

She pulled me into a hug.

The Eldrenne cleared her throat to gain our attention. "Don't forget, the details of the test are secret and not to be discussed." She turned to Hunter. "At the Witches Ball on Hallowe'en," she said, "I will make the formal announcement that you are the new high priestess, and I will introduce you to the coven members and the media then. Until then, you will keep a low profile and work with Lydia to tend to the remaining details."

"Yes, Eldrenne." Hunter was beaming. The grin on her face wouldn't have come off with a jackhammer.

Lydia touched my elbow and pulled me into a hug. "That was a damn fine effort," she said. "Thank you."

Into Lydia's ear I whispered, "She'll do a good job; you don't need to worry."

She pulled away. "Are you sure?"

"I learned a few things about her, saw the character in her." I squeezed her hands reassuringly. "She'll do right by the coven."

Despite appearing so very tired, Lydia seemed fierce. "I'm too old for coven-watching and keeping priestesses in line. If she doesn't, Persephone, I'll be expecting you to knock some sense into her!"

"Of course," I said softly. As the Lustrata, that'd probably fall under my jurisdiction anyway. But I didn't like the feeling I was being inveigled again.

CHAPTER TWENTY-FOUR

The sun was well up by the time I pulled into the driveway. Johnny's motorcycle was not there; it better not have been. The temptation to run over it might have been too much. Then I wondered if he'd stayed at Erik's again. Or someone else's. *Stop it.*

Inside, Nana sat at the dinette where I'd left her more than twenty-four hours before.

"You look like hell," she said merrily.

"Gee, thanks," I said.

She took a drag from her cigarette and sat it on the ashtray as she exhaled. "So you didn't sleep. That means you had to participate all through the night. Every round?"

"Every round."

"Well?"

"I'm not the high priestess."

Nana sighed.

"I'm the runner-up."

"Good. That's good standing, then."

I yawned. "I'd like to think so."

"Go. Sleep. We'll talk later."

• • •

I awoke that afternoon, showered, and headed down-stairs. Ares whined from his crate, which meant Beverley must be gone, so I went into Beverley's room and let him out, then started down again. Through Nana's open door, my eyes caught on the crystal ball on her dresser. I'd helped her pack it carefully away when she moved in with me. Perhaps she was telling Beverley about scrying or used it as a prop in a story. I continued, but midway down the steps, the pit of my stomach jumped and went cold. I stopped. Another step, another jump. I backed up. Nothing. I returned to the top of the steps, frown-ing. But by the time I reached the top, my stomach felt fine.

The protrepticus!

Taking it from the bedside table, I slid it into my back pocket and went slowly down the steps, without incident. I wondered if and when it would do something or if it would wait until I had a need. Did I initiate it, or did it work both ways? What, exactly, could it do?

I kept my eyes away from my couch as I reached the bottom of the steps. My feet turned me toward the kitchen where I discovered two notes. One was from Beverley letting me know that she and Nana had gone to the movies. The other was from Nana letting me know that Celia had called me yesterday morning, afternoon, and again in the evening.

I didn't want to talk to Celia yet. She'd either make things better or worse by telling me something about Johnny and the situation. I needed to come to terms with what I already knew before I let her add to it one way or the other.

I started to make a pot of coffee, but my palate was java-ed out. Juice sounded better. Checked the mail that had come yesterday, tended to some bills. Then, armed with the tape measure from the drawer, I sized the dining room, the doorways, and windows. A difficult task because Ares curiously followed me and obstructed the tape repeatedly.

Sitting down at the dinette with paper, pencil, and ruler, I drew it out. In half an hour, I had a good idea drawn up for making it her bedroom, with an attached bath—a new room jutting out from the house. I'd even made a list of contractors to call to get quotes from. It was Sunday, so I'd be ready to start tomorrow.

About that time, the moviegoers returned. Beverley dropped to her knees and hugged Ares, who greeted them with deep, happy barks and his tail wagging like a thick whip.

"Seph!" Beverley came and hugged me next, as enthusiastically as she had hugged the dog. "I missed you yesterday! How'd it go?"

"I came in second."

"Demeter and I went to the movies!"

"I got your note. Tell me all about it."

She was excited and animated as she told me about their day together. Nana watched from the doorway, smiling as Beverley acted out some of the scenes for me. Moments later, she was off to watch cartoons in the living room where Ares lay so she could use him as a pillow. Nana chuckled. "They're a bundle of energy at that age."

She dropped her jacket on the seat across from me, then dug her cigarette case from the pocket and placed it on the table. She didn't open it but watched me steadily.

When she opened her mouth to say whatever it was she was building up to, a combined buzzing and ringing erupted from my backside. It startled me so much that I jumped to my feet and jerked the protrepticus from my pocket. Its ring sounded like an old telephone with bells inside.

"You got a cell phone?" Nana asked, incredulous. "You?"

I held the buzzing thing out from me like it was a ticking bomb or a multilegged insect. "Um, no. I didn't."

"Then whose is it?"

"Well, it *is* mine, but—"

"Aren't you going to answer it?"

It stopped ringing. I set it on the table.

"Maybe they'll call back," Nana said, finally opening her cigarette case. "I thought you didn't want one of those?"

"I don't."

She cocked her head at me, eyes squinting at me as she held a cigarette to her lips. "Then why do you have one?" She flicked the lighter.

"It's not a phone. It's a protrepticus."

Nana was stunned silent for a long moment while smoke wafted toward the ceiling and her eyes darted back and forth annoyingly. "Xerxadrea was your Eldrenne. Damn." She breathed the last more than said it. "You said you weren't the high priestess."

"I'm not."

"Don't lie to me!" Nana shook her head. "When Xerxadrea is the overseeing Eldrenne, the high priestess always trots out of the competition with a protrepticus."

"Hunter and I both got them."

"Both?" Her features sharpened and she sat forward. "You mean the Eximium came down to a vote of the Elders?"

"Yes."

"Lord and Lady! What was the vote?"

"The Eldrenne's vote broke a tie between the two of us."

Nana pursed her lips, then loosed them to click her tongue.

"What?"

She took a long draw off the cigarette and rubbed at her knee. "She's always been partial to her sorcery, showing off, and doing her part to ensure the generations after her have had a taste of it. Those willing to accept the bargains get the rank. Of all witches, it had to be Xerxadrea on this Eximium." She shook her head. "I don't know if there's ever been a solitary to have a protrepticus."

"Is that a bad thing?"

"Probably not. But they all knew you were a solitary going in. You wouldn't both have gotten to keep them if you were going back to be in a coven as an underling."

"You're saying that in the end she voted for Hunter to be high priestess so she didn't have to take away my protrepticus?"

Nana fixed me with a stern look. "I'm saying she gave the prize position to Hunter because that way she could keep the ties to you both intact." She sat back and took another drag off the cigarette. "Xerxadrea saw something in both of you, something she wanted to hold on to . . . and she let you both succeed in order to not have to choose between you."

"Is she corrupt or something?"

Nana shook her head. "I don't think so. Though I knew her when I was sixteen. That was a long time ago. She was the high priestess of your great-grandmother's coven. She irritated me with her elaborations on every detail. Her rituals took hours." She rolled her eyes and made a flippant gesture. "Many things could have happened since then. Did you get a sense that she was corrupt?"

"No."

"You, being you, probably would have if she was. Forget about it." She waved her hand as if dismissing the subject. She pointed at the phone. "You did it."

"Yeah," I said softly. "Here," I said and showed her the drawing for turning the dining room into her bedroom. "That's what I think we should do. See how the bathroom becomes a new space added on there? You'll have that window, but the other will turn into a door for the bathroom."

"A private bath?" She sounded tempted.

I grinned. "Just for you. Jacuzzi tub if you want it."

"Look at this drawing. Is there anything you can't do?" she asked proudly.

"Keep a boyfriend," I blurted, then instantly regretted it.

Nana's happiness faded in an instant. "I—"

The protrepticus rang again.

Since it had stopped her from starting something I didn't want to talk to her about, I was thankful for the interruption, until she shifted gears and said, "Well, go on. Answer it. Introduce yourself to the spirit you got."

Resignedly, I picked up the phone, flipped it open, and stuck it to my ear. "Hi. This is Persephone."

"Now, more than ever," the spirit said, "I think you're gonna rot in Hell, little girl."

My eyes widened as I recognized the voice. Jerking the phone away and staring at the little color screen, my eyes beheld a pixilated version of the Reverend Samson D. Kline in a pale blue polyester suit. He waved at me and laughed. "Didn't expect me, did ya?" It came out in a Southern drawl, "dih-juh."

"Oh, fuck." I shut the phone and pushed it away.

Nana squealed, "Language, Persephone Isis!"

Before I could utter a word in my defense, the phone rang again.

Nana reached for it, but I was faster. I didn't answer it, just frantically turned it over and pushed buttons hoping to make it stop. It rang on and on.

"What is wrong with you?" Nana asked loudly.

"No," I groaned. "Why him?"

"You know the spirit?"

"Unfortunately." The phone was still ringing. I shoved it under my legs to deaden the sound. "It's the spirit of the man who came to collect the stake from me after Menessos helped with Theo."

"That pompous-ass preacher whose head ended up in your fridge?"

"Yeah." There was a mental flashback I didn't need. "Shit!"

"Persephone!"

I whispered hotly, "I vowed to investigate this spirit's murder and avenge him!"

The phone stopped ringing. My shoulders relaxed some.

"That's the trade-off you bargained for?"

"That's what he asked for. I thought that with me being the Lustrata it would be . . . okay," I said dully.

"You thought it would be easy."

"No, I didn't. I thought it would fit right in with my other tasks."

"And be easy."

"I never thought that word!"

"Definition's the same."

"Nana."

"I forget, which one was actually to blame?" she asked pointedly. "Menessos for actually killing him or Johnny for the deception that brought it all about?"

"Nana." Did she have to rub it in?

She pointed a finger at me. "You should know better! Witchery is natural; it asks the universe to align things as you will. Slow and steady, in good time, laying groundwork for what is to come. But sorcery's immediacy alters what *is*. Its cost is equally immediate! After the protrepticus is sealed, it's too late to change the terms of what you agreed to do."

I sat there feeling grouchy, then, "And what if his own stupid, brainless actions—and attacking a master vampire qualifies—brought about his death? What if no one is to blame but himself?"

Nana just stubbed out her cigarette. I could tell she had more to say—

The phone rang.

This time it wasn't the twitter of bells. This time it was some rap song about booty.

I flipped the phone open and dropped it on the table, disgusted.

"Hey, now. Not so rough." Samson stumbled around inside the square display screen. "Holy Moses! You're sweet as pie at first, but soon as something's not going your way, *pow,* you go sour as a wet cat."

That probably was his true perspective, as far as my encounters with him went. "What can I say? You bring out the best in me, Sam," I replied. Assuming he could see me, I added my I'm-being-polite-but-I-hate-you smile. Rev. Kline had seen it before.

"Women." He rolled his eyes; but being a spirit, he could literally roll them all the way back so the irises and pupils came up from the bottom. It made my stomach churn a little.

"I suppose your attitude is well earned," I said, employing a little psychology, "because this is how women have treated you all your life?"

"Not at all." He smoothed the lapels of his jacket. "Some women in my life were downright nice to me."

"After you paid them, right?"

"It's always a trade-off of one kind or another. Everything and everyone has a price. One way or another, what you want always has a cost; what you're willing to pay for it defines you."

My fingertips galloped irritably on the tabletop.

"Now," he went on, somehow managing to make that a two-syllable word, "you're not the first woman who can't understand men. And," I knew as he made that conjunctive monosyllable into a polysyllable, that he was going to drive me crazy with this diction. He grasped his lapels as if the gesture affirmed his right to analyze me, and finished. "Because of your lack thereof, you default to anger for your responses."

I said, "If you think starting off with 'You're going to rot in Hell, little girl' is getting things off on the right foot and isn't something that would make anyone 'default to anger,' then I think it's you who needs the lesson on understanding people, Sam. An insult and a veiled threat is always wrong."

"I'm a preacher, Ms. Alcmedi. Telling people the status of their soul is my job."

"Not anymore."

He glared at me.

Maybe I should drop the phone in the grove and run like hell, to break the binding. Let the Eldrenne know. Let her make me do another. It couldn't be as torturous as this. "Why aren't you and your soul in heaven, Sam? Why are you here in this phone, if your soul was so sanctified?"

Samson laughed. "Already figured that out, girly. The afterlife is different if you're murdered. And pondering the how-and-why of my being here doesn't change that I am here and you're stuck with me." Glowering, he continued in a prissy tone, "*I* can't go anywhere. Where you go, I *have* to follow. We're in this together."

He was right. Damn it.

"Good-bye, Sam." I shut the phone and shoved it into the back pocket of my jeans. Nana wasn't going to be able to keep quiet much longer. I started counting in my head. I got to four.

"Persephone, Johnny stopped in yesterday morning,"

Nana reached across the table and wrapped her warm old hand around my wrist.

Having anticipated she'd go on about the phone, I wasn't ready for the shot of regret her words left ricocheting around my heart. I stared at her hand, the skin like parchment, and wondered what, if anything, Johnny had told her.

She squeezed my wrist. "He took his things with him."

Some secret part of me had hoped there was some logic in Johnny's actions, something I didn't understand. Just then, that part of me shattered. And I realized that I wouldn't have been more stunned by Nana's words if she'd pulled out a gun and declared herself Jesse James.

"Persephone?"

"Good," I said.

With her other hand, she put the cigarette in the ashtray, then reached into her pocket. She pulled out an envelope and pushed it across the table toward me. "He said to give you this."

I stared at the rectangle of white. My heart wouldn't beat; it felt like a cold rock in my ribcage.

Ripping open the envelope, I removed the paper. It read:

Lustrata you are . . . and yet not.
You've come so far!
You are what I've sought.

Lustrata you see and are blind.
Your answer won't be inside your mind.
*   It's inside your heart.*
*   It's in knowing yourself.*

It's inside your heart.
Recognizing yourself.
  Seein' it.
  Believin' it.

You create your bound'ries. Will they be lines?
Lines you won't color outside of? Do you have a spine?
Lines you can step across? Can you not redefine?
You create your bound'ries. Will they be walls?
Walls to keep you safe within? Locked inside lonely halls?
Walls that must be scaled to escape? Don't fall. Don't fall.

Lustrata, you choose the limit.
The scope of your truths and your mental intent.
  Disclaim it or acclaim it!
  Blame me or reclaim me!
    But know yourself . . . see yourself.
    Know yourself . . . trust yourself.
It's inside your heart.
It's in knowing yourself.
It's inside your heart.
Recognizing your Hell.
  Seein' it.
  Releasin' it.
  Seein' it
  . . . and letting it go, letting go.

There were little marks, chords and notations, to the right of the page. It was a song. It was how he expressed himself best. *Musicians.*

Eyes burning, I folded the paper and replaced it in the envelope.

Nana was watching me intently. "You okay?"

No. Nope. Not at all.

I felt the hurt churning, turning. My heart burned and began to beat again. Angrily. Those shattered pieces, those fragmented shards melted and ran together, congealing and hardening like one big scab over a wound I'd never admit having. This song indicated I needed to rethink my perceived self. How *I* saw things? My boundaries were fine; his needed to be reexamined.

So what if he's supposed to teach me about fighting. I'd find someone else.

I was not about to cry over him leaving. After what he did, why would I even want him around? He *better* have gotten his shit and left. He saved me the trouble of throwing it out by the road.

"Persephone?"

"Yeah. I'm fine."

"You sure?"

I faced Nana squarely. "Yes."

CHAPTER TWENTY-FIVE

What happened, Persephone?"

"I don't want to talk to you about it." I kept my tone even and polite.

"Fine. I'll do the talking," she said cheerily. "Earlier, you said the only thing you can't do is keep a boyfriend. You knew he was gone, or was planning to go, before I gave you that letter. You're thinking about him, and whatever was in that letter. Am I right?"

I frowned at her. "He went wrong. It's not fixable."

She opened her cigarette case and lit another. "I need you to tell me what happened."

"I already know what went wrong, so *we* don't need to analyze it."

She took a long draw on the cigarette. "And?"

"And it's done."

"What's done?" Beverley asked, coming to the doorway.

I stammered. Nana said, "Her column. What do you need, honey?"

"I want to take Ares outside."

"Stay in the back," Nana said.

I watched Beverley head for the garage door, Ares following closely. "Still wearing your necklace?" I asked.

"Yup. I love it."

As soon as the door shut, Nana said tersely, "So long as you're thinking about him, it isn't done."

"He left, Nana. Whether or not I think about him, whether I'm glad he saved me the trouble of hauling his shit to the road, or whether I regret it, it's done." I left the table and carried my mug to the sink. I rinsed it out, wishing I could wash him from my mind and heart by turning on the tap. I smirked; I could try crying him out. But I hated crying.

"He's a wolf, Persephone."

I turned to her. "Duh."

"So stop thinking of him like a man. He isn't *just* a man. Even when he's not furry. He's still part wolf." She half-rose in her seat, checking on Beverley through the window. "And not just any wolf," she added.

I crossed my arms over my chest and leaned against the counter. "What does that mean?" I hadn't told her about the at-will partial change. Wait—the morning after we changed Theo, he and the other wolves had a discussion that made him uncomfortable. Had Nana overheard? "You mean his maintaining his human sensibilities while in wolf-form?"

Nana got up and shuffled over to open the refrigerator, and started rambling around. "You know so much about wæres. They tell you much and you're perceptive, you see a lot. But it's just the surface of things. The surface that the world, such as it is, can accept. They still haven't let you in. Not with your column."

"What about my column?"

"You're helping them. With things as they are." She set ground beef and vegetables on the counter.

My column created sympathy and humanized wæres despite much of society wanting to make them monsters. "Are you saying the wæres are using me?"

She pulled a deep pot from the low cupboard and a frying pan from the stove drawer. "No more than you use them to make your living."

"Now wait just a darn minute—"

"Persephone, the time for being naive has passed!"

My jaw clamped shut, teeth grinding tight to keep in the angry words wanting out.

What was wrong with me? Was my anger amped-up from the stain as well? If it was, then all my emotions were affected.

Aw, hell! Why wasn't there a *You and Your New Stain* handbook? Or a "Ten Things to Know about Your Stain" pamphlet?

Nana dumped the meat into the pan, then turned to chopping the peppers and onion. Her old fingers went through the motions methodically, dicing the vegetables precisely, deftly. It made me reflect and wonder: was she preparing me as deftly?

Maybe this was one of those times when I should just shut up and listen to her.

She put the lid on the meat, drained a little of the grease off into a second skillet, then added the pepper and onions to that one and stirred. I prompted her. "What do I need to know?"

Nana tapped the wooden spoon on the side of the pan and put it in the spoon rest. She shuffled back to the ashtray and lifted her cigarette. "I went to Columbus while you were gone yesterday. Beverley went with me and we did some research on the Lustrata."

"I thought we were talking about the wæres—wait. You went to the Archives?" There were dozens of witch archives across the country; Columbus was the closest one. "You drove all that way?"

"Oh, it's right down I-71. Straight shot."

"No one's going to be suspicious of me, are they?" So much for me shutting up.

"Don't worry. I told them I was pulling up the old legends to tell Beverley stories." She shrugged. "It's true."

Even if I wasn't certain that would negate any suspicion, it was already done and I couldn't change it. "And? How does that fit with me being naive about the wæres?"

She blew smoke at the ceiling and put the cigarette back in the ashtray. Shuffling back to the cupboards, she sorted through the variety of spices Johnny had bought. "Regardless of what else has happened, you need to get Johnny back over here. As soon as possible."

I held off saying it as long as I could, then, "I can't, Nana."

"You can't or you won't?"

I looked away.

Nana proceeded to open two cans of garlic-and-herb spaghetti sauce. She dumped them into the pot and added more chopped garlic. I resolved to wait for her to expand on her words, but she didn't. She stirred and stirred, leaning over the mix.

"Why? So he can cook?" I asked, hoping this was going to be that simple and knowing full well it wasn't.

"That would be another reason," she said, adding coarsely ground pepper to the mix before facing me with a critical expression. "But not the main one."

She checked the simmering meat and veggies, poured off grease again, then added them to the pot and stirred more. When she finally tapped the spoon off and laid it in the spoon rest, she adjusted the burner.

"If you want me to consider trying, you need to tell me why first—and it better be a hell of a reason," I said. When her critical face hardened with disapproval, I added, "What did you find?"

Nana returned to her cigarette and stared out the window. Her eyes darted this way and that, following the girl and the dog racing around the yard. She didn't answer.

"What does that have to do with the wæres not 'letting me in'? And why is this not the time for me to be naive?"

She sank back into her seat, ran a hand over her beehive hairdo. Only then did she face me.

"Sit down," she said, gesturing to the bench across from her. "You're not going to like this."

I sat.

"You've seen a coven, seen people come to a sabbat. Just regular people seeking a spiritual connection, a moment of solace, or a party. Whatever they are searching for, they can find it and go home and on about their way happily. You knew from the stories that the council was convoluted, but now that you've seen WEC Elders at work, do you think you've seen the deepest depth of their complex machinations?"

"Hell, no. With the lengths Desdemona and Vilna-Daluca went to simply to test a high priestess, I can't imagine what they do to certify an Elder, let alone an Eldrenne."

"Yet those 'practitioners' who simply come to sabbats to worship the Goddess . . . most of them never aspire to know more, never seek to see what you have seen."

"What's your point?" If spirituality was their goal and they received it, that wasn't a bad thing.

"You've glimpsed the *wyrd* of the Witch now, and you've come to know a little of the intricacies of the vampires."

"More than I want to, actually." I thought of Menessos making blood oath to Xerxadrea. Their history could be a part of those intricacies.

"You go in the light of day and peer into a stream and you're going to see your reflection. But you go in the dark of a moonless night and all you'll see is the stream bed. You've been exposed to the dark, so you're seeing below the surface, now, Persephone. You're seeing the beauty in the smooth stones and feeling the slime covering them. Slime that, if you're not mindful of your footing, will cause you to slip and plunge under the surface with them."

My thoughts turned to my namesake and her descent into the underworld.

"Do you think, Persephone, that the world of the wærewolves is any different?"

Sitting there, speechless and feeling small, my fingers gripped the edge of the bench seat. "I hadn't given it any thought."

"Celia and Erik were turned how long ago?"

"Five years."

"They were camping, so it was summer, right?"

"Late spring."

Nana's fingers twitched as she calculated. "Last year in the late spring or early summer . . . I assume they took a six-week vacation, right?"

How'd she know? My breath caught. "It wasn't a vacation?"

Nana shook her head. "Every wære I've ever known of started a six-week vacation that encompassed their fortieth and forty-first full moons, or the beginning of their fourth year as a wære."

"I thought you avoided wæres."

She rolled her eyes. "Doesn't mean I didn't know of things going on with the wæres other witches knew and befriended."

"Okay. And?"

"And, as we have covens, their kind have dens. Like us, they have a network much deeper than the surface shows and they must be indoctrinated in it. So, they maintain a 'normal' life, being guided and prepared by their den-keeper. It makes the surface reflect wæres as they would have themselves seen. It's no different for us. Witches want the non-magic-using humans to see us as beautiful and spiritual when young and as sweet, cookie-grannies when we grow old. But you and I know the truth is more complicated. The wæres want to be seen as average folk, but stronger and"—her voice mocked casualness—"oh, so what if they shed their skin for fur once a month? They kennel, so all is well."

Tone back to normal, she went on, "The vampires want to be seen as intelligent and gorgeous, as the wealthy elite, and they buy their blood to stem the slaughter. It's just business and everyday humans benefit, of course. While the fey, they're tooth-fairy delicate and harmless."

She poked her cigarette at the ashtray, pushing the ashes into a mound. "Even the non-magic-users. They puff up against us all like they have the law on their side. But it's not truly the laws that have kept the rest of us at bay. They're organized and we aren't . . . or weren't." She took a raspy breath. "We're people with power or wings or fur or fangs. But they're the people with weapons of mass destruction. The balance is so tenuous."

I was thrust back, to the memory of the vampire protocol test at the Eximium. When Heldridge asked, "Does your Goddess never cause harm?" I'd thought to myself that by allowing unpleasantness to transpire in small doses, a tenuous balance would be maintained. After spending a few heartbeats arguing with myself that this couldn't mean I was supposed to tolerate what Johnny had done and see it as "unpleasantness in a small dose," my voice came softly, if irritably, "What does this have to do with getting Johnny back here?"

She stubbed out the cigarette. "Bear with me; I have to set the stage a little. The Lustrata legend has two ancient documents to support it, but neither are whole. The Stellatus Tablets are broken, and the Lux Scrolls partially burned. The information is not complete and it is not perfect. Elders dispute over the translations and the guesses made concerning the fragments and the missing parts. They'll never know so they'll never agree because their agendas are all different."

"Okay," I said. "Your disclaimer is noted. What *do* we know?"

"There have been two previously documented Lustratas."

"Only two?"

"Are you going to interrupt every point?"

My mouth shut and my expression turned beatific.

Nana continued. "Stories are told, updated, and retold through bards, like Johnny. Though such references are few and mostly nonfactual, they remain far more numerous than the actual relics. Much of what bards and storytellers have told has come to be taken as fact, although it shouldn't be, as such folks do take liberties. Poetic license. These bard-stories mostly romanticized the Lustrata. Johnny, a wære, wrote of you as an enemy of the vampires. His lyrics went something like:

> *Impurity rising from under the world,*
> *Dead above ground, diseases unfurled.*

"But the vampire bards see you as the enemy of the wære. I found one who said:

> *Lustrata walks,*
> >*unspoiled into the light.*
> *Sickle in hand,*
> >*she stalks through the night*
> *Wearing naught but her mark and silver blade.*
> *The moonchild of ruin, she becomes Wolfsbane.*

"They see what they want to see, do you follow? They see you as the justice they want, not *true* justice. It's not simply these two either. I even found fairy references! And as I said, the Elders have conflicting takes on it—and Xerxadrea won't be oblivious to either side."

"You mean not even the witches agree?"

"They all have their own motives, their own agendas."

"So you're saying the different sides will try to get the Lustrata to choose them over another side or other sides?"

Nana made an uncomfortable face. "Yes and no."

"Nana."

"It's not that simple. It's not like two or three or five different factions will toady to you to gain your service. I mean, after they see the sign, some will, but—"

"But?"

"Some witches think the Lustrata is the enemy."

Of course. Can't be a simple, smooth path I must walk. "When you say some, how many do you mean?"

"I don't have a head count!"

"A percentage?"

She considered. "A third."

"That's a lot."

She waved off the idea. "Less than half and nothing you can change yet. Now listen." She rubbed her knee. "Even the regular mortal humans have a few obscure references that, in my opinion, are veiled links to the Lustrata though they'll never admit it. Bottom line is, we're *all* in this. We're *all* at risk." She stopped, turned her cigarette case over and over in her hands.

Something occurred to me. "Wait, wait! It's not just some witches either. When you say the wæres and vampires each have their ideas of justice, you mean that if I, as the Lustrata, don't agree with their purposes or if I act against them, then they will renounce me and become my enemy, right?"

Nana gave me a sheepishly sorry smile. "I hadn't thought that far into it." She rubbed her knee again. "I'll look into it."

And the truth that I hadn't seen hit me. "You've been using the scrying crystal."

Her expression turned stern but scared.

"Your door was open; I saw it sitting on your dresser." Now it all made sense. Why it was there, why her knees hurt. Scrying, like any other power, has a price. I was willing to bet the universe taxed her in the arthritis department. "What did you see?"

"Everyone's different agendas—and not just where the Lustrata is concerned—work against each other." Her wrinkled hand rose to her neck and her fingers worked as if she'd loosen a tightly wound scarf. But she wore no scarf. "You must find a way to maintain the balance," she said. "With the numbers the normal-humans have, and the technological destructibility at their fingertips, if you fail, the consequences will be insurmountable destruction."

CHAPTER TWENTY-SIX

My mind refused to acknowledge the mega-ginormous weight of her words.

Synapses filed it away as *Bad Things that Could Happen* instead of *End of the World.* "Okay," I heard myself say calmly, meanwhile thinking: *Why am I not running to hide under my bed?* "But still, what does that have to do with Johnny coming back here?"

"You need him."

"The hell I do."

Her mouth went crooked. "If not now, you will soon."

"Doesn't mean he has to live here."

"He is the chosen protector of the Lustrata. For that," she insisted, "he must be close."

"Says who?"

"Do you remember the Tarot reading I did for him?"

My eyes shut and my heart sank, knowing a long explanation was coming. "Yes. You found something in your research to corroborate or define or link to that?"

Nana leaned to look out the window. "I don't see Beverley!"

As soon as she said the words, panic rose up within

me. My feet had me moving toward the garage door. It opened and Ares pushed through; Beverley came in right behind him. "When's dinner?" she asked.

I nearly collapsed to my knees with relief. The adrenaline in my system stalled like lead in my veins. "Soon," I said, a bit breathless. "Go wash up."

Beverley and Ares charged into the house and in seconds the water was running. I was visibly shaking from the unused adrenaline. Nana got up and grumbled. "I'll get the salad together. You pour yourself a glass of wine."

Nana encouraging the consumption of alcohol? I just leaned on the counter.

A moment later, she shoved a glass into my hand.

"The tablet made a reference," she said as she started to tear lettuce into a bowl, "to an unburned portion of the scroll that has been translated: *the Lustrata, flanked by an aberrant pack of wolfen.* It's been taken to mean a pack that does not return to man-form. But I think it's a pack whose leader never loses his man-mind."

"That doesn't explain why he has to be *here*."

"He's a pack animal. He must be with his pack."

"So you want the lot of them to move in?"

"He must be with you."

"I'm not pack! I'm a witch. Besides, he obviously doesn't want to be with me."

Nana ignored my protest. "The Lux Scroll, being in poor condition, has been pieced together in places and in one such place the text makes reference to Lupercus. He's the god of shepherds to some, the wolf-god to others. Our translators have theories about how either of these meanings can be taken in the context of the scroll.

However, I showed a photocopy of that scroll section to Dr. Lincoln, and he, with his minor in Latin, said he thought it was two words: *lupus* and *erctum*. If you take the LUP and ERC most witches would assume it to be Lupercus. If Dr. Lincoln is right, *lupus* is, obviously, "wolf." *Erctum* or *herctum* is an inheritance. If Johnny has been given the wolf-inheritance that makes him retain his human sensibilities . . ."

"What if it's simply word-order confusion? Latin has convoluted rules for mixing and grouping words. It could be simple: as a wære he already has the inheritance of the wolf."

"Regardless, both the scroll and the tablets indicate that the Lustrata is somehow closely associated with a pack. And a pack needs a leader, an alpha. You don't have to be a member of the pack. You're their sovereign because you're *his* sovereign."

"His sovereign my ass."

Beverley giggled from the doorway. Nana pointed a finger at me. "I will start a swear jar if you don't mind your tongue, Persephone."

"Do I have time for more cartoons?" Beverley asked.

"Yes," Nana said. "I need to finish the salad then start the pasta."

"Can we have garlic bread too?"

"Good idea." Nana went to the freezer and pulled out a long red package and handed it to me. "Preheat the oven."

When Beverley had gone, she said to me, "In the Tarot reading I did, the fourth card, the base of the problem, the motivation that drove him was the High Priestess, your namesake. It was intuition. And I remember that

Prometheus was the sixth card, future influences. Johnny would have to sacrifice something to gain something else of greater value. And I told him the final outcome would be spontaneous and intuitive at the same time, but that intuition can be conflicting. Hermes on the Magician card meant his potential would be pointed out to him and that he would have to choose whether to develop it or not." She rubbed her brow. "Persephone, has he gone from here thinking that he's developing his potential somewhere else? Has he sacrificed what you two were building to gain something else?"

"Maybe." The band getting a recording contract would qualify. I took a big gulp of the wine.

"Can he not see that *this* is where the greater value lies, *this* is what he must develop, his position with the Lustrata?" Her eyes were moist, shining. "*So much* depends on it. You must make him see that!"

I put the glass down and took her hand in mine. "I'm not going to go running after him, Nana, but if he shows up to kennel tomorrow, I promise I'll try to talk to him."

I had to meditate. There was time before dinner.

I went up to my room and pulled the bed from the wall. Sprinkling coarse salt around it, I made a thin salt-circle, then lay down and whispered my meditation opening. The switch flipped, and I created my usual wakeful dreamscape. I washed my face with the cool water from the river beside the ash trees, then sat back to wait for Amenemhab. The sun was warm and bright and with my bare toes stuck in the water, I tried releasing my negativity, doubt, and fear, but it felt like my chakra-faucet was clogged.

When Amenemhab trotted up, I pulled my toes from the water and stood, putting my hand up to stop him before he spoke. "You were right. When I was here last, I was being stupid. I left resolved to face the problem and fix it." I started pacing. "But things came up. Johnny stayed with friends so I didn't see him. The band was being showcased Friday night at midnight. I went, intending to tell him once they finished playing." I stopped both talking and walking. My eyes were burning.

I forced down the tears and picked up where I left off but stood still. "When the set was done, he pulled these women up on stage. They pawed him in front of everyone before exiting the stage together. As they got to the backstage area, one of them kissed him. I went home, and proceeded on minimal sleep to the Eximium. And while I was there, Nana said he gathered his things and left."

Starting to pace again, I went on. "Nana also says I have to get him back to the house because he's some chosen protector of the Lustrata, but I don't know that I want him back at the house." I stopped, sank to the ground. "He used me." My fingers picked at the grass.

Amenemhab came alongside me and sat, ears pricked forward as he stared across the world before us. It made him appear stoic.

"You were right," I said again. "So much has changed and little of it was under my control. Last month, I lived alone. I wrote a small column, did some Tarot readings, and rented my acreage to local farmers. Now I'm responsible for Nana and Beverley, my column is nationwide. I'm stained and I know more about the vampires and WEC than I ever imagined I'd know. I wanted Johnny but I didn't know if it was right. I gave in and within about forty-eight hours, he—he couldn't even give me two days to wrap my head around *another* big change in my life." A few hot tears poured from my eyes. To my credit, though, I at least sounded angry and not pathetic. "That doesn't make me stupid. That doesn't make me weak."

"I agree. You have been rash and taking a short time to consider the ramifications and be certain before proceeding is practical."

My hand strayed over to stroke Amenemhab's back. His fur was coarse under my fingertips, but it soothed me anyway.

"Persephone," the jackal said softly, pushing his paw at the ground. "You went there to do the right thing, to take the risk with your heart. I encouraged you to do that, and for this pain, I am sorry. You cannot control the actions of others. You can only control how you respond."

"I know," I said quietly.

"I didn't realize you were this deeply invested already."

Invested? Was that the barren term society used now? As if emotions were a Wall Street transaction. Was the romanticism of "head over heels" gone? Was puppy love archaic?

I asked, "Do you know what it truly means to be bound to a vampire?"

He put a paw on my thigh. "Do *you* know what it truly means?"

Recalling the reactions I had to Menessos and jolts I experienced at the Eximium, I said, "I'm finding out."

"This is who you have chosen to be, is it not?"

"Yes, yes. We've been over that, but being bound to a vampire scares me."

The jackal cocked his head. "It should scare you. Menessos is infinitely more powerful than an ordinary vampire."

"The way I see it, that's all the more reason to fear and avoid him."

"The way I see it, that's all the more reason to want him *on your side*."

"*My* side?" I stood, incredulous. "My side? As if I'm the one recruiting him or forcing him against his will into the service of this mere mortal?" I shook my head. "No way."

Amenemhab looked at me as if uncertain. "You are no 'mere' mortal."

"If he knew I was the Lustrata, that'd be reason enough for him to want to control me." My voice went softer. "He'd use me too."

"You don't know?"

"Know what?"

"Of course . . . it all makes sense now."

"What?" I demanded.

"Persephone, you have been so busy trying to *define* who you've become that you can't *see* who you've become. You're not this or that, the supporting granddaughter *or* the role model to Beverley. Not the Lustrata *or* Johnny's lover. Not a marked witch *or* someone of interest to Menessos." He leaned closer. "You're all of that and more. Stop drawing those lines of separation and see what you are."

I couldn't help thinking of Johnny's letter/song. *You create your bound'ries . . . will they be lines you won't color outside? Lines you can step across? Can you not redefine?*

Amenemhab continued, "Justice is a woman. You've seen statues of Justice, haven't you?"

"Yes."

"Do you think this is coincidence?"

Justice held the scales; she balanced things. "No. But she's blind." I thought of the Eldrenne.

"No, she isn't. She's merely blindfolded. To show that she weighs the scales fairly, without favor to or fear of the parties involved. She is not swayed by their identity, nor their politics or wealth or power or lack thereof. Her decisions are based on solid facts, on truth, on actions and consequences. The blindfold is meant to keep personal feelings out of the equation and to let her double-edged sword fall equally without emotion."

"Without emotion," I repeated. "Johnny wanted me to learn to make my expressions blank so I didn't give my thoughts away to foes." Indifferently, I added, "That'll be the only expression he'll ever see from me again."

"There is value to his lesson, when facing an enemy. But your tone distresses me."

"Why? I'm to keep emotions out of the equation, right?"

"Wrong! Emotions *are* valuable! If you have nothing of your own to love, no pleasure to keep, no personal stakes to fight for . . . then why would you fight at all?"

Staring at him, I couldn't speak.

"You have the lineage of witches to empower you. You have the experience of your grandmother to guide you. You have a world to balance, and if you do, Beverley will inherit a better place." His voice softened. "But you can't do it just for them. You will *fail* if you are merely altruistic. Witches and wæres and vampires are a part of you. *You* bind all this together! You wouldn't relinquish your ties to Nana or to Beverley; you didn't relinquish the binding to Menessos and, no matter what, you are bound to Johnny now as well. This hurt will fade or fester, depending on how you choose to feel about it." He let that sink in. "You will come to see that all of it has been creating—and will continue to hone—the warrior you must become to be the Lustrata."

Amenemhab stood rigidly and spoke loudly, "Take off the blindfold, Lady Justice. See it. See yourself. See the power you have, the power you claimed *right here*." Amenemhab had tears in his dark eyes. "You claimed it when you accepted all the good and bad, when you took the burns into yourself. Have you not yet comprehended? You broke the shackles of the vampire that night! You freed yourself and made your former master *your* slave! He is bound to you now. You are the Lustrata and you are not subservient to anyone!"

I stared at him, openmouthed. My mind flashed through everything in seconds. The pain that was Menessos's to bear. His leaving because I told him to go. The gifts. Him protecting me during the test. Perhaps the scene with Xerxadrea's raven was somehow a part of him being enslaved. But my increased senses, my amped emotions, good and bad . . . the stain had flipped and I held the reins, I did not bear the yoke. I had stood up and declared that I would not be the servant. I had claimed a place of authority in the universe. And all the consequences, the benefits and responsibilities that came with it.

Oh. My. Goddess.

CHAPTER TWENTY-SEVEN

Lying on my bed, staring at the fading light on the wall, I heard Nana call Beverley to dinner. I'd be next. Dinner.

Such a *normal* thing.

I sat up, moved to the edge of the bed. My gaze fell from the wall to the floor, landing on my boots in the corner. They sat where I'd dropped them when I came in Friday night. One flopped on its side, sole exposed. The other stood upright as it should.

The Lustrata's shoes. Those boots . . . were me.

One part defeated and down, soul revealed, tread worn. And one part strong, upright, ready. Together, they fulfilled their purpose.

I didn't need to grow into the Lustrata's shoes. They already fit.

So mote it be.

Monday, with Beverley off to school, I began making plans. The next two days were going to be busy. Tonight, with the full moon, the wæres would kennel.

That meant popcorn and Disney with Beverley even if it was a school night. We'd started the tradition when Lorrie, Beverley's mother, had kenneled here. Beverley would stay with me in the house. The human cries and wolfish howls of the wæres' transformation were somewhat muffled by the cellar, but Mary Poppins singing "A Spoonful of Sugar" or Pumbaa and Timon rollicking through "Hakuna Matata," accompanied by the crunch of popcorn, drowned it out completely and kept a young girl's mind away from the change happening to her mother.

When we had magically forced Theo through a change in order to save her life, the other wæres had changed as well and Beverley had witnessed it. Now that she had actually seen the wæres change—not a pretty sight—it was probably even more important to keep her distracted.

When she slept, once the wæres were changed, I meant to take advantage of tonight's blue moon, the "extra" full moon in the calendar. Tomorrow I'd make the effort to talk to Johnny.

Because of that, I took out my Tarot journal and reviewed the reading that Nana had done for him. Nana was right about the sixth card being Prometheus. Yup, Johnny was clearly sacrificing what we had or could have had. But reviewing the reading didn't help me know what to say to him.

I put the journal away and took out my Book of Shadows. Flipping to the Wheel of the Year section, I opened the Hallowe'en/Samhain pages. Nana and I planned to introduce Beverley to a lesser-known part of the witch's celebration for Hallowe'en. Afterward, Nana would be taking Beverley to a costume party at a class-mate's home while I showed Hunter my support at the Witches Ball. All in all, it was going to be a good night.

But first, I had to deal with tonight. I started creating my blue moon ceremony.

Every year, there are thirteen full moons. That means in one month, there are two, and that second one is called the blue moon. To witches, this moon has special mean-ing and it is a time for uncommon rites and unique wishes. Of course, tomorrow the Covenstead would host the Hallowe'en Sabbat, but I planned to draw down the moon tonight.

Beverley and I were sitting on the couch watching *The Little Mermaid*. It was her favorite. "Should we decorate your bedroom in mermaid stuff? We could sponge-paint starfish and shells all around."

"I don't know. Maybe ponies."

Ares sat attentively before us, keenly waiting for pop-corn to be dropped. The Great Dane puppy was growing fast. Maybe we could saddle him for her.

That was when I felt the triad of energies combine in the heavens. The sun reflected perfectly on the moon, which reflected it perfectly onto the Earth. Reaching for the remote, I jacked the volume of the movie just as Ariel started singing. Between the television and the attempted sound-proofing in the cellar, I could barely hear the hoarse screams of humans transforming into wolves.

Still, Beverley leaned against me. "I never asked Johnny about it hurting when they change."

Arm going around her, I rubbed her shoulder. "You'll have the chance. Though tomorrow's going to be a full day for you: a party at school—don't forget to take the costume and the candy with you—and a costume party at Lily's."

"I like Lily. She was the first girl in my class to ask me to play with her at recess."

"That was sweet of her. I'm so glad you're making friends."

"She likes your jokes in my lunch too." She stretched, resettled. "Demeter said there was something you two wanted to do with me tomorrow."

"Yeah. It's important and it's going to be special."

"Give me a hint?"

"No way." I took a slurp of cider.

Beverley sighed. "That's what Demeter said. Pass the popcorn?"

A chorus of howls arose from the basement, despite the soundproofing.

With Beverley tucked in her bed, I took the basket of gathered supplies from my bedroom. Traveling through the garage and out the back door, I stepped into the yard.

I took a moment to look back at the house and imagine the add-on bathroom for Nana. I'd called and arranged for three contractors to come out to give me quotes on the addition and making the interior changes to give Nana a first-floor room. As I scanned around, it occurred to me that maybe I should get a quote on a deck also. Not that I'd have them build it until spring.

Hello, whispered the ley line. I smiled. "Hello."

My back pocket erupted with the sound of bells. "What do you want, Sam?" I answered, setting the basket down near my outdoor ritual spot.

"What-cha doin'?"

"It's a blue moon. I'm about to start a ritual."

"Oh. Well, hold up there. *My* job takes precedence."

"What do you mean?"

"Xerxadrea's calling."

A second of static was followed by, "Persephone?"

"Yes?"

"Are you attending the Ball tomorrow?" She sounded very happy.

"Yes. I thought showing my support for Hunter would be a good thing."

"I agree. Several members of my *lucusi* are flying in to attend. I look forward to introducing you to them."

I wondered if they were flying in planes or on broomsticks. With her, I wouldn't have been surprised to discover it was the latter. "I'm looking forward to it as well."

"Blessed be."

Static again. I pulled the phone away and saw Sam sitting before a switchboard with a headset on, acting like he was chewing gum and filing his nails. "Can you believe it used to be done this way?" he said as he jerked the wire from one spot on the board and plugged it into another. Then, with a bored expression he waved his hand and the props disappeared. He stood and the seat faded away. "Go on, get your wicked witchery done. I'm out of here." He walked out of frame.

Shoving the phone back into my pocket, I sorted

through the supplies and gave another thought to the Tarot card I'd pulled for a quick reading on what I was about to do. It had been the nine of wands. It meant steadfastness despite resistance; it meant acquiring leadership, a journey, a new and freer way of thinking. To me, it embodied encouragement to proceed.

Not long after I moved into the farmhouse, I had created a ring of mortar and topped it with various stones. Inside the ring the grass grew just as it did outside of it. Admittedly, mowing the interior wasn't easy. Measured precisely, the mortar had the compass points clearly marked, and five equidistant holes. Taking an eight-inch iron spike wrapped in copper wire from the basket, I dropped it into the first hole, leaving about an inch sticking up. After placing the other four spikes, I put candles on each compass point. Placing a tray in the center and assembling my supplies, I slipped out of my shoes, curled my toes in the cold grass, and began.

A new moon symbolizes the universe's natural and unrefined resources. It's a time to work, to begin projects, and apply that energy to good use. But this was the full moon, the manifestation of what was begun, and the answer from the divine. It was my intention to draw that culmination of events to me and embrace it as the Lustrata should. Through this ritual I would demonstrate my acceptance to the Goddess.

I cleansed and blessed the space with each element, lit the illuminator candles on the tray, and cast my circle just outside the mortar ring. Then, after lighting the quarter candles and calling the elemental spirits to guard my circle, I lifted a spool of glittering, silver ribbon. My fingers unwound it slightly and secured the end to the spike to my left. I unwound the ribbon to cross the circle and wind it around the right-side spike, repeating the move until I created a silver-ribbon pentagram. Starting from the left, this was also an invocation of water—the predominant element connected to this ritual's aspects.

My astrological correspondences were such that the sun had entered Scorpio and the moon was passing through Taurus. Though I'm not the sharpest witch when it comes to astrology, my experience tells me the sun-sign lends regeneration and resourcefulness at this time. The moon-sign influence made me see that what mattered most is ending the suffering that people—be they normal, furry, winged, or fanged—cause each other.

This was the night to ask for the wisdom to discern where instincts can help or harm. Recognizing and controling impulses was the only way to bring balanced co-existence to all. Combine all that with the wish-making of a blue moon and it was an opportunity I couldn't miss.

Stepping over ribbon to stand in the center of my circle, the center of my pentagram, I lifted my arms high and said, "I call upon the Mistress of the Mysteries! Upon She who is the Three Who are One! Past, Present, and Future . . . Queen of Heaven, Earth, and the Underworld. Maiden, Mother, and Crone! Queen of Witches! My Goddess, Hecate!"

Face to the moon, my breathing slowed and I centered myself, grounded myself. "As I draw down the moon, free its light, release its energy, impart your silver and gold power, entrust it to this body, and let it fill me."

I kept my eyes focused on the bright moon above. My

mouth opened and my lungs drank the moonlit air. As if my spirit could stretch out from my lifted arms and brush fingertips across the lunar surface, I reached *above*. Setting my will into the astral, my wish under this blue moon, I let the words sing through my mind and leave my lips in a whisper, "I accept the mantle of the Lustrata. Place it upon my shoulders and grant me the wisdom to keep my feet upon this path that I may be what You have made me, that I may accomplish the goals You set before me, that I may be Your instrument, humble and just, and that I may fulfill my purpose."

Above myself, I saw my wish, my words, tumbling in the astral air. Symbols glowing, this pattern of light filtered down into the ethereal. There, to my amazement, each symbol became a circle. They looped in on themselves and linked together forming row after row like chain mail. Then this armor of light sank through the ethereal and down to my shoulders, my words, manifest. A badge with the balanced symbol of the scales rested over my heart.

Feeling this approval, this gift of Hecate, I felt my knees bend and I knelt.

"If I may be granted a wish, grant me knowledge that I may know when to dispense swift justice and when to offer aid. I wish to know my heart and trust it to be strong, to lead me well, and not to betray my purpose with foolish emotions. May my heart know the difference."

CHAPTER TWENTY-EIGHT

The next morning, while Beverley brushed her teeth, I carried the box of doughnuts and two six-packs of orange juice around to the storm cellar. Cars were lined down one side of my driveway as they usually were for the full moon. Two of them I didn't recognize. Assuming one belonged to Theo, she'd had to replace her wrecked SUV, the other made me mildly curious. It wasn't unusual for some wæres I didn't know to occupy the spare kennel. If they became regulars, though, it meant we'd have to add another section of caging to stay ahead.

Quietly, I descended the steps into this underworld of snoring wæres, pulling the cellar door shut behind me. Though I'd have preferred to let the light in, the cool air would follow me and I'd rather let them sleep. Their suitcases and duffels were piled near the steps. I stepped far out and around them as my eyes hadn't adjusted to the near-dark. I set the food and drinks in the center, then approached the first cage. Here, a black couple I didn't recognize cuddled together on the hay. After unlocking it, I moved on. Next, Celia and Erik spooned on their sides. Tom and Jericho Patrick—we called them Tom and Jeri like the cartoon—lay in the next kennel, and after them was Theo, lying with one leg over Feral, who sprawled on his back, legs and arms flung widely outward. I averted my eyes and tended the lock.

Lastly, I turned to the darkest, rearmost cage, knowing it was where Johnny always kenneled.

Even without their pom-poms, I recognized the blond twins that lay spooning on either side of him.

Busily attending the lock, my fingers performed the function automatically. Insert key, twist, pull.

Someone stirred in the hay. I looked down.

"Red," Johnny whispered. He stretched, remembered he wasn't alone, then seemed to realize what I was seeing. His mouth opened and closed but nothing came out.

"If you're able to talk before you leave, there's a conversation we need to have," I said softly, giving him the blankest of expressions.

I left the cellar.

An hour later, someone knocked on my door.

From my bedroom where the busywork of sorting laundry kept me from nonproductive pacing, I'd heard the cars leaving and expected this. I'd asked Nana to remain upstairs so we could have privacy. She promised.

At the bottom of the stairs, though, I grew worried. The shadows beyond my door meant far more than one person was waiting. And I could hear them whispering hotly back and forth.

I opened the door to see Theo and Celia in front, Erik and Johnny behind them.

Before I could ask them to come in, Theo stepped forward. "What the fuck did you do to us?" Her tone wasn't aggressive, just concerned.

"What?" Was something wrong with the doughnuts?

"When you did the spell that forced us all to change."

Oh. This was the first regular change the four of them experienced since Theo's accident. "You better come in," I said, proceeding down the hall.

The four of them followed me into the kitchen. "Coffee?"

"No, just answers," Theo said.

"I want coffee," Erik said.

Celia cut around me, putting her hand on my arm in passing. "I'll make it, Seph."

"Thanks." To Theodora I said, "Tell me what's going on."

She sank into a chair at the dinette. "I remember last night. All of it. We all do."

I wanted to make a wisecrack, but refrained. Last time this group sat around my table, Johnny admitted that even in wolf-form he kept his human sensibilities. I slid into the bench seat and scooted down. I asked him, "Anything different for you?" *Aside from sharing your kennel, that is.*

He shook his head. "No." His eyes flicked to the empty portion of bench beside me as if he were thinking of sitting there. But he didn't.

"This is what it's like for you all the time?" Theo asked. "Never losing yourself to the wolf?"

"Yeah."

"I can't kennel with Feral ever again," she said, running hands over her hair and clasping them at the back of her neck. Her elbows hugged around her head as if she could hide her face.

"Why not?" I asked.

"He wouldn't stop trying to mount me!" She peered through her arms at Johnny, who'd taken up a position in the doorway to the dining room. "Ugh! And Tom and Jeri, and Steve and Cherynna—all they did was mate!"

Johnny shrugged and said, "That's what you guys always do. That's why I always . . ." He couldn't say he always kenneled alone anymore. His arms crossed over his chest and studied the floor.

Behind me Celia took mugs from the cupboard and set them on the counter none-too-lightly. Tense silence followed, broken when the coffee started perking. The smell of it seemed strong and ashy, repellent to me. "The soundproofing isn't there only because you howl," I said quietly, noting that Steve and Cherynna must be the new couple I saw. "It's also there to mask the mating sounds."

"If it's the four of us, it has to be because of the spell you did," Theo said.

I didn't doubt her logic. "I didn't know it would have this effect."

"I don't understand," Celia said to Theo. "Are you unhappy about it? Do you not want to keep your sensibility about you?"

"It felt like I was trapped with a rapist all night, Celia!"

"Oh, god." Her tone faltered. "I didn't, I mean . . ."

"Forget it. It's fine."

"Let me get Nana," I said, scooting from the bench. "Maybe she'll be able to shed some light on this."

I explained to her what was going on as we came down the steps. Entering the kitchen, I resumed my spot on the bench. Nana stood there considering the wæres. "Well," she said to Johnny, "if Seph did this to the rest of them, who did it to you?"

Good question.

"And when?" she added, shuffling over to sit beside me. "And why? And did they know it would have that effect?"

"I've struggled with those questions for eight years, Demeter."

"Can we assume, since Johnny maintains his sense of self, that we will likewise be aberrations from now on?" Erik asked, sipping coffee Celia had poured him.

Nana hit the tabletop and stared at me. "An aberrant pack of wolfen!"

"What?" Theo asked.

"I did some research on the Lustrata and—"

"And," I cut her off, "before we get sidetracked, I have to ask something." I paused. "I know I'm not supposed to know. I know you won't want to tell me. But we've deepened the level of trust among us in the last month. Witches have their legends. Wæres must have theirs. Don't they tell you about them in the six weeks you're gone for your fortieth full moon?"

Looks shot around like wild pinballs. No one spoke. I turned to Celia, thinking she would be the one to break, to show me she trusted me. We'd been friends since college.

But it was Johnny who spoke. "No. The purpose of the den is other," he said.

"Johnny," Celia protested.

"She's the Lustrata!" He came forward. "She must have a foot in our world."

"What if that's all bullshit?" Erik asked. "No offense, Seph, but this hero-witch business isn't easy to accept."

"No offense taken," I said.

"She is," Johnny insisted. "She gave you the *gift*, how can you not believe?"

"Gift?" I asked.

"Everyone knows wæres lose their humanity—body and mind—when they transform, but don't you realize you have been given half of that back?" He faced Erik. "Once you told me that when the beast rose the man sank and it left you feeling robbed. Now you'll be a man, always! You won't act like an animal, unless you choose to," Johnny said.

I decided to remember that last remark for later. "What about your at-will partial transformation?" Okay, it was a dirty Nana-trick to ask him in front of everyone, knowing he'd be forced to respond because everyone would pressure him if he didn't, but I intended to get my answer. "Can they do that too?"

Johnny glared at me.

I glared back.

"You can do that?" Theo asked him pointedly.

Johnny turned like he would walk out, but his feet didn't carry him away. He spun back, angry. Jaw closed tight, breathing hard through his nostrils, his forearms crossed before him, he made fists so hard he shook. With a low growl he lowered his arms, opening his hands as he did. Nail beds narrowed and elongated, fingers went dark and slightly furry. Bones popped as his fingers grew thick and long. He shouted and fell to his knees, panting. His head hung.

Stunned, we were all silent as his arms hung limp at his sides and claws reverted to normal hands.

"Domn Lup," Nana whispered.

"How the hell did you do that?" Erik demanded, moving to offer Johnny a hand.

"Will."

"Can you go all the way?"

Johnny brightened, opened his mouth, surely to say something lewd, but shut it without uttering anything. His answer was simply, "Not yet."

"Yet?"

"It's easier when I'm angry. I haven't been *that* angry."

Celia asked, "Does the *dirija* know about any of this?"

Johnny shook his head no.

"Dirija?" I asked.

"The title of the local supervisor."

"And you're pushing me to out myself to the Elders," I said flatly.

"Speaking of the Lustrata," he said, his attention transferring to Nana, "what did your research reveal, Demeter?"

"Oh no," I cut in. "You still haven't told me what goes on with the fortieth full moon and all."

Hands on hips, he said, "At the end of our third year as a wære, the beginning of our fourth, we are called to participate in a group training exercise called the *luna patruzeci*. It means simply fortieth moon. We retreat to the *Grimasa-azil,* it is our home. The name means 'grimace sanctuary' because we change together, unkenneled, as a group. I attended the *luna suta* or hundredth moon, before I started kenneling here."

"What kind of training exercise?" Nana asked.

"They say they're teaching us for a worst-case scenario, but bottom line is, as men and women, we are taught to wage war."

Nana twisted in her seat to stare and me and ask, "*Now can I tell them?*"

I conceded with a small nod.

"I have foreseen the hostilities. They must be avoided at all costs." She pursed her lips, then went on. "There are strong personalities among you. Strong minds. There are things you must do, things that may not soothe your nature, but will stir its opposition. And still it must be done."

"What must we do?" Theo asked.

"You are a pack. More than that, you are the Lustrata's pack. And she will have need of you."

"You mean we're her pets?" Erik asked, his tone clearly offended.

"Not pets," Nana said, "but you must honor her summoning."

Erik came forward. "No." He stopped, facing Johnny. "No. For years we've worked on what we wanted. On the contract we now have in hand. I know, man, you've spent years on this Lustrata thing, but you can't tell me you'll blow off the label—your shot at fame—to stay in a farmhouse in Ohio and be the watchdog of a witch."

Johnny hadn't been slumping, but he rose up, shoulders squaring, chest broadening. Wordless, his posture said everything.

Erik asked, "You're going to let this ruin the deal for the rest of us, aren't you?"

Johnny didn't flinch or blink.

"Celia," Erik said, and left.

Head down, she followed him out.

"Nana, let me out." I was going after them.

She didn't budge from the end of the bench.

"Give him time," Theo said. "He'll cool down. They'll be back."

CHAPTER TWENTY-NINE

Johnny turned and strolled into the living room, biker-boots tapping each slow step down the hallway.

Nana got up and motioned me to get off the bench.

"What?" I asked. She hadn't moved an inch when I wanted out, but now she wasn't giving me an option.

"Go talk to him," she whispered.

After a glance at Theo, I scooted from the bench. Behind me, Theo asked, "So, Demeter, can you tell me about the spell that did this to us?"

Johnny stood in the living room. I couldn't tell if he was staring out the picture window, with its view of Erik's Infiniti just pulling out of sight, or if he was looking at the couch where we'd had sex.

I picked up the receiver from my desk phone and dialed his number. Suddenly the sound of Motley Crüe's "Looks That Kill" filled the living room. He turned and looked askance at me. I shrugged. "I wanted to know what my ringtone was."

He turned away. I hung up the phone and walked into the living room.

"So you got a contract. That's fantastic." I wished it

had come out more enthusiastically. *Something of greater value.*

"Haven't signed it yet."

"Why not?" I asked, surprised. "It's what you want, isn't it?"

"I want a lot of things."

The muscles in my neck and shoulders felt so taut they might snap. I moved past him and sat on the couch, off to the far end. "I have something to say. And I don't want you to interrupt me." He nodded. "I couldn't figure out if I had done what we did because I wanted to or if the stain was in charge. I had to sort some things out and, until I knew for certain, I couldn't falsely let you think all was perfect. I see now that my reaction may have made you think I was regretful, childish, and scared. I don't know if I was more afraid that it was the stain or more afraid it would be just me because then, if it was me, then what I felt would be . . . real.

"I came to the show to tell you that I'd figured it out." I paused. "I hadn't heard the band before. You guys sound great. Celia had said you were a great singer but I didn't know how . . ." I struggled for the right word.

"Look Red, Celia told me she saw you at the show. And that you hightailed it out of there after we left the stage."

Realizing my lowered eyes was a defeatist position, my chin raised to face him squarely. I'd done nothing to be ashamed of. I wouldn't be the embarrassed one here. I put on a mirthless smile. "My exit was so fast I left my leather blazer in the coat check."

"I know what you saw," he said, hands sliding into his pockets. "And I want to explain."

"You don't have to. You don't owe me anything." My voice was flat, firm, and void of emotion.

Those Wedjat-tattooed eyes fixed on me. "Yes, I do."

I waited, unaffected. Blank.

He knew I had mastered the skill he'd taught me; the sorrow he couldn't hide made it clear. "They are Samantha and Cameron Harding, Sammi and Cammi."

"As in Harding Bank?" I'd seen their commercials.

"Yeah. They're the forty-something twins whose rich daddy died and left them his banks, so they kind of don't live in the same world we do, if you know what I mean. They've been wære for six years and even bankrolled an underground vault with kennels inside for wære employees to use. They're good friends of Celia's; she often refers clients to their banks for financing. They put the money up for Lycanthropia's CD."

I waited, hands in my lap.

"I thought it was cool they'd got all Gothed up and come to the gig. I pulled them up onstage so they could go back to the Green Room with us. That kiss was totally unexpected. After seeing you, Celia came back in and ripped them both a new one." He chuckled. "You should've seen it."

Seeing Celia get mad was an uncommon thing, but I knew from our college days she was formidable.

"Turns out they'd been seeing some guy for years, a happy threesome, kenneling with him and all, and they had just broken up with him. Guess they decided to make me the next object of their affection. Celia disabused them of that pretty damned fast. Maybe a little too harshly considering the business relationship and all."

He turned his head and looked out the window for a moment.

"Without the boyfriend, they couldn't exactly kennel with their employees, and had no backup place to go. They asked Celia if they could join her and Erik—she said she tried to call you. Anyway, Celia couldn't tell them no. She wanted to mend the business fences but she'd already said the other couple—Steve and Cherynna—could come."

I looked him up and down, taking in his posture, his expression, but I kept my thoughts to myself. He had more yet to explain.

"So, they kenneled here, and yeah, they kenneled with me. There was nowhere else for them to be. I couldn't give them my kennel and hang with another male; he'd just want to fight. If I'd known Celia and Erik would retain their human minds, we could have kenneled together and dealt with the teasing. But I didn't know that. I just knew I could kennel with the twins without incident. No mating happened, and if you don't believe me, any of them who kept their minds can tell you. Theo had one wolf trying to mount her; I had two trying to get under me. My solution was to curl up and sleep, snarling at them if they got too close. I figured they'd wake up and assume whatever they wanted, but I'd know the truth." He waited for me to say something.

I said, "So what advice did Celia give you about explaining all this to me?"

He came closer and lowered himself to sit on the floor with his back to the couch. Though he was facing away from me, I could hear him clearly as he said, "Grovel at your feet." He laid his head on my knee.

"Johnny, stop." My irritation was clear and he turned quickly. "The Domn Lup doesn't grovel at anyone's feet."

"Damn what?"

"You know what I said. You've researched the Lustrata; you know what the Domn Lup is and you know you are he."

"Wolf King."

"So get up."

He made a swift little bounce of a move and was on the couch next to me. The furniture frame creaked a complaint. "Red, this is miscommunication, pure and simple. I want it to be right again."

I stood up and paced away, arms wrapped around myself. "You moved out fast enough to make it seem like you were eager to get out." I turned back.

"Let me see," he said, crossing his arms and placing one finger thoughtfully at the corner of his mouth. "Live at my own place or be obligated into tooling around town in a rusty Le Sabre all winter? Tough decision."

He was trying to be funny, but I wasn't into it. "Pardon my self-centeredness, but didn't I figure into that equation at all?"

"I didn't take *everything*. After what you'd seen, I figured you might throw my guitar outside or something. If it didn't break, the neck would warp." He got up and came to me. He put his hands on my arms. "I only took the stuff I didn't want to risk losing. The guitar was pretty much it. And some clothes."

Things weren't as I'd feared and I could accept that. He sounded like he wanted to come back. Nana said I needed him here and, just then, I felt like it might work.

But, as Amenemhab had said, I couldn't control how other people reacted. I had to know if he could take it, if he could handle my connection to Menessos. Not that I wanted to provoke him, just I needed to know. "I saw Goliath at the show," I said. "Made sure Menessos knew about the fairy's warning."

"That's—that's good." I could see that he was trying to be cool about it.

"He said that was a regular thing for them, getting threats. That I'd better get used to it."

"I still don't think the fey are any threat to them."

Looking over his shoulder and through the window, I saw a white van slow down on the road and pull into my driveway. The side of it read INCOMPARABLE DELIVERIES, LTD. "Just a minute," I said.

At the door, I waited as a little man in dark blue coveralls and matching cap carried a long, wide rectangular box to the porch. Grinning, he said, "Ms. Alcmedi?"

"Yes?"

"These are for you, miss." He handed them over.

Though the box was about four inches deep, it wasn't heavy. "Do I sign?"

"No. That's all taken care of, miss. You have a good day, now." He was already on his way back to the van.

"You order something?" Johnny asked.

"No." I set the box on the chair, checked the label. "Oh." The descending note of my voice belied my dissatisfaction.

"What?" he asked, coming closer.

"It's from Menessos."

Instantly, I could feel jealousy jacketing his aura. "Open it up," he said.

It seemed he was going for cheerfully-okay-with-it but what came out was I-hate-his-evil-guts. "I need scissors."

"Here."

Before I could move away, Johnny offered me his pocketknife. "Thanks."

Inside the cardboard box was a white box. I tried to remove it, but Johnny stepped in to slide the outer box away while I held the inner one. It was similar to a department store dress box, but the embossed seal in the top wasn't one I recognized. Lifting it gingerly, I set the lid aside and peeled back the different shaded layers of purple tissue paper. Inside was a costume gown of black and copper velvet, including the matching mask and shoes. Even jewelry.

"Oh my."

"Figures," Johnny said. He pointed at Ariadne. "More gifts to obligate you."

My anger was rising. The heat in my core was like a just-stoked furnace. "You know, I don't try to foster your jealousy but I have to talk to someone about what's going on in my life, and that's a part of the job I thought you wanted. I've been tiptoeing around it, and that's *over*. You could certainly choose to fight that emotion and do better than just giving up in the face of it, Domn Lup."

"Are you going to taunt me with that title now?"

"Not if you act like the king you are."

"You're bound to that vamp. I don't want to watch you succumb to his ploys!"

"Because I'm just a dumb little girl who doesn't see him for what he is?"

He straightened. "No. The Lustrata is not a 'dumb little girl.' " He started to add to that, but I spoke first.

"When are you going to succumb to trusting me?" My shoulders squared.

Johnny shut his mouth. He didn't look happy.

"It's as simple as making that choice, isn't it?" I paused, but he still said nothing. "I've learned my lesson. Waffling over things that should be clearly black and white, smearing it until everything is all gray, is bad. It leaves me uncertain what to think about it, let alone what to feel about it."

He put hands on hips and managed to seem irate *and* thoughtful.

"Do you think I can control what Menessos does?" I didn't have to tell him that to a degree, I possibly could. "Should I wave my wand and make him stop sending me things because it makes you feel bad? Or should I wave my wand and make you grow up?"

"Are your pretty painting and your pretty costume worth the rest of your life?"

A personal confrontation with someone I'd been intimate with usually made me cower, made me back down and give in just to stop the fight. But not now. Not as the Lustrata. "Worth?" I repeated. "What *is* the value of the Lustrata's life, Johnny?" Sauntering close and glaring up at him without fear or anger, I said, "I'm not sure what it's worth, but I am well aware of what price must be paid. I am aware the due bill will only get longer, never shorter. And I am aware that your jealousy vexes me." I nearly spat the last before returning to the box and gazing down into it. "There are things you don't yet understand."

"Then enlighten me." He sounded mesmerized. Maybe

on some level he could detect the change the glowing armor-mantle of the Lustrata symbolized.

I said:

> *"Lustrata I am . . . and yet untested.*
> *I've come too far to not be invested*
> *Deep in the role that is consuming*
> *My remade life while Destiny's looming."*

He whispered, "Enlighten me!"

Did I tell him that Menessos was mine to control and not the other way around? More secrets wouldn't help. *Ease in to it,* I thought. "I figured out my troublesome issues with the stain."

"And?"

"You have no reason to let any stab of jealousy wound you."

I expected him to ask why, to press me for every detail, and I was prepared to tell him. But he stood there with this look of awe on his face. When he spoke, he said, "Do the right thing, for the right reason. It's not just words to you. It's a way of life."

"And *that* is why I'm asking you this: Is the recording contract worth the rest of *your* life?"

"What do you mean?"

"You need to check into exactly who offered you the contract. Maybe Theo can dig up the truth, but Goliath was entertaining A&R friends at the Rock Hall that night. It's cause for suspicion."

CHAPTER THIRTY

Not one light was on in the house, but it was aglow with burning candlewicks. The scents of pumpkin pie and licorice and spices made simply breathing a pleasure.

In addition to the real pumpkin pie, Nana had made us a feast of pork, her version of colcannon (which was just mashed potatoes with fried onions on top), and peas and cornbread. While pork, like the pie, is a typical Hallowe'en staple, the colcannon is specifically Celtic. The rest was typically Nana.

I filled a plate with some of each item, then set it to the side and picked up one of the smaller plates and put a slice of pie on it, added a dollop of whipped cream.

Beverley asked, "Are you eating the meat?"

"Nope," I said.

"Is that mine or Demeter's?"

"Neither."

"Is Johnny coming back?"

I hesitated. "Not tonight."

"Then who's it for?" she asked suspiciously.

I handed her the small plate. "Follow me."

Leading her to the dining room, I set the plate at the

head of the table, where I'd already arranged the silverware, and poured a glass of wine. Nana came to stand beside the table.

"On Hallowe'en," I said, "the veil between the worlds is said to be at its thinnest. So on this night, we set a special table for those we love who have passed on."

Beverley whispered, "This is for my mom."

"It is."

She turned and bolted so fast I feared the pie would hit the floor. Nana and I shared a look; neither of us had expected she'd react like this.

"Beverley—" I stepped back into the kitchen and stopped, seeing the girl rummaging through the spices.

"It has to be right. Give me a minute," she said.

"Okay."

I slipped back into the dining room and waited beside Nana.

When Beverley returned with the pie, cinnamon was sprinkled over the whipped cream. She set it reverently on the table beside the plate of food before stepping back.

"That's the way she liked hers." I could hear tears in her voice.

"This place at our 'special gatherings' table is set for Lorrie Kordell. We ask you to visit us, Lorrie, and we honor your memory in hopes you will join us."

We passed the tissue box around, then filled our own plates and sat at the dinette in the kitchen. "Can I sit in the dining room with Mom?"

"Of course," I said.

Beverley picked up her plate.

"Do you want us to join you?"

She turned back, smiling despite the tears on her cheeks. "Yeah. We'd like that."

After dinner, Beverley went upstairs to get her costume on.

Nana said, "She's strong, that girl."

"I know." I admired her.

"As strong as you were as a girl." Nana left to go and help Beverley.

By the time I had the kitchen cleaned up—except for Lorrie's plate, which would sit overnight—I heard them at the top of the steps, singing a song from the movie we'd just watched. Nana's singing voice was a raspy, gravelling undertone to Beverley's breathy falsetto.

Hurrying down the hallway, I grabbed the digital camera and started taking pictures as they descended. Beverley was a lovely mermaid of green and gold with a dozen strands of Mardi-Gras beads around her neck. It reminded me of Aquula's pearls. I wondered what Beverley would think if she ever met Aquula.

"You look fantastic!" I said.

"You think?"

"Absolutely!"

Suddenly, Nana stumbled on the last step.

Lunging forward, I caught her under the arm and kept her on her feet. I didn't even drop the camera.

"Oh my," she said, hand over her heart.

"Are you okay?"

"My knee. It just gave out."

"To the couch," I said, not fully releasing her as I helped her get there and sit.

Wide-eyed, Beverley asked, "Wow, Seph. That was fast."

"And lucky for me," Nana said.

I said, "It's time to put the crystal away, Nana."

She wouldn't meet my eyes, so I knew she'd been peeking into it.

Not wanting to take a chance she might end up with a broken hip or worse, I left her and went up to her room. Taking her crystal from the dresser, stand and all, I placed it in a shoebox on the top shelf of my closet.

As I returned to Nana, I noticed movement in the dining room. Beverley's hand was curled on the top of the chair-back, her head tipped as if she were laying her head on someone's shoulder. "I miss you so much," I heard her whisper.

"The contractors will be here to give me quotes over the next few days. Let's keep your trips on the stairs to a minimum until we can get the addition done for you, okay?"

Not one to appreciate being made to feel old or feeble in any way, Nana simply nodded.

Beverley joined us. "Can you still take me to Lily's party?"

"You bet I can," Nana said and stood, resolve hardening her features.

It was six forty-five and as I watched them go, I noted that the sun had set, and that the sky was a beautiful shade of blue and growing ever darker. I heard rustling in the corn, but again, the stalks were too thick to see the deer.

Inside, I carried my box from Menessos up to the bedroom. Now I had to shower, get ready, and do something with my hair that would work with a tie-on mask.

With a soft towel wrapped around my now-clean body, and my blow-dried hair wrapped around hot rollers, I studied my costume. The clear shoe box, with pointy-toed black stilettos, made me frown. Cinderella's shoes weren't quite this high-heeled, and she'd run out of one on the steps. My feet wouldn't know how to function in that position. I'd likely fall and break my neck before I ever made it near the stairs. Those shoes were going to miss the Ball and take up residence in the back of my closet.

The jewelry boxes, however, did not make me frown.

My fingers caressed the soft, soft velvet of the costume before I lifted it by the shoulders. The skirt slid away, and I discovered that the bell-sleeved bodice was a separate piece. The sleeves were an amazing vibrant copper color, the cuffs midnight black. The bodice portion was also black, except for the center front portion with a long diamond of copper there.

Holding it up revealed that the bodice was short enough to leave quite a bit of midriff exposed once it was laced up the back. Elaborate black and gold embroidery surrounded the brassy grommets that the silk cording zigzagged through. This was never going to get tied properly with me being alone. I'd have to do my best; maybe Lydia would adjust it for me at the Covenstead. Still, I loved the bell sleeves, though highly impractical, bearing a larger version of the elaborate hand-stitched embroidery all along the draping cuff.

I set it aside. The sleeves would get in the way of putting on the skirt.

Taking up the skirt, my examination of it revealed it was short in the front with two daring slits, and the back had flowing length. All of it was lined with a glossy silk.

I was *not* wearing that skirt.

Turning to my closet, eyes scouring everything, I came up with a pair of black velvet, narrow-leg pants. Paired with my low-heeled leather boots, the modified ensemble might work.

Putting the "bottom" items on first, I saved fighting with the bodice for last. I ended up with it knotted tight and my breasts accentuated more than I preferred, but it was knotted. I'd require help to undo it. I stood back and checked myself in the mirror.

A belt.

I needed a belt. Not that the pants were falling, they weren't. But something shiny to break up the darkness of the velvet. Again to the closet. Nothing. Then I remembered something I'd come across in helping Nana unpack. Going across the hall, that unsettled feeling sent me back for the protrepticus from my jeans pocket. Able to move safely to Nana's closet, I found her fancy copper scarf of sheer material with tassels on the ends was perfect.

It matched the copper velvet, so I tied it around my waist, angled it on one hip. In my room, I took out a black pouch I used at Renaissance Faires when I read Tarot, tied it to the scarf, and slipped the protrepticus inside.

Standing again before the mirror, this time I was satisfied. It was like half of me was pirate and half of me was Guinevere.

Guinevere. To Menessos's Arthur? *Not.*

After arranging my hair much as I had for the Rock Hall showcase and applying a little makeup (I did line my eyes a little heavier because of the mask), I returned to the jewelry box. I lifted the heavy choker of triple-row onyx beads interspersed with nickel-sized rounds of bright topaz. The weight of it was mostly in the huge piece that hung from the front center of the choker and rested on my sternum. A large topaz set in gold, surrounded by onyx. A matching headpiece fit into my hair like a web of jewels glittering there. A topaz from it hung in the middle of my forehead.

After adding the rings and rubbing at the scrapes still on my right-hand knuckles, I slid the matching bracelets of burnished gold and flat, wide pieces of onyx onto my wrists, and was on my way, mask in hand.

My arrival was a little past fashionably late; the doors had opened at eight and it was now just before nine o'clock. The ritual wasn't going to start until midnight. Still, the Covenstead parking lot was nearly full. The two media vans on the lot didn't surprise me.

I flipped down the illuminated vanity mirror on the visor and put on the mask. It was the fabric tie-on kind, made of silk, and covered my face from nose to brow. The mask was adorned with small copper sequins and glitter across the brow, and thin lacework and a row of tiny black beads looped down on my cheeks. It was lightweight and not as uncomfortable as I had expected.

I added a stroke of coppery lipstick to my lips, replaced

the visor, and exited the car. Signs indicated that admittance was through the north doors only.

This was an annual affair, open to the public so the curious could observe what witches do in their rituals. As I understood it, Vivian had used her flair for the dramatic and people had come to expect a show. I wondered what Hunter had come up with—it was clear the sales were good, which meant expectations would be high. That was great, as ticket sales were the coven's major fundraiser. Lydia had sent me a complimentary ticket in the mail. As I approached the north doors I slipped it from the Tarot pouch.

Inside, a tunnel of fabric and fake webbing had been erected, and eerie music was softly playing, an underlying reminder of the holiday's inherent scariness. Mandy and another girl sat in witch costumes at the ticket-table, chatting. Mandy's hair was smooth and healthier looking, a shade or three darker. She looked great.

I offered her my ticket. She accepted it, and stamped my hand with a black pumpkin. "When you pass this doorway," she said mysteriously, "you are entering another world."

The other girl added, "The world *between.*"

"Do you understand?" Mandy asked, seriously.

They were surely hinting at the décor, theme, and tone of the party. Along with the soft music, they set the mood. "I do. Thank you, Mandy."

She squinted at me. "Who are you?"

"Persephone."

"Oh! I wouldn't have known! Wow, you look awesome!"

"Thanks. You too. You doing all right?"

"Yeah," she said, smiling. "Hunter's not been a bitch like I expected at all. She's been . . . fantastic, actually."

"I really like your hair; it looks great."

"Hunter. She took me to a salon and had them do something, and it's like hair again. Not straw."

"It suits you."

"Have a Ball."

At the end of the tunnel, the doorway was covered with layers of dark gray cheesecloth. Fake fog curled underneath. I brushed the strips aside with my hand to enter. They felt like a mummy's wrappings would feel, dry and brittle, despite the cold dankness the fog machines created.

Immediately past the entry, wrought-iron fencing had been erected. Glowing jack-o'-lanterns peered eerie faces through the fog. The din of voices seemed far away. The walkway ended in tall iron pillars adorned with fodder-shocks and more pumpkins.

I emerged into the Covenstead's Great Hall and was awestruck. Before me was the pentagram on the floor, with the five pinpoints of light shining down from the ceiling to highlight each point on the star. Beyond it was more iron fencing, shorter, maybe two feet high, with eight-foot-tall candelabra spaced along it. Each held three pillar candles: one white, one red, one black. There were more carved pumpkins glowing along the fence, bright-colored leaves scattered around, and baskets of red and yellow mums. The center section had a double gate thoroughly covered in creepy webbing, but there were arches along the way to allow people to wander through.

Beyond the fencing was a stage, set for a band. Cauldrons sat to the far right and far left, and each had rows of large pumpkins encircling its base, cut to look like licking flames. Smaller pumpkins, also cut to resemble fire, sat inside the larger shells, completing the look of brewing cauldrons. Fog billowed up and over the cauldron edges, rolling across the stage and spilling down on the floor. To either side of the drum riser, someone had stacked pumpkins with wolf faces carved into them.

"Persephone! I'm so glad to see you!" I turned to see Hunter approaching dressed as Isis, but without the enormous horned-disc headdress the Egyptian goddess was usually portrayed wearing. Her gold-accented white gown was flowing and feminine. In the darkened room—which I realized then had some black lights added in the domed ceiling—the white gown glowed slightly, ethereal and ghostly. A golden mask was tucked into a jeweled belt.

"How'd you know it was me?" I asked. "Mandy didn't recognize me."

"Mandy doesn't know about your scraped knuckles."

I glanced down. The bell sleeves stopped just above the scrapes. Under the strange lights, the scabs seemed more prominent. "True. You did an incredible job decorating the Covenstead."

"I love that choker."

"Thanks." Glancing around, I asked, "Who carved all the pumpkins?"

"We had a community-welcome pumpkin carving last night. One of the coven members bought hundreds of pumpkins. Another donated carving kits. We had people come in with their kids. They carved two pumpkins each, took one, left one, and *poof,* we have décor. Plus we had a fun event for families. Tonight's for the grownups only, of course. Come with me to the photo op?"

"The what?"

"I want a picture." She took my arm and led me toward the east-side doors where a backdrop was set with hay bales and more pumpkins and corn and fake crows, more flowers, webs, and glistening lights under more fog. There were people waiting in line for the photographer to take their photos.

"Wow, you've had some great ideas here. A band, even."

"Yeah. I'm so excited. I've been lucking out. One of the coven members donated two hundred caramel apples. Even the liquor in the cash bar was donated. I came up with the idea for the table arrangements, but volunteers just kept showing up to put them together. I know these wealthier members making donations aren't sure where they stand with Vivian missing, but, hey, it's still help. I appreciate it. Some of the locals who drifted away to be solitaries have offered up some interesting details about my predecessor."

"Where'd you get the band?"

"Even that was a lucky fluke. When I called the radio station to tell them about the Ball and ask them to mention it, I asked if they knew of a good band that might be available. The DJ told me about this local group who were just showcased at the Rock and Roll Hall of Fame and Museum in Cleveland. I called the contact number he gave me and they didn't have a Hallowe'en gig."

I stared at her open mouthed. "Lycanthropia?"

"How'd you know?"

I pulled Hunter aside. "The name's not just a gimmick, you know. They're wærewolves. The ritual—"

"Relax. I know. They're playing a set at ten, and another, shorter set at eleven. They'll be gone before the ritual even begins. We planned time for them to vacate the premises." She stepped back into line. "You've seen them?"

"Yeah," I said. "I went to the Rock Hall showcase." Johnny must have settled things with Erik. Or maybe not. Weren't bands notorious for playing gigs while hating each other?

"I never would have guessed you'd be into that kind of thing."

We moved up as the line progressed. I shrugged. Opening my mouth would have revealed more than was necessary.

"If you've seen them, then you know the singer is *hot*." She overemphasized the *T*. "They were here setting up and doing sound check earlier and, wow." Hunter leaned closer. "Lydia insisted they were loud and filthy, but after the radio stations started announcing the band was playing here tonight, the online ticket sales zoomed. We're going to be packed!" She studied the area behind us. "I should've had more tables."

To either side of the long entry were tables, each with black cloth, a wisp of webbing glowing under the blacklights, and a raised circle with black candles and gourds over purple, red, and orange mums.

The tables were mostly filled already. Costumed people—young and old—laughed and talked over their beverages. There was free punch and a cash bar had been stationed in front of the west-side doors.

The media crews were set up on the catwalk over the north entry, cameras aimed at the stage. "Media coverage, radio, online ticket sales. You're going to make this work, Hunter. Congratulations." I couldn't have come up with all these ideas.

"My predecessor had a fabulous list of contacts," she said as the line moved again. "She may have flaked out and disappeared, but she was organized."

I could see how that would be like a roadmap to success for someone with Hunter's skills. All I knew about her test for dealing with a threat from the vampires was that, as the voting went afterward, I'd won that round. Eventually she would face real adversity—something more than scheduling a band or a last-minute caterer. Then we—the coven members and solitaries—would see what Hunter was really made of. When the time came, I felt certain we'd all be proud of her. "I'm glad the locals are coming back. That's very encouraging."

"How do you like your new phone?" she asked.

I knew she meant the protrepticus, but in the photo line where I wouldn't know coven members from the public at large, such things should not be discussed. I replied cryptically, "I think I have a few bugs to work out."

"Connectivity problems?" she asked.

"It connects to the network all right, just I'm not certain I got the right calling features."

"I hear you."

The frustration in her tone made me feel better about my situation. "That new compact of yours . . ."

She thought about it and cocked her head as she answered, "I can't begin to tell you how much such a little thing has come to mean to me."

"It's special to you, then?" I wasn't quite getting her meaning.

"Yes. Like an heirloom already. I feel a weighty responsibility about tending it, not physical, mind you. Just mentally."

"I know exactly what you mean."

After we took pictures, Hunter was off to meet and greet others. I found Lydia sitting with a couple dressed as Bo Peep and a sheep at one of the tables. They were an older couple, and it made their matching theme costumes cute. But it made me glad I didn't have to match my costume with anyone. Lydia was dressed in a flannel nightgown and robe, complete with sleeping bonnet. She even had the small wire-rimmed glasses to suit her character. "Is Grandma still looking for Red Riding Hood?" I asked.

"Who's asking?"

"Persephone."

"With your tummy bared! Lord and Lady, I'd never have guessed!" She introduced me to the couple and then made polite excuses that we had business to attend to. As we strolled away she said, "I'm more comfortable tonight in this costume than I have been all week." She even had house slippers on. "And I can go home and go straight to bed."

"There is that," I replied.

"You, on the other hand . . ." She gestured at me.

"Oh, that reminds me—I want you to loosen this bodice in the back a little. I had to put it on alone and got it too tight."

"Can you breathe?"

"Yeah."

"Then it's not too tight. Besides, you're young enough to enjoy the interest."

"But—"

"What superhero are you, anyway?"

"I thought it was pirate-y."

She gave me the once-over again as we walked. "You were right. About that and about Hunter. I am so pleased I could burst."

"I wouldn't have done this well, Lydia."

She gripped my arm, stopping our strolling. "You have other commitments. If you wanted this like she did, you'd have done *better*."

I was about to reply, when I felt something. The fine resonance was occurring again, rising up my spine.

Menessos was here.

CHAPTER THIRTY-ONE

Turning to face the entryway, I waited only a moment before he entered the Covenstead and stepped down the foggy walkway. He was dressed as a king, in a copper velvet shirt with a black velvet cape and pants. The crown upon his head was adorned with topaz and onyx, and Goddess help me, it was like Arthur strode into the hall.

I couldn't breathe. My eyes felt dry and refused to blink. My body wouldn't move, not even to flee. The vibrant sensation had wended all through me and was now beginning to converge into the heat of desire. I began to crave his touch.

And then I realized our costumes matched.

I should have known he'd planned it this way.

Lydia followed my gaze and put it together. "He sent you this costume?"

"Most of it, yes." Denying it would have been childish.

She squeezed my arm. "I am so sorry! If I hadn't insisted you participate in the Eximium, he'd never have met you and you wouldn't have to bear his notice now."

"Lydia, it's all right. I just thought—"

"He's a vampire. A dangerous one!"

"I know. Trust me, it's under control." I moved away.

She didn't release my arm. "He'll let you think it is until it's too late."

"Thank you for caring about me, Lydia." I let her see the truth of that statement in my heartfelt smile. It made her grip weaken, disappear. She was surely putting it together, knowing that I had a protrepticus, a connection to Xerxadrea, and that Xerxadrea had a former connection to Menessos. It was the wrong assumption, but based on what she knew, it was a good one that should satisfy her. "I have some work to do while I'm here. I'm sure you understand. . . ."

"Yes. I do now." She didn't seem to like it. "Take care with your work, Persephone."

"I will. Thank you."

When I left her and approached Menessos, Goliath, dressed as a knight in armor that I'd have bet was real and heavy, had joined him. Menessos offered his hand to me as I neared. "No skirt?" He sounded disappointed.

"I don't much care for them." I accepted his warm hand. It surprised me; I expected it to be cool or cold. "Thank you for the bodice and jewelry."

His eyes were locked on my cleavage. "You lend credibility to the theory of euhemerism."

It meant something about the belief that ancient heroes were deified mortals. "Bombastic as ever, Menessos. No mask for yourself?" I asked, reaching to take the mask from my own face. Few others were wearing them.

"Leave it," he said abruptly.

"Why?"

"Because I like it very much." He slipped my hand onto his arm and walked slowly away with me. "Grant me this one indulgence, please?"

"You're not wearing one. Goliath's not."

"True." He didn't elaborate.

"That's a small response. Monosyllabic, even."

"Concupiscence distracts me."

His fancy way of saying he lusted for me reminded me that he was the one with the stain, now. It was his libido that should be amped. Mine was more than libido, though. I felt . . . *powerful* in his presence. Like my ego was sexually aroused.

No wonder vampires were so egotistical. In a room full of their stained underlings, they'd feel a rush of invulnerability and confidence. I would have to keep this in mind and not let it rule me.

Time to see who knew what was actually going on. I halted the promenade and pulled away. "Goliath, would you get me a drink, please?"

He glared at me and made no move to do as I asked.

"Bottled water." I did not resign, but waited expectantly. Menessos whispered, "Goliath."

The knight turned with a sneer. Goliath probably thought I was testing my favor with his master, and for him to have to fetch me a drink would gall him. He didn't realize *I* was the master. But Menessos did. And now Menessos knew that I knew.

We spent a long moment, the vampire and I, standing in the Covenstead staring at each other, gauging each other. I kept my shoulders square and my head high as if to say that I would not be manipulated by him.

The protrepticus rang. Thankfully, it was the ringing sound of an old telephone again.

I was not about to answer it here, in front of Menessos—Samson D. Kline's murderer—and certainly not with the chance of Goliath returning.

"Aren't you going to answer?" Menessos asked.

"No."

Just then, I caught movement on the stage. Johnny was removing guitars from cases and putting them in stands. He hadn't passed us, so the band must have access through the south doors.

Hunter stood before the stage, chatting with him. When he finished placing his instruments, he sat on the stage left steps. I watched them talk and trade polite smiles. Hunter moved closer. She put her hand on his knee for an instant as she spoke, then removed it. Flirtatious prep-move.

"Interesting," Menessos said. "Someone's flirting with your wolf, and your pulse hasn't changed at all."

Still watching the stage, Hunter did it again, but this time her hand lingered.

Johnny reached toward her hand and her smile broadened. That is, until he carefully removed her hand and placed it on the stage beside him.

"Excuse me," I said to Menessos.

Hunter had taken the rejection well but found a reason to be on her way as I started crossing the Covenstead. Johnny walked to the front of the stage and turned to check the backdrop and the scene from an audience viewpoint. His arms were crossed over his chest.

Pausing beside him I said, "You patch things with Erik?"

"Theo checked on the contract. You were right."

"If it's what you guys want . . ."

"He's not sure now that he knows the vampire connection. Feral's not sure either."

"What do *you* want?"

He turned and took a good look at me as if he hadn't realized I was in costume until then. "Wow." His awareness lingered in my chest area too. "More of what I already had."

My cheeks flushed. "Would you settle for a dozen or so of your remaining kisses?"

"Wanna see my tour bus, little girl?"

After glancing at the front of his pants, I said, "Didn't I already take a ride on your bus?"

He laughed, low and hungrily. "Well, the one parked out back is almost as big."

"Almost?" I laughed.

He grabbed my hand and led me around the stage to the south doors and out. "I stopped at the Rock Hall and retrieved your blazer."

"You did?"

It wasn't a bus, but a box truck that sat with the back open like a black, gaping mouth. "That's what a good boyfriend would do, isn't it?"

"B-boyfriend?"

The Covenstead door clanged shut behind us, and he grabbed me into an embrace. "Yeah," he whispered. His hand was hot on the back of my neck as he held me and kissed me with an intense passion. I felt as if I were melting. When he finally broke away he said casually, "You know, ma'am, I'm eager for the position and I think I'm very qualified to do a satisfactory job."

"Yeah," I said. My semi-molten brain wasn't up to witty rejoinder.

The night was bright with the just-past-full moon to light it and the air was cool as it swirled around us, lifting the cedar and sage smell of him to my nostrils. My ears gave a little pop like a bubble bursting. It reminded me of Aquula's bubble in the grove—

The protrepticus rang again.

Johnny broke off. "You got a cell?" he asked, incredulous.

The ringtone wasn't antique phone this time; it was something else.

"And your ringtone is an old Black Sabbath tune?"

I heard lyrics about fairies wearing boots.

Fairies. *Oh Goddess.*

CHAPTER THIRTY-TWO

Hearing a muffled scream, I pulled away from Johnny and moved around the box truck. I heard Johnny right behind me.

Beyond the parking lot, in the grass of the Covenstead grounds stood three short, costumed teenagers, and one of them was restraining Beverley, still in her mermaid costume.

They weren't teens. They were fairies.

The brunette male growled as Beverley struggled against him. She almost slipped away, but his slightly elongated fingers stayed fastened over her mouth and he jerked her roughly against him. I saw that his dark vest glinted with gold embroidery as did his breeches. A large jeweled brooch gleamed against a lacey cravat.

The female stepped forward. "We've lost *our* mermaid. So we took yours." Even in the distorting illumination I could tell her skin was red and her hair a shade of the same. She wore a wreath of tiny flowers in her hair and a gossamer tunic dress that matched her coloring.

"Release her!" I demanded. Johnny, standing just behind my shoulder, gave a low growl.

"Come and make us," the red fairy said.

I didn't exactly know how to stop fairies. My mind blanked.

She answered my hesitation by saying, "Cerebrosus, the honor is thine."

The third fairy, a light-haired male with yellowish eyes that afforded him an air of uncontrollability, stepped up beside the female. He wore breeches with a shirt under a brocade surcoat. He leered at me as she offered him a sheath.

Suddenly, many things happened at once. My mind registered the weapon and Beverley's danger. I started forward. Though running, time seemed to slow, and all sounds became muffled. The yellow-eyed fairy pulled the dagger from the sheath. The southern doors opened behind me. . . . I *felt* the air current of their movement. I *felt* Johnny at my heels. I heard Menessos's voice, chanting, loud through the fog that had filled my ears. The yellow-eyed fairy turned and raised the gleaming dagger, ready to strike Beverley.

I was too slow. I could not speed myself up. I would not make it to Beverley in time.

The fairies suddenly blurred toward me, like ink smearing in water. Lines of color slid over the cars separating us.

Beverley fell to the soft grass.

I was there, picking her up. "Beverley, honey, are you okay?" A second later, Johnny was beside us.

"Yes." She hugged me so tightly. "I was so scared. I'm sorry. I'm sorry."

"You have nothing to be sorry for."

"I took it off. The necklace Demeter gave me. I didn't wear it because of my costume. And the fairies took me, just like in the story."

Johnny put his hand on my back and we both sighed with relief.

But it was too soon.

The sounds of fighting came from behind us.

Menessos, Goliath, and Aquula were fighting the three fairies.

Aquula?

And then I understood. Menessos had used his bond with them; he'd called them all to him as if to guard a circle. He'd done it to remove the threat to Beverley.

Aquula's blue tail flipped and caught the red fairy in the jaw, sent her up in the air twenty feet. Wings shot from her back and she laughed, producing another dagger.

"Stay with Beverley," I said to Johnny and was up, running across the lot. Putting the toe of my boot on the fender of a sedan, I charged up and across a car, launching myself into a flip even as the red fairy dove down. From the side, I collided with her. The dagger tumbled from her grip and she crashed into the fairy with the vest and cravat.

"Persephone," Menessos said, giving me a hand up. His crown was missing and his tunic was ripped.

Beyond him, though, I saw the fairy named Cerebrosus bolt away from Goliath to the south doors, and into the Covenstead.

I was moving again, running after him.

Inside, screams and shrieks erupted. I charged around the stage at a run, but pulled up short. This fairy had

sprouted wings as well and, fluttering, they held him perhaps fifteen feet above the floor.

Xerxadrea was just arriving and being guided through
the entrance aisle. He swooped down to hover in front of
her. "Where is it?" he demanded, his hands—yellow, I
could now see, as was all his skin—pawing at her robes.

He backhanded her raven, knocked her staff from her
hands, and lifted the ancient Eldrenne into the air. She
screamed. Her raven fluttered about, pecking and clawing
at the fairy, but the fairy twisted Xerxadrea this way and
that to block the bird. "Where is it?" he demanded again.

Flying backward toward the stage, Xerxadrea in his
clutches, he snarled, "It will be the end of all witches!"

I eased up the stage-left steps.

"Ha!" he said, dropping her even as the stage came
under her feet. Lucky for her too. Instead of falling six
feet down, it was as if she merely stumbled and fell to her
hands and knees.

"Ha, ha! I have it!" he shouted to everyone, shrinking
as he spoke. "The end of the witches is at hand! Or is that
at handkerchief?" he asked, laughing and waving a black
cloth at the throng staring at him.

I darted forward, grabbed the handkerchief, and ran for
stage right.

Behind me, the fairy growled angrily, wings flapping
to pursue me. Nearing the edge of the stage, though, I
remembered here there were no steps like there were on
stage left. I went down and slid like a baseball star aiming for home plate. The fairy shot past over my head. I
jumped up and ran back across the stage to the steps.

Halfway across, the fairy dropped into my line of sight,

flipping head over heels to kick at my face. I ducked to the side, narrowly avoiding his boot; I felt the ankle brush over my earlobe. *Fairies wear boots,* I thought, even as he grabbed my foot from behind and tripped me.

Rolling with the momentum, I came up with my shoulder against the tip of one of Johnny's guitars in its stand. It was the wicked-cool axe-shaped one.

Then the fairy was on me. "Give me that cloth!" he demanded. We grappled for it. He was small but superhumanly strong, agile and fast. He yanked on the cloth but I held tight. With my other hand, I punched him in the chest, knocking him back. I used the instant to shove the cloth down into the bodice firmly between my breasts.

He was on me again in a flash. I crossed my arms to block him. Amid a flurry of pinching and grabbing strokes of his hands, I rolled to my stomach and pulled my knees under me. He kicked at my stomach, but wasn't big enough to make it count. He moved to kick at my head but was too late. Having gotten one foot flat on the stage, I pushed up, took a boot to the shoulder, and swung my fist.

He retreated to avoid the strike, then lunged at me. I threw another punch, added a kick. He lunged again, and we repeated our measures. With each lunge he grew a little bigger.

His boot heel hit the corner of my mouth. I tasted blood, but snatched him by the ankle. With a savage jerk, I slammed his back against the stage, wings fanned flat under him. "Stay down!" I commanded, standing over him.

He lay still for a heartbeat or two, then his mouth moved once and an ornate dagger appeared in his grip.

"Don't," I said, kicking at the weapon.

He shrank again, changing the distance needed for my kick to succeed. As my follow-through brought my leg past him, he rolled clear and leapt to the air. The blade glinted in the light. He came after me.

Slicing X shapes in the air, the fairy had me backpedaling across the stage. Hands reaching back, searching for something, I thought if I came up against the amplifiers I'd duck and roll. Instead of amps, my hand found the neck of the axe-like guitar in its stand. My fingers wrapped around it.

The fairy's X-move ended to my left; I ducked to the right, rushing forward and dragging the guitar with me. I righted myself and ran. Again, everything slowed.

I heard the flap of his wings behind me. I heard my breath in my ears.

I ran for the drum riser. In my mind's eye, I could almost see myself one step ahead, see what I was planning an instant before I did it. My foot lifted, one big, slow step directing my motion upward. The fairy gained on me. The next step was slow as well, but it started me across the riser. Two steps and I pulled up short, twisting around, while the guitar in my hand came up.

Even as I guided the guitar into position, like a baseball bat over my head, I started toward the fairy. His legs moved as if he were skidding on air trying to back up. I launched myself off the riser, swinging the guitar overhead, aiming for the dagger. Like a giant fly-swat, it crashed down, squashing the fairy like a bug center-stage.

CHAPTER THIRTY-THREE

Johnny's guitar was broken and a yellowish green fluid was all that remained of Cerebrosus. The brocade surcoat, breeches, all of it was gone, replaced by gooey fluid leaking from under the guitar. I released the instrument and hurried to where Xerxadrea lay on her side.

"Eldrenne? Xerxadrea, are you okay?"

"Persephone? Is that you, dear?"

"Yes, Xerxadrea. You took a fall—anything broken?"

Her raven cawed and jumped up on her arm. "I feel fine. Help me sit up."

"I think you should wait. Let us—"

"Help me up!" Her hand reached out and I took it, helped her sit up. She sucked in a breath.

My heart leapt, thinking her quick breath was due to some pain.

"Did the fairy get away with my hanky?" she asked.

"No. I have it." I started to retrieve it from my bodice but I saw Johnny past the end of the stage. Beverley was beside him, holding Aquula's hand. Menessos and Goliath were just entering, each restraining one of the other two fairies. To the side, I detected people drifting close, chattering like people do after something has stunned them. A glance let me know Hunter and Lydia were hurrying over.

Then the fairies realized what had happened to their comrade and they went into fits of rage and grief. The red one burst into flames and tore herself away from Menessos and turned on Goliath, who threw the other male into the air. "This night, we have been summoned into a circle on Covenstead grounds," the red fairy shouted as the flames around her hardened and became her wings. "And a witch has murdered one of us! The Concordat has been broken and the consequences shall be wrought upon you!" She and the other darted behind the stage backdrop and the south doors were thrown back on their hinges and bounced closed.

A mist around my feet made me glance down, and slowly Xerxadrea rose to standing. The mist disappeared up under her dress as it had when she entered for the Eximium. "Where's my staff?"

"Lydia's bringing it," I said.

Johnny stepped up onstage. "You two all right?" he asked.

"Yes," Xerxadrea answered.

"Yeah," I said. With a sheepish attempt at a smile I added, "Sorry about your guitar."

"Hell, I'll make another one," he said. Before taking me into his arms, he gestured at the news crew on the catwalk opposite the stage. "I just hope they got that footage. Pete Townshend's got nothing on you."

News crew? Oh, crap—

Then I heard the splattering sounds of palms against

palms, growing into the unmistakable rain of heartfelt applause. They—at least the mundanes in the crowded Hall, including the media—had taken it all for one hell of a great Hallowe'en treat complete with spectacular special effects.

They'd gotten the expected show. And I had been the star.

We witches assembled in Hunter's office, with Xerxadrea being guided to the big chair behind the desk. Johnny remained with Beverley and Aquula, while the vampires were asked to quietly secure the stage area and let no one near.

"What the hell happened out there?" Hunter demanded.

"They kidnapped Beverley and brought her here. They tried to kill her."

"Who's Beverley?" Hunter asked.

I sank into the chair that, a few days before, I'd sat in when I'd come to decline the nomination. I pulled the mask off and held it in my lap as I rolled the fabric up and squeezed my fingers into the silk. The stress of everything that had happened and could have happened felt like lead weights holding me down. "The daughter of a friend of mine."

Lydia put her hand on my shoulder. "Her friend was murdered a few weeks ago and Persephone has become the child's guardian."

Hunter was taken aback. "And on top of that you entered the Eximium?"

Shaking my head I said, "No. On top of that Lydia nominated me."

"Did the fairies have something to do with her mother's death?" Hunter asked.

"No, they weren't involved."

"Then why would they try to kill her?"

"Were they trying to sacrifice her?" Xerxadrea asked before I could answer. "On Covenstead grounds?"

"It wasn't ritualistic, so 'sacrifice' might be the wrong word, but they drew a dagger and . . ." I let it trail off, unsure whether telling them about Menessos was necessary.

Xerxadrea's fingers tapped on her staff. "That makes no sense. To sacrifice a virgin child on coven grounds is an act of war."

"And instead, one of them was killed inside the Covenstead." Hunter crossed her arms and gave me a petulant look. "My Covenstead."

"I haven't announced that yet," Xerxadrea said pointedly. "If you'd like to decline—"

"No!" Hunter's arms dropped to her sides. "I'm not giving it up."

Xerxadrea seemed to study Hunter, as if her filmy eyes weren't blind at all. "You would accept the position even with the instigation of a war lying at *your* feet, having occurred on *your* watch?"

I realized Hunter's moment of real adversity had just slapped her in the face and I had helped it happen. I held my breath.

The new high priestess met our eyes in turn. "My name is Hunter," she said sharply. "Let any who bring hostility to my coven's door or to my witches discover it the hard way."

Lydia gripped my shoulder. "You were right," she whispered to me.

She was with me. Not against me. My held breath escaped slowly. "Eldrenne. He called them to him, as if for a circle, to displace them so they could not kill Beverley."

"And this, too, was done on Covenstead grounds?" Xerxadrea asked. She knew who I meant.

"Yes. It was the only way to stop them."

"The Concordat accounted only for witches," Xerxadrea's cheeks rounded slightly and her tone conveyed an air of secretiveness. "I knew this day would come. I knew that, aberration that he is, he would be held accountable by them."

"Let me make sure I've got this straight," Hunter said. "The fairies were going to kill a kid on Covenstead grounds, which we would take as a violation of the Concordat and an act of war against us. But that vampire from the Eximium intervened, and he just happened to be able to call fairies to him. That's supposed to be impossible, right?"

"Supposed to be," I answered.

"By calling those particular fairies to him he saved the kid's life."

"Right."

"But his calling them as if to guard a magic circle is an act in direct violation of the Concordat and can therefore be taken as an act of war against the fairies. And in the end, you"—she pointed at me—"killed a fairy inside the

Covenstead, which is also a direct violation and an act of war. Right?"

"He was trying to kill me—that was self-defense," I said.

"The two fairies who saw the aftermath did not see him after you. They will not tell the other fey you had just cause," Lydia said.

"The Concordat was violated twice against them," Hunter said.

"In order to stop them from violating it and killing a child!" I argued. Rubbing my brow I added, "I bet the news crews have already broadcast the footage with a 'Breaking News' banner under it. Shows it was self-defense."

Lydia put a hand over her mouth.

Hunter said, "I saw people with their cell phones out. I'm sure it's on YouTube already. They'll know it was self-defense."

Xerxadrea pulled her staff in front of her and gripped it with both hands as she stood and started working her way around the desk. She stopped in front of me. "Most are not aware that you have come or that your trials have begun. Some of us already know. Though many will see the events of this night, Persephone, only a few will understand what they are viewing. Your enemies will recognize you first." The lines on either side of her mouth deepened. "It is always that way. You've already been forced to share your secret with the few who have earned your trust. But you're going to have to expand your consortium. You might as well begin in this room."

I hesitated. My stomach felt like fire and ice were warring inside it.

"What are you talking about, Eldrenne?" Hunter asked.

"Tell them, Persephone. Say the words here, among your friends, for practice, child. For my *lucusi* will be next. Only by revealing yourself to them all will you keep your enemies at bay, and draw your allies near."

I stood. I paced away from them. Hands on hips, my brain searched for a way out of this. But there was none. I knew what had to be done. "Xerxadrea."

"Yes, child?"

"Are you with me?"

"My *lucusi* amd I are all with you."

I faced her. "As for those against me, how do I protect the ones I love from becoming targets?"

Her hand passed before her, palm toward me. "You already have."

"What do you mean?"

"Anonymity," she said. "With your mask, your face is hidden, like the face of Lady Justice—and yet *you* see." She tapped the staff on the floor. "Come."

The orb glowed softly when I stopped before her, and she whispered words that I could not understand to the light.

Then the Eldrenne reached out slowly. I moved my hand to accept hers, but she paused with her palm hovering over mine, whispering. The scent of anise and nutmeg changed to raisin and currant cakes.

Suddenly she grabbed my arm, and I hit my meditative alpha like it was a swimming pool I'd just belly flopped into. Not only was the wind knocked from me, but I felt *different* . . . cold and wet as if my clothes were soaked and clinging, yet I was dry. The ground beneath my feet wavered as if quaking. Power like I'd never felt before, *Her* power, arced over me, dragging me into her bright meditation, into her illuminant sacred space.

It was as if we had not moved, but the entire room had become a place of harsh light, yet . . .

Could we be inside the glowing orb atop her staff?

"My face," her voice croaked. "Look upon my face, child. Do you see Me? Or do you see your own soul?"

It was no longer the Eldrenne who held my arm. A figure of darkness stood before me. Not dark-clothed. She *was* darkness alive. Everything else around us was like overexposed film, as if all color and tone had seeped into creating Her as a living statue of ebony.

A breeze that could not touch me blew around Her, lifting Her dark hair and obscuring Her ever-changing face. Eyes closed, She seemed at rest. Or was She waiting for something? Surely the changing of her beautiful face—as if aging a lifetime in a second and reversing it equally—meant something.

"I am waiting for you. . . ."

"Your face," I whispered. I didn't want to see my soul. Not yet.

Then the eyes of the figure of darkness opened. When I have finished meditating after gazing at a candle's flame, a color unlike any other has haunted my eyes for a time afterward, a reddish-yellow-green afterglow that wasn't pretty. Her irises were *that* color, with no pupils at all. And where that color ended was not white, but a crackling of jagged blue and green flames retreating into blackness so dark and void it seemed there was no orb to Her eye, just the flat, tricolored iris hanging in the space of Her eye socket. These were eyes that had stared, unafraid, into the sun for eons. These were the eyes of the moon. It had to be Her face. It couldn't be my soul.

"I am Hecate. I am Queen of the Underworld, the Goddess of Witches, and you, Persephone," She said my name slowly as if savoring the sound of it, "aptly named Persephone . . . you are mine. I came to you, I began all that is, but you have not yet come to Me. Not in *My* place. But you will. You will call upon Me and you will seek Me out at My crossroads. And you . . . clever you . . . will find Me." She laughed. Her grip on my arm tightened like a vice. "You will find Me in the darkness. In *your* darkness. I am there. When you are ready to see your own soul . . . I'll be waiting."

I blinked.

"Persephone," Xerxadrea's whispery voice came to my ears.

Everything seemed normal again, and the Eldrenne was just herself. Harvest spices—anise and nutmeg—were all I could smell. "Yes?" I said, trying to shake off that eerie feeling.

"Say the words."

An alarm went off then, beeping from Lydia's watch under her gown's flannel sleeve. She clicked it off. "It's time for me to remind you," she said to Hunter, "to check on the band and get ready to be announced as the new HPS." To Xerxadrea, she added, "And to get you on the stage to make the announcement."

"Can we reconvene this after the band's set starts at eleven?" Hunter asked. "I have to mingle after the announcement is made. There are some people out there who contributed a lot to this party and they expect me to show how grateful I am and make assurances about the future of this coven."

"Tend to them, Hunter. Let them believe they saw performers acting out a show—"

"Some out there know better than that," Lydia said.

"And they will wisely keep their mouths shut," Xerxadrea said confidently. "We'll reconvene after the Ball," Xerxadrea said. "And those of my *lucusi* who are here will convene with us."

Hunter left. I held the door as Lydia guided Xerxadrea from the room.

CHAPTER THIRTY-FOUR

Xerxadrea took center stage with all the slow pomp of an Eldrenne in full dress. The assembled crowd gave her the respectful silence she deserved, until she said, "I'd wager you didn't think an old crone could do her own stunts."

The laughter and applause she received in response fully restored the party mood of the room.

I watched from under the catwalk, undetected by the camera crews above me. I'd put the mask back on, simply because it made me feel safer and hidden. Johnny brought Beverley to me then hurried backstage. She clung to my arm and whispered, "Johnny called Demeter to let her know I'm okay."

"Good."

"I can't believe it! Did you see Aquula?"

I went down on one knee beside her, to hear her better. "I did."

"She's a *real* mermaid! Did you see her skin, all glittery? And her eyes? Wow! She was *sooo* much cooler than Ariel."

"Did she like your costume?"

Beverley nodded. "She said I was adorable."

I stood, rubbed her hair, and pulled her closer to me, relaxing some muscles I hadn't realized were still taut. But in my heart, I still worried. How could I be the Lustrata and avoid endangering her over and over? I had to figure out an answer to that.

"I'm delighted you enjoyed our show," Xerxadrea was saying as I focused on the stage again, "but I am even more delighted to introduce to you the new High Priestess of Venefica Coven . . . Hunter Hopewell."

Hunter crossed the stage, at ease under the bright lights. The applause seemed to embolden her, where it had embarrassed me. Yes, she was perfect for the job. She declared her gratefulness to all the appropriate people, dropping the names of those who donated to the party— who were surely satisfied to hear themselves called out— and singled out those who gave of their time. Then, she announced the band to riotous applause and cheers.

Only a few measures into the first song, the Eldrenne and a handful of other women were making their way toward us, going down the steps into the office where most of the music's volume would be blocked. I stayed under the catwalk, knowing Beverley wanted to listen to at least a few songs.

Momentarily Goliath, minus his master, joined us. The armor part of his knight costume had been removed, leaving only the undergear. Though I knew the specific names of the pieces he wore, I couldn't recall them just then. My brain was too preoccupied by the many trains of thought zooming about on multiple tracks inside my head and trying to figure out which of them to follow. Goliath lifted

Beverley onto his shoulders so she could get a better view of the band.

I stood there, letting my mind wander a bit, as I watched the crowd for a sign that someone among them had understood that what they'd seen wasn't a show. All eyes were on the band.

All eyes, that is, except Menessos's. Moving directly toward me, I let him have my attention. Beverley was alive because of him. He had red marks on his face, thin burns from the fairy. The crown was gone. In a torn tunic, he should have seemed haggard; but he didn't. He looked battle-worn, but victory clothed him as clearly as the fabric. It made heat rush through me like a jolt of courage.

Then I remembered myself and pulled the shield around my aura like a curtain.

But Menessos wasn't one to let a little metaphysical shielding get in the way. Stopping with only inches between us, he raised one finger and traced my jaw from chin to earlobe. My shields held off the effects until he touched my neck. I felt too tired to fight anymore, and ripples of heat crossed my body. I couldn't stop the sigh from escaping my lips.

"You're more than I dared to hope for," he whispered.

"What does that mean?"

He took my hands and kissed the back of each. "It means enjoy the rest of your evening, Persephone. Goliath." At his name, the other vampire turned. "It is time to go."

Goliath set Beverley down, said something in her ear. She grinned and nodded in response. Then Goliath joined his master in leaving.

I watched them go, not sure if I was sad or relieved.

When I turned back, Beverley was yawning. It was late and technically a school night, though after all she'd been through, I wasn't sure I could make her go to school tomorrow.

Then she put her hand in mine and said, "I'm tired."

I led her down to the office. Surrounded by the light of a dozen candles placed around the room, the Elders sat on chairs arranged in a circle. Vilna-Daluca immediately announced, with a knowing smile, that she'd fetch a cot for Beverley. I pulled the mask off and tucked it into my Tarot pouch.

"This is part of my *lucusi*," Xerxadrea said. "You know Vilna-Daluca. This is Silvana, Jeanine, Celeste, and Ludovika." Each nodded at me as their names were said. I tried to repeat their names to myself so I'd not forget. Talk quickly turned back to commenting on the wonderful turnout, the lovely decorations, and the loud music. Through it all, Vilna-Daluca smoothed Beverley's hair over and over until the girl was sleeping.

I was about to nod off too, when Hunter and Lydia finally joined us. From the buzz of the outer office's windowed door, it was clear the band's second set was roaring. Introductions were made again for Hunter, as the newcomers took the open seats.

"The Ball proceeding well?" Celeste asked politely.

Pleased by the inquiry, Hunter gave her a brief rundown. When she finished, though, Xerxadrea impatiently pointed to me and said, "Tell them."

They all turned to me expectantly. My chest went tight. A cleansing breath—in, then out—helped as I willed myself to relax. I stood, because, well, it felt appropriate to say this on my feet. "I . . . am the Lustrata," I said.

For a moment there was silence. Only Lydia and Hunter looked surprised. I don't know what I expected, but *some*thing would have been better than the nothing I got. In the silence that followed, I resisted the compelling urge to start spewing reasons and citing occurrences from my life that seemed to validate the claim. Keeping my mouth shut wouldn't give them ammunition to tear me down.

At first they were all openly staring at me, then, moment by moment and one by one, they turned to Xerxadrea. She sat with her head angled so the brim of her hat hid her face. The raven upon her shoulder resettled its feathers but was silent.

"The Redeemer? The Bringer of Justice and Light?" Lydia asked, finding her voice.

I wondered if everyone was going to have a different moniker for me.

"Yes," Xerxadrea said.

"Are you certain?"

The Eldrenne tapped her staff and held her hand out toward me, murmuring. The orb atop the staff began to glow softly and I felt a glittery, shimmering cold upon my skin. I began to glow and those gathered gasped as the Goddess's mantle appeared on my shoulders. Each circle of the armor that had come to me under that blue moon gleamed in the soft orb-light.

When their shock ebbed, the light faded.

I asked. "So . . . did I screw everything up out there?"

Silence.

"You killed a fairy on these grounds," Ludovika said.

"An act of war," Celeste murmured.

"It was not my intention to start a war," I said firmly. "I was ending the threat they posed to Beverley." My eyes went to the girl sleeping on the cot.

"It was inevitable," Xerxadrea said.

"The fairies *will* retaliate," Jeanine said.

"Earlier, Xerxadrea, you said I'd protected those I care about with my anonymity. But the fey took Beverley, they already know who I am."

"Other witches do not. The news media do not."

My brows furrowed. "Are you suggesting that other witches and humans are more dangerous than the fairies?"

"I am saying the fey will make a grand plan and they will use a secret to their advantage, as leverage. And knowing that, we can use it too."

"Beverley and my Nana must be safe." I disliked how thin my voice sounded.

"We will see to that," Vilna-Daluca said. She and Xerxadrea exchanged nods.

"Hunter, you and Lydia will be conducting the public ritual shortly," Xerxadrea said. "Afterward, Hunter, you must remain."

"You want to clean up tonight?" she asked with slight exasperation. "I hired a crew to come in tomorrow to do that."

I remembered her cleanser allergies and wasn't surprised by her strategy.

"This isn't cleanup," Vilna said. "We're initiating you and Persephone into the *lucusi* tonight."

• • •

I stayed with Beverley. Johnny, hair dripping with stage sweat, peeked in for an instant to say he'd be back in an hour when the ritual was concluded. "Don't leave without me," he said and shut the door. I didn't get to say anything before he'd taken off again.

With the comfy desk chair near Beverley, I arranged another chair so I could prop my feet in it. My fingers stroked Beverley's head as Vilna's had.

She had to be safe.

I killed a fairy. I took a life! Instigated war. Nana had warned me.

The weight of it all filled my chest, tightened my throat.

I won't cry. I'll fix it. No matter what. I'll find a way.

I drifted to sleep. Even when Johnny's voice whispered my name, even when I smelled the cedar and sage and freshly shampooed aroma of him, even as I felt his callused fingers on my cheek, I thought it was a dream. Then Beverley giggled and called me "Sleepyhead."

I sat up.

Johnny kissed my cheek. "They wanted me to leave, but I insisted I had to see you."

"Who wanted you to leave?"

"The witches. They're getting ready to do something up there, so I can't stay. They allowed me to come and wake you, but they also said I could take this drowsy mermaid with me." He poked Beverley in the ribs.

"Do I get to ride your motorcycle?" Beverley asked, eyes widening.

"No, take my car," I said quickly, reaching into the Tarot pouch for my car keys.

"Aw," Beverley whined.

"I don't have a helmet that'd fit you, anyway," Johnny said. "And your eyes won't stay open. You nod off on a bike wearing an oversize helmet and you'll dump yourself on the road!"

"Then how will Seph get home?"

Johnny said, "We could wait?"

"We'll see that she gets home," Vilna-Daluca said from the doorway. "Come with me, Beverley, and give them a moment?"

She followed Vilna from the office.

I stood, stretched my arms high. Johnny's warm hands on my waist preceded the kiss he planted on my cheek.

My arms fell about his shoulders.

His arms wrapped around me too, then his hands cupped my backside. "Oooo. Velvet."

When we left the office and emerged at the base of the eastern stairwell, a black-robed woman whose face was hidden in the depths of her hood stood silently waiting.

"This is where I move along," Johnny said. He squeezed my hand and took the steps two at a time with Beverley running and giggling behind him. "See you at the house."

The woman before me, obviously one of the *lucusi,* lifted another cape just like her own and offered it in a manner that said she would put it on me. I went forward and slipped into the soft cape. She then turned me, fastened the front at my throat, and lifted the hood, positioning it to hide my face. I could see out clearly even though my eyes were hidden in the depths. Lastly, she pushed the cape's length behind my shoulders, so my arms could move freely.

She led me up the stairs, where another cloaked woman stood beside Hunter, who I recognized only because of what I could see of her Isis costume.

I took in the Covenstead. The hush of emptiness had fallen and four women, all cloaked with hoods up, waited around the pentacle in the floor. It was only the eight of us now.

The two women led Hunter and me across the Covenstead floor and indicated where we should stand. I was surprised our places were not on any of the star's points, but rather in between them.

The women who'd led us took places at the points, and the other four filled in the other points, leaving one, where Xerxadrea with her staff and raven took up a position to triangulate mine and Hunter's.

Xerxadrea called up a circle, then strode around us making her quarter calls and Goddess invocation. Then, around us, the five women on the points began chanting. Their movements were stiff, but it was clear they were calling up energy from the nucleus below. I could feel something physical manifesting with their sorcery. In moments I could see a dark mist floating in the center, but where Xerxadrea stood she blocked what was forming from my view.

The Eldrenne chanted with them, a separate chant, one that almost mocked the meter and tone of their chant, but her words were old words and they worked efficiently.

"For you," the ley line whispered. Power shot upward, like a geyser erupting at the center. White light shone from it. Mist curled around our feet.

The chant ended and the hooded women stood with their arms outstretched before them.

"A gift," Xerxadrea called. "By accepting this gift, you are inducted into my *lucusi*," she said. "And on your honor you vow to follow my commands." She paused. "Do you so swear, Hunter Hopewell?"

"So I swear," she said.

"Do you so swear, Persephone Alcmedi?"

I wanted to know what they had created, but I trusted Xerxadrea. "So I swear."

Immediately, two brooms skittered across the floor and rose up, broomsticks in Xerxadrea's hands. She offered the brooms to us.

From the broomstick tip to the dried straw making its base, it was black. In my palm, the broomstick was smooth despite the beautiful symbols etched along its length. And, as newly created matter, it was warm. This symbol of women's labor tingled in my hand.

"Thank you," I said. Hunter did likewise.

"You are welcome," Xerxadrea said. Then each of the *lucusi* members repeated her. They had all created these, for us.

"Awaken them," Vilna-Daluca said.

Holding the broom before me, I whispered, "Awaken ye to life."

The end lifted into the air. The broom floated in front

of me, suspended horizontally about two feet above the floor. I looked up to the assembled women, to Hunter. They laughed. So did I.

"Is this what I think it is?" Hunter asked.

Xerxadrea gestured to the eastern doors and they flung open. "Try them out," she said.

And the *lucusi* materialized their brooms, spoke the awakening, and sat on their floating broomsticks. Hunter and I still stood stunned and motionless.

Then the witches flew out into the night.

Hunter and I exchanged a look before hurriedly mounting our brooms.

I sat upon the straw where it was bound to the broomstick. It held my weight easily, steadily. Copying what I had seen the others do, my legs bent so my knees pointed down, and, hovering there, I tucked my toes under my bottom. "East," I said.

I rode the broom from the Covenstead as if I'd been doing it all my life.

CHAPTER THIRTY-FIVE

The other witches were nowhere to be seen. Hunter waved and sped off to the north. I turned the broom southeast, toward home.

I rose high, leveling my ascent as the air grew cold. Cruising slowly along, I turned my face to the moon. Just past full, it was still almost whole. And it was beautiful.

Nana had said there would be a sign, and with one wide swing of a guitar, the Lustrata had left a green-and-yellow—blooded announcement: *I'm here.*

Many witches, and some of the wæres and vampires, would recognize what they had seen. Among them would be those who feared and loathed what I represented. . . .

I had an opportunity, with the fey, to show all the other-than-mere-humans what I meant when I said "justice."

Nana had said, "Everyone's different agendas work against each other," and that I must find a way to maintain the balance. She said she'd seen the hostilities and that they "must be avoided at all costs." She hadn't indicated that I'd be the start of it.

Another broom came alongside me. "May we join you?" Vilna-Daluca asked.

"Absolutely."

Jeanine and Ludovika were with her.

"Xerxadrea wanted me to remind you that time runs differently in the world of the fey. We hope to have a week before they take some action, but that is not a guarantee. Boost your wards, link them to the protrepticus. We will come to you in the morning."

"Dawn?"

She sighed. "I would love to sleep in, but Xerxadrea isn't fond of it." After her words faded she kept gazing at me. She didn't seem starstruck exactly, but it was something akin to that. Like a devotee. It made me uncomfortable. I looked away.

"Is my first landing going to be a problem?" I asked.

"The brooms drive on intentions, so that's up to you."

"Thank you."

"You may thank me tonight, Lustrata. But soon we will all be thanking you," she said.

"I don't know if I can bear it," I muttered.

"And that's why I like you, Persephone." She nodded. "Until tomorrow?" she asked.

"Until tomorrow."

The three of them left me. Apparently, speed is part of that intention too. They zoomed like silent black rockets and were out of sight.

Broom-riding, I found, was actually a lot of fun and no matter how dismal the future might loom, I was in *this* moment.

Dipping, turning, following familiar roads from a

brand new perspective, I was soon laughing out loud, going fast enough the make my new cape's length flutter out behind me. It reminded me of a roller coaster without the click of wheels on the track. It was a buoyant kind of motion, fluid. Maybe it was more like surfing, but I wouldn't know.

It wasn't long, however, before I saw a Toyota Avalon on a certain country road.

Flying low and pulling alongside, I noticed Beverley lying curled up in the backseat, her head on the pull-down armrest in the middle. Then I pulled slightly ahead.

Johnny did an open-jawed double-take at me before a grin spread across his face. He called to Beverley, who sat up and looked out her window. I saw her mouth move in a slow "Wow." Then she reached up front and took the cell phone Johnny was offering her. I could guess who she was calling.

When we came up the drive, Nana was waiting on the porch.

"Lord and Lady!" Tears brimmed in her eyes. "Riding a broom!"

After all the explanations were spoken, all the hugs passed around, Nana sent Beverley upstairs and shuffled out of the living room to follow her. In the doorway she stopped, though, and assessed Johnny and me standing there. I wanted to ask her about what she had seen in the scrying crystal, if she'd known I would start it, if she knew how it would turn out. But I didn't want her querying the crystal ball again. At least not until after we had the dining room renovation done. No, not even then. I didn't want to risk her getting hurt.

I needed her.

She said, "I'm proud of you, you know."

"I know."

"I let my resentment of your mother blind me. I'm sorry if I—"

"Nana. You molded me, for better or worse, into who I am." I held back the tears trying to get out. "Apparently, it's good enough. There's no sorry to be said."

She gave me a small, brief smile, then left Johnny and me alone.

He wiggled his eyebrows at me and, said, "Um, hey, where's that mask?"

"I still have it." I patted my black pouch. "Why?"

"Could you put it back on?" he asked.

"Why?" My suspicions were on alert.

"Because, I keep telling myself I had a normal childhood."

I blinked a few times rapidly but couldn't make the connections or guess where he was headed with this. "What has *that* got to do with the mask?"

"The way I figure it . . . every red-blooded boy wants to make out with some hot heroine from the comic books. So, you could, you know, fulfill that dream for me. *Please.*"

I crossed my arms disapprovingly, knowing that it would increase the ample amount of cleavage already showing. "I think you used up all of your kisses the other night."

He grinned and nodded vigorously. "Yeah. I did." He took me into an embrace despite my crossed arms, arched his neck to peek down at my cleavage, then cuddled me a little and said, "I just figured that, instead of buying me a new guitar, I'd take what you owe me in trade."

There were all kinds of protests I could make about the

selling of my kisses. But I didn't want to protest, even for fun. Still, my arms were trapped and I couldn't just pull him into a kiss. So I went on tiptoe and puckered up.

Johnny kissed me, once, very chastely. Then he completely released me. "That should do it," he said.

My turn to arch a brow. "Just one?"

"Hey now, we *are* talking about a high-quality, American-made guitar. While competitively priced, I'd never call them cheap."

"So you mean my kisses are quite valuable?"

He wistfully played with a lock of my hair on my shoulder. "Priceless, actually. But I lost a guitar, so I have to get something. One of your kisses seems fair."

"Yeah, but I distinctly remember you mentioned making out."

"That was with a hot, masked comic-book babe. But you are maskless." He leaned down. "You . . ." He breathed the word into my ear. "You are the Lustrata. One kiss from you outweighs a boy's dream version of a lengthy makeout session."

"So mask on, we make out, and mask off, it's just one kiss?" I reached for the mask in the pouch.

He gave me his most charming grin. "I think it's time I show you my apartment. Will that broom seat two?"